THE
WOLF PRINCESS
AND HER SISTER

THE
WOLF PRINCESS AND HER SISTER

EDDI REDD

iUniverse LLC
Bloomington

The Wolf Princess and Her Sister

iUniverse books may be ordered through booksellers or by contacting:

iUniverse LLC
1663 Liberty Drive
Bloomington, IN 47403
www.iuniverse.com
1-800-Authors (1-800-288-4677)

ISBN: 978-1-4917-0768-5 (sc)
ISBN: 978-1-4917-0769-2 (e)

Printed in the United States of America

iUniverse rev. date: 01/09/2014

CONTENTS

This story is dedicated to my family, who always supported me.
And to the real "Candace MacKline" who always believed in me.
I Love You All.

Brenna's leg and hands were throbbing as she battled the wicked Laird Griff Cray. Suddenly he swung his broadsword with such ferocity that when their blades met Brenna lost her grip and her sword flew from her hands. With another heavy blow, Griff Cray brought his sword back cutting diagonally down from her upper-arm and across her ribcage. If Brenna hadn't leapt back he would've spilled her entrails.

Griff Cray leapt forward as well and gave her a hard, cruel headbutt that knocked Brenna back against the wall behind her. She let out a moan as she slid down into a sitting position. She sat there, clutching at her wounded arm which was squeezed hard against her bleeding side.

Griff Cray hovered over her, sword raised and asked, "Did you really think you could best me?"

Just around the corner, unknown to either of them, Brenna's twin and only sister Candy was fighting Griff Cray's right-hand man, Dritt. He flipped the sword out of her hand with an unusual twist and kicked her so hard that she fell back against the castle's gray-stone wall. She stood there, knowing that her life now hung by a thread.

Dritt raised his sword and smirked, "Well now, Princess, I suppose this is the end."

Griff Cray looked down at Brenna, watching as the crimson, sticky liquid seeped out from between her fingers, a smug grin on his countenance. Brenna returned his gaze, utter and bitter hatred in her eyes.

"You have a choice Wolf Princess," he sneered. "Join me and become an unstoppable force, or die! Which will it be?"

CHAPTER ONE
GENESIS

Lightning split the sky, the thunder roared, the wind howled like a wounded, lonely wolf and the rain pounded down on the roof of the castle.

The laird of this castle, Laird MacKline, paced nervously up and down the hall outside his bedchamber. The storm without only served to add to his discomfort.

He was a tall man with a deep chest and broard shoulders. His neatly clipped beard was dark as night, matching his hair that came just shy of reaching his strong shoulders. His dark eyes were angular and reflected the strength of a true warrior, as well as the aprenhension he felt at this moment.

A maid with blond hair exited the room and hurried down the stairs, nearly colliding with another maid who sported thick brown locks as she ascended the steps with a pot of steaming water. The maids ignored their laird only concerned with the task at hand, caring for the Lady of the house.

After a few minutes the eldest of the maids, who'd once had hair like fire but was now quite gray emerged with a wriggling bundle. Anne, for that was her name, was one of Laird MacKline's most trusted servants. She'd served as midwife when his son Lewis was born nearly four years earlier, and there was no one that he trusted more with the birth of his children.

She gave a small grin as she looked at the laird.

"Milaird, your wife has been delivered of a daughter." she told him as she held forth the infant in her arms.

Laird MacKline took the baby girl in his arms and gazed down at the chubby face. She was unmistakably his daughter. Even though she was a newborn in swaddling clothes, her countenance were simply an infant, feminized version of his own. He even saw some bits of dark hair on the top of her head and smiled. Her hair would be like his, like his father and his father's father.

"My sweet girl." he said, tears in his eyes as he kissed her soft forehead.

The wind no longer howled like a beast and the thunder was softer. The laird turned to the window when he heard a real wolf howl and felt the child in his arms stir at the wild sound. He looked skyward and saw that the storm was moving out to sea. As the sky cleared he saw that there was a dim star above. A dark star as many people called it in those parts. Just then the infant, whose eyes had been closed in slumber until now, opened them and stared at the dark star. The laird looked down at his new daughter and saw the star reflected in her bright eyes. He smiled at the sight, thinking how mystical she appeared at this moment.

At that moment Ivy, the young maid with blond hair who was rather superstitious, came bursting through the door to the laird's bedchamber and exclaimed, "Miss Anne, you must come." Her voice was worried.

Anne and Ivy disappeared back through the door. The laird felt anxiety building up within him as a series of worried questions raced through his mind.

The babe in his arms gurgled, which served to distract him. He turned back to look up at the still clearing night sky. As the dark clouds moved farther away he noticed another star, which was very bright. A few seconds later Fiona, the brown haired maid who was between Anne and Ivy's ages emerged with a second bundle.

"'Tis another girl sir." she said, holding the infant so the laird could take her in his free arm.

"Two." he whispered in disbelief, gazing in wonder at them both. "Two." he breathed again as he turned once more to the window, then watched as the second babe opened her eyes and stared at the star filled sky, her gaze fixed on the bright star.

The laird turned back to Fiona and inquired after the condition of his wife.

"She's a strong lady Milaird. She's tired, but other than that she just need's to rest for a few days." the maid told him, quite proud and pleased with her lady. "Some women would've died just trying to bring one child into the world. But Her Ladyship has remained strong even after bringing forth two."

Just then, Ivy came out and said, "Milaird, Milady wishes to see you and the children."

Laird MacKline entered his bedchamber, walked across the thick dark blue rug that adorned the smooth wooden floor and sat on the edge of the bed. He gazed lovingly at his wife and offered her the younger of the twins. The younger of the girls was nearly the image of her mother. As much as the elder twin resembled their father, the younger resembled their mother.

Lady MacKline had warm, loving eyes that could draw even the strongest warriors in and calm their anger. Her soft dark hair came to the small of her back and served as a frame for the fair and gentle face which bore high cheek bones as well as full, smooth lips that only enhanced her already great beauty.

The younger girl smiled an infant smile and cooed, her tiny face already showing the signs of one day growing to surpass her mother in pshycal attractiveness.

"They're both so tiny." Lady MacKline sniffed, feeling tears of joy burning in her eyes. "What will we call them?"

Just then in came Darsy, an herbalist who traveled all over the countryside. He was well loved by many and was a good friend of Laird and Lady MacKline. He had a dark, a neatly clipped beard and dark hair that fell just passed his shoulders. His dark eyes seemed almost to sparkle with a sort of youthfulness, as well as great wisdom.

"How are the new arrivals?" he grinned when he saw the infants.

"They're fine." Laird MacKline smiled. "Well met Darsy."

Laird MacKline handed his eldest daughter to his wife, who took her eagerly. She watched happily as her husband went over to embrace Darsy warmly. They pounded each other on the back heartily and each gave a happy laugh.

"Are they boys or girls?" Darsy asked.

"Girls." Laird MacKline stated with obvious pride. "And they're already as beautiful as their mother." the laird added as he looked at his wife and gave a boyish wink.

Lady MacKline gave a mock glare and said, "Oh, flattery will get you nowhere!" Then she gave a small smile and winked back at him.

"So what brings you out here at this time of the year Darsy?" asked the laird.

"I've told you both of my Master, who dwells far from here in the eastern lands." Darsy said.

The laird and lady both nodded, recalling the many times that Darsy had spoken of his master.

"He sent me to give you his best wishes, a blessing for the children, and to help you name them." Darsy explained. "So, I came. I believe my Master is very wise."

"He is indeed." Lady MacKline said.

"I still have trouble understanding how you are a free man but still have a master." Laird MacKline said scratching his dark beard thoughtfully.

"It's thanks to my Master's deeds that I am a free man. I owe him my life and much more. That's one of the reasons I offered him my service. He treats me like I was his son." Darsy said with a contented smile, his dark eyes shining.

Laird and Lady MacKline both noticed how fondly Darsy spoke of his master. He always pronounced it with a capital M. This was one of the reasons why they treated their servants so well. Most servants in this country were little better than slaves. But Laird MacKline had been taught long ago by his father that 'if you starve and work your servants to death, they won't be as productive,' and 'if your castle ever falls to an enemy you'll want loyal, trustworthy serfs to help you defend your land, not back-stabbing, hateful slaves to betray you.'

Just then four-year-old Lewis, the Laird's eldest child and heir, entered the room rubbing his little eyes and asked, "Mum, Da', am I a big bwoffa yet?"

"Aye dear." Lady MacKline said in her motherly voice. "Come and see your new baby sisters."

Lewis walked over to the bed and tried to crawl up next to his mother. It wasn't until his father came over and lifted the four-year-old up onto the large bed that little Lewis was able to look down at the babies in his mother's arms.

"Dey pwitty." he said. "Wha' duh names?"

The laird and lady looked at each other.

"They need names." Lady MacKline said softly. "What do we call them?"

"Wha's dat?" asked little Lewis, pointing at the collarbone of the baby nearest to him.

The laird came back over to the bed followed by Darsy. Laird MacKline scooped up the elder of the two girls. They all looked down at where Lewis pointed on the younger baby. There was a birthmark just below the collarbone in the shape of a horseshoe.

The laird looked down at the same place on the daughter he held and saw a birthmark shaped like a wolf's paw print. This mark was darker than the one that her sister bore.

"Look." he said. "She's marked too. But it's darker."

Darsy smiled, "Perhaps you should name them something that has to do with light and dark."

"Like what?" asked the laird.

"Trouble and death." Ivy mumbled.

"Did you say something Ivy?" said Anne, her voice showing her authority.

"No Miss Anne." Ivy said, lowering her eyes submissively.

"Uh, Miss Anne, should Ivy and I go fetch some more blankets for the twins? It's rather cool tonight since we had that storm." Fiona said wisely.

Anne nodded, "Aye. That's a fine idea Fiona. Please go and fetch some."

The two maids curtsied and left the room. Once they were out of hearing Fiona said, "Why did you call the twins 'Trouble and Death?'"

Ivy was completely caught off guard, "What?"

"I heard what you said in there. Why?" Fiona pressed.

"They were born under those stars and they're marked. They have an evil destiny. We are doomed as long as they live amongst us. They will carry bad luck with them wherever they roam." Ivy blurted out.

"Oh really?" said Fiona in an unimpressed voice. "And how would we correct this catastrophe?"

"Kill them. Especially the older one that was born under the dark star. She's the more dangerous of the two. But we should kill them both just to be safe." Ivy said rather quickly.

"Ivy you bite your tongue for even thinking such a thing. The very idea of harming innocent children. Pray that His Lairdship never finds out what you said. He'd have you banished for such thoughts and Her Ladyship would have you whipped before you left. To be honest I wouldn't blame them." Fiona scolded.

"But the stars and the markings," Ivy started, but Fiona cut her off, "Silence! Not another word! Just fetch the blankets!"

Laird and Lady MacKline were asking Darsy if he knew any names that had to do with darkness and light, which he did.

"Hmm." Darsy stroked his bearded chin thoughtfully. "Ailbhe means 'noble or bright.'"

Lady MacKline said, "I don't think I can pronounce that."

"Alright how about Aileen, 'light?' Or Alba, 'white?'"

"Those just don't feel right some how." Lady MacKline sighed. "What about the darker one?"

"Well, Darsy means dark." Darsy grinned like a wicked child. "And Kerry means 'dark-haired.'"

"Kewy is a boy's name!" Lewis stated with displeasure.

Darsy frowned, "What about Darsy?"

"I knew a ge'l named Dawsy, but she fell down the cwiff into duh sea and was 'wept away." Lewis explained with great enthusiasm.

"Ah, well, I only know one other name that means something dark." Darsy said, quickly changing the subject back to the unnamed infants. "It actually means 'Raven or black-haired.'"

"What is it?" asked Laird MacKline with slight curiocity.

"Brenna." Darsy said simply.

"Brenna." the parents said together, testing the name.

"I like it." Laird MacKline smiled. "But what about her?" he nodded at the younger baby.

"Well there are many names that mean white and light. May I tell you my favorite?" said Darsy.

The parents both nodded.

"It means, 'Brilliantly white.' Candace."

"I love it." Lady MacKline said happily. "We can call her Candy for short."

"Candy and Brenna." Laird MacKline said softly. "I like it." The laird held the baby that resembled himself up so that they were face to face. "How do you like that Brenna?"

The infant reached out and grasped weakly at her father's dark beard and gurgled her approval.

"I think she likes it." he chuckled.

"What about you Candy?" said Lady MacKline, holding her baby close and kissing the velvety soft forehead. The babe made a joyful squealing sound and reached up to touch her mother's kind face. The lady smiled and said, "Well that settles it."

"Brenna and Candy MacKline." Laird MacKline grinned and walked over to a beautifully carved wooden cradle in the corner to put the baby down for the night.

The instant that she was laid down, Brenna let out a loud wail of dismay, and then Candy followed suit, screaming at the top of her not so tiny voice.

Laird MacKline was about to scoop Brenna up again when Darsy said, "Wait," and marched over to the bed where he scooped up little Candy, then walked back to the cradle and lowered her down next to her sister. The infants instantly quieted.

Laird and Lady MacKline stared in astonishment at a smiling Darsy.

"They were born together, named together, so it makes sense they'd want to be together when one's not being held."

The MacKlines chuckled. Anne suggested that Darsy find some place to sleep in the servants' quarters and that young master Lewis go back to his room so that Lady MacKline could get some well deserved rest.

In the cradle, unaware of what the adults were talking about, the babies stared at each other before drifting off to sleep.

Unknown to anyone, a young man named Dritt was delaying Ivy as she gathered blankets for the newborns.

"Come on Ivy-love, just one more kiss." Dritt said, putting his arms around her waist from behind and pressing his lips to her neck.

"Dritt I can't. What if Fiona or Miss Anne catches us?" Ivy said, pretending to struggle. "The baby girls need these blankets."

"So it was girls that were born." Dritt said rather thoughtfully.

"Oh aye. But one of them was born under a dark star, and they're both marked." Ivy said fearfully. "So they must have evil destinies."

"Really?" he said, a smile playing on his lips. "You're not afraid are you?"

"Aye, quite." Ivy said, then grinned and leaned against him, saying rather dramatically, "Protect me Dritt. You're so strong."

"Protect you? From infant females?" said Dritt with a snort. He lightly touched his lips to hers, then left.

Silent as a cat stalking a mouse, Dritt sneaked through the gate to the castle grounds. Once outside he went flat on his stomach and crawled to the path that led to the beach below. He glanced once back up at the dark shape of the castle, to make certain that no one was watching him. The towers stretched upward, a shadow against the night sky. The massive fortress was imposing and forboding as he looked away from it.

He crawled to the shore, then leapt to his feet and jogged to a shelter in the sea cliffs where he'd left his steed tethered.

There were few people who'd ever seen a animal such as this one. From the tips of it's ears to the underside of its sharp, cloven hooves it was the darkest horse-like creature anyone could ever dream. Although this beast was more like something from a nightmare. This creature wasn't nearly as majestic as a real horse, though its body had a similar shape. It's eyes were a deep blood red. It was as if someone had placed two rubies deep into a face carved of ebony. Its teeth were far sharper than any normal horse and the beast snorted more like a carnivorous hunter than a prey animal. But the strangest things about this beast were the large pair of bat-like wings that projected from its withers. It was called a harpisus, named so for it seemed like a harpy and pegasus combined.

Dritt mounted up and the creature's wings began to beat the air. Then they rose from the ground toward the stars and flew north-northeast over the forest and toward the mountains. They flew to Castle Cray, to Dritt's true master, Laird Drac Cray.

Laird Drac Cray was about forty years old with a hard, cruel face and an even harder, crueler heart. He was more than twice Dritt's age, who was not yet eighteen.

Drac stood in his great hall with his fifteen-year-old son Griff, who had a kinder, gentler face than his father. It had been kinder still when he was a child and his beautiful mother still lived.

Lady Cray was said to have had the face and the heart of an angel. She'd had beautiful auburn locks that were silky to the touch and nearly fell to her ankles. Her eyes had been sapphire-blue and her skin was lightly freckled yet rosy and soft as flower petals.

But even though she was more gracious and loving than beautiful, Drac had been wicked and cold-hearted before and after he'd married her. All she was worth in his mind was someone to provide an heir. She'd done that, and died one decade later trying to bring Griff's baby sister into the world.

Ever since his mother's death, Griff had only learned bitterness from and for his father along with cruelty. Griff very much resembled his father, but his eyes were like those of his mother, only colder since her death and filled with hatred for his sire.

Dritt entered the hall and knelt before his master, then said, "Milaird, I've brought news from Castle MacKline."

"Has the lady bore a child yet, or died trying to?" Drac growled then chuckled cruelly.

Griff wrinkled his nose and glared in his father's direction. He always hated being reminded of how his own mother had died.

Drac knew this but said it anyway, then returned his son's glare until Griff dropped his eyes.

"Aye sire. 'Tis twins." Dritt answered, knowing better than to acknowledge the obvious disdain between his master and the master's son.

"Twins!" Drac snarled angrily, throwing wine-filled goblet across the great hall. His son merely stepped aside without flinching as the purple sticky liquid spattered across Lady Cray's oil portrait. Griff's disaproving glare went unnoticed as his father continued ranting, "Now there are two more brats to bare the name of MacKline! Two more heirs to battle and kill to get that land!"

"Not necessarily sire." Dritt said with a sly grin.

"What?" said Drac raising a brow.

"Look to the sky sire. To the northwest."

Drac and Griff turned to the huge window that looked northwest, moonlight pouring into the great hall making silver marble floor shine.

"Do you see the stars sire? The dark one in particular?" Dritt asked, still grinning.

"So?" Griff shrugged, his tone unipressed.

"The elder of the twins was born under that star, and bares a mark." Dritt's grin broadened in a wide smile.

"What of the other child? Is he marked?" asked Drac, now thoroughly interested.

"Aye sire, but the twins are female." Dritt said, sounding quite pleased with himself.

"Girls?" said Drac with a loud snort as he headed for a large richly carved table. Then he laughed after thinking about it for a moment. "Girls! What luck! They will be no match for us, and even if they are, they're marked and are certain to have evil destinies, just like us, ah son."

Griff knew that his father meant the birthmarks they both wore. Drac bore his on his right hand; Griff bore his on the side of his neck, not far below his ear.

"Laird MacKline's undoing will come not only from within his castle walls, but from within his own family." Drac said delightedly.

"We won't know anything until they're adults." Griff shrugged as he and Dritt came to stand near the huge dining-table.

"Just wait. In a few years time we'll see if these, infant girls, are worth our consideration. If they are, they will join us." Drac said with a wickedly cruel smile.

"And if they don't sire?" asked Dritt.

Drac drew his dagger and stabbed an apple on the table that was laden with food. "Then they will greet their ancestors," Drac said simply as he held the apple and squeezed it in his vice-like grip until it exploded, spraying Dritt and Griff with juice and tiny bits of apple.

Griff looked toward the window, examining the stars and wondering if his father had been this worked up for his own birth. Or if he'd plotted things for his future as passionately as this.

CHAPTER TWO
THE FIRST BATTLE

It's amazing how much things change in just a few years. Both of the girls grew and changed from infants into young women, but they were as different as the sun and moon.

Brenna grew tall and dark, in both complexion and in temperament. She was unmistakably the daughter of Laird MacKline. She grew until she was nearly as tall as he was. She had dark hair and eyes that made her look even more like her father, though she'd inherited more than a few freckles from her mother. But she was as fierce in combat as her sire. The deadliest thing about her was her accuracy when throwing a knife or a dagger.

Candace, who preferred to be called Candy, never grew as tall as her sister, nor was her temper so fierce. But she was as beautiful as her mother with dark, silky hair and the kindest eyes anyone's ever seen. But she was, no mistake, a warrior and wielded a sword as well, if not better, than her father. There were few people in that land who could ride as well as she could. Candy was always less competitive than Brenna, though she did enjoy a good victory.

It was early in the morning and the sun was just peaking over the horizon. Brenna was still in bed, but Candy was up and dressed. She wanted to have an early morning ride before breakfast, but just as she opened the bedroom door, she heard it. The alarm bell.

Candy ran out the door to the nearest window in the corridor. She looked out into the large courtyard and saw the soldiers barricading the massive main-gate. Others were standing on the wall, firing arrows at whoever was attacking the ancient oaken door. Kavan, captain of the guard was barking out orders to his men as they rushed across the hard-packed dirt floor of the courtyard.

His second in command, Angus, took twenty men to the east wall. Laird MacKline himself took two score of men to the north wall. The invaders had ladders and were coming up the outer walls determinedly.

Candy heard a loud 'BAM! BAM! BAM!' Then she realized that whoever was attacking had a battering ram. A large battering ram by the sound of it. She turned and ran back to the richly decorated bed-chamber to retrieve her sword and wake her sister.

"Brenna! Brenna wake up!" she called as she fastened her sword-belt and hid a jeweled dagger in her boot.

Brenna stirred and mumbled something that Candy couldn't understand. In frustration Candy yanked the blankets away and shouted, "Brenna get up!"

Brenna jumped, startled by the yelling, and fell out of bed onto the thick silver-blue rug that covered the floor. She lay there on her stomach. The pillow fell from the bed and landed on her head.

Candy took a deep breath, closing her eyes to calm herself. She looked down at her sister and stomped her foot as she roared, "Brenna MacKline, we're being invaded! There's a battle outside!"

These words woke Brenna completely. She sat up and threw the pillow onto the polished wood floor.

"A battle?" she said excitedly.

"Aye!" said Candy, almost in a growl of exasperation.

Brenna leapt to her feet with a laugh of delight and ran to where her sword lay.

"That's the best news I've heard in weeks." Brenna almost cackled, strapping on her sword-belt. "I've been dying for some excitement. Let's go."

"Uh, Brenna," Candy started, but Brenna cut her off by saying, "Come on. I don't wanna miss all the action."

"But Brenna," Candy tried again.

"What?" said Brenna from the doorway.

"Look down!" Candy stated desperately.

Brenna looked down at her attire. She saw a silver-gray woolen nightgown that fell just a few inches below her knees and a pair of bare feet in desperate need of a bath. She'd buckled her sword-belt on over her night-garment.

"Oops," Brenna said rather sheepishly. "I need five minutes."

"You don't say." Candy said with a sarcastic giggle.

"I'll meet you outside." Brenna told her. "Save a few invaders for me, alright?"

"Alright." Candy smiled, then dashed out the door. Within moments she was at the tower with its long spiraling staircase that led down to the first level of the castle. She ran down to the second floor and then through the main hall to the front door.

Out in the courtyard Laird MacKline and Kavan were doing their best to defend the castle. Laird MacKline's fourth and youngest child, a son named Konroy, was on the east wall with Angus firing their bows and sending arrows down into the mass of invaders.

Konroy's dark eyes flashed as the morning breeze blew through his dark hair. He was careful as he aimed and loosed each arrow on the enemies below, careful to dodge any return fire.

"Get down!" yelled Angus shoving Konroy down and throwing himself on top of him as a shower of the long, deadly shafts came whizzing up over the wall, narrowly missing them both.

"Thanks." Konroy said when the rain of arrows had ceased.

"Well young sir, if I don't keep you safe my hide will be hung out to dry." Angus panted, giving a weak smile as he got to his feet.

"Father's not that cruel." Konroy told him.

"I wasn't talking about you're father lad." Angus chuckled as he loosed another arrow into the mass of invaders below.

Konroy also chuckled as he fitted another arrow to his own bowstring. Angus was right. Protective as Laird MacKline was of his children, Lady MacKline was like a mother bear protecting her cubs, fierce and not one to be challenged.

Konroy took aim and loosed his arrow. He was a fair shot, but the axe was Konroy's weapon of choice. He was deadly with it and had quite a collection of them. He was wishing he could use them now instead of arrows.

The battering-ram made a very distinct 'BOOM! BOOM! BOOM!' sound now as it collided with the severely damaged gate.

Laird MacKline and Kavan had done as much as could be done to barricade the crumbling gate, but it was all in vain. The gate was being battered to splitters.

Kavan looked at his laird who he'd served since childhood. Laird MacKline was more than a laird and master, he was Kavan's oldest and dearest friend.

Laird MacKline stared almost in disbelief at the shattering gate, then he looked at Kavan and nodded. Kavan nodded in respect, then turned to the brave men who'd been working so franticly to keep out the invaders.

"Draw swords!" Kavan ordered.

The men obeyed. Not ten seconds later every single man held forth his gleaming blade.

"My friends," the laird called out, "If we die today, let it be as free, honest men. If death comes, I am proud to fall with such honorable men as you."

All of the men nodded, proud to be serving this great man.

The gate gave way under the pressure and the invaders poured into the courtyard, screaming their ferocious battle cries and brandishing their weapons. The defenders charged, meeting their oncoming foes with a magnificent clash of steel on iron.

A huge, wild looking man with a long, jagged scar down his ugly face came straight at Kavan, waving his monstrous, bloodstained club and roaring like an animal. His breath was like raw onions and stung Kavan's eyes.

Kavan raised his sword defensively. The scar-faced man brought down his mace with a deafening clang on Kavan's sword. Kavan backed up, his arm throbbing from the impact, but he managed to keep his sword raised. He continued to retreat as his adversary advanced. Their weapons met once again with a fantastic clang, forcing Kavan back even farther. Kavan suddenly felt his back hit the castle's wall. Kavan saw that to his right were the stairs that led up to the castle's main entrance. The huge man stood two paces in front of him and jeered, still like a wild, savage beast, smiling to reveal yellow-brown tooth-stumps. Still smiling his tooth-stump smile, he raised his club. Kavan held his sword up, bracing himself for the bone-crushing impact and his almost certain death.

"Castle MacKline!!!"

Everyone who lived within these walls knew that battle-cry as well as it's owner. The two men looked up the stairs and saw Candace MacKline skidding down the fincly carved stone banister, one foot in front of the other. She was upright with her sword at the ready as she descended rapidly. Her sword, Calma, which means valiant in the ancient tongue we know as Gaelic, gleamed in the morning sunlight. There were legends that the swords which the MacKline family carried had been forged by the elves in older times, and that there was even some elven blood in their ancestry.

Kavan ran the huge man through just as Candy launched herself from the stone banister and kicked the large man over. Then with a swing of her sword, Candy relieved the huge man of his head. She stood on the now dead man's body, her chest heaving as she turned to look at Kavan.

"It's about time you showed up and saved the day." he smiled, a little out of breath himself. "Where's the Wolf Princess?"

Because of her warlike nature and the fact that she always imitated a wolf howling when giving her battle-cry Brenna was known as the Wolf Princess, a title that she was proud to have.

"She's on her way. You know Brenna, she hates to miss a skirmish." Candy smiled.

At that exact moment Brenna was in the middle of a skirmish. She was locked in combat with a stubborn boot. She was hopping on one foot over and over, trying to pull it on when she lost her balance and fell flat on her stomach with a loud thump.

Just outside the now splintered gate stood a young man peering into the courtyard as he watched the battle. He was somewhere between the age of twenty-one and twenty-five. He was tall, broad shouldered and strong. His intense eyes were blue-gray, like the sea after the rain has stopped. His hair was messy and dirty, but when it was caught in the sun his hair was the color of sand, and his face was slightly smeared with dirt.

Laird Griff Cray, laird of castle Cray since the death of his father five years earlier, came to stand beside the young man. Griff was muscular like his father, though he had to hold his back straight to match the height of the younger man. His pale sapphire eyes were narrowed as he thoughtfully stroked the rough tuft of dark hair that grew from his chin.

"Which one?" the young man asked.

"That one." Griff answered gesturing toward Candy as she dueled a much larger foe.

The young man wrinkled his nose and snorted, "A girl? You want me to capture a girl? Do you think so little of my warrior's skill!"

"She's not just any girl, she's the twin of the Wolf Princess." Griff told him. "And she's almost as deadly from what I hear. But she's far more merciful than her wolfish sister."

The young man snorted again, "I've heard the stories about the Wolf Princess, and that's all they are. Stories. Tales to scare small children with when they're naughty."

"Well, then go and capture her, if you can." Griff smirked.

"This is a waste of my talents," the young man almost snapped. "Find someone else, someone weaker."

"You go in there or I'll sell you as a slave to the next ship headed north," Griff growled.

The lad stood there speechless, his blue-gray eyes wide.

Griff continued, giving the younger man a hard clap on the back, "You remember that life, don't you." Griff's tone was taunting as he grinned when he saw the lad wince knowing that he was in pain from the smack on his back.

"I'll have her in three strokes," the young man boasted, straightening his sore back and drawing his sword menacingly.

"There's a good lad." Griff said, squeezing his shoulder non-too gently. "And Mitch, if she doesn't do as she's told, you know what to do."

Mitch nodded once, his messy sand-colored hair dropping down in front of his eyes. It was in desperate need of a trim as he brushed it aside to look into the courtyard. He located his target and pursued her.

Brenna, having finally won the battle against her stubborn boot, was now running down the spiraling stairs of the south tower, the sound of her footsteps echoing in her ears. She reached the bottom and approached the great oak door that led into the main hall. She hesitated when she heard footsteps in the hall. They were going away from her, but she didn't think about that. She drew the jeweled dagger from her boot and flung the door open.

She saw the figure of a young man walking away from her. Even though his back was to her, she could tell it was her elder brother Lewis. She sheathed her dagger and ran to join him.

"I thought you'd be outside by now." she teased.

"I thought you'd be out there. What happened? Your boot get stuck?" he teased her back, then winced as she punched his upper arm.

"Ha, ha! What's your excuse, oh future laird?" she accused him.

"I was coming to get you," he grinned, "in case you needed some back up."

The hall echoed with Brenna's sarcastic laughter.

They were just coming around a corner, when they came upon three invaders who had somehow managed to get inside of the castle's main building. But they were near the main door, so Brenna and Lewis knew that the invaders hadn't been inside long. One of the three had only a crossbow, and he aimed it menacingly in Brenna's direction.

"Well look what we've found boys." he laughed wickedly, his finger on the trigger.

"Lookout!" Lewis yelled, shoving Brenna out the way as the man loosed the small arrow. It was just in time, for the short shaft would've buried itself in her ribs otherwise.

The man growled angrily and began to reload his crossbow hastily. The other two invaders drew their swords and charged. Brenna and Lewis drew their own swords and met their oncoming foes.

Brenna's sword, Ceartas, the Gaelic word for Justice, clanged against the invader's blade. She shoved him back a pace. He lunged. She sidestepped this attempt and caught him in the ribs with her sword tip as he passed.

Lewis was driven back slightly. His opponent was larger than Brenna's but he quickly regained some ground and relieved the invader of his left arm. His enemy screamed in anger and pain, swinging his sword at Lewis, seeking revenge. Lewis leapt back just in time to avoid the sharp blade.

The now one-armed man roared with utter hatred burning in his eyes as he pursued Lewis. The man's face was quickly draining of all color. Lewis knew that his foe was near death and in agony. He frowned as he relieved the man's suffering.

Brenna dealt her enemy another blow, driving him back a pace and a half. He was strong and well skilled with his sword. But Brenna was unwilling to surrender and shoved at him ferociously though he'd planted his feet now.

The man with the crossbow had reloaded his deadly weapon and now aimed it at Lewis. Lewis sidestepped to avoid the oncoming arrow, but not quite fast enough. He grunted as it grazed his ribs leaving a hairline gash.

Brenna decapitated her foe, then ducked to avoid another arrow as she drew her jeweled dagger from her black leather boot. She hurled it toward the invader as he tried to reload his crossbow again. He didn't even cry out, just slumped backward. Brenna strode over, and knelt to retrieved her blade from the man's skull. She wiped it clean on the corpse's clothes, then looked back at her brother.

"You all right?" she asked, a little out of breath after the recent combat.

"Fine. You?" he panted, leaning against the wall.

"Clean as the day I was born." Brenna grinned.

Lewis chuckled, "You were filthy the day you born."

"I'm fine too." she growled playfully. "Come on. Let's go find some."

As she turned and rushed down the hall, Lewis lifted his left arm slightly and examined the hairline gash across his left side, just above the hip. It was dangerous to go into battle already wounded, but it was his responsibility as future laird to protect his home. Keeping his wound covered with his arm he ran to join his sister.

Candy had just run an enemy through with her sword when she heard someone laughing behind her.

"Not bad, for a girl." said a mocking voice.

She turned and saw the owner of the voice, a young man with yellow-brown hair and blue-gray eyes. He flashed his white teeth as he grinned at her. Candy couldn't help thinking that if his messy hair were trimmed and washed he might be handsome. His smile might've also been attractive if it weren't a mocking grin.

"I'm a princess!" she stated firmly.

"Oh, well pardon me, your highness," he said sarcastically, giving a mock bow as he smirked, "Not bad, for a girlie princess."

"Well this 'girlie princess' could beat you in a fair fight." Candy snorted.

"Oh really?" his voice still held a note of sarcasm.

"Aye, really. Face me in combat, unless you're afraid of losing to a 'girlie princess.'" she said mockingly, trying not to show how angry she felt. It would've been more convincing if she hadn't been glaring at him so coldly.

"Very well." he shrugged carelessly, raising his sword.

Candy's anger got the better of her and she lunged prematurely. Mitch easily sidestepped her thrust and smacked her seat with the flat of his blade as she passed. Candy gave a surprised and angry gasp when she felt the hard blow. But she wouldn't allow him to hear a cry of pain. She gritted her teeth in anger, then gave an upset grunt as she stood up straight and turned to face her grinning foe. She rubbed slightly at her throbbing seat and glared at him icily. A mocking laugh rumbled deep in his chest.

"How dare you," she growled.

"I dare just fine." Mitch grinned.

"Ooh!" she growled, starting to lunge at his right side and then quickly changing direction. As he moved his sword to the right to block her, she dodged to his left and with the tip of her sword, she clipped a bear-claw fastener from his buckskin shirt. She smacked his seat with the flat of her sword as she passed him. She grinned when she saw him jump out of the corner of her eye and heard his surprised grunt.

Mitch turned to face her, his smile gone and brow lowered. Laird Griff Cray had been right. She was a warrior to be reckoned with. His sore seat was in agreement with him on that point. He decided that he wouldn't let her pass him again.

"How do you like it?" she grinned at him.

Mitch stood holding his back straight, his eyes burning with frustration. But he forced himself to appear calm. He wasn't about to show her any of his weaknesses.

"Like what?" he said simply, as though she hadn't touched him.

She lunged at him again. Once again he dodged. She turned to face him, careful to keep her seat away from his sword-flat. Mitch swung at her. Candy ducked and thrusted forward at his gut. Mitch leapt backward, out of range. Candy stood up straight and rushed him. Mitch brought his sword down on top of hers, forcing it's tip to the ground. Mitch put his foot on the end of the blade and grinned at Candy in triumph.

"Call the surrender and maybe I'll ooph . . ." Mitch's negotiations were interrupted by Candy's fist connecting with his jaw.

Mitch reeled backward, his jaw throbbing. He felt lightheaded as he steadied himself. He caught sight of Candy raising her sword to strike. Mitch raised his own sword defensively just in time. He shoved her back. His hand went to his mouth, then he spat red liquid on the ground.

"You drew first blood." he said, raising a brow. "Not bad, princess."

"Just wait 'til I get warmed up. You'll be lying in a puddle of it!" she spat at him, then lunged.

Mitch put up his sword once again and the two stood there, pushing at one another as they tested each other's strength. They gritted their teeth and glared at each other angrily over the place where their swords crossed.

Mitch's brow shot upward. It was the way that the sun was hitting Candy's face as she stood there, and the way that the breeze caught her hair so that it framed her face perfectly. This was the same image he'd seen more than two years ago. In his mind's eye, he saw another young woman, about the same age as Candy but with long auburn hair. She had looked at Mitch with such tenderness and love in her eyes, and in each other's arms they had known true joy. But Mitch had been embittered by her death two years earlier.

When he saw Candy the way she was now, he remembered his beloved Babbette. Candy suddenly disappeared and was replaced by Babbette. She had tears in her eyes and looked at him as though she was asking for help. Without thinking Mitch began to lean forward, in order to kiss the woman he'd loved and lost. It was the way he'd always comforted her.

Candy didn't know what was happening. One minute this man was trying to kill her, the next he was leaning forward as though to kiss her. What was wrong with him? But she didn't have time to think about that.

"What're you doing?" she almost shouted at him in alarm.

The nearly desperate tone of her voice brought him back from that dream-world where you see those that you haven't seen in years. Mitch stepped back, blinked, and stared at Candy. She stared back questioningly.

"Let's finish this," he said, trying to growl.

Candy wasn't sure what had just happened, but there was something in his eyes. A grief. A pain. Something very much like despair. She couldn't figure it out. She simply raised her sword to continue the battle, but her heart wasn't in it anymore. Neither was his.

Brenna and Lewis came out at the top of the stairs that led from the castle to the courtyard and scanned the battlefield.

"There's Father." Brenna pointed to their left, "and good ole Kavan."

They saw that the two men were fighting back to back, with Kavan taking the brunt of the battle in a most protective manner. Laird MacKline was like a brother to him and Kavan would've sooner died than allow his laird to be wounded by an enemy blade.

Lewis chuckled, "Look at Konroy."

Brenna looked to their right where Lewis pointed. Konroy was in the courtyard now swinging his battle-axe at every foe that dared to get too close. He drew a small double-bladed axe-head from the back of his belt. It had been his first axe several years earlier but he'd used it so much that the handle had fallen off. He now used only the head, usually for throwing like a knife-thrower uses a knife. He now hurled it at an invader that held his sword up to strike a young servant girl with dark blond hair. The man dropped his sword and slumped forward narrowly missing the girl, who was one of a few that had braved the battlefield to help the wounded. She nodded her thanks to Konroy who was suddenly swept up in the battle again.

"I don't see, wait, there's Candy." Brenna said, pointing directly in front of them, halfway between the castle's main building and the splintered gate.

Mitch looked toward the gate momentarily and saw Laird Griff Cray, a loaded crossbow in his hand and a look of impatience on his countenance. He glared at Mitch, warning him to hurry. Mitch became more vigorous, slashing violently at Candy, who backed away. Having been caught off guard she didn't see the dead body sprawled behind her. Mitch did. He swung his sword with all of his might and knocked her weapon from her hands. Using his shoulder he rammed into her, causing her to trip backward, knocking her to the ground.

Candy was bewildered for a moment, having had the breath knocked out of her, but quickly regained her bearings when she felt Mitch's sword-tip at her throat. She glared up at him defiantly as he spoke.

"Well now, princess, will you call out the surrender, or do I have to kill you?" he smirked cruelly.

Candy drew back her lips in a snarl showing her white teeth. It was a little trick she'd learned from Brenna who often made faces similar to a wolf's.

"Never surrender," she growled through gritted teeth. "Death first!" Then she spat on his sword blade disrespectfully.

Mitch raised a brow in surprise. Where did such courage, such defiance come from? Did she not know that her life hung by a thread?

"Fine!" he said, raising his sword. "Have it your way."

Candy closed her eyes and set her teeth, knowing that her death was near. Mitch thrusted his sword downward and felt it connect. Candy heard the sound of the blade sinking into something. She opened her eyes and saw that the sword tip had sunk into the blood soaked soil nearly three inches from the right side of her neck. She stared up at Mitch, her eyes questioning. That pain, that grief, it had come back into his eyes.

His lips moved slowly, "I can't."

The moment Brenna saw Candy fall she knelt and drew the jeweled dagger from her boot, then stood and raised it over her head, aiming for the lad. How dare he threaten her sister! Brenna froze, her blood running cold when she saw the young man's sword come down on her sister's neck. A tear came to her eye at the thought of Candy being dead.

Lewis looked on in disbelief. Candy, gone? No! That just couldn't be.

Brenna focused and saw that the sword hadn't touched her. The blade was in the mud not her sister's throat. Candy was still alive, and Brenna planned on keeping it that way. Taking aim, she threw her dagger with all of her strength.

Had Mitch not moved in that moment, the blade would've certainly sunk into his heart and killed him instantly. The dagger's impact with his upper arm knocked him off balance. In a second, he found himself on his own back, staring skyward.

Candy sat up and wondered if he was dead. She hoped he wasn't. She wasn't sure why she hoped that he was still alive. But she did hope all the same.

Brenna was down the stairs in a heartbeat and began shoving her way through the dueling mass on her way to her sister's side.

Candy got to her feet and retrieved her sword. Then she approached the still form of Mitch. She was startled when he sat up and pulled the dagger from his arm. He struggled to his feet, holding his sword in his left hand while he clutched at his bleeding left arm with his right hand.

Candy met his gaze, his eyes the color of smoke. There was a great blaze behind them she could see as he stared back.

Candy didn't see exactly where she came from, but suddenly Brenna came charging, sword in hand. Mitch switched his weapon back to his right hand and raised it defensively. The two blades met with a tremendous clang. The Wolf Princess and the Northman stood eye to eye, quivering as they pushed at each other, testing one another's strength. Brenna was shocked when she felt herself shoved back a pace and a half. Mitch came at her, swinging his blade. Their swords clashed again, and this time it was Mitch who found himself giving ground.

He was confused. This person looked like a woman in the face and had long, black hair, but she was dressed almost like a man. As she came at him, he ducked and punched her in the ribs. The air left Brenna in a rush, but she dodged his next oncoming blow in spite of this. Then she rammed into Mitch as hard as she could. Mitch landed on his injured arm. Pain shot through him, as he cried out. He released his sword as he lay there writhing in agony. His ribs ached. He hadn't seen the flat stone on the ground. He'd landed squarely on it and had nearly broken five ribs. He raised his head once and looked at Candy. Then he lowered his head to the ground and stopped writhing as the darkness closed in around him. Candy gulped as she stared at the motionless young man.

"Is he, dead?" she asked haltingly.

"He will be in a minute." Brenna growled, still holding Ceartas. "Try to kill my sister will you!"

She raised her sword to kill him, holding it high over her head. But as she tried to bring it down, she felt a hand close over her wrist and heard Candy say pleadingly, "No! Don't! Please?"

Brenna turned to her sister with wide, questioning brown eyes.

"What? Let go!" she said, pulling her wrist free.

"Don't kill him!" Candy continued. "He doesn't deserve to die!" Candy stood in front of her sister now, blocking the young man from her sister's wrath. "Please!"

"Move Candy!" Brenna said sternly, narrowing her eyes.

"No!" Candy stood firm. She'd never argued with Brenna like this.

Brenna's brow rose for about three seconds, then lowered farther than before as she fixed her sister with a cold glare. Brenna had never glared at her twin so coldly.

"Move aside Candace MacKline!" Brenna's voice was low and angry.

"No!" there were tears in Candy's eyes as she gave her defiant answer.

"He almost killed you!" Brenna stated.

"But he didn't want to!"

"Who cares?" Brenna growled. "Look! He's one of those savage Northmen!"

Candy gazed down at Mitch. When he'd fallen, the medallion that he wore under his shirt had come out. It hung from a chain on his neck down across his slowly rising and falling chest. The medallion was solid gold, round and flat with the image of a ship sailing across the sea carved into it. Flying above the ship was a dragon, longer than the vessel it soared over.

Brenna had no sympathy or love for the men from across the northern sea. For the past thirty years, they'd come and gone, taking whatever goods they took a fancy to, including slaves which were once free and noble people. All they'd leave in their wake was devastation, death, and misery. Remembering the friends and relatives she'd lost because of these invading barbarians, Brenna curled her lips and sent a gob of spit in Mitch's direction. It spattered across his dirt smeared cheek.

Candy had no great love for these robbers and slavers either, but she felt great compassion for the wounded lad lying less than two feet away from where she stood.

"He deserves a slow, painful death!" Brenna spat.

Candy's mind raced. She owed him her life. He'd had the chance to kill her, but had spared her. How could she save him from Brenna's anger and wrath? How?

"Wait!" she said as she saw Brenna pushing past her, sword raised. Candy swallowed and continued when she saw that she had Brenna's attention. "We should keep him. He might know something. Maybe we could use him to trade for one of our own."

A thoughtful light came into Brenna's eyes, "You think he has information we could use?"

Candy swallowed again, "He might. In any case, he's a prize fighter, and somebody might be willing to pay a ransom for him."

Brenna raised a brow and locked eyes with Candy, "There's something more I think. What is it, really?"

Candy lowered her eyes and blushed, "There's nothing more."

"Truly?" asked Brenna. "Honestly?"

Candy was silent as a tombstone as she slowly met her sister's gaze with large pleading eyes.

Brenna's brow lowered as she heaved a frustrated sigh, "Fine, I'll spare him. But he's your responsibility. Keep him in the dungeon and away from me. Understand?"

Candy nodded vigorously, hiding a smile, "I understand. Thank you."

"Get him out of here." Brenna said, rolling her eyes. "And watch your back."

"I will." Candy promised as she sheathed her sword.

Brenna groaned and went off in search of another foe with whom to do battle. She needed to let off some steam.

Candy put her arms around the young man's chest from behind and dragged him toward the dungeon. It was hard going. Mitch was at least a half a foot taller than she was and about twenty-five pounds heavier. It was difficult not to get caught in a skirmish as the battle raged all around them.

Lewis's side was throbbing as he swung his sword at the invaders who were trying to surround him. They'd seen that he was wounded and had made him an automatic target. But Lewis was a fierce, formidable warrior, and his foes fell as they tried to close in on him.

Konroy saw his brother in the invaders' midst, and cut his way to his brother's aid.

The two stood back to back, and cut down anyone who came too close that didn't belong to Castle MacKline.

At last, their enemies retreated. It was then that Konroy noticed that Lewis's side was bleeding. He would've told him to go inside, but he knew that would only make Lewis more stubborn about staying out and fighting. Out of the corner of his eye, Konroy saw Candy trying to drag a young man toward the castle and not quite succeeding. He decided to kill two birds with one stone.

"Lewis," he said, "Candy needs some help. I think I'll be all right on my own for a while. You can go and give her a hand."

"I'll be back." Lewis promised, turning to aid his sister in her plight.

Candy accepted his help gratefully. Wounded though he was, Lewis easily supported the unconscious lad. In a short while Mitch was lying on a pile of straw in a cell below the castle.

"Are you sure that you want him in 'this' cell?" asked Lewis.

"Aye." Candy stated rather firmly.

Lewis raised a brow questioningly.

"Lewis, he doesn't know about, 'that.'" Candy pointed out.

The 'that' and 'this' they were referring to, was a secret tunnel that led to the stables and another tunnel that led to the beach below the cliffs that the castle was built on. This was an easy escape for the family if invaders captured them, as long as they were put in this cell. It was also a way to get back inside the castle if they were chased out.

Candy was right though. Mitch had no clue that there was a hidden tunnel leading out of the cell. But even if he had known, he was in no condition to use it. He lay there, unconscious and wounded.

Out in the courtyard Brenna dealt out hard blows on the invaders that came within range of her sword. With every death-blow she threw back her head and howled like a wolf. Konroy had joined her and laughed as their enemies scattered in fear of the Wolf Princess and her allies.

Just outside the shattered gate, Laird Griff Cray watched with interest. He raised a brow at Brenna's unique fighting style. He was impressed. Most impressed. Yes, she would do nicely. Quite nicely indeed.

He picked up the hunting horn that hung from his shoulder, put it to his lips and gave three long blasts. It was a hauntingly dark sound that came forth from the instrument. It filled one with dread to hear it. But upon hearing it his men instantly gave up the fight and retreated out through the splintered gate.

Brenna roared and chased the last of the men out, swinging her sword high over her head.

"And don't come back!" she bellowed threateningly, then she threw back her head and gave her battle-cry howl.

The rest of the warriors in the courtyard began cheering, knowing that they had won the day. But Brenna's eyes were focused elsewhere. She saw a man standing near the gate, watching her. She stared at him. He stared back, then smiled and bowed before turning to follow the rest of his comrades. Brenna wasn't sure who that man was, and she didn't care. She'd won, and that was what mattered. Besides, she'd probably never see him again anyway. She joined in with the rest of the cheering army, celebrating their victory.

Down in the dungeon, Candy and Lewis heard the cheers and knew that those within Castle MacKline had been victorious against the invaders. It was at that moment that Candy noticed how Lewis was favoring his left side and holding his arm tight against it.

"Lewis," she asked, "are you all right?"

"I'll survive." Lewis said, holding back a groan of pain.

"Let me see." Candy insisted, lifting his arm and gasping at what she saw. "Lewis!" she scolded.

"It's just a scratch," he said with a slight moan.

"Come on," she said, steering him toward the stairs.

"Where're we going now?" he asked in an annoyed tone.

"To the infirmary." Candy said firmly.

Konroy with the help of another soldier named Bricker, was helping a limping Angus to the infirmary, where Darsy the herbalist was tending to the wounded. Angus groaned as he sat down on a cot and removed his arms from around Konroy and Bricker's shoulders.

"If you'll pardon me Master Konroy, Cap'n Kavan needs my assistance with barricading the gate." Bricker said, giving a slight bow.

"Aye. Thank you Bricker." Konroy said kindly.

"Thank you sir." Bricker said, then straightened up, turned and marched out of the infirmary.

"Ooh, I should've seen that arrow coming." Angus grunted, holding his right thigh. Dark, sticky blood seeped out from between his fingers as he clutched at the wound made by an enemy shaft. "You're a good lad Master Konroy. Most other lairds' sons would've left a common man like me behind for someone else to help."

"What was I supposed to do? Leave a wounded man on the field to die?" Konroy said, then turned toward the door.

He stopped in mid-turn when his eyes fell upon the blond slave girl he'd saved earlier. She was giving water to the wounded men. Her name was Erica, and she'd come from the far Northland several years ago as a child slave. Konroy thought that she was the most beautiful girl he'd ever seen, with her dark blond hair, blue-green eyes and smooth, blush colored lips.

She smiled at a man who called her an angel of mercy, then turned to continue her task. She stopped when her eyes met Konroy's. He saw her eyes widen as she gulped, then she blushed and lowered her gaze. Konroy lowered his eyes as well, then walked toward and then past her.

"Master Konroy?" he heard her voice.

He stopped and turned to look at her, "Aye Erica?"

She looked at him for a moment, then lowered her eyes before asking, "Would you like some water sir?"

Konroy smiled, "Aye. Thank you."

Erica dipped a carved wooden ladle into the bucket of water she was carrying and offered it to him. Konroy accepted it and drank deeply. As he handed the ladle back to her, he intentionally brushed her hand with his own, thinking of how soft her skin was in spite of all the hard work she did every day.

"Oh." Erica gasped.

"What?" he asked, wondering if he'd frightened her.

"Your hand is bleeding." Erica said, her voice laced with concern.

Konroy looked at the back of his right hand and saw a three-inch long cut. It was a little wider than the width of a hair, and as crimson as strawberry juice.

"Oh, that." Konroy said, relieved that he hadn't frightened her. "It's just a scratch really. A sword glanced off my axe and slid down the handle. It cut my hand as it passed, but I'm fine." he brought himself to his full height, trying to look brave and strong, feeling quite pleased by her concern for him.

"Please, wait a moment." Erica said, putting down the bucket and turning in the direction of the linen shelves and cupboards.

Konroy watched her go to a nearby cupboard and take out some bandages and a small vial of some sort of liquid. Konroy wrinkled his nose at the sight of the vial. Inside the small vessel was a mixture made from herbs boiled with seawater. The smell was tolerable, but when poured over an open wound there was a sudden stinging sensation. His mother had used that medicine many times on his countless cuts and scrapes during his childhood. He'd dreaded those times and that awful mixture. He had become more careful in his games just to avoid that awful, stinging medicine. But he wouldn't show cowardice now. Not in front of Erica.

She returned, vial and bandages in hand. Konroy drew his lips into a thin, tight line, gritting his teeth behind them as the liquid made contact with his damaged skin. An involuntary moan escaped through his tightly clamped lips as the pain started.

"Are you alright sir?" she asked softly, trying to hide the concern in her voice.

Konroy forced a smile and nodded. "I'm fine!" he said through clenched teeth.

After applying the oil, Erica carefully and gently bandaged his hand.

"There." Erica said triumphantly, having finished her role as nursemaid.

"Thank you." Konroy smiled.

Erica curtsied, but Konroy thought he'd seen the hints of a smile playing on her lips. Then Konroy was left alone as she took up her bucket and returned to her old task.

Candy was having a hard time getting Lewis to the infirmary.

"Lewis, come on!" she groaned irritably.

"Candy," he complained, "I'm just fine. I'm a grown man,"

"Who's behaving like an infant!" she interrupted.

"I am not!" he snorted.

"You are too!"

"Am not!"

"Are too!"

"Hey, you two are having a fight and didn't invite me!" Brenna's voice came from behind them in the hall. "What's going on?"

"Lewis is hurt and won't let me tend to the wound!" Candy stated firmly, glaring at Lewis coldly.

"It's just a scratch. She's over reacting!" Lewis said, rolling his eyes.

"I am not!" snorted Candy angrily.

"You are too!" said Lewis.

"I am not!" growled Candy.

"Are too!" stated Lewis.

"Am not!" snorted Candy.

"Are so!" said Brenna, grinning like a naughty child.

Lewis and Candy stared at her in confusion.

"You think I'm over reacting?" said Candy, raising a brow.

"No, I just wanted to join in." Brenna grinned mischievously. "Wow, is that the wound?" her voice taking on a more serious tone. "That's one big scratch Lewis, and that's coming from me."

Lewis rolled his eyes, "I'm fine. You two are acting like a pair of mother hens. Bunch of girls!"

"Uh oh." Candy said, eyes widened as she took a step back toward the hallway wall.

"What now!" It was more of a statement than a question that Brenna directed at her elder brother. "Did you just call me a 'mother hen?' Candy did he just call me a motherly bird?"

"I think he's wishing he hadn't." Candy said, hiding a smile.

"Aye, look at him. He's scared." Brenna smirked.

"Me? A grown man scared of a girl?" said Lewis.

Candy covered her eyes and turned away, "I can't watch."

"Ooh, I'm shaking in my boots." Lewis said in mock fear.

Brenna glared coldly at her older brother, then charged at him. In an instant, Lewis found himself flung over Brenna's shoulder and being carried into the infirmary. He flailed his limbs this way and that, protesting with every step.

"Hey! Put me down! Put me down! I'm a grown man!" he growled threateningly. "Put me down or else!"

"Or else what you big baby?" Brenna's tone was every bit as threatening as his. "You don't scare me!"

She threw him down on an empty cot with a resounding thump.

"Ow!" he grunted.

"That's not a grown man's sound." Brenna said smugly, leaning forward as she put her hands on her hips.

"Uh huh, and you'd know wouldn't you." Lewis said just as smugly.

"Whoa! Easy Brenna, easy!" said Candy, rushing to stand between her two siblings. Brenna was glaring at her brother, teeth bared and fists balled, ready to punch Lewis's smirking face. The only thing that stopped her was Candy restraining her.

"Go on Candy, let her go. I'm not scared." Lewis chuckled, though he hoped that Candy would continue to hold the angry Brenna back.

At that moment Candy saw Konroy placing the vial back in the cupboard.

"Konroy, get some bandages and bring me that vial!" she called to him.

Lewis's eyes grew large, "That vial? No! No! Absolutely not! It's nowhere near that bad." Lewis's voice had taken on a whiney tone. "I just remembered, I have something to do, somewhere else." Lewis tried to stand, but at that moment Candy released Brenna who leapt upon Lewis and sat down on his chest keeping him from escaping to anywhere.

"Get off me!" he bellowed.

"Make me!" Brenna snorted in a rather smug manner, crossing her arms stubbornly.

Lewis struggled, but in truth they were both about the same height, weight, and were equal in terms of swordsmanship, horsemanship, and speed. This was mostly because Brenna was very competitive with her older brother. If he climbed a tree, she'd climb a taller one. If Lewis rode his horse for an hour, Brenna rode hers for two hours. It was all of this physical activity that had built and hardened their muscles, causing them to be such close equals in both strength and endurance.

Konroy handed Candy the bandages and the vial, then watched as she instantly went to work.

"Candy? Candy no. You wouldn't! I forbid it! Don't you dare Candace MacKline! Ouch! Ooch!" Lewis moaned and groaned as the stinging mixture was applied to his wounded side. Soon after Lewis sported a fine, clean bandage.

"Alright Brenna, let him up." Candy said, going to the cupboard to fetch more bandages.

"Do I have to?" Brenna said in a whiney voice. "He's so comfortable."

"No I'm not comfortable! You're sitting on me!" Lewis nearly yelled.

"Exactly. You're a great seat-cushion." Brenna grinned mischievously.

"Get off me!" Lewis roared. "Candy, tell her to get off! Candy? Candy?"

There was no answer.

CHAPTER THREE

MITCH

C andy had taken the vial and some more bandages down to the dungeon in search of another patient. She was careful not to jingle the keys as she approached the vertical iron bars. She inserted the brass-colored key into the lock and turned it until she heard a click. She silently entered the cell that held Mitch. He lay motionless on a pile of straw, with the damp stone wall behind him. He looked as if he hadn't moved since she and Lewis had brought him down here. For one terrible moment Candy was afraid that he might be dead. Relief surged through her when he stirred and mumbled a name.

"Babbette." he half moaned half gasped.

He was dreaming of his lost love. Her hair was a swirling mass of shining auburn, glorious and bright when it was caught in the sunlight. It framed her gentle face and her eyes shone like stars as they gazed lovingly at him. Her perfume filled his nostrils, it was intoxicating and he loved it. Her lips, red and soft as two rose petals, smiled at him kindly. Then she was kissing him tenderly.

They were in each other's arms once again. He felt her hand on his shoulder, then a stinging pain broke the spell and his eyes flew open.

He beheld the young woman he'd battled earlier. She was pouring something on his wounded shoulder, but stopped and drew back, startled when their eyes met. His shoulder was throbbing but he pushed himself up with an effort, grunting in pain as he did.

"What're you doing here?" he asked defensively and untrusting.

"Tending to your wound." Candy said simply.

"Why?" he said raising a brow, still sounding a little defensive.

"Because you're hurt." Candy shrugged carelessly.

"You should be trying to kill me." Mitch stated very matter-of-factly.

"Why?" Candy sounded puzzled.

"Because we're enemies." Mitch said simply, as if it was the most obvious fact in the entire world.

"Well, we're not enemies now." Candy said, coming closer and starting to bandage his wound.

Mitch held still as she applied the cloth strips to his aching arm. There was a sweet gentleness about this girl that made him feel more relaxed somehow. She was so kind in her actions toward him.

There was something wrong here. Why was she being so nice? This had to be a trick. She was going to try and get some information out of him.

Well that's not gonna happen! I don't care what she does! This girl is my enemy, and will never be my friend! No matter what! he told himself firmly.

"There. You'll be right as rain in a few weeks." Candy said proudly as she tied off the end of the bandage. "Does it hurt?"

"Who're you to care?" snorted Mitch.

"I'm Candace MacKline. Who are you?" she said simply with a hint of cheerfulness. She thought Mitch looked like he could use some cheering up.

"You have a short memory if you can't remember dueling with me a little while ago!" he snapped at her, then added under his breath, "Empty-headed princess!"

Candy took a deep breath, forcing herself not to show how much he was irritating her with his cold remarks, then said in a very calm voice, "All right. What's your name?"

Mitch was silent. He had no intention of revealing his identity to an enemy. His only response was to fold his arms across his chest in a most decidedly stubborn manner and glare rebelliously at her.

"I'd like to have you're name so I know what to call you." Candy said kindly.

Mitch was still stubbornly silent as he rolled his eyes at her.

"I suppose I could just make one up for you, couldn't I?" she said with a sly grin.

Mitch tried in vain not to stop glaring.

"Let's see. What would suit you?" she said thoughtfully. "Hmm, 'Lost to a girl'? No, that's too masculine. Oh, I'll name you after my favorite pig. We roasted it last week for my birthday. We called it Pickle Face. How do you like your new name, Pickle Face?"

"How is that less masculine?" said Mitch, raising a brow.

"It was a female pig, Pickle Face." Candy grinned.

"Don't call me that!" he snarled.

"Well I don't know what else to call you Pickle face."

"Fine! Just shut up!" he growled, then sighed, "My name is Mitch."

"Mitch? Is that all?" she asked.

Mitch thought for a minute.

"Mitch Pickle," Candy started.

"Learicson!" cried Mitch. "Mitch Learicson."

"Well then, welcome to Castle MacKline, Mitch Learicson." Candy said kindly.

"Some welcome." Mitch snorted, touching his aching arm. "Who was that throwing knives? Is he insane?"

"It was a dagger not a knife, and 'she' is my sister." Candy told him.

Mitch's eyes widened, "Your sister's a knife-thrower?"

"Dagger, and don't you forget it." Candy said firmly. "Aye. That's Brenna, the Wolf Princess."

"The Wolf Princess is your sister?" Mitch said in surprise. All of those stories hadn't just been tales to frighten naughty children. So Griff hadn't been lying.

"Aye. She's my twin sister, though we look quite different." Candy shrugged.

"The one born under the dark star?" he asked curiously.

"Aye." Candy said, raising a brow. "You've heard of her?"

"Of course I've heard of her. I just didn't think she was real."

At that moment Mitch's stomach growled, reminding him of how hungry he was. Candy looked at his abdomen then back at his face. Mitch's cheeks were bright-red with embarrassment.

"I was gonna go get some breakfast," she smiled, "would you like me to bring you something?"

"How do I know that it won't be poisoned?" he smirked.

"If I wanted to kill you, I wouldn't have to waste time with poison or be trying to heal you, would I?" she said, patting her sword's hilt.

Mitch raised a brow, then smiled a very small smile, "Well, I am hungry."

Candy gave a small half smile, "I'll bring you something later."

Mitch watched her go, locking the cell door behind her. It had been a long time since anyone had been kind to him. No. It was all an act. She was his enemy, not his friend. That was a fact of life. Enemies could never be friends under any circumstances, and no matter what she did or said he would betray nothing.

Candy entered the kitchens and saw several serfs and wounded men sitting, standing or walking around. It wasn't overly crowded, since the kitchen area was quite spacious and was always warm due to its many fireplaces always being lit. Even in the winter this kitchen easily heated the entire castle through several vents leading upward and side to side.

Miss Anne was cooking a hardy stew over one of the fires while Fiona and Ivy were making fresh bread. It smelled heavenly. Better than heavenly if you were as hungry as Candy was.

She took a bowl of the steaming stew and a large chunk of still warm bread, then sat down at one of the many tables to enjoy her breakfast. It was wonderfully good. But about halfway through her meal, Candy was interrupted when she felt something nudge her leg. She looked down and saw her wolfhound, Bonnibel.

"Hello Bonnibel." Candy said, stroking the hound's silky head. "Hungry girl?"

Candy tore off a piece of bread and fed it to the light gray dog, who ate it gratefully then started sniffing the floor under the table for more.

"Did you save some for me?" she heard Brenna's voice from the direction of the doorway.

Candy turned to see her sister entering the kitchen, her own wolfhound on her heels.

"Come on Dooley." Brenna called over her shoulder to the nearly black dog that followed her faithfully.

Brenna got a bowl of her own and some bread, then took the seat next to Candy. She threw a crust to Dooley after having him do a few tricks then began eating her own breakfast.

"So what did you do to Lewis after I left?" Candy chuckled.

"I didn't do anything. He started squirming and it just wasn't comfortable anymore. So I called him a worm and left," Brenna explained in between and during mouthfuls.

With how competitive the Wolf Princess had been with her brothers, her table-manners left something to be desired. The dogs didn't mind though. They were rather pleased as each time that she opened her mouth, crumbs and bits of half chewed food fell to the floor for their dining pleasure. They gladly cleaned up the Wolf Princess's mess.

Some of the more refined people in that area thought that she must have gotten her title from her awful eating habits rather than from her fighting skills. They weren't far wrong. There had even been times when she'd growled jokingly at the table when one of her brothers pretended to steal something off her plate.

"So where did you go?" Brenna asked. "You just disappeared."

"I had to take care of someone else's wound." Candy shrugged.

"Who?" Brenna asked curiously.

"Mitch." Candy said simply before spooning another bite of warm stew into her mouth.

"Oh." Brenna said around a mouthful of stew soaked bread, delighting the hounds with a shower of crumbs. "Who's Mitch?"

Candy lifted the bowl to her lips and drained its contents, then stood and went to the stew-pot to refill it.

"Candy?" Brenna said a little more seriously, disliking the feeling of being ignored. "Who's Mitch?"

"A very hungry man." Candy said, taking up a second chunk of bread and turning toward the doorway.

"Candy wait." Brenna called, rising from her seat only to trip over Dooley and to find herself lying flat on her stomach. She lay on the kitchen's hard-packed dirt floor with Dooley sniffing at her ear.

"Ow!" she grunted. "Dooley!"

Brenna could hear the sound of her brothers' chuckling as the sound echoed through the kitchens. She looked up and saw them in the doorway, their dark eyes dancing with merriment.

"What's so funny?" she growled up at them from the floor.

"The wolf is brought down by the wolfhound." Lewis snickered.

"Even the Wolf Princess isn't safe from the ferocious hound." Konroy grinned.

Both of their faces were turning red as they tried to hold in their laughter.

"Start running lads!" their sister bellowed, jumping to her feet and chasing after the laughing young men, who were now running through the courtyard as though their lives depended on it.

Candy had reached the cell where she found Mitch sitting near the bars. She handed the bowl and bread through to him, then watched as he ate like a starving animal. Within a minute his meal was in his stomach and the empty bowl was back through the bars in Candy's hands. Then Mitch issued forth a very loud, yet satisfied belch.

"You're welcome." Candy said, raising a brow and wrinkling her nose at him as she thought, **And I thought that Brenna had bad table-manners.**

Mitch moved the back of his hand across his mouth and gave a quieter burp, "Well if it was poisoned, I should be dead soon."

"I think it's more likely that you'll die from a stomach-ache, the way you eat." Candy said, wrinkling her nose again.

"Oh have I offended you your highness?" his tone was a sarcastic one, filled with contempt.

"I just don't want to see your breakfast come back up." Candy said, a little annoyed. "Pardon me for caring."

"Why do you care so much anyway?" he snorted. "Feeling guilty about something are we?"

"No, it's because you're a human being." she stated firmly. "And you care."

"I don't care about you princess." Mitch snarled.

"Then why didn't you kill me?" she almost yelled.

Mitch was struck to silence.

"Whether or not you want to admit it, you spared me." Candy continued. "So now I'm sparing you." That being said, Candy turned and left the dungeon. That Northman. He was so aggravating to talk to.

"I'm so mad I could just spit!" she muttered as she began her ascent up the stairs that led out of the prison and into the courtyard. "Maybe I should've poisoned him!"

Brenna had been chasing her brothers for about ten minutes, when she tackled Konroy and put him in a headlock.

"Surrender!" she ordered.

"Never!" he bellowed defiantly, trying to loosen his sister's tight grip. But Brenna was too strong and too stubborn to let go before he admitted defeat.

"Say it!" growled Brenna. "Say it!"

"No!" roared Konroy.

"Say it!" she said tightening her grip.

"All right! Fine! Eel stew and starfish mush are delicious!"

"And?" Brenna reminded him of the second part.

"And I'm in love with a mermaid," Konroy muttered.

"What was that? I couldn't hear you." Brenna teased.

"I'm in love with a mermaid! Now lemme go!" he yelled, squirming against her grasp.

Brenna released him reluctantly, "Now, where'd Lewis get to? Aha!"

She'd spotted him ducking into the stables and pursued him. She rushed into the stable and ran smack into MacKurk.

MacKurk was about six feet tall, had shaggy blond hair, blue eyes, lightly tanned skin, and a smile that would make even a selfish hag's heart turn over.

"Oof!" said MacKurk.

"Oh I'm so sorry MacKurk!" gasped Brenna, blushing slightly. "Are you alright MacKurk?"

"I'm fine. I took a kick from Lightningbolt earlier and I'm still standing." MacKurk chuckled.

MacKurk was one of the best stable-hands in Castle MacKline, and most of the young maids that served there were half in love with him. Even Brenna couldn't help noticing how very attractive and muscular he was.

The Lightningbolt that he was referring to was Brenna's black stallion. He was as dark as a starless, moonless night, except for a zigzagging stripe down his face and four white socks. He was a tall, strong and proud horse, and he had spent many a happy hour out running along the beach with Brenna on his back.

Candy had always accompanied them on her golden-chestnut mare named Dutchess. Dutchess was a sweet pony/horse mix with one white rear foot. Her mane and tail streamed out behind her, and when they were caught in the sunshine, they were the color of gold and as soft as velvet. Some even said that there was unicorn in her ancestry and that was why she was so gentle and beautiful.

But Brenna wasn't thinking about horses right now. She wasn't thinking about much of anything other than MacKurk's smile and blue eyes.

"Well, I'm glad he didn't hurt you." she smiled at him.

"Me too." MacKurk chuckled again.

He has such a wonderful laugh. Brenna thought. Out loud she said, "You're so strong." Then she tried a very poor attempt at flirting by stroking the bare part of his arm with her fingertips.

"Well being strong, I need to go and fetch some water. Good morning Princess." MacKurk said kindly, brushing past her.

Brenna watched him go and sighed, lightly biting on her lower lip.

He's so handsome. she thought.

"Oh MacKurk, take me in your strong, hairy arms, and kiss me you fool. Ha, ha, ha!" she heard Lewis doing a bad impression of her voice.

She turned and saw him laughing hysterically behind a pile of straw. She leapt upon him and put him in a headlock as she had done with Konroy earlier.

"All right, say it you sack of dirt!" she growled.

"Brenna loves MacKurk. Brenna loves MacKurk." Lewis said in a singsong voice.

"Shut up! You know what I want to hear, now say it!" she snarled.

"Eel stew and starfish mush are delicious, and I'm in love with a beautiful mermaid named Colleen." Lewis laughed.

"Eew!" yelled Brenna jumping away from him.

Colleen was a beautiful young woman who had been betrothed to Lewis since they were both about two years old. They'd been friends as children, until they were old enough to understand what being betrothed meant. After that, they were never really certain of how to behave around each other. But Lewis knew that talking about his love life was a sure-fire way to get Brenna to leave him alone.

This was mostly because it reminded Brenna that she was also betrothed. But while Colleen was kind and beautiful, Brenna's betrothed was annoying and regardless of whether or not he was handsome, it was impossible for Brenna to get along with him. Each time they met, he tried to kiss her and followed her like a starving puppy follows a butcher. Worst of all, he insisted on calling her by a nickname that she absolutely despised. More than once she'd wondered why, of all the men she could've been betrothed to, her parents had chosen this one.

"Brenna, Lewis, Da's gonna take a score of men out to make certain that the invaders are gone. Want to come?" they heard Konroy call.

The two young people answered as one, "Aye!" and went to saddle their steeds.

Lewis was extremely proud of his bay gelding, called Loch King. This horse was one of his closest companions, and he quite enjoyed riding him out across the fields and over the hills. But he mostly loved this horse because it often beat Brenna's stallion in races.

Within an hour the party was out searching the surrounding area for any hidden invaders. Konroy was riding his liver-chestnut colt, named Starwalker for the mark on his forehead and his fancy trotting.

Candy came bounding on Dutchess right passed them. Nothing cheered her like a good ride on her beloved horse. It was a good day for riding. The sun was shining down on them, the sky was clear and the gentle sea breeze was rustling through the treetops.

But as fine a day as it was, after about fifteen minutes of combing the hills Brenna became bored and started challenging Lewis to a race.

"Come on Lewis," she said in a pouting voice. "This is so dull I want to scream."

"No!" he said irritably with an annoyed grunt. "Now keep your eyes pealed for any signs of those invaders! I wonder what they wanted?"

"Who cares? They're gone now. We should be celebrating. Let's race!" his sister persisted.

"For the last time Brenna, No!" he told her.

"Fine!" she sniffed. "If you're not up to the challenge."

"What challenge? Loch King beats Lightning two out of every three times." Lewis snorted.

"And yet you're too cowardly to race us." Brenna smirked. "What a shame."

"I'm not a coward!" Lewis stated firmly.

"Prove it!" Brenna challenged.

"Fine! Konroy!" he called over his shoulder.

"What?" Konroy called back, riding up alongside them.

"Say go." Lewis said simply.

"Are you two racing?" Konroy asked eagerly.

"Aye." Brenna smiled smugly.

"Well I want to race too." Konroy said quickly. "Get someone else to say go."

"Fine." Brenna sighed irritably. "Candy," she called over her shoulder.

"I'm coming. What is it?" answered Candy as she came up beside them.

"We're racing and need someone to say go." Brenna explained.

"Where are you racing to?" asked Candy.

"Uh." Brenna hadn't thought about where to race, just the race. "How about around the Old Oak and back here past the Big Rock?"

There were murmurs of agreement as they formed a line next to the Big Rock and waited for Candy's signal.

"All right. Ready? On your mark. Get set. Bye!" Candy yelled as she sunk her heels into Dutchess's sides. "Go!" she laughed over her shoulder to them as she bounded ahead toward the Old Oak tree.

Her three siblings were on her heels in a second, sending up a spray of dirt and grass behind them. The horses galloped toward the huge, ancient tree, their riders encouraging them every step of the way.

Brenna and Lewis broke away from the other two riders and were suddenly ahead by about two yards. Still neck and neck, they approached the mighty tree, slowing their pace so that they could turn with ease.

Some people said that this tree, christened the Old Oak, was at least five-hundred years old. It certainly looked that old with it's gnarled branches reaching ever skyward, it's huge trunk nearly six feet thick, and it's large roots stretching out in all directions, each one as thick as a grown man's torso.

As they rounded the ancient oak Brenna suddenly leaned forward and squeezed with her knees. This was the signal for which Lightningbolt had been waiting. The signal to speed up. Less than a minute later, Brenna had taken the lead.

She passed Candy and Konroy who were slowing to round the giant tree. She knew that Lewis was right behind her and trying to pass.

"Go Lightning! Come on boy!" she encouraged her steed.

To anyone watching that race, Brenna and her stallion would've appeared to be nothing more than a large, black blur. Brenna looked to her right and saw the Big Rock go by. She slowed Lightningbolt to an easy trot. They were both panting and sweating. The sea breeze was a welcome, cooling sensation.

"Good boy Lightning." Brenna gasped as she patted his neck affectionately.

Lightningbolt gave a small whinny in agreement as he trotted toward the Big Rock.

The Big Rock was a large brown piece of sandstone, likely left there after an attempt to build a castle. There were no other ruins to prove that it was anything more than a failed attempt, but it was a landmark that was nearly impossible to miss, due to it's size. Thus it had been christened by the locals, the Big Rock.

"Not bad." Konroy called, as he rode up next to sister.

"That was amazing." Candy agreed, close behind Konroy.

"I want a rematch." Lewis complained from where he and his mount stood next to the Big Rock.

Brenna started laughing, "And I thought you won two out of every three races."

"Hey." Konroy said in a startled voice.

"What?" asked Candy.

"Didn't you see that?" he asked.

"See what?" said Lewis.

"It looked like a wolf." Konroy told them.

"Oh, a wolf. Well that's very strange." Brenna said sarcastically.

"Aye. You don't see one of those in the woods every day." Lewis chuckled.

"But, it wasn't a normal wolf. It looked like it had, wings." Konroy said, lowering his eyes.

The three eldest MacKline children stared at their youngest sibling, questioning whether or not they'd heard him correctly.

"Are you feeling alright Konroy?" asked Candy.

"I'm not ill. I saw a winged wolf!" he told them.

"Konroy there haven't been winged wolves in this area for over a hundred years." Lewis said very matter-of-factly. "Now if this is some sort of a joke," Lewis started, but was interrupted by Konroy pointing and shouting, "Look! There it is again!"

They all looked toward the woods and saw something small and gray make a dash from behind an elm into the tall, thick grass near the tree-line. It looked like a wolf. A very small wolf, but, were those bat-wings folded down on its back?

They all stared in disbelief at where the small creature had vanished.

"Do you think that's where it's den is?" said Lewis.

"I'll be right back." Brenna said as she kicked Lightningbolt into a gallop, heading toward the exact spot that the small gray creature had just been.

Something in the treetops caught Candy's eye at that moment. Something had glinted. Flashed in the light. It was horrible to realize that it was the sun reflecting off of something medal. It moved upward. It was a sword blade. All through the treetops

Candy could now see dark clad archers drawing their arrows back, ready to fire. What were they waiting for? The sword. They were waiting for the sword to signal them.

"Brenna wait! It's a trap!" she yelled, spurring Dutchess forward.

Mere moments later she was by her sister's side.

"Fire at will!" a voice bellowed from the treetops.

The air was suddenly filled with a rain of arrows whizzing toward them.

"Run!" yelled Brenna, burying her heels in Lightningbolt's ribs.

The girls rode back toward their brothers, dodging the arrows as best they could. Candy grunted as a shaft grazed her right thigh and tears of pain came into her eyes as another nicked her upper right arm.

Brenna cried out as an arrow pierced her upper left arm. She swayed on Lightningbolt's back, but did not fall. Lightningbolt, aware of his mistress's wound, slowed for a moment, then sped up, turning in the direction of the castle.

The entire group from Castle MacKline turned to follow, escaping the shower of deadly shafts. The cheers of their attackers were echoing in their ears as the party entered the castle gates.

Lightningbolt stopped near the stables and whickered in alarm at the feeling of Brenna swaying on his back. Dooley the wolfhound came bounding from the kitchens and let out a howl of dismay when he saw his owner's wound.

Lewis, Konroy, and Candy all quickly dismounted and rushed toward Brenna, but halted when Candy dropped to her knees, looking deathly pale. Lewis knelt beside her, quickly followed by Konroy.

"Candy?" Lewis asked fearfully. "Are you all right?"

"I feel like I'm going to," Candy never finished whatever it was she was going to say, for she was interrupted by suddenly having to vomit.

Konroy moved just in time to avoid being sprayed by the smelly mess. If he'd remained where he was the vomit would've surely landed in his lap.

Because of all the noise, MacKurk came hurrying out of the stables. He saw the wounded Brenna swaying in the saddle and rushed over to catch her as she fell from the horse's back. He supported her easily.

Brenna could feel herself drifting in and out of consciousness, but wasn't completely sure who was holding her. She forced her eyes open and gazed up at her rescuer.

"MacKurk?" she said weakly, not totally trusting her eyes.

"Aye Princess." MacKurk said honestly.

Brenna knew no more as the darkness closed in around her.

MacKurk watched helplessly as her eyes glazed over and rolled into the back of her head. Then she went limp in his arms.

Candy's eyes were wide as she stared at Lewis.

"Lewis I can't see you!" she gasped fearfully.

"What?" said Lewis disbelieving that this was really happening to his sister.

"I can't see you!" she said, turning her head so that she was facing Konroy, and said, "All I can see are dark shapes with the sun behind them."

Then her eyes glazed over and rolled into the back her head as she collapsed into her brothers' waiting arms.

CHAPTER FOUR

A DEAL FOR A CURE

Mitch had been sleeping fitfully for about two hours when he was rudely awakened by a sharp kick to his back. He grunted partly from pain and partly from grouchiness. He sat up and glared coldly up at his attacker.

Lewis and Konroy looked back down at him with icy-cold glares.

Mitch looked them up and down, concluding that they were sons of the laird due to their fine attire and weapons. No lowly servant carried swords with gold and silver on the hilts, and jewels for the pommel-stones.

"What do you want?" he snorted, lack of sleep having made him irritable. "Isn't it below you to be down here? Or are you two just giant rats?"

"Can I kick him again Lewis?" growled Konroy, clapping a fist to his open palm.

"Steady Konroy." Lewis said, putting a hand on his younger brother's shoulder.

"Well, while you boys argue, I'm going back to sleep." Mitch yawned. "Goodnight."

"Kick him again Konroy," said Lewis.

"Alright, what do you want?" Mitch groaned. "Ow!"

"Thank you Konroy. No more kicking please." Lewis said, completely emotionless. "Some of your 'friends' ambushed us out near the woods and our sisters were shot."

"So? What do you want with me?" said Mitch, raising a brow.

"The herbalists say that the arrows were poisoned. Since they were arrows from your friends you need to give us the antidote." Lewis explained, his tone threatening.

"And what do I get in return for this valuable information?" Mitch asked, raising a brow.

"I won't kick you again." Konroy said threateningly.

"Konroy, go out for a bit." said Lewis.

"What?" said Konroy, sounding confused as he raised a brow. "But,"

"Konroy, just go." said Lewis in a voice that was low and serious. Konroy knew better than to question his elder brother when he took on that tone.

Lewis took off his sword and handed it to his brother, causing Konroy to stare at him worriedly.

"I'll be fine Kon, just take a walk." Lewis said in that same low, serious tone.

Konroy left reluctantly, leaving Mitch and Lewis alone in the dank cell.

When Konroy was out of sight, Lewis smiled slightly down at Mitch.

"What's your name?" he asked the prisoner.

"Mitch." Mitch shrugged. "What's it to you?"

"Well, Mitch, it's in your best interest to help me with the antidote." Lewis told him, his voice was still threatening dispite his smile. He knelt in front of Mitch, leaning toward him imposingly.

"And if I don't?" said Mitch, glaring up at him defiantly.

Mitch was caught completely off guard as he was grabbed by his shirt collar and dragged to his feet. The air left him in a rush as Lewis's fist met his gut and Mitch suddenly found himself shoved back against the cell's damp wall. Mitch stared at Lewis, who had brought his face within inches of his own. Mitch felt a hand closing around his throat.

"If you don't, I'll squeeze your neck 'til your eyes pop out!" Lewis growled menacingly, the smile gone from his face.

Mitch clawed feebly at Lewis's tightening grip. When this failed Mitch spit in Lewis's eye and kicked him in the shin before he punched his wounded side. Lewis bent double, clutching at his now throbbing ribcage as he gasped desperately for air.

Now free of Lewis's grip Mitch rubbed at his bruised neck, panting. Seeing Lewis bent double Mitch kicked Lewis in the face. Lewis's head was spinning, but in spite of his sudden dizziness he saw Mitch coming at him, fist raised. Lewis ducked and rammed his shoulder into Mitch's stomach as hard as he could. Mitch was bent double. Lewis stood tall and brought down both of his fists square on Mitch's back. Mitch lay flat on his belly, face down in the moldy straw. Hands flat on the cell floor he started to rise, but Lewis put his foot on the small of Mitch's back and pushed him back down.

"Now," Lewis panted, tasting blood, "how about that antidote?"

Mitch, still gasping for air, almost yelled in defeat, "All right! I'll tell you what to use!"

Lady MacKline had been weeping ever since she'd heard that her daughters had been shot with poison-tipped shafts. She sat by their bedside bathing their feverish brows as tears streamed down her cheeks. She noted that Brenna's brow was hotter than Candy's, and that Candy wasn't shivering and writhing the way that Brenna was. Every so often Brenna's eyes would snap open and she'd sit up so fast that she'd sometimes fall out of bed, though it seemed more like she'd thrown herself from the bed.

Laird MacKline entered the chamber, closely followed by Darsy.

"I came as soon as I heard." Darsy said.

"How are they?" asked the laird, coming to stand by his wife.

"Candy seems to be healing slowly, but there's been no change in Brenna." Lady MacKline told them. Her voice was shaking so fearfully that it was difficult for the men to understand what she was saying. "When she opens her eyes, it's like she can't see me. She doesn't know me." Lady MacKline buried her face in her hands, sobbing inconsolably.

Laird and Lady MacKline had become slightly gray in the last twenty years since their daughters' birth, but Darsy didn't look like he'd aged a day.

Darsy approached the bed and looked down at the sweat-covered faces while Laird MacKline tried to comfort his weeping wife.

"Do you have one of the arrows?" he asked. "Maybe I can identify the poison."

Laird MacKline nodded at a table by the far wall, reluctant to leave his wife. Darsy saw a long, black arrow with dark raven feathers and a sharp steel tip lying on the tabletop. He walked over to the table and picked up the arrow. As he looked it over his eyes grew wide and he shook his head in disbelief.

"Is something wrong Darsy?" Laird MacKline asked as he came to stand by the herbalist, leaving his now slightly calmer wife to care for their ill daughters.

"Were all of the arrows like this one?" asked Darsy with a shudder.

"Aye." the laird nodded. "Do you recognize it?"

"I do. There's only one clan that makes their arrows like this. The Raves Clan and those that follow them." Darsy said, still shaking his head at the arrow. "They're a dangerous people."

"Do you know what kind of poisons they use?" asked Laird MacKline hopefully.

"Aye." Darsy said simply.

"And how to cure it?" Laird MacKline's voice was more hopeful than before.

Darsy turned his dark eyes to the laird. Laird MacKline saw a great sadness on the herbalist's face. "I know of things that slow it, but nothing that will save them. The Raves keep their antidotes secret. Very secret." Darsy's voice was uneven as he spoke. "I don't know what to do for them."

"I have someone who knows." Lewis called from the doorway.

The laird, the lady and the herbalist all turned their eyes toward the three young men who had just entered the room.

"Lewis your nose is bleeding!" cried Lady MacKline, rushing to her eldest son.

"Mum I'm fine." Lewis said rolling his eyes. "Kon, keep your axe on him!"

Konroy nodded, pressing the flat of his axe a little harder against Mitch's back. Mitch flinched. His back and gut still ached where Lewis had punched him.

"Who is this filthy dog you've brought before us?" growled Laird MacKline, stomping over to where the young men stood. He fingered the medallion that hung from Mitch's neck. Mitch glared hatefully at the older man.

"So you're one of those Northmen." the laird nearly spat the word 'Northmen' as he spoke, glaring back at Mitch just as hatefully.

Mitch took the medallion in his hand and hid it under his bearskin shirt.

"He knows the antidote." Lewis said, dodging as his mother pursued him with a wet cloth.

Laird MacKline's face didn't soften as he spoke, "Is this true?" It was said as more of a threat than a question.

Mitch, still glaring, uttered one word, "Aye."

"Then tell our herbalist! Now!" said the laird, shoving Mitch toward Darsy.

Mitch stumbled, but quickly regained his footing. Darsy tried to put his arm around Mitch's shoulders to steady him, but Mitch shrugged him off.

"Tell me my son, what do I need to cure these girls?" Darsy asked, gesturing at the girls.

Mitch stared at the girls on the bed. He recognized Candy, and then slowly the other girl came back into his mind. She was the one who'd knocked him over earlier.

Her hair was a tangled web framing a sweat glistening face. Her lips weren't as red as her sister's, nor were her eyelashes as long. Her skin was more freckled and bore the signs of previous sunburn, while Candy was lightly tanned.

Mitch approached the bed, taking a closer look at Brenna. So this was what the fierce warrior who'd been given the title 'Wolf Princess' had been reduced to. She didn't look very threatening now. She seemed quite gangly to him as she lay there rasping painfully.

He was startled when her eyes shot open and seemed to be staring at him. He took a step back as she leaned over the edge of the bed and regurgitated her half-digested breakfast on the floor. Then she laid back down on her pillow, eyes closed and her breathing ragged.

"Well?" said Darsy, bringing Mitch's attention away from the mess.

"Give them well boiled dandelion tea." Mitch said simply.

"That's all they need?" asked Darsy, sounding inquisitive.

"At this point," Mitch explained, "she's beyond anything else." He motioned at Brenna. "Make sure there are nettles in it too, and honey might make it go down smoother."

Darsy put a hand on Mitch's shoulder and smiled, "Thank you lad."

Mitch wasn't sure how to react. What was wrong with these people? He was their enemy. Couldn't they see that? At least the laird and his sons knew what was what. They at least treated him like an enemy. But Candy and this man acted as though he were an ally.

"Where did you find him Lewis?" Laird MacKline asked in a hushed tone, standing very near his eldest son.

"I helped Candy put him in the dungeon earlier." Lewis explained, also in a hushed tone.

"Give him some food, drink and a blanket, after you put him back in his cell." Laird MacKline said reluctantly.

"Aye sir." Lewis said. "Alright Mitch. It's time to go."

Mitch's brow lowered, then he saw Lewis fingering his sword hilt. Mitch left the room obediently, pausing at the door just once to gaze back at the girls. Then he felt Lewis and Konroy's weapons at his back and moved forward.

Darsy started preparing the herbs for the tea while Lady MacKline sent for some boiling water from the kitchen.

"Help from a Northman." Laird MacKline snorted. "They're all traitors and murderers."

"Not that one." Darsy said softly.

"What makes you say that?" asked Lady MacKline.

"There was something in his eyes that spoke of pain and loss. That boy has suffered." Darsy said. "I can feel it. He has been through something that no man should go through."

Mitch was grateful for the food and blanket, but was still uncomfortable in his cell. It was damp, dank, cold and foul smelling. The straw that he slept on was moldy and uncomfortable. The scent of it made him feel ill, but he'd been too hungry to care.

After eating and drinking, he wrapped himself in the blanket that Lewis had brought him, laid down on the disgusting straw pile and tried to sleep. But sleep wouldn't come. The image of the Wolf Princess haunted his thoughts. Those eyes, those big brown eyes. He'd seen eyes like those before, and their owner still haunted his dreams.

Later that afternoon Candy was feeling well enough to get up and walk around. Soon after that Brenna felt better as well, but began protesting when their mother insisted that they both stay in bed for the remainder of the day. Candy was content to lay back and relax while Brenna argued with Lady MacKline for nearly ten minutes.

Brenna finally laid back moodily, crossing her arms and putting a most decidedly sour expression on her face. The unhappy look only disapeared once she fell asleep.

It was about sunset when Laird MacKline was called to the gate. A messenger from the Raves had come demanding an audience with the laird. Laird MacKline came, his eldest son at his side.

"Laird MacKline, my master, Laird Griff Cray, has something that you need. By this time, you'll have noticed that your daughters are frightfully ill and likely near death. My master has the antidote. He is willing to save their lives in exchange for your surrendering the castle to him." the messenger explained. "What say you?"

Lewis hid a smile as the laird stroked his chin thoughtfully, then said, "He can keep his antidote."

The messenger, whose name was Vrant, was taken aback by these words. "You'd rather have two dead daughters than give up your castle?"

"My daughters aren't dying." Laird MacKline smiled.

Vrant's eyes widened, "No one is strong enough to survive that poison. You must be lying to yourself."

Laird MacKline's smile widened, "My daughters are strong enough, and I am no liar."

Brenna had woken up just before sunset and thinking of her stallion in the stable, she refused to stay in bed any longer. She rose and dressed in her black breeches, shirt, boots, and long vest and sword belt, then she went to the door.

"Where're you going?" asked Candy.

"To check on Lightningbolt. I don't know if he got shot." Brenna told her.

"I'll come too. I'd like to see Dutchess." Candy said, rising and pulling a long, light gray, sleeveless dress on over the top of her nightgown, then she strapped her belt around her waist. Lastly, she slipped into two dainty buckskin shoes.

The two walked down the corridor side by side and descended the long winding staircase in the south tower.

Vrant couldn't believe the sight he beheld as the two princesses exited the Castle and started toward the stables, as if they had never been wounded. Brenna was the first to stop when she saw her father speaking to a man she didn't recognize.

"Candy, do you know who that is?" she asked, nodding toward Vrant.

Candy raised a brow and shook her head, "I've no idea."

"As you can see, we've no need of your master's cure." Laird MacKline nearly sneered at the messenger, then added in a low, dangerous tone, "So you can tell your 'Laird Griff Cray,' that if he ever comes near my family, my people, my castle, or my land again, he won't live to regret it. Make certain that he understands that, messenger-boy."

Lewis felt true pride in his father as the enemy messenger's face almost turned a vivid shade of purple with rage.

"This isn't over yet MacKline." Vrant snarled. "My master will gain your castle, lands, and you and yours will be his slaves."

"Leave now or you will leave with a flogging." growled the laird. "It's your choice."

Vrant threw Laird MacKline an icy glare over his shoulder as he exited through the gate. Laird MacKline returned the glare, his eyes never leaving Vrant's figure until it was beyond his sight. He knew that Vrant was right, this wasn't over.

Brenna and Candy were pleased to find their horses in good condition. Brenna was even more pleased to find MacKurk working hard in the stable. She watched the way that his muscles flexed as he hefted a pitchfork of straw into an empty stall. She was startled when he looked over at her. She felt herself blush but forced herself to keep looking at him.

"Did you need something princess?" he asked, wiping sweat from his brow.

Brenna felt her breath catch, "Well, maybe you could meet me here tomorrow night to help me with Lightning. There's something he does that I'd like to show you."

"All right. If that's what you'd like princess." MacKurk shrugged.

Brenna left the stable with a smile on her face. Tomorrow night she would be alone with MacKurk. He and she would talk and perhaps, he would fall in love with her.

CHAPTER FIVE

MIDNIGHT IN THE STABLES

The next day felt as if it would never end. The day seemed to drag on and on. All Brenna could think about was the coming evening with MacKurk. But her daydreams were interupted by a servant delivering a letter through the side gate, since the main gate was now baracaded after being splintered.

She knew this servant, his name was Delaney. He was somewhere between twenty-five and thirty years old, tall, broad shouldered and had dark auburn hair.

"For you my lady." he said kindly, offering the letter to her.

The Wolf Princess gave a discontented sigh, knowing that the letter must be from her much disliked betrothed since Delaney was his most trusted servant.

"Good grief, what did Lynch write this time?" she said, taking the letter and opening it.

"My young master asks that I bring him a reply." Delaney said kindly.

Brenna scanned the letter's contents and frowned.

"He wants to see me in a fortnight?" she groaned.

"He thought that two weeks was enough time for you to prepare." Delaney said kindly.

"I don't think, I mean, I'm busy that day." Brenna said, stumbling over her words as she struggled to find an excuse.

"How about the week after?" Delaney asked hopefully.

"That would be perfect." said Lady MacKline, coming over to stand near them. She ignored the unhappy expression on her daughter's face as she continued, "Tell your master we'll be expecting him."

"Uh, thankyou Milady." said Delaney, raising a brow as he mounted his horse and rode through the side gate.

"Mum," Brenna whined.

"You need to get used to each other's company if you're going to get married someday." her mother said simply. "Your father and I did, and it made our marriage much happier. Now go through your wardrobe and start thinking about to wear that day."

"It's three weeks away." Brenna grunted.

"I could always have a new dress made for you." Lady MacKline smiled. "A nice pink dress with ribbons, bows and lace."

"I'll go through my wardrobe." Brenna said quickly.

"Good g'el." Lady MacKline said cheerfully, embracing her eldest daughter.

Brenna's mind began racing for a way to avoid Lynch's upcoming visit, and slowly a plan took shape in her mind. She decided that tonight in the stable, she would put her plan into action. She only hoped that MacKurk would go along with it.

"Are you all right?" she asked.

Mitch rolled his eyes, "I'm fine."

"So I owe my thanks to you. Or so I hear." Candy smiled.

Mitch lowered his gaze refusing to look at her and saying nothing.

"You saved my life, and my sister's." Candy continued. "How do I repay you?"

"My freedom." Mitch said, locking his eyes with hers.

"Would you return to the Raves?" she inquired.

"Never!" he almost snarled, griping the bars of the cell. "They abandoned me here! I'll go my own way once I'm free. Ask your father to release me."

Candy lowered her eyes, "He'll never permit it. Not for a Northman."

"Then how do I gain my freedom?" Mitch's knuckles turned white as he tightened his grip on the cold iron bars that seperated them, bringing his face close to hers.

"I'm thinking," she said, a little startled by his tone. "You'll need some new clothes, a few days worth of food and water." She thought for a moment, then got to her feet and said, "I'll be back." Then she was gone.

He watched her go and wondered what she had in mind.

Candy went straight to Lewis's room. She peaked inside. He wasn't there.

Good. she thought.

Silently she slipped into the room and went to her brother's trunk. She opened it and took out a pair of breeches, a shirt, and a jerkin. She closed the chest as quietly as she could and hid the clothes beneath her coat. She peaked out into the hall. It seemed empty enough, so she slipped out and closed the door behind her, then headed toward her room. As she rounded a corner, she almost collided with Lewis.

"Oops!" he said. "Sorry Candy."

"It's all right. See you later." she said quickly, brushing past him and quickening her pace.

Once she'd reached the door to her own room she would've rushed inside and hidden the clothes. But the door was bolted. She knocked on it.

"Go away!" she heard Brenna yell.

"Brenna, I need in there." Candy answered.

"No!" came the sharp reply.

"Come on Brenna, please? It's important." Candy pleaded.

"All right, fine. But only if you promise not to tell anyone what I look like right now!" Brenna's voice came through the heavy oak door as she unlocked it.

"Since when do you care about looks?" asked Candy as the door opened.

As she entered the door quickly closed behind her and was instantly rebolted. Candy stared wide-eyed at Brenna. There was a brush tangled up in her hair and she was wearing a dress. Candy couldn't believe it. Brenna absolutely hated to wear anything feminine, or to brush her hair.

"Don't look at me like that," Brenna complained.

Candy could see that Brenna's eyes and face were red with weeping. She'd obviously been having a rough time getting her hair smooth. Candy had never seen Brenna cry before, not even when they were seven and Brenna had fallen from her favorite climbing tree. She'd nearly broken her leg, but she still hadn't cried.

"Would you like some help?" Candy asked sympathetically.

Brenna was silent, but nodded in spite of her pride.

"All right. But uh, why are you doing this?" as Candy spoke the clothes under her coat slipped out and fell to the floor.

Brenna raised a brow and said, "Aren't those Lewis's clothes?"

"I need them."

"For what?"

"I won't ask about why you're dressing up if you won't ask me about these." Candy said, gathering up the clothing.

"Deal. Help me get this thing out of my hair." Brenna said, pointing to the brush.

Candy laid the clothes on their bed and went to work on loosening the brush from Brenna's hair.

"Ow!" Brenna winced.

"Sorry." Candy said, trying to work the brush out of the tangled mass as gently as she could. "When was the last time you washed your hair?"

Brenna shrugged, "A couple of months I think."

"Ew!" said Candy, quickly drawing her hands away from Brenna's greasy hair. "No wonder the brush got tangled up in your hair. You need to take a bath and wash your hair before you can brush it out."

"A bath? No! I won't do it!" Brenna nearly shouted, crossing her arms stubbornly.

"Brenna, I don't know what your plans are, but obviously you're trying to look nice for some reason. Unless you take a bath and wash your hair you can't accomplish that." Candy said just as stubbornly. She'd learned a thing or two about how to deal with her sister.

After another ten minutes of arguing Brenna finally agreed to a bath.

It took around two hours to do it all. Candy helped Brenna to wash her hair and then to dry it. It was an unusual sight to see Brenna completely clean and wearing a dress. It was one of the few dresses she had that still fit her, and Candy was surprised her sister was allowing her brush and style her hair.

When Brenna looked at herself in the full-length mirror she nearly gasped in shock. She turned this way and that, admiring the cornflower blue fabric that she was now wearing. She couldn't believe how beautiful she was, with as plain as the dress was made. Things of the feminine nature had never really mattered to her. But to see how attractive she could be almost made her wish that she'd cared sooner.

"You're absolutely beautiful." Candy said softly.

"Really?" asked Brenna, refusing to take her eyes off of her reflection, as though she were afraid that when she'd look back it would've vanished.

"Aye. Just look at you. You look, well, like a princess."

They both gave a small giggle over that.

Brenna thanked Candy and continued to look in the mirror, admiring her reflection while Candy folded up the clothes and put them in a drawstring bag.

"Well, have fun with, whatever you're going to do." Candy said as she exited the room.

"You too." Brenna's voice was in a dreamlike tone. How would MacKurk be able to resist her now?

Candy made her way back to the dungeon where she found Mitch asleep, wrapped up in the blanket that Lewis had given him.

"Mitch." Candy called to him softly, kneeling down and placing the bag on the floor.

Mitch stirred, stretched, then blinked at her as he sat up and yawned, "What?"

"I've got some clothes in this bag." she explained, pushing it through the bars. "Change into them, then push hard on that smooth rock that sticks out funny."

Mitch crawled to the bars and put his hands on the bag, "Then what?"

"Part of the wall will open and reveal a tunnel that leads to the stables. I'll meet you there with a sack of food and a skin of water. Then I'll distract the sentry so that you can slip through the gate." Candy explained.

Mitch nodded and began to pull the bag toward him, but stopped when Candy tugged on it. He looked at her questioningly. Her hand came up to stroke his cheek. Mitch closed his eyes and leaned his cheek against her soft palm.

"I haven't known you very long Mitch, but I'm glad that we've met. I just wish that it had been under different circumstances." she said softly, drawing his face toward her.

Mitch opened his eyes and looked at Candy as she pushed her face through the bars and kissed the side of his mouth. He wasn't sure why he did it. Maybe it was because he hadn't been kissed in so long. Maybe it was because she reminded him of his now dead Babbette. Whatever caused it, Mitch turned his head slightly and opened his mouth to hers.

Their lips brushed for only an instant before she drew back and said, trying to keep her voice calm, "I'll see you in the stables."

Then she stood, turned and rushed back up to the castle, her cheeks burning. That had been her first kiss.

Brenna was walking toward the stairs when she crossed paths with Konroy.

"Whoa!" he whistled. "Who are you?"

"Shut up!" she almost growled.

"No! Seriously, who are you?" Konroy chuckled.

Brenna growled and took hold of her younger brother's shirt collar. Konroy felt his feet leave the floor as his sister brought her face close to his.

"Brenna?" he gasped in disbelief.

"If you tell anyone that I look like this, I'll beat the stuffings out of you, you little scarecrow." Brenna growled, shoving him away.

"Your secret's safe with me." he said, straightening his shirt.

"It better be!" she snarled as she began her descent. Poor Konroy was still in such shock that he that had to put a hand on the wall to steady himself. He then nearly bent double and started laughing as he thought about his sister's appearance.

Candy was in the Kitchen packing a few loaves of bread and some dry salt pork into a sack when Lewis came in, startling her.

"Lewis! What are you doing here?" she said, hiding the sack under a table.

"Looking for you. Some of my clothes are missing. Do you know anything about it?" he asked.

"What do you mean?" Candy asked timidly.

"Well you were up near my room earlier, so I was wondering if you'd seen anything . . . strange?" he said slowly.

Candy gulped as her mind raced for an explanation.

Mitch had just exited the tunnel and entering the stables. He glanced at his surroundings. The stables were too dark at this hour of the night to make out anything more than shapes and shadows. The smell of hay, straw, grain and horses filled his nostrils. He could feel dry straw crunching under his boots. He could taste the fresh sea breeze that drifted through the openings of the stable doors and windows. He could hear the horses making soft sounds to one another, and footsteps.

Footsteps? It must be Candy coming. But the steps were heavier than Candy's and swifter. It had to be one of the guards. They must've discovered that he'd escaped and were coming for him. Surely they'd never recognize him in the dark, especially now that he was wearing Lewis's clothes. But he knew that they mustn't find the tunnel. Then they'd know how he'd gotten out and his only chance would be gone. He quickly kicked the cover back over the hole in the floor, and stepped back in the darkest part of the stable where he wouldn't be seen so easily.

Brenna paused outside of the stable's main entrance and took a deep breath. She looked up at the stars, hoping that her plan would work. Then, eyes forward, she entered the stables, her thoughts on MacKurk.

MacKurk was at this exact moment, with a young woman that he was promised to marry. Her father, Hagan the head stableman, was deathly ill. He had no sons, only his beloved daughter Elsa. But MacKurk had been his foster son since his own parents had died. As Hagan lay on his deathbed, he asked MacKurk to care for the widow and orphaned daughter that he was leaving behind. MacKurk gave his word that he would.

MacKurk, Hagan's family, as well as Laird and Lady MacKline were the only ones who knew anything about this, and where MacKurk truly was at this moment. So Brenna went into the stables, believing that the first person she'd see would be MacKurk.

Candy was being detained by Lewis, so Mitch was certain that the figure of a woman entering the stable and coming in his direction, obviously looking for someone, had to be Candy. Mitch couldn't imagine who else it could be.

She looks taller somehow, he thought, stepping out of the blackness of the corner.

The darkness in the stables only served to convince Brenna that it was MacKurk she was approaching. She came to stand in front him now that she saw where he was.

"Evening." she said softly.

"Evening." he said, a little above a whisper. "I'm glad you came."

"Really?" she said, feeling her breath catch.

"Of course." he said, sounding confused.

"Then you feel the same way I do?" she gasped happily.

"What? How do you feel about me?" he asked backing up into the dark corner again, until he felt the wall behind him.

"I'm betrothed to a man I can't love. I can't stand to be near him, even for a minute." Brenna said, taking a step closer to him. "I need to escape him. I feel so trapped."

"I know how you feel." Mitch said, pushing himself back as far against the wall as he could. Brenna reached a hand up and stroked his cheek tenderly. He flinched uneasily at her touch.

Her hand feels rougher. he thought.

"Then let's rescue each other." Brenna said breathlessly, then wrapping her arms around his neck she kissed him.

Mitch thought to push her away, but couldn't bring himself to do it. He put his arms around her and held her tight. Then the image of his lost love came back to haunt him and he pushed the young woman in his arms away as gently as he could.

"Uhm, I," he started, but Brenna cut him off with another kiss, this one much more passionate than the first.

Mitch was once more caught up in the moment and the emotion of the kiss. He had to force himself to push her away again.

"Candy, I really have to go." he said, his voice still a little husky after that kiss.

Brenna couldn't believe her ears, "I'm not Candy!" she nearly hissed, shoving him back harder against the wall.

Mitch grunted, then his eyes widened and strained in the darkness as he gulped, "You're not?"

"No!" she growled, glaring into the darkness.

"Oh no!" Mitch said worriedly. "Who are you?"

"Brenna!" she snarled angrily.

Mitch's heart sank, "Oh no!" he clapped a hand to his forehead. "I'm a dead man." he moaned.

"All this time you thought I was Candy, MacKurk?" she snapped.

"I'm not MacKurk." The words were out of Mitch's mouth before he'd had time to think about them. He instantly regretted that he'd spoken.

Brenna drew back in shock. She'd just kissed a complete stranger.

"Then," she began, pausing for a moment from the shock. She took a deep breath to steady herself, then forced herself to continue, "then, who are you?"

"I'm," he was being a little more careful with his words this time. After all, this was the Wolf Princess, the same girl who'd stabbed him just yesterday.

"I'm a friend of Candy." he told her "She was supposed to meet me here."

"What's your name?" she insisted.

"Uhm." Mitch stuttered.

"Your name is 'uhm'?" she said annoyed.

"It's Mitch." he answered reluctantly.

Brenna was backing up, "She told me she had a friend named Mitch, but she didn't say anything about meeting him tonight."

Mitch was stuck for an answer.

"Come into the light, where I can see you." she said, her voice commanding.

Mitch stayed where he was. What if she recognized him? He'd be a dead man that's what.

"Come this instant or I'll call the guards!" There was a danger in her voice.

Mitch didn't dare refuse. Slowly, he came forward, following her out of the stables. It was a clear night and the moon was full and round, making it easy to see. Brenna's mouth dropped open when she beheld his face and realized who he was. The Northman! That horrid Northman! She'd shared he first kiss with a Northman! She suddenly felt ill.

"You!" she whispered.

"I can explain." Mitch said hopefully.

"You!" Brenna said a little louder. "You!" she roared, anger lacing her voice like lumps of sugar in a cup of tea. "Guards!" she bellowed.

Mitch turned and ran toward the gate. Ten yards. Nine yards. Eight yards. Seven yards.

"Oof!" Mitch was struck to the ground by Kavan's sword-hilt.

"What should I do with him?" Kavan asked Brenna as two soldiers picked up Mitch's limp form.

"Put him back in the dungeon!" Brenna yelled, disliking the shocked expressions they were wearing as they stared at her feminine attire. "Now!"

Then she turned and ran toward the castle, tears burning in her eyes.

Candy had finally eluded Lewis, but froze in mid-step when she saw the guards carrying Mitch's limp body toward the stairs that led down into the dungeon.

"Kavan, what happened?" she called.

"Apparently this fugitive attacked your sister in the stables." Kavan answered. "I don't know how he got out though."

Candy was dumbstruck as questions raced through her mind. Had Mitch really attacked Brenna? What had Brenna been doing there in the first place? Could Mitch really be so untrustworthy?

Candy shook her head and gathered her wits, asking, "Where's Brenna now?"

"She ran to the castle Milady." Kavan said simply.

"Thank you!" Candy called over her shoulder as she rushed toward the castle.

Candy couldn't believe the sight that she beheld when she arrived at the chamber she and Brenna shared. Brenna was sprawled across the their bed, weeping uncontrollably. Brenna wasn't one to cry over just anything.

Candy dropped the sack of food that she'd been carrying and rushed to the bed. She sat on the edge of the blanket covered mattress and laid a hand on her sister's trembling back. Brenna started when she felt the caress, but refused to turn her tearstained face toward her would-be comforter.

"Brenna, what happened?" Candy asked gently.

Brenna was sobbing so hard into her pillow that it was difficult for Candy to decipher her shakey words. The words she caught were, "Wrong one." "Not there." "Horrid Northman." and "First kiss ruined." But they were so muffled by Brenna's face being buried in her pillow, that Candy wasn't even sure that she'd heard those words correctly.

Lewis and Konroy came in, having heard of the incident and wanting to see if Brenna was well, but they stopped dead in their tracks at the door.

Lewis couldn't believe his eyes, "Is Brenna wearing a dress?"

Brenna sat up and tried to glare through the tears, which made her look feirce and frightening. She took up her pillow and hurled it at her elder brother with enough force to knock Lewis onto his seat. The air left him in a rush as it hit him in the gut.

Brenna buried her face in Candy's pillow and continued sobbing. Candy motioned to the boys that they should leave.

As the boys exited, Konroy looked back and asked, "Is she gonna be all right Candy?"

Brenna growled into the pillow.

Konroy made a hasty retreat, closing the door behind him just in case Brenna should have any other, more dangerous missiles other than a pillow.

"What do we do?" he asked Lewis.

"We pay Mitch a little visit." Lewis said, rubbing his sore abdomen.

Candy continued trying to calm Brenna down, with little success.

"Brenna, please talk to me?" Candy said pleadingly.

Brenna leapt up almost violently from the bed in such a way that it frightened Candy a little. Brenna opened the drawer on her side-table and took out a crumpled ball of paper, which she tossed to Candy. Then as Candy tried to flatten it out so she could read it, Brenna went behind the screen they used for privacy and began tearing off her dress.

The paper was the letter from Lynch, and as Candy read it she teetered between understanding and confusion. Brenna reappeared from behind the screen, dressed in her plain black fighting clothes and came over to stand by the bed.

"Is this the letter you got earlier?" asked Candy.

Brenna nodded solemnly, her face more angry and frustrated than sad.

"So why did you dress up if you hate Lynch so much?" Candy asked, raising a brow.

Brenna sighed and sat down on the edge of the bed. Then, because Candy was truly her best friend, Brenna told her the whole story, and then listened as Candy told her own.

Mitch was startled awake by a bucket of water splashing on his face. He sat up, rubbing at his eyes while coughing and snorting out the water that had gone up his nose. He looked up at the lad holding the empty bucket.

"Thank you Konroy." Lewis said, patting the boy's shoulder.

"My pleasure." Konroy said, glaring down at Mitch. "Just let me know if you want me to bash him over the head with this." he lifted the heavy wooden bucket menacingly.

Mitch scooted backward until his back was against the wall, constantly watching the two brothers.

"What do you want?" Mitch asked, his eyes darting back and forth between them.

"What did you do to our sister?" Lewis said, fighting to keep his voice calm.

"I didn't do anything to her." Mitch said honestly.

"Don't lie to us, you dog!" roared Konroy, hefting the bucket. "We know you attacked her!" Konroy took a threatening step toward him.

"I did nothing to her!" Mitch yelled in self-defense. "She kissed me!"

"You lair!" Konroy started to charge, but Lewis held him back.

"It's the truth!" Mitch continued.

"Our sisters are both betrothed and neither one, especially Brenna, would ever kiss a Northman!" Lewis stated firmly.

"She didn't know it was me." Mitch said a little more calmly. "She'd gone to meet someone else."

The MacKline brothers rolled their eyes.

"A likely story." Lewis snorted.

"She did! She called me MacKurk!" Mitch told them, desperate to be believed and to avoid another fight with Lewis.

Konroy snorted, but Lewis stared at Mitch curiously.

"Are you sure that's the name she used?" Lewis asked, his voice nearly shaking.

Konroy raised a brow at his brother, but Lewis kept his eyes on Mitch, who was nodding his head vigorously.

"Aye!" said Mitch. "MacKurk!"

Konroy and Mitch both heard Lewis's sharp intake of breath.

"She kept talking about wanting to be rescued from a betrothal to a man she couldn't love." Mitch said, trying to prove his innocence.

"Shut up!" Lewis yelled. "I've heard enough! If you're lying, you'll pay!"

Mitch's jaw tightened as Lewis glared at him. Lewis turned on his heel and stalked out of the cell moodily.

"Come on Konroy!" he yelled over his shoulder.

Konroy looked at Mitch, then his leaving brother, then back at Mitch. Konroy shot Mitch one final glare before turning to follow Lewis.

Once they were gone, Mitch rubbed the back of his neck where Kavan had struck him. Leaning his head back against the wall, he gave a sigh of relief. Lewis seemed to truly believe him. For now at least.

CHAPTER SIX
INVASION AND NEGOTIATION

Laird Griff Cray stood just within the treeline of the forest across the open ground from Castle MacKline, staring at the mighty fortress. It was well illuminated in the light of the full moon, making it easy to see the enormous scale of the building as it stood against the dark sky. It was a massive fortress built of grey stone with high walls and tall towers. It reminded Griff of the castles in the books his mother had read to him when she was still alive.

He forced the memory from his mind and focused on the main gate. He noted that the gate was still splintered, but barricaded and heavily guarded. Getting in was going to be difficult, but not impossible.

"Dritt," he nearly hissed into the darkness.

"Here sire." Dritt came forward obediently.

"Is everything ready?" asked Griff.

"Aye sir." Dritt replied, nearly smiling.

"Then let's conquer a castle!" Griff grinned.

On the wall and gate barricade, soldiers sat or stood watch. They were tired and bored, but forced themselves to remain vigilant. Angus, who was taking his turn on watch with Bricker like so many others, saw it. He was the first to see it, Bricker was the second.

"Fire arrows!" shouted Angus. "Sound the alarm!"

Bricker rushed to the bell-tower on the south wall in order to ring the bell and call his fellow soldiers to arms.

"Kill him before he rings that alarm-bell!" Griff barked at Vrant, who holding a crossbow.

Vrant raised his crossbow, took aim and fired.

Bricker knew a sudden stinging pain as the arrow pierced the flesh of his upper right arm, and he felt the arrowhead enter his ribcage. He managed to ring the bell once before he fell to the battlement, passing out of consciousness due to the agony.

"Now!" said Griff, sinking his heels into his mount's ribs. His winged steed left the ground, rising into the air. His men mounted on similar beasts followed.

Nobody knew how the Cray family had domesticated these fierce creatures known only as the harpusia. But they had, and many believed that they had some how mutated the animals to be even more ferocious than in the wild. In all honesty they had.

While the sentries and most of the rest of the guard worked franticly to put out the now burning barricade, the Raves on their harpusia flew over the walls and landed silently in the courtyard.

"Dritt, you take sixty men into the castle and capture the family." Griff whispered. "Vrant, you take another sixty into the servants quarters and capture those that are loyal. I'll take the final eighty men and capture the guards. Now go!"

"Aye sir." both men whispered as one.

The group split up, each following its leader. Every man crept along, not daring to make a sound. They knew that Griff Cray's punishment for giving away their position was quite severe. It was an appointment with Dritt and his barbed whip.

Griff halted his men, waiting for the sentries to finish putting out the barricade fire. He saw a small gate to his right. It was a side-entrance near the stables, usually used by the servants and huntsmen. He signaled two men to go over and motioned for them to open it. Then he had them step outside and signal the rest of his army to come in.

As soon as the flames were put out, Griff gave the word, and the soldiers of Castle MacKline were surrounded and disarmed. Angus put down his sword reluctantly, glaring hatefully at Griff.

Vrant and his men had gathered all of the servants and the remaining guards that were in the servants' quarters on the first level. At the sound of his follow soldiers cries, Kavan had leapt out of bed and began arming himself. He was one of the first to be captured, having been caught in the corridor. Vrant himself knocked him unconscious with his sword-hilt. Within an hour everyone who served the MacKline family was a prisoner.

Dritt knew the upper levels of the castle well. He'd been exploring them for over twenty years, all the time, having everybody within the walls convinced that he was just one more servant. He sent twenty men into the master bedchamber to capture the laird and lady of the house. Then he sent another twenty into the princesses' room. The final twenty he divided in half so that there were ten men to go to each of the boys' rooms.

Having heard the alarm, Laird MacKline was arming himself when the invading men burst into the master chamber and surrounded him and his wife. Lady MacKline screamed as she ran to her husband's side as he slowly reached for his sword, which hung from his belt.

One of the Raves came forward like lightning and struck Laird MacKline to the floor with a blunt club. For a moment, the laird saw nothing but stars as he lay on the floor. Clutching his sword he tried to rise. Another blow from the club and he saw nothing as he was lost to unconsciousness. Lady MacKline scrambled to her wounded husband's side. She stiffened when she felt a sword-point on her back.

"Prepare to march down to the courtyard. We shall bring your husband." said a harsh voice.

Brenna and Candy leapt off of their bed and took up their swords as the Raves entered their chamber. They soon found themselves surrounded and outnumbered. Dritt himself came in to disarm them, jeering triumphantly when he saw that the Raves had hold of Candy and were closing in on Brenna.

Candy was the first to recognize him, "Dritt? You're with them?"

"Traitor!" Brenna roared, changing at him.

Dritt dodged and gave Brenna a shove that sent her rolling. She leapt to her feet and charged again. Once more she was knocked to the ground, though this time not far from Dritt. With a swipe of her legs under him Dritt was knocked to the floor as well. Brenna leapt on him and they went rolling. Dritt growled and drew his dagger as he pinned his wrestling opponent to the polished wood floor.

Candy somehow managed to break free of her captors and grab hold of a sword. She rushed toward them as Dritt raised his dagger menacingly.

"Dritt!" she yelled, hoping that he'd jump away from her sister.

Dritt looked from Brenna to Candy, his dagger still raised. The blade dropped from his grasp and his hands shot to his face as he screamed in agony. Brenna scurried out from underneath him as he collapsed and began writhing in pain.

Before she could be stopped by the Raves, Candy had cut down diagonally the length of Dritt's face. Crimson liquid seeped out from between his fingers. It would be a horrible jagged scar when the wound healed, if it healed at all. It started on the right side of his forehead, slanting downward across his left eye, dividing his left cheek into two hills of flesh with a crimson river between them. The awful gash finally ended at his jaw-line.

Dritt lay on his side, still moaning and clutching at his now ruined face.

"My eye!" he cried.

"Sir! Sir!" came a voice from the corridor. "The lads' rooms are empty!"

"What?" Dritt roared, jumping to his feet. He stuck his blood-covered face out into the hall and yelled, "They must be here somewhere! Start searching the other rooms! Find them! Now!"

Konroy and Lewis had quickened their pace when they heard the alarm bell ringing. But had stopped just inside the door that led to the stairs of the dungeon when they saw the black winged creatures descending into the courtyard. They watched in horror as two hundred dark clad figures dismounted from the backs of the large beasts and split into three groups. The lads flattened themselves against the wall as two groups passed the doorway, one heading toward the servants' quarters, the other in the direction of the upper levels where the rest of their family was.

The two young men started to discuss their battle plans once the Raves had finally passed by.

"Konroy, you're the best climber. Scale the wall, get through a window and warn the others." Lewis told his young brother. "There's no sneaking past those men without getting caught."

"But someone needs to help the servants." Konroy said worriedly, his thoughts on Erica.

Lewis raised a brow as though he could read Konroy's mind.

"I've thought of that. I'll go. I'm no good at climbing." Lewis said kindly.

"You'll make sure that, 'everyone' is all right?" asked Konroy with a small half-gulp.

"I will." Lewis smiled. "'Everyone'. I promise. Now go."

The boys went their separate ways then. Konroy scaled the wall, climbing toward his window on the third level, while Lewis entered the servants' quarters cautiously.

It was hard going up the wall, even for an experienced climber like Konroy. It was a straight vertical ascent, and as he got higher the wind seemed to grow stronger. He clung to the wall each time that the gale-like force picked up, and nearly fell more than once. But soon he was at his window. He was just about to climb through, when he saw his door opening. He ducked, and was glad he had when he heard the Raves' angry voices.

"Where's the runt?" snapped one.

"Check under the bed!" snarled another. "Children always hide under their beds when they're afraid." he added with an amused, yet cruel chuckle.

The air was filled with the sound of clattering and thumping as the Raves tore his room apart in their desperate search for the youngest MacKline.

Konroy's heart sank when he heard his mother's scream. It was all he could do not to jump through the window and rush to her aid. He listened as the Raves smirked about the sound, as though someone else's dismay was pleasurable. He felt the urge to go in and punch them all in the nose.

Konroy heard Brenna roar a word that he couldn't decipher because it was muffled through the walls. But knowing Brenna it was probably a good thing that he couldn't understand it. Not long after that he heard a man's cry of pain. Konroy tried not to giggle, but he was sure that Brenna'd had something to do with the man's distress.

"Let's go! He's not here! Maybe the others found him in his brother's room!" said a gruff voice.

Konroy was sure that there were at least ten pairs of feet shuffling as the Raves exited his chamber, and then he heard his door squeaking as it closed.

He peered over the sill. His room was a mess, but nobody was in there. As quietly as he could, he crawled through the window, then tiptoed to his door. He heard someone yell, "What?" And knew that he'd have to hide for a few minutes until they'd gone.

He knew that his family had most definitely been captured. Tiptoeing back over to his bed, he sat and buried his face in his hands. He didn't know what to do. He sat there, racking his brain for a solution, a new plan, anything to rescue his family. But nothing came. Nothing but hopelessness.

Lewis crept down the passageway to the servants' quarters, ears constantly listening and eyes always moving, scanning ahead for enemies. He heard a muffled grunt as he approached a corner. Back against the wall, he peered around a corner and saw a group of Raves standing over an unconscious Kavan.

"Tie him up and bring him along." said a man as he kicked the captain's limp form.

Lewis recognized that voice. It was that messenger who'd been there the previous day threatening his father. Lewis followed at a safe distance as the men moved on, trying to think of how best to take on twenty men.

One after another, all of the servants were captured. It was easy work as nearly all of them had been sleeping and the few who'd been awake weren't prepared for battle.

Lewis saw Erica in the mass. Her blue-green eyes were wide with fright. Lewis swallowed. If anything happened to her Konroy would never forgive him.

Konroy heard them searching the other rooms. Then heard someone yell, "They're not on this floor Sir."

"Let's go below. They couldn't have gone far!" he heard somebody roaring.

Konroy looked out of his window, then felt the wind rise, almost as though it was mocking him. He most certainly wouldn't be going back down that way. He stuck his head out into the corridor. They were going down the main stairwell. When they were out of sight, Konroy left his room and made a mad dash for the side-stairs in the tower. He ran down the spiraling staircase so fast that he nearly tripped several times. When he reached the bottom he paused at the door and peaked out into the hall. He didn't see anyone. There was nothing but silence. He stepped out through the door and looked around. Then he heard footsteps. He ran.

Lewis ducked into a side-room as the Raves herded the now bound servants out of the first level of the castle into the courtyard. Lewis waited until they were passed, then he slipped out into the corridor and followed the group. He could see Erica. She was obviously afraid, but unharmed.

He paused just inside the open doorway, looking out into the night. The guards and servants were made to stand in the very center of the courtyard surrounded by men in black. Children whimpered, staying as near their parents as possible. Young women sobbed fearfully, tears pouring down their faces. Men's faces were pale with fright as they struck protective poses, staying in front of their families.

These were Lewis's friends. People he'd grown up with and played among for years. To see them reduced to this, such fear on their countenance, it was almost more then he could bare.

Just then, there was a commotion.

"Sir!" one of the men shouted to Griff, pointing at the castle as he did.

Lewis looked toward the castle. His heart sank. It was Konroy in the open doorway.

Konroy was halfway down the outer staircase when three Raves, at Griff's command, rushed to the bottom step blocking his way. Konroy backed up as they advanced. He looked back at the top step. He saw Dritt with his ruined face holding onto Candy. Candy stared at her younger brother, then shouted, "Konroy, run!"

Konroy leapt over the railing, managing to land on his feet, and started to run in Lewis's direction. Vrant charged and knocked him to the ground, drawing his sword.

"You little scum!" Vrant roared.

They were about three steps from where Lewis was hiding. He drew his own sword and charged to his brother's defense, knocking the sword from Vrant's hand and stabbing him in the thigh.

Vrant hit the ground clutching at his wound, crying out in agony.

"Stay away from my brother!" Lewis growled. "Release my family or else he dies!" he bellowed, putting his sword-tip to Vrant's throat threateningly.

The rest of the MacKline family was among the other prisoners now. Griff marched over to them, sword drawn and put the blade to Lady MacKline's throat.

"Lay down your weapon and allow yourself to be captured, or the woman will never speak again!" he called.

Lewis stood still as a statue. He couldn't let his mother die. But could he really just, give up? Yes. He had to. Surrender was his only option. Lewis threw down his sword and bowed his head in defeat. Not five seconds later, he and Konroy who had just stood up, were tackled and their hands were bound behind their backs. They were dragged over and shoved amongst the rest of the prisoners.

"Oh, my brave boys." Lady MacKline sobbed, wishing that her hands were free so that she could hug her sons.

Laird MacKline and Kavan lay side by side on their stomachs, still unconscious. They started to stir and moan. As Dritt passed them he gave them each a swift kick. Brenna came to their defense, spitting in Dritt's face. The gob hit him square in his good eye.

Dritt clapped a hand to his face and swiped at her with his free hand. Brenna ducked, easily avoiding the blow, and head-butted him in the gut. Dritt found himself sitting on the ground, rocking back and forth, holding his sore abdomen.

Candy came forward and knocked him flat with a kick to his face. Dritt clutched at his bleeding nose and glared hatefully at the two girls with his only eye. He now covered his ruined eye with a strip of black cloth, torn from his sleeve.

"Before this is over, I'm going to kill one of you brats!" he growled, then spat blood at them.

Griff came over just as Brenna roared her reply.

"You don't scare me, Dritt dog!" she spat the words hatefully. "I'm not afraid of any of you! Especially your leader, whoever he is!"

"I am the leader of the Raves, Laird Griff Cray," Griff said, raising a brow. "And you should be afraid. Very afraid."

"Oh you're the leader?" said Brenna, wrinkling her nose. "I was expecting a man."

All of the Raves' eyes widened and their jaws dropped open. They all watched, certain that the Wolf Princess had spoken her last words.

Griff narrowed his eyes, "I could say the same of you, but that would be a lie." Griff fought to keep his voice calm.

Brenna gave a half-smile, Griff was angry. Her grin widened as she said, "I appreciate your honesty, Griffy!"

Griff glared at her, "Griffy?"

"That doesn't bother you, does it, Lady Griffy?" Brenna brought her face close to his. "Ooh!" The air left her in a rush as Griff's fist connected with her stomach. Brenna bent double and fell to her knees gasping. Then her head snapped to one side as the back of Griff's hand slapped the right side of her face. Her cheek burned as his hand came back, striking her once more. Brenna looked up and as his hand descended a third time, she opened her mouth and leaned up. She caught his hand in her mouth and bit down as hard as she could. She smiled at the taste of blood and the sound of his pain-stricken cry.

"Aah! Get her off! Get her off!" Griff screamed as he tried in vain to free his hand. "She's biting my hand off!"

Vrant and Dritt both volunteered to help their master. Working together, they pried the Wolf Princess off of their laird. Brenna glared hatefully at Griff as he nursed his bleeding hand. She spat his own blood at him, hitting him in the face with the crimson spray. Griff blinked through his now blood covered face at her, brow lowered.

"She is a wolf." Griff muttered.

Brenna bared her bloodstained teeth and growled like an animal. Her eyes were wild and red liquid dripped down her chin as she taunted, "Oh, does poor Lady Griffy have an owie on her dainty hand? Will she still be able to embroider her pink lace handkerchiefs?"

Griff ground his teeth angrily, his eyes burning with utter and complete contempt.

"Do we kill her sire?" grinned Dritt, drawing his hunting-knife and holding it near to Brenna's neck menacingly.

"As tempting as that is Dritt, we do nothing 'til she's heard my offer!" said Griff, motioning for his second in command to sheath his knife.

Dritt obeyed reluctantly, his eye on Brenna's throat.

Just one slash! he thought. **The day will come when the earth drinks their blood.**

"What offer?" Brenna asked, raising a brow.

"You were born under a dark star, were you not?" said Griff.

Brenna stared at him, a confused expression on her face, "What does that have to do with anything?"

"Is it true?" Griff pressed, drawing his sword and pointing it at Brenna's chest.

"Aye. But,"

Griff cut her off, "And you bare a strange birthmark. Am I right?" As he spoke, he used his sword-tip to pull her shirt collar down slightly, revealing the wolf paw-print birthmark just below her collarbone.

"Aye." Brenna said simply, feeling uncomfortable with her shirt being pulled slightly aside. "But what's your point?"

"Don't you know what that mark means?" hissed Griff.

Brenna shrugged and gently shook her head from side to side.

"It means that you have a dark destiny." Griff said very matter-of-factly, as though it was the most obvious thing in the entire world. "Just like me."

"I am nothing like you!" Brenna snarled, shaking her head. "We are nothing alike!"

"Oh aren't we?" he said, turning his head to reveal the reddish-pink patch of skin on the left side of his neck, just below his left ear.

Brenna stared at the mark. Could something physical that you had no control over, really define whether or not you were evil? That just couldn't be.

"My offer, is for you to join me, and together we shall conquer all of the world. What say you?" asked Griff.

"You want me . . . to join you?" she asked in shock, her forehead wrinkling.

"Aye. And from what I've seen, you and I will be a force to be reckoned with. None would stand in our way." Griff continued.

Brenna's mind was racing. The idea of power was tempting, but could she really stand for evil? Would the power, if she ever gained it, truly be hers if she just took it by force? In her mind's eye she saw herself and Griff fighting side by side in several different places. They always won and left a wasteland behind.

For a mere mortal to rule the world, is to make it a graveyard and then to rule over the tombstones. she thought.

"None would stand in our way?" she asked.

"Aye. None!" said Griff, thinking that she was ready to join him.

"I stand in your way!" Brenna said lowering her brow as she struggled to her feet. "I will not join the Raves or anybody else that stands for evil! And I'll fight you 'til my last breath!"

Griff sighed irritably, "Well, its come to this has it?"

"If you're gonna kill me go ahead. I fear death even less than I fear you, Griffy." Brenna snorted, flashing her bloodstained teeth.

"Oh, it's not you who will die this night." Griff said, nodding toward Lewis.

Brenna's eyes shot to her brother. Vrant had gone over and taken a handful of Lewis's hair, yanking his head back until the eldest son of Laird MacKline was staring skyward at the stars.

Vrant's dagger was out flashing in the moonlight as he pressed the cold, sharpened edge against Lewis's throat.

Brenna's eyes widened as Dritt did the same to Candy. There were other men doing the same to Konroy and their parents. The Raves all jeered at her as they threatened her family, knowing that they now had the upper-hand.

"No! Don't! Please!" Brenna yelled franticly, trying to run to her family but held back by the two Raves behind her.

"Oh." Griff said mockingly. "You wish to save their lives?"

"Aye!" shouted Brenna, tears slowly building in her eyes.

"Then join us or their blood will be on your hands!" snarled Griff.

Brenna shot him a hateful look.

"Is that a no?" he said, glaring coldly at her.

"It's a big decision. I want a few days to think it over." Brenna said, trying to keep her voice calm.

"No! I want an answer now!" Griff snapped, holding his sword so that the tip touched her chin.

Brenna's mind raced, "If you kill me and my family now, it'll be a waste, and you'll be left to wonder what my choice might've been for the rest of your life. All I'm asking for is a couple of days. If I say aye, you'll be glad that you waited. If I say no, you can kill me and be no worse off than before. Either way, you win the castle."

Griff contemplated Brenna's words. He liked them. But his impatience got the better of him.

"I want an answer by tomorrow!" he stated firmly.

"I need more time than that." Brenna said desperately.

"I want it by tomorrow or I will kill each member of your family in front of you, one by one!" he snarled cruelly.

Brenna drew her lips into a tight line. Eyes on the ground, she nodded sadly.

Griff grinned triumphantly, "Take them to the dungeon. But, treat the Wolf Princess like royalty. Put her in her own privet cell, away from the others." Griff ordered.

Several of the Rave guards laughed as they started herding the MacKline family toward the stairs that led down to the lowest level of the castle.

"Split the rest of the family up as well. This 'brave warrior," he jeered at Lewis, "May stay with his sister, the one that Dritt seems to hate so much. As for this young rooster," he smiled coldly at Konroy, "he can stay with his Mummy and Daddy."

Lewis and Konroy glared at Griff with such iciness that the leader of the Raves had to look away. All the strong, able-bodied men were imprisoned as well too avoid an uprising.

Brenna was escorted down to an empty cell and locked in. The sound of many people protesting and Rave guards growling filled the air as she sat there alone, thinking and worrying. How was she going to get out of this?

CHAPTER SEVEN
WE MUST ESCAPE!

It was then as she lay on the cold stone floor that she remembered what she kept in her boot. The jeweled dagger that her Uncle Allen had given her for her thirteenth birthday. Lying flat on her back, she twisted and turned until her hands, still bound were in front of her. She drew the dagger from her boot and carefully placed the hilt in her mouth, holding it firmly with her teeth. She worked the rope between her wrists back and forth along the blade until it was severed. Then dagger in hand, she approached the cell door.

Reaching out through the bars, she inserted the tip of the weapon into the lock, and moved it around until she heard it 'click' open. She put the dagger back in her boot and slowly pushed the door open. She looked up and down the passage. No one was coming. She crept up the passage silently, constantly listening for any sign of trouble. She kept looking to the left and right, searching for her family. She finally found Lewis and Candy in the same cell as Mitch. She raised a brow when she realized that he was untying their hands.

When Mitch's eyes met Brenna's, she glared at him icily, dispite the fact that he was helping her captive siblings. He narrowed his eyes before lowering them. Brenna drew her dagger and picked the cell lock before entered the barred room.

"Are you two all right?" she whispered.

Candy and Lewis both nodded. Then all went silent when they heard footsteps. Brenna closed the cell door, and heard the clicking sound as it locked.

They all scooted to the back wall, Brenna staying behind Lewis and Candy. They all watched as Rave guards guided Angus and Kavan along the passage, passed their cell. Two Raves carried poor wounded Bricker after them. Once they were gone, they all relaxed once more, at least until Brenna and Mitch caught sight of each other again.

"So what's the plan?" asked Lewis.

Brenna drew her dagger again, "We get out and rally the rest of the clans. If no one else, Uncle Allen will help us."

"Clancy and Glen will help too. I'm sure." Lewis put in.

Brenna rolled her eyes, "You just wanna see Colleen."

Clancy was their father's cousin, and Colleen and Glen were his children. Clancy had married Lady MacKline's cousin, Lady Meave, who was quite beautiful and had the kindest disposition of all their mother's cousins. Lewis's betrothed, Colleen was every bit as beautiful and kind as Lady Meave. At the mention of Colleen's family, Brenna couldn't resist teasing her elder brother, in spite the circumstances.

"Clancy's a good man with many followers." Lewis insisted, his cheeks reddening.

"I agree." Candy said solemnly. "But what about Mum, Da' and Konroy, and everyone else that's been captured?"

"I don't know where they've been taken. It would take too long to search all the cells. We'll just have to leave them and hope for the best." Brenna said logically. "Right now, the main thing is getting out of here. Any ideas?"

Lewis and Candy started thinking, but remained silent. It was Mitch who was the first to speak.

"What about the tunnel to the stable? That's how I got out." Mitch said.

"This is none of your business Northman!" Brenna snapped.

"Oh do shut up Brenna!" grumbled Lewis. "You're just mad 'cause you didn't think of it first, Stableman-romancer!" his tone wasn't very pleased.

Brenna blushed to the roots of her hair. She glared at her brother, then turned away and folded her arms moodily.

"I am not!" she snorted.

Candy rolled her eyes and sighed, then nodded at Mitch, "That's a good idea Mitch, but if so, why are you still here? Why didn't you try to escape after they put you back in here?"

Mitch rubbed the back of his neck, almost sheepishly, "I thought that there might be guards watching the stable after what happened earlier. But as long as the Raves don't know about the tunnel, it should be safe to use it."

"But once we're out, what do we do next? We still have to get through one of the gates." Candy said thoughtfully.

"The side gate is right next to the stable." Lewis said, rubbing his chin as he always did when he was in deep thought about something. "If we're very quiet and careful not to be seen, we could open it and slip right out. We could even get our horses and ride out."

"It sounds good to me." Candy said cheerfully.

"I agree." Mitch put in.

"What?" Brenna's voice had a sharp edge to it as she turned back to them. "He's coming too?"

"You really think I'm gonna stay here?" Mitch said, spreading his hands and raising a brow.

"I'm not riding with him!" she stated firmly, turning away again.

"You don't have to." Mitch snorted. "Just get me out of here and you'll never see me again."

After a few more minutes of Brenna protesting, she finally agreed and they crept through the tunnel into the stables. They quietly saddled their steeds, careful not to jingle the bridles.

Brenna finished first, and walked silently to the stable entrance. She stood still as a statue when she heard the approach of footsteps. It was three Raves, holding three very familiar swords. She recognized her sword first, Ceartas. Next she saw Candy's sword, Calma, then Lewis's blade, Dana, the Gaelic word for Intrepid.

The three men were chuckling as they pretended to duel, doing impressions of the three eldest MacKline children.

"I'm not afraid of any of you!" snickered one. "I am the Wolf Princess, and I'll bite you. Grrr!"

"Release my family or he dies!" giggled another.

The third one laughed and said, "I hear it was that one born under the bright star that ruined Dritt's face. What an improvement."

"Poor Dritt! Beaten by a girl!" said the first and all three started falling over each other and had tears streaming down their faces as they laughed uncontrollably.

The rest in the stable had finished saddling their mounts and came forward, having heard the mockery. Lewis and Brenna both looked at each other.

The three men didn't seem to be in any rush to leave. Five minutes passed. Ten minutes. Fifteen. Twenty. The men were still there, and worst of all they were coming closer.

"Let's see what kind of horse flesh they have." one of the men said.

Lewis signaled for everyone to hide. They all darted into the shadows just as the Raves reached the stable entrance, still laughing. Once all were inside the stables, the four lying in wait set upon them. It was a very short struggle. The three Raves were knocked unconscious, gagged and all were bound and laid behind some barrels. There was no short supply of rope in the stables, which made binding their captives an easy task.

The four escapists in the stables led their steeds out silently. Brenna held Lewis's reins while he unlatched the side gate. She was quite pleased now that she'd reclaimed her sword. She almost smiled when she thought about having a fine, quick ride out across the fields and hills. All they had to do was make it to the woods and they could disapear. If only that Northman wasn't there. After kissing him she felt much more aware of him. She didn't like noticing him. But that didn't matter right now. He'd soon be gone, and be out of her life forever.

Candy stood nearby, only wishing that she knew what had happened to her parents and Konroy. She hoped that they were all right wherever they'd been taken.

Aside from being a little shaken up they were fine. Konroy had done the same thing that Brenna had, managing to get his hands in front of him. It was difficult, but even with his hands still bound he untied his father's bonds. Laird MacKline then loosed his wife and his son's bonds and they all huddled together for warmth in the cold cell.

Lady MacKline was nearly sobbing, but Laird MacKline did his best to comfort her. Konroy was the one who succeeded in drying his mother's tears.

"Mum, Lewis, Brenna, and Candy won't fail us." he said. "They'll think of something. I know it."

Konroy felt relief when his red-eyed mother managed a weak smile.

Lewis was slowly lifting the latch, thankful that it hadn't squeaked thus far. But just as he started to open the heavy oak door, the rusted hinges gave a loud groan. The noise hadn't mattered when the Raves had opened it, due to all the commotion at the burning barricade. But in the silence of the late evening the groan might as well have been a roar.

Brenna heard somebody on the wall yell, "Halt! Who goes there?"

"Hurry Lewis!" Candy whispered franticly.

"Quick!" Brenna urged.

Lewis swung the door wide open, not caring who heard now. Then he rushed back and leapt onto his horse's back.

"Let's go!" he yelled, sinking his heels into Loch King's ribs.

The four riders darted out through the gate. Candy could hear somebody bellowing, "Stop! Stop! Escape! After them!"

They were riding straight for the forest as fast as their mounts could go. Candy chanced a look over her shoulder, and to her dismay she saw four dark forms pass in front of the full moon. It was an eerie sight that brought a chill to her blood.

"We've got company!" she called to the others.

The other three looked up and saw the four Raves mounted on the frightening harpusia closing in from above. The beasts flapped their bat-like wings furiously, kicking as though they were running on an invisible floor in the sky. The men on their backs had large crossbows, loaded with long wicked-looking arrows that were drawn back on the string.

Without warning, two of the pursuers swept low and grabbed up Candy and Mitch. The two struggled, but with a swift blow to back of each head the two escapees went still and were laid across the front of their captures' saddles.

Brenna and Lewis forced themselves to keep going. The now riderless horses galloped onward and into the forest until they were lost to sight.

Brenna looked up and saw the other two riders sweeping low. She knew that if they were captured, they were finished and all hope would be lost with them.

"Lewis!" she screamed. "We gotta split up or we'll be caught."

"All right!" he answered. "Be careful and watch yourself!"

"Only if you watch yourself!" she called back to him. Then she leaned forward to cut down on the wind-resistance as Lightningbolt bounded toward the forest.

Just as the two Raves got close, their prey turned sharply in different directions. Brenna suddenly went right and Lewis went left. The Raves had to split up as well if they wanted to catch them. Just as the Raves tried a second time to capture their query, they suddenly had to pull up to avoid the thick forest canopy.

The other two riders carried Candy and Mitch back to the castle and put their unconscious forms into the first empty cell they found. Little did the Raves know, this was the same cell they'd just escaped from.

Brenna couldn't see Lewis anymore. The trees to her left were too thick. She looked overhead. As long as she couldn't see the sky clearly, she knew that the Rave couldn't get to her. Suddenly the trees left some open space above. There was a wide river running through the middle of the forest, which pushed the trees back revealing the starfilled sky. Brenna knew that this must be Murky River. It was the only one that she knew of in this area.

Brenna kept scanning the dark heavens for her enemy, but didn't see any sign of him. She slowed Lightningbolt to an easy trot, keeping as close under the branches as she could without being scratched by the rough limbs.

Her horse was still panting after their escapade. Brenna could feel her heart racing like a frightened rabbit and the now cold sweat dripping down her back only added to her uneasiness. At least while they kept near the river they knew where to find water if they became thirsty.

They trotted for about ten minutes, then slowed to a walk for another ten minutes. Brenna kept looking to the sky and listening for the sound of beating wings. The sound of the river filled her ears and made it difficult to hear anything else. This was probably why she was so surprised when an arrow suddenly came whizzing from above and buried itself in a tree-trunk near her head.

"Go boy! Go!" she cried as she sank her heels into Lightningbolt's sides. The black horse began to canter forward. More arrows came raining down through the branches as they tried to escape.

Lightningbolt was galloping now as they raced along the riverside, the roar of the water becoming all that they could hear. Brenna suddenly let out a cry of anguish as she was hit in the right thigh by one of the black shafts. Another arrow whizzed down, narrowly missing her, but cutting into the saddle strap.

The saddle slipped from the black stallion's back and Brenna with it. She plunged into the ragging river, limbs flailing as she tried to keep her head above water. She went under for a moment, then managed to get herself back to the surface. Coughing and sputtering, she tried to get her bearings. Her thigh was throbbing as she tried to swim through the freezing water. She tried to gain a good foothold, but found that the river was too deep.

She noticed that the river was beginning to flow faster. She looked around wildly and to her dismay, she saw that she was about to go over a high waterfall. She tried her hardest to fight against the current, but it was all in vain.

As she went over, she reached up for something, anything, to grab hold of to save herself. She felt something brush her left hand. She grabbed it and looked up. It was one of Lightningbolt's reins. The brave horse had followed her loyally to the cliff's edge where the waterfall started. Now he was leaning his head down, dangling the reins within her reach.

"Good boy Lightning!" she called up to him happily as he started to back up slowly, pulling her upward to safety.

But misfortune reared its ugly head once more as the rein snapped and she fell down, down, down. Lightningbolt whickered after his mistress as she vanished into the mist below, still clutching the piece of leather that had snapped.

CHAPTER EIGHT
OF CANDY AND OF MITCH

"Candy? Wake up. Candy are you all right?"

Candy's head was so achy that she wasn't sure if the voice was inside her mind or if somebody was truly speaking to her. She opened her eyes slowly and found herself looking up at Mitch.

"Wha, what happened?" she groaned.

"We were caught and put back in the cell. That's what happened." Mitch explained in a discontented tone.

"Ooh, my head." she moaned, then asked fearfully, "What about Brenna and Lewis?"

Mitch lowered his eyes and shook his head sadly, "I don't know. But I think they got away." He said this to reassure Candy more than anything. In truth he was almost certain that both Brenna and Lewis were either captured or dead.

He was very nearly right where Brenna was concerned. She wasn't sure how she'd survived the huge drop over the waterfall. In those first few moments Brenna wasn't entirely certain where she was or even who she was. All she knew was that she needed to keep her head above the icy, churning water, but she was too tired and in too much pain to do it. The weight of the sword attached to her belt made swimming all the harder.

She fought to stay on the surface, looking around wildly. She saw the shore, though it was getting hard to see due to the massive pain in her thigh. She started swimming toward the river's edge. The darkness was closing in around her as her hand touched something solid. She grasped it and laid her head on it as she was lost to exhaustion. She closed her eyes and knew no more.

Griff was yelling at the two Raves that had returned empty handed after their chase.

"But sire, after she went over the waterfall, she just, disappeared." said one. "She's almost certainly dead."

"Silence you incompetent fool! 'Almost certainly' isn't good enough. Did you see a body?" Griff shouted angrily.

"Sir I tried to go down the waterfall, but the mist was too thick to see through, and it was as though," the Rave's voice trailed off and he lowered his eyes.

"As though what?" snapped Griff.

"As though the mist rose as soon as I got low enough to see her in the river." said the Rave. "Like it was working against me somehow."

"Superstitious coward!" snarled Griff turning to the other man. "And you! You lost the boy! How could you lose the boy?"

"Sire, forgive me. I don't know how he escaped, but there was a fog that came upon the forest as I swept low. One minute he was there, the next he was gone." said the second Rave. "But I know that my arrow found its mark in his chest. He can't long survive a wound like that. If only that fog hadn't risen at that moment I could've caught him."

"Fog! Mist! How could two Raves, no, two men, be defeated by fog and mist?" bellowed Griff. "That girl, Candy, she'll know where her sister will go if she's alive. You there, bring me the Wolf Princess's sister for questioning! Now!"

"Aye sire." said a man, rushing out of the room to do his master's bidding.

"Dritt, go get your whip." said Griff, his voice little more than a growl.

"With pleasure sir." Dritt grinned, then bowed before leaving to retrieve the long whip that he used when 'questioning' a hated enemy. He would have his revenge. Revenge for his lost eye. Revenge for his dignity. But mostly, revenge for the painful and burning scar that was now upon his face. He would give her many a scar this day. Perhaps if he was lucky, he would claim her life as well.

"Did they take your sword?" asked Mitch.

"I don't think so." Candy shook her head. "There's a sheath on Dutchess's saddle, and that's where I put the sword."

"Who's Dutchess?" asked Mitch, raising a brow.

"My horse. Unless they brought her in, my sword is still out there with Dutchess." Candy explained. "If we can get out of here and find her, we'll have a weapon."

"How are we supposed to find a loose horse running wild in the hills?" Mitch said sarcastically.

"If she's within earshot, she'll come when I whistle."

"Well, how do we get out of here? They're sure to be watching the stables and gates now." Mitch said in a nearly hopeless tone.

"You're such a wet blanket." Candy nearly snorted, then whispered, "There's another tunnel that leads to the beach. We'll have to walk up the cliff path into the woods. If we're careful, we won't be spotted."

"All right, let's go." Mitch whispered eagerly.

"Shh! Listen!" she said softly.

As they listened, they heard footsteps approaching in the passage. A tall man with a cruel face appeared at the cell door. He smiled a very crooked smile, showing them several brown tooth-stumps in his lopsided mouth.

"Come now, me pretty bird. His lairdship and his whip wish to speak with you." he said smiling at Candy in a sickening way. "Come on now. Come to old Slimp."

Mitch's eyes grew wide, "Dritt's whip?" he asked.

Slimp's stump-toothed grin widened as he said, "Aye lad."

Mitch grew pale at the memory of several men's bodies lying on the ground. Their bodies broken after their encounter with Dritt's whip. He knew this would be Candy's death.

Slimp was in the cell now, preparing to bind Candy's hands behind her back. Mitch saw the fear in her face and a tear roll down her cheek. Mitch's lost love had looked just like that when she lay dying in his arms. Mitch knew that he needed to act now if he was going to save Candy. He leapt on Slimp, knocking him to the ground.

"Candy, get ready to escape. Don't look." Mitch grunted as he struggled with his enemy. Candy turned her eyes away when she saw Mitch put the man in a headlock.

Slimp squirmed and tried to call for help, but suddenly went quiet and still. He would never move or make a sound again. Candy turned and watched as Mitch moved his hand down the now dead face, closing Slimp's eyes forever. She wasn't sure, but she thought that she saw Mitch lower his head and shudder.

"Come on." he said, rising from where he was. "We need to get out of here."

Candy opened the entrance to the secret tunnel and they crawled through, leaving Slimp's corpse in the cell. Candy could feel herself shaking as she led the way through the dark tunnel. Mitch had just killed for her! Killed! She felt much more afraid of him now than she'd ever felt before. She was all-alone with him in a dark tunnel and he was capable of murder. Was she safe? Had she made a mistake in protecting him from Brenna? She didn't know. All she knew was that she wanted out of that dark enclosure.

She was relieved when they crawled out into the stable, but her relief was short lived as they uncovered and entered the next tunnel that led to the beach. Her heart pounded and she could feel her fear rising even more with every crawling step.

Finally she could see the end of the tunnel as they continued forward. She let out a sigh of relief. They were almost there. Almost out. As they reached the opening, Candy crawled out onto a ledge, then she began to climb down toward the beach below. She was eager to get away from Mitch now that she knew he was willing to kill.

The tunnel-mouth was some fifteen feet up the cliff-face, and it was a rather steep climb. Candy gulped as she looked down at the sandy ground and felt apprehensive about continuing her decent. Then she looked up and saw Mitch exiting the tunnel, and decided to continue downward.

"Careful." she warned him. "It's slippery."

Mitch was a champion climber. He watched his step and made sure that he had a good foothold before moving onward down to the beach. As he looked down their steep path, he noticed something. Something that any well-experienced climber would notice and avoid. A small part of the ledge was obviously loose. One could and certainly would turn an ankle if they put their weight on it.

"Candy watch that bit there." Mitch warned just a second too late.

"What bit?" Candy said, looking up apprehensively at Mitch and putting her foot down on the very spot he'd been trying to warn her about.

Candy suddenly let out a little cry of pain and began falling downward. Mitch reached out and grabbed her hand. For a moment she was just dangling there on the face of the cliff, then she found a foothold and Mitch released her.

"Are you all right?" he asked.

Candy didn't answer at first, but then she gulped and nodded, "I, I think so. My foot hurts though."

"It's not far." Mitch said encouragingly. "Just watch your step."

Mitch joined her on the ledge and helped her to the next one. They continued like this until they were almost four feet from the ground. Mitch jumped from the ledge to the ground, then held out his arms to Candy. She stared at him. What was his intention? Could she still trust him after he'd killed someone?

"What are you doing?" she asked.

"You can't walk on that foot. I can see the blood in the moonlight." Mitch explained.

Candy put her throbbing foot forward and examined it in the pale light. It was unmistakable. She'd scraped her foot quite badly on the rocks above, and the crimson liquid was easily seen. Now she knew why it ached so much.

"Come." Mitch said simply, arms still extended.

Candy stared at him, fear in her eyes. Mitch saw how her gaze went to his hands. Hands he'd used to commit murder. He suddenly knew why she wasn't coming to him.

"Candy, are you . . . afraid of me?" he asked hesitently.

Candy looked away, "You killed that man." she said timidly.

"I did it to save you. Dritt has never left a victim alive after whipping them. I'm not proud of what I did. I wish that I didn't have to, but it's done and over and we're wasting time. So come on." Mitch explained.

Candy lowered herself into his arms without a word. Mitch carried her, following the line of the cliffs toward the forest. Then he carried her up the path into the woods. After about an hour's walk, he sat her down on an old fallen tree and tore a strip from his jerkin to bandage her foot.

"I'm sorry I didn't do it sooner." he said regretfully.

"I'm fine." she smiled in the darkness, then gave a whistle.

"What was that for?" Mitch asked, raising a brow.

"I'm calling Dutchess." Candy told him.

"Your horse?" he asked.

"Aye." she said then whistled again. "She's not nearby." Candy sighed sadly.

"Well, then let's go find her." Mitch said, lifting her into his arms once again.

"Am I too heavy?" she asked, a little concerned.

"Not a bit." Mitch said kindly. "We'll travel a bit, then you can whistle again. We need to keep on the move. They'll be sending out scouts to look for us soon, and if we're caught again," he stopped in mid-sentence, not wanting to finish it. "We'll find a safe place to sleep for the night too. We'll both need some rest before dawn."

"Why are you helping me?" Candy asked.

"Why did you help me?" he asked simply.

She smiled at him in the moonlight, and she saw him return it. It was a happy, kind smile. She was glad to see that in his face. It helped her to forget the unpleasant incident in the cell earlier. She laid her head on his shoulder. It felt good. No. Better than good. She felt so safe. So secure in his arms. He was so strong and kind, and handsome. She blushed when she thought this. But it was true. He'd done nothing but protect her since she'd saved his life. In that moment, she knew she was safe with him. She decided then and there to trust him.

CHAPTER NINE

NICK GARTHSON

Nick Garthson knelt by Murky River with his faithful friend Marie. Marie was truly a remarkable person, because in truth she wasn't a person at all. She was a gray wolf with large black, bat-like wings folded down on her back. She sat by his side gazing into the water.

"Now!" she said, and Nick stabbed the water with a short makeshift spear, catching the fish that swam in front of him.

Nick had gone blind at the age of seven, and Marie had been his eyes ever since. Now in his early twenty's he was well adapted to life as a blind woodlander.

"Aha! Got it!" he laughed triumphantly.

"What the," started Marie.

"What is it Marie?" asked Nick, grabbing up his staff. "What's wrong?"

"It's a girl, in the middle of the river." Marie said. "She's clinging to a log."

The log was the thing that Brenna had grabbed hold of and laid her head on. Unconscious, she had no realization that the log was actually drifting in the middle of Murky River. Disoriented as she was, it was a miracle that she'd been able to grab hold of anything. Clinging to the drifting wood, she'd floated down the river through the night and into the morning.

"Nick, I think she's hurt." Marie's voice was concerned.

"Where is she?" he asked, throwing down his staff and wading into the river, hands outstretched.

"A little to the left. More. Oops, too much. To the right. A little more. There! Forward. Wait! You got her." Marie instructed.

"I can feel that Marie." Nick grunted, as he lifted Brenna from the log.

"Careful. There's an arrow in her right thigh." Marie called from the shore. "Bring her here."

As the young man did this he said, "I don't think she's breathing."

He laid Brenna on her left side and removed the arrow under Marie's instructions.

"Careful now. I'm holding her. Just give it a good yank." Marie told him as she laid herself across Brenna's ribcage. "Prepare to hear a yell."

Nick did so, but there was no cry from the woman who lay on the riverbank.

"Something's very wrong." Nick said, rolling Brenna to her back. He put his ear near to her mouth and nose, listening intently. There was no sound. "She's not breathing. What should I do?" he asked.

"Blow into her mouth." Marie said simply.

"What?" he almost shouted his voice full of shock.

"Put your mouth on hers and blow into her lungs." Marie told him.

"You want me to kiss her?" he said, still in shock.

"No. Breath life into her!" said Marie, a little frustrated. "Do it or she dies."

Finally Nick did as Marie told him. Surprisingly, to him at least, it wasn't a completely unpleasant experience. Not until Brenna started coughing up an unbelievable amount of water splashing him in the face did it become unpleasant.

Brenna rolled to her side, clutching at her wounded thigh and gasping for breath. Nick patted her back until all of the liquid was out of her lungs. Brenna, half wheezing, half sobbing, lay there shaking like a leaf in the wind.

Nick took his coat which was lying nearby on the river-bank, and covered her trembling form. Brenna opened her eyes for a moment and gazed up at her rescuer.

Nick was tall and had thick, messy brown hair, eyes as dark as coffee, and was as handsome a man as Brenna had ever seen. Then her head fell to one side and her eyes closed as she surrendered to the overpowering weariness.

Candy and Mitch had found a large tree with low branches hanging over a dry, mossy place. They had laid down, back to back and fallen asleep for a few hours to ease their exhaustion.

Mitch was the first to wake and see the sun rising. Careful not to wake her, he lifted Candy into his arms, laying her head on his shoulder and started Northward through the thickly wooded forsest. He remembered that had been the direction they'd been riding in the night before, and he hoped that was the direction the horse had taken.

As he held her in his arms, the memories of his beloved Babbette flooded into his mind. She'd been twenty, about Candy's age when the tragedy had occurred. He'd even held her in his arms this way during those last few moments.

What he remembered most vividly were her eyes. Those beautiful eyes and what was in them during those last minutes of her life. The fear. The pain. The grief and sorrow. Then the glaze of death as it claimed her and she went still forever.

He looked down at Candy. When he saw that she was still asleep, he allowed a single tear to escape from his eye. He felt an ache in his chest. A deeply familiar and painful ache.

Candy stirred and he forced his countenance back into a calm, passive expression. He would never let his heart be broken again. Never. No matter who he met.

He kept on marching, carrying Candy until she woke and insisted on walking for herself, at least for a while. It was painful, but she wasn't thinking about that now. Her mind, as was Mitch's, was on food.

They found some wild berries and picked the bushes clean. A few berries does little for an empty, growling stomach, but it cheered them up as they continued onward. But those few berries didn't last very long and soon they were hungrier than before.

"Look." said Mitch. "There's smoke over there."

Candy saw the dark column of smoke rising above the treetops. Her stomach growled and her mouth watered at the thought of food cooking over an open fire.

After some debating they decided that it would be best to go toward the smoke and see if they could get some breakfast. Mitch pointed out that if whoever had the food turned out to be an enemy, they could do a little raiding if they had to. Candy said that she agreed as long as this person had some to spare, and they moved toward the smoke.

Brenna awoke to the smell of fresh fish frying over an open fire and a slight ache in her right thigh. Fortunately the arrow hadn't caused much damage in her leg and it hadn't been poisoned.

The heat from the fire warmed her flesh as she rolled to look in the direction that the smell was coming from. She saw a young man holding a frying-pan over the fire with a fine looking fish in the bottom of the pan. Next she saw two wolves with large, bat-like wings folded down on their backs, who were both eating large, browned trout. One of the strange creatures was larger than the other. The bigger of the two looked up and said, with a sort of smile, "Ah, so you've decided to rejoin the living have you Miss?" her voice was rather cheerful. It had a voice?

"Is she awake now Marie?" said the lad by the fire.

"She is indeed Nick. Let's see if she's hungry." said the creature, who was apparently called Marie.

Brenna sat up, staring at the wolf, "Am, am I still dreaming?"

The smaller wolf leapt behind the larger one and screamed, "Aah! It talks!" then she came out laughing at Brenna's expression.

"Dawn, mind your manners." Marie nearly hissed, then she returned to her cheerful tone as she turned back to Brenna. "It's no dream. We Bulves have always been able to talk. Though some of us don't use proper manners when we do so." She glared at the smaller creature, who was apparently named Dawn.

"Manners yourself, bug-face!" said Dawn, who then stuck out her tongue at the elder Bulf and spit while making a very rude sound.

Nick chuckled, "Don't let Dawn bother you. She's always like that. Hungry Miss?" he held forth the newly fried fish, but he seemed to be looking passed her.

"Are you all right?" asked Brenna, raising a brow. "Can't you see me?"

"I haven't seen much in the last fourteen years. I'm blind." Nick said, his voice taking on a bitter tone. "Are you hungry?"

"Aye." Brenna said softly, feeling her cheeks turn red as she took the fish, now cooled from the breeze. "Thank you."

"You're welcome." Nick said stiffly, though it almost sounded like a snort. Then he stood, taking up his staff and walked off moodily.

Dawn shook her head and looked at Brenna, "Boy are you stupid!"

"Dawn!" scolded Marie.

"I'm sorry. I didn't know." Brenna said in self-defense. "Will he be all right?"

"He just needs some time alone to cool off." Marie told her. "He'll be back in a little while."

Candy and Mitch approached the camp cautiously, ducking behind bushes and trees. They could see the glow of the fire through the thick foliage now and the smell of fish frying made them even hungrier than before.

They could see that the camp-fire was in a small clearing lined with pines, oaks, beeches, birches and maples, their branches spreading into a dome of foliage that provided a massive amount of shade. The smoke billowed upward through a small opening in the center of the leafy dome, nearly blotting out what little sunshine was filtering through the branches.

"Can you see anyone?" asked Candy in a whisper.

Mitch shook his head, "Not yet. But we'd better keep on the lookout just in, ooh!" Mitch was interrupted by a sharp blow to his back. The air left him in a whoosh as his feet were swept out from under him and he landed on his back.

Candy turned to face their attacker, then ducked as a long staff was swung at her face.

"Who are you?" she yelled at the brown-haired man wielding his staff.

"Nick Garthson!" he bellowed. "Why're spying on my camp!"

"Please, we're just hungry." Candy said, dodging another swipe from his stave.

"Don't plead like dogs you spies!" he snapped.

"Who're you calling a dog you slap-happy-woodsman!" Mitch snarled from the ground.

Before Nick could throw back another insult or respond in any way, Mitch kicked his legs out from under him. As soon as Nick hit the ground, Mitch leapt upon him. The two lads went rolling, punching at each other. Mitch felt a tightly clenched fist connect with his gut, and for a moment he couldn't inhale. Then Nick threw his opponent over his head, sending Mitch rolling. Nick sought his stave, crawling on his hands and knees.

Mitch jumped to his feet and leapt at Nick once again. Nick heard him coming and flipped to his back. Bending both knees, Nick kicked out and both of his feet hit Mitch square in the stomach. Mitch fell back a pace and a half, his face red as he tried to breath. Nick jumped to his feet having found his staff, and began swinging it over his head.

Brenna, Marie, and Dawn came bursting out of the shrubbery, having heard the racket. The moment the two sisters saw one another they embraced, overjoyed to see each other alive and well.

"Brenna!"

"Candy!"

"You know this girl?" asked Nick, lowering his stave.

"This is my sister, Candace." Brenna explained.

"Is this man a friend of yours too?" Nick said, his tone untrusting.

Mitch folded his arms across his chest and glared in Nick's direction, unaware that Nick couldn't see him.

Brenna was silent, so Candy said, "Aye. He's trustworthy."

Mitch rolled his eyes at Brenna and snorted. Brenna lowered her brow and glared coldly back at him.

"Well, in that case, they may as well join us for breakfast." Nick said. "Marie, we should probably go catch some more fish."

"I could catch some fish." Dawn said quickly.

"You shouldn't be here." Nick said sternly. "You're still on restriction after that stunt you pulled a few days back."

"But Nick . . ." Dawn whined.

"No. Go back to the fireside." Nick said, unyieldingly.

With her ears and wings drooping, and her tail between her hind-legs, Dawn turned and slowly walked back to the camp.

"That was just cruel!" Candy said, putting her hands on her hips.

"Pardon me?" said Nick, his forehead furrowing.

"How can you be so, so mean?" said Candy, who had such a great love of animals that she didn't think about the fact that these wolves had wings. "She looked so sad when she left."

"You don't know what she did. Thanks to her, some innocent girl got shot by one of the Raves a couple of days back." Nick said.

Brenna suddenly remembered that day when she'd gone riding with the group to search the surrounding land. Then how she'd seen a small gray, winged animal before being shot while coming closer to investigate. But she felt sympathy for the young creature.

"How did you know that? You're blind." Brenna regretted her words almost instantly when she saw the hurt expression on Nick's face.

Mitch's eyes were wide with shock, "He's blind? But he almost killed me." Mitch said, rubbing his sore abdomen.

Nick turned his face in Mitch's direction, "Thanks, I think. You weren't so bad yourself."

"How did you know where I was?" asked Mitch, who was now thoroughly interested.

"Your breathing. It gets heavy when you're angry." Nick shrugged.

"It gets heavy when he's excited too." Brenna smirked sarcastically, brushing passed Mitch, intentionally bumping his shoulder with her own.

Mitch inhaled sharply, not even trying to hide his disdain for Brenna. Then he gave a small half-grin, "And you start talking about being rescued and running away together when you get excited."

Without turning around to look, he could tell that he'd angered her and that the Wolf Princess was glaring at him.

A smile creased Mitch's face as he said, "Want some help with those fish, uh, Nick, was it?"

"Aye. What's your name?" said Nick, leading Mitch down toward the riverbank.

"Mitch. And you've already met, Princess Brenna." he laughed over his shoulder, catching the aggravated expression on Brenna's face.

"Ooh!" she growled, stomping her foot. "He's so, so, gragh!"

Brenna turned and stomped back to the fireside, closely followed by Candy and Marie.

Marie introduced herself as Marie the Bulf, then excused herself as she turned to join the boys down by the river.

By the time they returned with a bounty of fish, already gutted and cleaned, Brenna's anger had eased somewhat. It was difficult to be angry when Candy was around, unless she was also angry.

The two young men had seemed to become the best of friends in that short time, and were speaking to each other as though they'd known each other all their lives. They sat there by the fire talking and laughing while they cooked and ate fish.

Brenna and Candy had exchanged their stories of the previous night's events, and were now debating where to go next. Brenna thought that they should continue north-northwest to the mountains and seek out Uncle Allen, who was her favorite uncle. But Candy disagreed, insisting that they should go due west around a swamp to Uncle Garvey's village, because it was closer.

The two argued for about five minutes, until they were suddenly interrupted by a huge black arrow planting itself within an inch of Brenna's foot.

"Raves!" shouted Marie. "Scatter!"

Mitch kicked a bucket of water that was next to the fire, instantly extinguishing it and sending up a billowing cloud of gray smoke. The smoke covered the entire camp, filling up the dome of foliage as the Raves charged. All was in confusion as the Raves ran straight through the smoke and tripped, falling face down into the river, or smack into the sides of trees.

Coughing and sputtering, three figures exited the smoke on the west side of the encampment into a small, green glen. They were Marie, Nick, and Candy.

Candy looked around franticly, "Where's Brenna?"

"I think I saw her running north with Mitch and Dawn." Marie said.

"We should get moving before the smoke lifts and we're seen." said Nick. "They seemed pretty anxious to catch or kill us."

"But what if they caught Brenna?" Candy said worriedly, touching Nick's arm. There were tears in her eyes and voice.

"I doubt that they got anywhere near her." Nick said. "And even if she has been captured, then our best chance would be to get help from this, Uncle Garvey person you two were arguing about."

Candy couldn't disagree with that logic. Heading due west, the three of them set out. A Bulf, a blind warrior, and a warrior princess not knowing what was to come.

Brenna, Mitch, and Dawn came out of the smoke into a large clearing and scanned their surroundings. Brenna's reaction to not seeing her sister mirrored that of Candy's.

"Where's Candy? If one of those dirty rats has laid a hand on her, they're great grandchildren will regret it!" Brenna snarled.

"I saw her and Nick running west with Marie." Mitch said. "Don't worry."

"Don't worry? Don't worry?" said Brenna in an aggravated voice, then turned to Dawn. "Did he just tell me not to worry?"

"I think so." Dawn said, a little uncertain as to why she had to answer such an obvious question.

"She's got a blind man and a, a flying wolf to protect her," Brenna started, having turned back to Mitch.

"Bulf. Not flying wolf." Dawn corrected, interrupting.

"Shut up!" said Brenna, glaring at Dawn, then she turned back to Mitch, still glaring and snapped, "And you tell me not to worry?"

"Nick and Marie are tough warriors. She's as safe as if she were home in bed." Dawn told her.

Brenna glared at the small creature, then turned her anger on Mitch as he said, "I'd definitely agree about Nick."

"Whatever." Brenna growled. "So, what're we gonna do now?"

"Go north to that uncle you were arguing about." Mitch almost snapped.

"North-northwest." Dawn corrected again.

"Just stay out of this!" the two humans said as one.

"Well at least you two finally agree on something." Dawn snorted, then spread her wings and launched herself into the air.

"Shall we?" said Mitch, giving a mock bow and extending a hand northwest.

"We shall!" snapped Brenna, stomping passed him in the north-northwest direction.

Mitch shook his head and gave a slightly mischievous grin as he followed her. This was going to be a long trip. So the three of them headed toward the mountains, a Bulf cub, a Northman, and the Wolf Princess.

CHAPTER TEN

SWAMPS AND RIVERS

"I'm not going in there!" Candy stated firmly. "Let's just go around."

"Are you afraid of the swamp?" asked Nick.

"Of couse. Ever since I was little, Uncle Garvey warned me about the dangers of the swamp. Quicksand, large water-lizards, spiders the size of my fist." Candy was talking so fast she wasn't sure if Nick could understand her. She gave a little shudder at the thought of those huge spiders crawling about.

"It's all right. Just step where I step and you'll be fine." Nick said in a kind voice.

"You've been in there before?" she asked apprehensively.

"Several times." Marie shrugged. "We lived in there for three months the last time the Raves upset our camp."

"Three months? In there?" Candy said in complete shock.

"Come on," Nick said kindly, "if a blind man can live in there for three months, surely you can survive for one day."

Candy took a deep breath and said, "All right. But if we die, I'm gonna kill you."

Nick tried not to laugh, "Dually noted. Come on." He offered her his hand a little more to her left than to her. Candy couldn't help smiling as she moved slightly to the left and took his hand. Marie rolled her eyes and trotted into the swampy woods that lay before them, followed by Candy and Nick.

"It's so dark." Candy said softly. "How do you see at night?"

Nick turned his face toward her, a blank expression on his countenance.

"Oh right." Candy said sheepishly. "Sorry."

"Just walk where I walk." Nick said simply, releasing her hand and marching ahead on the muddy path.

Candy followed obediently, disliking all the mud that squished beneath her boots.

The swamps seemed to mainly consist of muddy ground, thick thorny bushes, and ugly gnarled trees, most of which had lost thier leaves yet still seemed to blot out the sun. It gave the entire place an eerie sense of foreboding.

Candy shuddered and hoped that they'd soon be out of this dreadful place.

The Raves had found their way out of the smoke and had now split up into two groups, each following the tracks left by the fugitives.

Dawn was the first to notice the pursers as she looked back while soaring above the treetops. She swooped low and landed rather awkwardly on a thin tree-branch in front of Brenna and Mitch.

"They're right behind you." she panted. "You can't outrun them. We gotta hide. Fast!"

"What do you mean we can't outrun them?" said Brenna, ignoring the pain in her thigh.

"Aye," said Mitch. "We've got a head start on them."

"There's five of them on horseback, galloping up here." Dawn told them. "We need to hide now!"

"Where?" Brenna and Mitch asked together, having no desire to try and outrun horses.

"Follow me. There's an old dead tree up this way. It's hollow." Dawn called over her wing as she awkwardly launched herself from the narrow branch. "I used to hide there to avoid chores. It's the perfect hiding place."

Brenna and Mitch exchanged a glance, then followed quickly as the small animal moved at an amazing speed.

The tree was a huge oak that had obviously been dead for many years, yet still stood tall and strong. The first five and a half feet of the trunk was as solid as a rock, but above that was a hollow cavity that Brenna and Mitch had to squeeze into at the sound of approaching hooves. They saw a group of five men pass them on horseback.

It felt strange to see that they were on regular horses, unlike the harpusia they'd ridden the night before. Brenna, Mitch, and even Dawn who'd taken refuge in the upper branches, held their breath until their enemies were out of sight. All three of them let out a loud sigh of relief.

"Aha!" a Rave shouted, leaping up and giving a smug grin at the hiding duo. "I've found them!"

Brenna let out a small yelp of surprise and Mitch sent the man flying with a swift kick to his face. Mitch leapt from the hollow cavity onto the man and started punching him in the face until the Rave was unconscious. He leapt to his feet and ran back to the tree.

"Come on!" he called, stretching out his arms as if to catch Brenna.

"You can't be serious!" Brenna said, almost glaring at him.

"There's no time! Just get down here!" he nearly growled in frustration.

"Fine!" she snorted, preparing to jump.

When Brenna did make her flying leap, it knocked Mitch to the ground when he caught her. The two of them lay flat, Brenna atop Mitch making him feel crushed. She put her hands flat on the ground on either side of his shoulders, and pushed herself up, then looked down at Mitch. Their noses were only four inches apart, and Brenna suddenly found herself staring into those blue-gray eyes of his.

Mitch stared back up at her and felt his pulse quicken. Babbette used to look at him like that. The familiar ache in his chest returned strongly. Then the two suddenly remembered where and who they were, and jumped away from each other. Leaping to their feet they ran northward.

"They must be following our tracks." Mitch panted.

"Oh, so we'll just stop leaving tracks then!" Brenna growled sarcastically, the pain in her thigh increasing as they continued to run.

"You're right." he said, grabbing her hand and pulling her in another direction.

"What're you doing? Let me go!" Brenna demanded, struggling against his grip.

"I saw a river over here." Mitch explained.

"It's the Roaring Eagle River." Dawn called from above where she soared.

"There it is." Mitch said triumphantly. "Let's see them follow our tracks in moving water."

"What? No! I almost drowned last night, I'm not going back in the water!" Brenna protested.

"This is different water." Mitch said.

"That's not the point!" she stated firmly.

"There they are!" yelled one of the Raves from about thirty yards behind them.

"Come on, Princess!" growled Mitch, dragging her toward the river.

The two young people rushed to the river and waded in. The water felt freezingly cold, but they didn't care about that right now. All they cared about was getting away from the pursuing Raves.

At first the water was only lapping their shins, but soon it was up passed their knees as they ran with the current. It was almost up to their waists when Brenna noticed something troubling. The speed of the river's current.

"Is the water moving faster?" she asked, her voice a little shaky.

"I think so. There're some rocks up ahead. Let's get out for a minute." Mitch's voice was shivering. Clearly the cold was getting to him as well.

They climbed up onto the nearest rock and began jumping from stone to stone. Brenna's teeth chattered as a strong breeze picked up and made her loose, wet clothes flap against her flesh.

The spray from the river made it difficult to see properly and the roar of the rushing water made it hard to hear. The river was flowing westward and the current was speeding up.

Mitch cried out painfully and knelt on the rock he'd just leapt onto, clutching his right upper arm. Brenna turned and saw that an arrow had obviously grazed his arm, leaving a scratch and a torn sleeve in its wake.

"Let's give 'em a volley!" one of the Raves shouted from upstream. "They're sitting ducks."

The river was more than five feet deep here, nine feet wide and moving at an incredible speed. The water was foaming and bubbling, looking terribly dark and forbodding.

"We've gotta go back into the water!" Mitch shouted over the river's roar.

"Are you insane? That's suicide!" Brenna yelled back.

"As opposed to staying here?" Mitch growled.

"Men, take your aim!" yelled one of the Raves.

"Come on!" Mitch yelled.

"Ready. Fire!" yelled the Rave upstream.

Brenna and Mitch both dove into the frothing current just a second too soon for the Raves. Just as the rain of dark shafts came clattering down on the rocks, Brenna and Mitch were being swept away by the raging river, lost to their enemies' sight.

It was hard work going through the dark swamp. The mud was thick, the trees and bushes were dense, and Candy felt her skin crawl everytime a large spider came into view. The humans trudged onward, while Marie flapped overhead calling out encouragement.

"Are you sure this is the right way?" Candy asked tiredly. "That spot over on the left looks dry and easy to walk on."

"Show her Marie." Nick called without stopping or slowing his pace.

Marie swooped and took a large, dead bough in her teeth. Carrying it as she flew, she flapped over the green, mossy place that Candy had indicated, and dropped the piece of wood. For a second the wood rested on the moss, then rapidly started sinking into the quicksand beneath.

Candy stared in disbelief, "But, it," her voice trailed off.

"That's one of the benefits of being blind." Nick said, still marching onward. "You don't trust what your eyes see. Don't trust the ground in these swamps. They're treacherous Miss Candy."

"But, how do you know where to walk?" asked Candy.

"The trees." Nick said simply.

"What?" she asked, sounding confused as she raised a brow.

"Trees only grow in solid ground." Nick continued to explain. "This ground is just very, very muddy."

Until now, Candy hadn't noticed that every tree Nick passed he'd touch its trunk.

"Stay where the woods are thickest, and you're in the safest place in this swamp." Nick explained.

"I'll remember that." Candy smiled.

"Shush!" said Marie, landing daintily on a nearby branch. "I saw some Raves about half a mile back. They're tracking us!"

"Come on." said Nick, holding out his hand toward Candy.

She put her hand in his, and the two started moving as fast as they could through the knee-deep mud. It made a sickening squish-squash sucking sound as they rushed forward.

The Raves were having a much more difficult time as they trudged through the muck. It wasn't easy to follow these fugitives. The thick mud would instantly refill whatever footprints were left behind. They had to depend on the broken branches and disturbed shrubbery.

"I'm going over here! This path looks easier!" groused one of the men, heading for what looked like a dry, mossy path.

"I don't care where you walk, just keep moving!" Dritt roared.

Dritt himself had come out on the hunt, determined to avenge his lost eye and ruined face. He covered the now empty socket with a black sash rather than the torn piece of sleeve he'd used earlier. This made him look even more sinister than before. His encounter with the sister of the Wolf Princess had hardened him, leaving a burning anger in his remaining eye.

He curled his lip in a sneer as he fingered the coiled whip that hung from his belt. He would find that girl. That horrid, hated girl who had stolen his precious eye. He would find her, and she would beg for death before he was done. Then he would gladly oblige her request. She would die with an expression of fear on her countenance. A slow, painful, agonizing death. That would suit her nicely.

"I'll give ten gold pieces to the first man who brings me that girl alive!" he bellowed.

"Aah!" screamed the man who'd gone to the apparently dry path.

The group of men all stopped and looked over at the man who'd left the main party. He was up to his waist in quicksand and still sinking rapidly.

"Help me!" he screamed, his hand outstretched toward Dritt. "Get me out! Please!"

He was in up to his chest and seemed to be sinking even faster than before. One of the men rushed over as fast as the knee-deep mud would allow.

"I'm coming Glac!" he called to the man in the quicksand.

"Just get me out!" Glac yelled. "I don't want to die here Jep!"

"Hang on Glac!" said Jep, trying in vain to grasp Glac's hand.

Glac was up to his chin, his hand raised only inches above the sucking ooze. Jep tried to take hold of the outstretched fingers, but only managed to brush them with his own. Then he watched as the head and fingers disappeared beneath the mucky surface.

All of the Raves who'd witnessed the event stood stalk still, eyes wide and mouths open. They all stood there in the mud, frozen in shock.

"Let's get going!" snarled Dritt. "Remember, ten gold pieces to the one who brings me that girl alive!"

None of the men dared to defy him. They all trudged after him fearfully. His one good eye burned with an eerie madness and hatred. Hatred for that horrid girl.

"And they just kept going?" said Candy, not believing the report Marie had just given them.

"One tried to save him, but the leader, a cruel one-eyed man with a whip, did nothing. Once the man was gone, he told them to just keep moving. No speech. No may he rest in peace. Nothing. He seems very intent on catching you." Marie explained, looking at Candy.

"Me?" said Candy in surprise. "Why would anyone want me?"

"I don't know, but he's after you." Marie said simply.

Candy was thoughtful for a moment, then her eyes widened. "Did you say that the leader is a one-eyed man?"

"Aye." Marie said, nodding her wolf head vigorously. "And he's put a price on your head. Ten gold pieces to the man who brings you to him alive."

"Dritt." Candy gulped, feeling the color drain from her face.

"Dritt? Who's that?" asked Nick, sounding confused.

"The one-eyed man. He's coming for me." Candy said, fear evident in her voice. "He wants me dead, I'm sure."

"Why?" asked Nick.

"Because I'm the reason that he only has one eye. I had to save my sister! He was going to kill her!" Candy almost shouted as she hastily explained. "Marie, about how far back would you say they are?"

"About a third of a mile back. That 'Dritt' person is driving his men as fast as the swamp will allow them to go." Marie said simply. "We'd better pick up the pace if we're gonna stay ahead of them."

Candy let out a groan of weariness, "Pick up the pace?"

Nick offered his hand, "I'll help you. Marie, you keep an eye on our guests while Miss Candace and I go ahead to Dead Lizard Grove."

Marie gave a wolfish grin, "Oh. All right."

She quickly launched herself into the air.

"What's at Dead Lizard Grove?" Candy asked, thinking that was a strange name for a grove.

"A welcoming party." Nick grinned.

Dawn soared over the raging river, scanning the rough current for any sigh of Brenna and Mitch. Each second was agony as it slipped by. Dawn had nearly lost hope, when sweeping low she saw Mitch's head bobbing in the middle of the river.

Mitch came up and took a breath, then was sucked back down by the undertow. He fought against the current and popped back up just as his lungs started to burn. He finally managed to stay on the surface and began looking around wildly.

"Mitch!" Dawn cried from above. "Where's Brenna?"

Mitch was coughing and sputtering, but managed to answer a little above a croak, "I don't know."

As Brenna surfaced she bumped into Mitch from behind and they both were drawn back under. They both struggled back to the surface, gasping for air. Brenna instantly went down again, dragged beneath the surface due to the weight of the sword attached to her belt. She fought her way back up, barely managing to keep her head above the water.

"Over this way!" called Dawn, hovering above the riverbank to their right.

The two young people paddled toward the shore, exhaustion overwhelming their limbs and lungs.

Mitch crawled halfway out of the water and collapsed, then with an effort he flipped to his back, his chest heaving. He closed his eyes and lay still, grateful for the fresh forest air that filled his burning lungs.

Brenna didn't crawl as far out of the water, but unlike Mitch, she didn't watch where she fell. Her arms ached and gave out under her weight as she moved out of the river on her hands and knees. She collapsed and Mitch let out a grunt as her head landed on his chest. Both were too exhausted to care about where they landed, who they landed on, or who landed on top of them.

Brenna would've never admitted this to anyone, but the 'thump-bump, thump-bump,' of Mitch's heart was a relaxing comfort. Within a few minutes they were both lost in slumber.

Dawn flew high above the treetops and looked back upstream from where they'd come. The Raves were gone. She flapped the great distance back to the place where they'd been. There were tracks going in the opposite direction.

She followed them and found the group of Raves halfway between Nick's campsite and Castle MacKline. She soared back to where she'd left Brenna and Mitch, then landed on the river-bank.

The humans didn't look like they'd moved. Mitch was snoring softly, and the two seemed so peaceful that Dawn couldn't help smiling at the memory of their argument earlier.

She looked around the clearing on this river-bank and found that it was really a grove beech, willow and pine trees. Dawn settled on a thick willow branch and tucked her head under her wing before going to sleep. It had been a long morning.

Dawn knew that they'd be safe for a while, since the Raves had retreated back to the castle. The only thing that bothered her was not knowing what had happened to Nick and Marie, and that Candace person.

She hoped that wherever they were, they were safe. Her thoughts were still on them as she fell asleep.

"Hurry up!" Dritt roared angrily.

These men weren't moving fast enough! How was he going to catch that awful girl and have his revenge if these cowards didn't stop whining about quicksand and march faster? In frustration, he unfurled his whip and cracked it over his head.

"Get a move on, or I'll tear out your guts and feed 'em to ya'!" he bellowed ferociously, cracking his whip again.

This caused the men to rush forward, terror in their eyes and fear in their hearts. Dritt would show no sympathy if they dared to stumble. He would have the sister of the Wolf Princess today, and nothing was going to stop him.

CHAPTER ELEVEN

DEAD LIZARD GROVE AND
ROAST RABBIT

"Is this Dead Lizard Grove?" asked Candy, staring at the semicircle of skeleton trees before them. It seemed to be the only place in the entire swamp that had enough space between the trees to let the sun shine through.

"Shh." Nick whispered. "Wait a moment."

He whistled a long, low whistle. Then he turned his head and listened.

Candy's eyes widened and she stared in disbelief at the creature that arose from the mud. It was at least seven feet long and four feet tall. It was a giant, scaly, mud covered lizard. It opened its huge mouth wide and flicked out a long tongue, grabbing a large spider with the very tip. Drawing its tongue back with lightning quickness, the beast snapped its jaws shut with a sickening crunch. The creature licked its chops, then opened its mouth again and issued forth a loud, long, high pitched whistle-like sound.

A smile slowly spread across Nick's face, "Aye. We're here."

"What is that thing?" Candy almost sobbed in fear.

"A mud-whistler. They're giant lizards that thrive in the swamps." Nick explained. "They mostly live in this grove."

"Do they eat, anything besides spiders?" Candy gulped, her voice nearly failing her.

"Anything they can get their tongue around." Nick said simply.

Candy gulped again, "So, how do we get passed them?"

"We climb." Nick said, tapping a tree trunk with his stave. "Come on."

They climbed up into the branches, and started moving across the mucky grove from tree to tree by way of the thick branches. About halfway across Nick stopped.

"What's wrong?" asked Candy, feeling concerned.

"How much does your dress mean to you?" he asked.

"What?" Candy said raising a brow.

"Your dress? Would you miss a part of your sleeve if it was gone?" he asked.

"I don't know. Why?" Candy shrugged.

"Tear off part of your sleeve and toss it down there." he explained.

Candy loved the dress she was wearing. It was a beautiful pale blue and aqua, but the hem was torn and the skirt was crusted with mud up passed her knees. She tore off a couple of inches of her sleeve and threw it down into the center of the grove. It drifted down toward the muck and landed on what appeared to be a muddy mound. Candy gasped when the mound shifted slightly.

"I think it landed on one of the lizards." she said timidly. "Why did I have to do that?"

"So that when the Raves come this way, they'll think you were eaten and give up the search." Nick said logically.

Candy felt ill at the thought of being eaten by one of those monsters. She had trouble moving across the branches again until Nick called softly, "Come on."

"Move you scum!" shouted Dritt, cracking his whip.

The group of men trudged onward, more willing to deal with quicksand and giant spiders than Dritt and his whip. They were all constantly looking around, hoping to spot Candy so that they could go back to the comfort of Castle MacKline, not caring who got the ten pieces of gold.

Jep was the first one to see the torn piece of fabric in the middle of the grove they'd just found.

"Sir," he called to Dritt. "I can see a piece of cloth in there."

Dritt turned his gaze in the direction that Jep pointed. His eye widened.

"Isn't that the same color that girl was wearing sir?" Jep asked.

"Aye." Dritt growled. "She must've gone through here. Forward men. She's near. I can feel it. And remember, ten gold pieces to the one who brings me that girl alive!"

A wicked smile creased Dritt's scared face. Revenge was near. He knew it. The last thing that dreadful girl would ever see, would be his smug grin as he took her eyes, just as she'd taken one of his. Then she would stumble in utter and complete darkness, while he would laugh and mock her as he pushed and tripped her. Her cries for mercy would be music to his ears. Only after he'd had his fun he would take her life. These evil thoughts pleased him greatly.

"Aah!" Jep's cry cut into Dritts awful thoughts.

Dritt looked around. As soon as he found that whiner he'd give him a thrashing he wouldn't soon forget. But where was he?

"Where's Jep?" he bellowed angrily.

"I don't know." one of the men answered honestly. "He was right behind me. Jep? Jep?"

"Uh! Get it off me! Get it off me!" another man screamed.

All eyes turned to the screamer and most of them started laughing as he danced around with a huge, black spider on top of his head.

"It's not funny! Get it off!" the man screamed.

"All right mate. I'll help you." said the man who'd been walking in front of Jep as he walked toward his friend's back, ready to remove the spider.

"Ah! Thanks! You're a true mate Killis."

Killis stared at the back of his friend's head. The spider was gone, but Killis hadn't done a thing.

"I, I didn't touch you mate." Killis said in a confused voice.

Then they heard a long, high-pitched whistling sound. The two men turned toward it and saw the face of a giant lizard.

The beast's mouth opened and closed slightly, changing the whistle's pitch. More lizards rose from the mud and the small group of men screamed in horror as the long slimy tongues shot out of the huge reptiles' mouths, and coiled around them.

Candy and Nick could hear the cries from where they were hiding. They sat in a hollow crevice in the face of a large rock near the grove, while Marie perched on a branch nearby. The cries of the Raves were bone-chilling. Candy covered her ears, wishing that she'd never asked for a rest.

"Can we go now?" she asked, trying not to sob.

"Are you strong enough to continue?" said Nick, his expression blank and emotionless.

"I won't be if we have to sit and listen to this much longer." Candy sobbed, unable to hold back the tears any longer.

"All right then." Nick said kindly, putting a hand on her shoulder. "Let's go."

Dritt ran as fast as he could through the knee-deep mud, stumbling back the way he'd come. All twelve of the men who'd been with him were now dead, swallowed up by those monsters. When one of those creatures lashed out with its tongue, he'd drawn his sword and cut through the slimy flesh that coiled around his thigh. The lizard had let out a blood-curdling scream. His head still pounded as that anguished cry echoed through his mind.

Before turning to run, he'd seen the girl. That horrid, hated girl. She was climbing down a rock-face on the other side of the grove. It had only been a glimpse, but it had been enough to spur him on. He'd charged forward, but the lizard he'd severed the tongue of stood in his way. Sword still in hand, he'd separated the monster from its head.

When he'd looked back at the rock-face, she was gone, and there were at least ten more mud-whistlers in his path. He'd had no choice but to run for his life. He would return with more men, and he would find her. He would find her, and destroy her.

Candy was tired, but would not dare to ask for a rest again. The last time she'd asked she and Nick had taken shelter in the rock-cleft and been forced to listen to the Raves' screams of death. But in spite of herself she was exhausted. Marie noticed this and swooped low, hovering by Nick's left shoulder.

"Miss Candace needs a rest." Marie whispered.

"We just had a rest." Nick whispered back, sounding confused.

"We didn't rest long enough, and how can you rest when people are dying?" she replied softly. "She's not as strong as you are Nick. She hasn't faced what you have."

Nick nodded slowly and whispered, "Granted. We'll take a break at the Fallen Giant. We can camp on the Moss-trail tonight if we need to. Once we're out of the wet it'll be easier for her."

"Sounds good. The Fallen Giant is about thirty paces ahead. I'll round up some lunch." Marie said, beating her wings in order to gain more altitude.

"Is it really noon already?" Nick asked in surprise.

"Aye." Marie called from above.

"What were you talking about?" Candy asked from behind, sounding tired.

Nick thought for a minute, then said, "Marie is going to find some food, and we're going to stop for a lunch-break at the Fallen Giant."

Candy looked ahead and saw a huge tree lying on its side. She couldn't tell how long it was since the brush was too thick and tall.

"Do you mean that huge tree up ahead when you say, 'Fallen Giant'?" she asked.

"Aye." Nick said simply, not slowing his pace.

When they finally reached the fallen tree, Candy collapsed across its trunk.

"Are you all right?" asked Nick.

"Just tired." Candy said wearily.

"Here," said Nick, pulling her into his arms and carrying her to a hallow space of the tree. "Get some sleep. I'll wake you when Marie gets back."

"Thank you." Candy said, unable to keep her eyes open.

"Goodnight Miss Candace." Nick said softly.

"Mmm, please, just call me Candy." she yawned.

"Alright, Candy." Nick smiled.

Candy didn't respond. She was too tired to speak. Nick could hear her even breathing and knew that she was asleep. He felt a breeze on his cheek and heard Candy shiver. He removed his coat and wrapped it around her.

The action woke Candy, but she didn't say anything, only smiled at the kind gesture. She was surprised that he'd give up his jacket when it was so chilly. Candy gave a small sigh of contentment as she watched Nick.

Nick couldn't help wondering what Candy looked like. Soon the curiosity that he felt got the better of him. He knelt at the mouth of the hollow space, his sightless eyes twinkling with intrigue. He reached out a hand and touched Candy's face. His brow wrinkled as he tried to paint an image of her face in his mind. Her skin was soft and smooth against his rough palm. Candy closed her eyes as his hand passed over them. Rough as his flesh was, his touch was gentle, and in a way almost pleasant.

She had long, soft lashes he thought. His hand moved down over her nose. He could feel her warm breath against his palm. His hand moved lower and traced her lips.

Candy wasn't certain, but she thought that he spent a long time on her mouth, and thought that he seemed to blush for a moment.

Nick cleared his throat quietly and touched her chin gently, then traced her jaw-line with his fingertips.

Candy could feel herself blushing and was relieved that Nick couldn't see the redness of her cheeks. She stared at him, trying to read his thoughts. His expression appeared to be approving. There was the hint of a smile playing on his lips.

Candy felt somewhat pleased that he approved of her looks. She watched him as he scooted back, stood, then turned and walked back to the center of the trunk. He tore a branch from the long dead tree, pulled out his hunting knife and began sharpening one end.

Candy closed her eyes and was lost to sweet slumber.

Mitch stirred, dreaming of beautiful Babbette and how she used to rest her head on his chest as they slept. He put his arm around the girl that now lay by his side. He felt her head shift to his shoulder. He turned his head slightly and brushed her forehead with his lips.

Brenna's eyes fluttered open. She moved her head so that she could see the man who was kissing her brow.

Mitch happened to open his eyes and look at the girl in his arms.

The moment that their eyes met, they widened. They both yelled and leapt apart, splashing into the shallows.

"Uh! Ew!" Brenna grimaced.

"Ick!" gagged Mitch, then stared at her, "Hey wait a minute, what do you mean 'Ew'?"

"It's disgusting! We were hugging and almost, kissed! Ew! Yuck!" she shuddered.

"Yuck?" Mitch said defensively, glaring at Brenna. "I saved your life and your sister's."

"So?" Brenna said, splashing him.

Mitch blinked through the water dripping down his face and gritted his teeth.

"So," he said, "you owe me!" Mitch growled as he splashed her back.

Brenna's mouth dropped open in shock, "I owe you nothing!" she growled, splashing him in the face again.

Mitch returned the splash, only to receive another face full of water. He splashed her again and said, "You're right! I owe you!"

Brenna stared at him curiously, "What?"

Mitch touched his bandaged shoulder, "I owe you a cut!"

"What?" Brenna said, trying to keep her voice calm.

"I owe you a cut!" he stated, getting to his knees. "Come here!"

Brenna suddenly realized that he was serious and scrambled out of the river. Mitch pursued her up the embankment. He wrapped his arms around her waist from behind and lifted her off the ground. But the slope of the bank combined her weight threw him off balance and they both fell backwards.

"Ow!" said Brenna as she fell on him with a thump.

Mitch said little above a gasp and then a groan as the air left his lungs, crushed under Brenna's weight. Brenna broke free of his grasp and ran toward a tall beech tree. She swung herself up onto the lowest branch and reached for the next.

Mitch had gained his second wind and was up again, chasing after her. He grabbed hold of Brenna's foot just as she was trying to pull herself up onto the third lowest branch.

"Get back down here!" he growled, tugging hard on her booted foot.

"Let go of my foot!" Brenna growled back, pulling her foot upward.

"Come down!" Mitch demanded, pulling harder.

Brenna almost lost her grip on the branch as she yelled stubbornly, "No!" and tried in vain to regain her foot.

The two tugged and pulled until Mitch found the ground with his seat, with an "oof!" and then a "plop!" sound. Mitch looked at the object in his hands. It was Brenna's boot, which had slipped from her foot during their tug-of-war.

Brenna had nearly fallen out of the tree when she was released from the pulling force. Quickly regaining her footing and grasp, she climbed upward out of Mitch's reach, her sword clacking against the branches in the scabbard as she went.

Mitch leapt to his feet, threw down the boot angrily and began climbing up after her.

Brenna grabbed a handful of the prickly nut-husks and started throwing them at the ascending Northman.

"Ow! Ouch! Stop that!" Mitch protested, raising a hand to shield his face. "Cut it out!"

"Then leave me alone!" bellowed Brenna, hurling another handful of husks at him.

"Ow! Alright! Ow! Stop it or I'll, aah!" Mitch fell as the branch he'd been standing on snapped beneath his weight with a loud 'crack.' Mitch hit the ground with a resounding thump.

Brenna peered down through the branches at his still form.

"Northman?" she called. "Northman?"

No answer.

"Northman?" she called a little louder. "Mitch?" she tried, hoping that his name would gain an answer.

There was only a moan in response.

Brenna climbed down and cautiously approached where Mitch lay.

"Mitch?" she asked, trying not to show the concern that she felt growing within her. "I mean, Northman, are you alive?"

"I think I landed on some of those seeds." Mitch groaned. "Ooh!"

Brenna couldn't help giggling at the situation. She covered her mouth with her hand to muffle the sound.

"It's not funny. They're sticking in my back." Mitch growled painfully.

"You, uh, also have some in your hair." Brenna chuckled.

Mitch raised a brow as he moved his hand through his hair, combing the prickly husks out. He sat up slowly, grunting or groaning with each movement he made.

"How did all of this start again?" he moaned.

"I'm not sure." Brenna giggled, shaking her head. "Need a hand?"

Mitch's eyes darted from Brenna's face, to the hand that she held out to him, then back to her face. She seemed sincere enough. But then a thought entered his mind and he smiled.

"Aye. Thank you." Mitch said, taking her hand and yanking down as hard as he could.

Brenna hit the ground as Mitch released her hand, sending the Wolf Princess rolling. Mitch shook with laughter when he heard a loud splash.

"You rat!" Brenna roared from where she lay in the river-shallows, pounding the river's surface with her fist.

"You humans act strange when you're hungry." Dawn's voice echoed from above them. "Yuck! Beech tree seeds? I didn't know you were that hungry."

Mitch and Brenna looked up at the sun's position and saw that it was half passed noon. Mitch heard a gurgling sound and rubbed his empty belly. The fish he'd had for breakfast seemed so long ago.

"Here." Dawn said proudly. In her paws were two plump rabbits. "If you two build a fire, you can cook them for lunch."

"Is there enough for all three of us?" asked Mitch.

"I've already had mine. All three of them were just bouncing in a meadow over toward Wolf mountain. I just swooped down and caught 'em all before they could get to their burrows." Dawn explained happily.

"All right, I'll gather some wood and clean the rabbits." Mitch said.

"And what do I do?" said an irritated Brenna as she climbed out of the river, dripping wet.

"Dry off. This is man's work." Mitch said, standing up straight and squaring his shoulders. "And you're a girl, I think."

Brenna glared at the grinning young man, then smiled and walked passed him, intentionally knocking her shoulder into his, saying in her sweetest voice, "Takes one to know one."

Mitch's expression changed from surprise and shock at her bold, harsh words, to anger and frustration.

"Women!" he almost snorted, rolling his eyes.

Brenna and Mitch gathered armfuls of wood and would've probably spent a good fifteen minutes arguing about who'd gathered more wood if they both hadn't been so hungry. Then they argued about who would get to use the dagger to skin their rabbit first, since Brenna was the only one who had a blade.

"Just give it to me for five minutes." Mitch growled irritably.

"I'm not giving my favorite dagger to some Northman." Brenna snorted.

"I know how to use it." Mitch stated.

"Are you saying that I don't?" she growled, pointing the dagger at him.

Mitch stared at the sharp point. He touched his bandaged shoulder where that very dagger had stabbed him not four days earlier. He swallowed noticeably, still watching the weapon.

Brenna raised a brow at him, "Afraid of blades?" she said, not realizing what a ridiculous question it was.

Mitch raised his eyes to meet hers, "Afraid? It's common sense to avoid sharp blades." Mitch opened his shirt to reveal an eight-inch long scar that went straight down his chest. "But sense or not, I fear no sharp edges."

Brenna eyed the massive scar, "How did you get that?"

Mitch's face went blank for a moment and his eyes seemed very distant, then he finally blinked and asked, "Do I get to use that dagger or not?"

Dawn suddenly came winging in overhead and landed next to Mitch, dropping a large carving knife next to him.

"Here." she said. "Just stop fighting."

Brenna and Mitch lowered their eyes, feeling a little ashamed that they'd lost their tempers so easily over something so simple.

"Where'd you get this?" asked Mitch, trying to change the subject by picking up the knife.

"It was back at Nick's camp." Dawn said simply.

"Any sign of Candy? Or Nick?" asked Brenna, rather intently.

Mitch raised a brow at her, "Or Marie?" he added, keeping his gaze on Brenna as he spoke.

Dawn shook her head sadly, "No. They must've left."

They were all very quiet as the fire was lit, the rabbits' were cleaned and speared on long sticks, and then slowly turned over the flames. Brenna had found some wild potatoes while gathering wood and thought they'd go nicely with the rabbits. There were six piled by the fire, and she decided to show off a little. Taking up two potatoes she began juggling.

Mitch looked up from the roasting meat and stared at her, careful to keep his expression passive and unimpressed. He watched the motion of her hands and the potatoes. The objects went up and down in an oval shape in the air. When she tossed a potato, she quickly grabbed the potato in her other hand, then caught the potato in mid-air with her empty hand.

After a few minutes, she stopped and smiled smugly at Mitch, then sat down across the fire from him, still grinning slightly. Mitch nodded at her, then stood.

Taking up three potatoes he began juggling in a much more impressive way then Brenna had just done. His hands moved up and down and side to side, until the objects were just a brown blur in front of him.

Brenna's mouth dropped open as she watched. Mitch finished and put the potatoes back on the pile, then sat back down keeping his eyes on the fire.

"If you want to eat those, you should probably wash them before you cook 'em." Mitch said, turning the spit and watching as the meat dripped sizzling fat into the flames as it roasted.

Brenna wrinkled her nose as she gathered up the potatoes and took them to the river. As she rinsed them, she looked up at the blue sky and wondered if Candy was all right wherever she was. Brenna certainly hoped so.

Candy awoke to the smell of roast duck. She blinked her eyes and looked over at Nick and Marie who had built a fire and were now roasting what looked like two small marsh-ducks over it.

"Ah, look who's awake." Marie said cheerfully. "As you can see, I've caught two marsh-ducks."

"They look delicious." Candy smiled, crawling out of the hallow space in the Fallen Giant.

"They are. I caught one for myself earlier." Marie said, licking her wolfish lips. "Marvelous. Quite marvelous."

Candy and Nick both chuckled as Marie continued to describe how tasty the duck had been. By the time she'd finished speaking, Nick was handing Candy her roasted duck and Marie, having made herself hungry again, flew off in search of another delicious waterfowl.

"Thank you for the coat." Candy said after a few minutes, draping the garment across his shoulders.

"You're welcome." he said softly.

They ate in silence for a few minutes. The meat was juicy and tender. It calmed the gnawing ache in their empty bellies with each swallow.

"Mmm!" said Candy. "This is good."

Nick nodded in agreement, then spoke around a mouthful of roasted duck, "Marsh-duck usually is. But venison is better."

"I prefer a nice piece of mutton myself. But venison is good with boiled potatoes and onions." Candy paused to take another bite of duck. "We always have roast venison prepared that way for New Year's day."

There was silence again, then Nick spoke, "May I ask you something?"

"Of course." Candy shrugged.

"How did you and your sister, being princesses and all, get mixed up with the Raves?"

"Laird Griff Cray invaded our castle." Candy said simply, lowering her eyes.

"I know that, but why?"

Candy swallowed, "I suppose he thinks of himself as a conqueror."

"There's more to it than that." Nick pressed.

"He thinks that because Brenna was born under a dark star, that she has a dark destiny." Candy explained reluctantly, glancing at his face.

Nick's expression was one of astonishment, "So she was the one born that night, and you're the one born beneath that bright star."

"Aye." Candy said, raising a brow. "You know the stars?"

Nick was quiet for a minute, then said, "My father knew the stars. He told me about the stormy night when the sky cleared and the two stars appeared side by side."

"I think I should speak to your father." Candy said. "If he knows the stars, he must be very wise."

Nick looked sad for a moment, then they both heard the familiar sound of Marie's wings beating the air. She landed between them, her stomach bulging. She'd obviously found more marsh-ducks.

"Ah," she said, licking her chomps in a most satisfied way. "Full belly feels good. So, are you two about done eating?"

"I am." Nick said, standing and scattering the gnawed bones into the mud below. "Miss Candace?"

"I can eat on the move." Candy said, rising to her feet.

Marie kicked some mud over the fire, sending up a cloud of gray smoke, "Then let's go."

The three moved forward through the shin-deep mud. It was easier going now that the mud wasn't so deep. Nick led the way Candy following while she ate the remainder of her duck, and a plump, waddling Marie trotting by her side. In between mouthfuls Candy spoke with the Bulf.

"So, what's Nick's family like?" she asked.

Marie's eyes grew wide, "Shush!" Marie's eyes darted to Nick. He didn't appear to have heard Candy's question.

"What's wrong?" whispered Candy.

"I think I can trust you. But you must promise that you won't tell Nick that I told you." Marie said softly.

"I promise." Candy said quietly.

"It was fourteen years ago." Marie explained. "Some bandits came to his family's home and killed everyone in sight. Nick was only seven. While trying to protect his sisters he was knocked to the ground and hit his head on a rock. The bandits must've thought that he was dead or he wouldn't be here now. When he woke up, he said that everything was blurry, and then it all went black. I found him crying over his mother's body, trying to wake her. Dawn and I are his family now."

Candy's heart went out to the blind man who walked ahead of her. He'd lost so much, but here he was walking tall. She suddenly felt a deep admiration for this young man.

Brenna and Mitch had finished their meal and were now traveling north toward the mountains once again. The great gray peaks loomed ahead of them, the very tops hidden by a ghostly mist, making the mountains appear eerie, yet beautiful. As they continued northward the trees thinned out into a sparce woodland of pines and maples, many of them still just saplings.

Dawn trotted nearby, rolling her eyes as Brenna and Mitch argued.

"You follow me!" snorted Brenna.

"Why should you lead?" growled Mitch.

"'Cause I know where we're going!" she groused. "And I'm a better cook." she grumbled under her breath just loud enough that Mitch could hear.

Mitch glared at her. The rabbits had been very tasty, and Mitch wasn't a bad cook. But Brenna wasn't about to admit that fact openly.

"At least I can juggle." Mitch muttered.

"I juggled!" Brenna protested.

"And it was very poorly done, Princess."

"I'd rather be a princess than a scruffy-looking, rude, smelly Northman!" she growled.

Mitch raised a brow, "Smelly? I just had a bath."

"And at least my mother is a lady of noble birth, and not some dog!" Brenna said in smug tone.

This was the breaking point for Mitch's patience. He took an angry breath, then hissed spitefully, "My mother was a pure, honorable woman, and she always checked to make sure that she was kissing the right person."

Brenna glared coldly at the Northman, who stared back at her smugly.

"But you wouldn't know how to do that, would you?" he started to grin.

"Shut up!" Brenna yelled.

"Make me!" Mitch taunted. "And about that kiss, did I feel tongue?"

Mitch hadn't actually felt any such thing, but he'd been enraged by the Wolf Princess's words and all he wanted at this moment was to upset Brenna. He was succeeding, as Brenna's expression showed that was most certainly upset.

"I did not! There was no such thing, you, you pig!" she bellowed.

"Well that makes you a pig-kisser." Mitch snorted. "So which is worse?"

"Oh aye?" she snarled.

"Aye!" he sneered.

"I am not!"

"You are too!"

"Am not!"

"Are too!"

This went on for another several minutes, but long before that Dawn had torn up two dandelions and stuffed them into her ears. She shook her head and groaned, thinking that humans must be the most willing to argue type of creatures in the world. She launched herself into the air, deciding to fly ahead for a while until they calmed down.

The argument was only ended when Brenna, who had somehow gotten ahead of Mitch, suddenly felt something go tight around her booted ankle and yank her foot upward, out from under her. She wasn't entirely certain what had happened, so she screamed, but then she noticed that the entire world was now upside-down. She quickly realized that it was she who was upside-down, caught in one of her uncle's large snares.

"What're you laughing at you stupid Northman?" she snapped at Mitch when she heard his laughter. "Get me down!"

"Now why would I want to do that?" he chuckled. "What's in it for me?"

"Northman!" she growled threateningly.

"As long as you're just, hanging there," Mitch said, picking up a large piece of dead wood, "let's get one thing straight. My name is Mitch, not Northman, Mitch. Understood, Princess?"

Brenna drew her lips into a tight line and glared defiantly at him, which looked fierce in spite of her awkward position.

"What's that Princess? You want me to beat you with this stick until you have splinters? All right then." Mitch grinned, gently thumping the piece of dead wood against his palm.

"Fine, Mitch." Brenna grunted angrily.

"You mean I can still beat you with a stick?" his mischievous grin only broadened.

"No. Now get me down."

"I don't know. You look pretty good hanging upside-down." Mitch laughed. "I think I'll leave you that way."

"Mitch, you get me down this instant or else!" the Wolf Princess shouted angrily.

"Oh and why should I?" he asked, coming toward her. "All you do is bark orders and complain. Well I'm sick of your arrogance, so I'm gonna give the orders from here on ooow."

His sentence was cut short by his booted ankle also being caught in a snare, and in an instant he was dangling upside-down next to Brenna, who burst out laughing.

"Well, well, well, look who's upside-down now." she smirked.

"Ha, ha." he said sarcastically. "Now that you've had your laugh, how are we gonna get down?"

"We?" she said.

Mitch stared at her.

"I don't know how you're gonna get down, but you won't be getting any help from me, Northman." Brenna spat.

"Mitch!" he snapped, shoving at her, which caused her to swing away from him.

"Fine, Mitch!" she replied as she came swinging back with an outstretched fist. "Take this!"

Her fist connected with his ribs. He grabbed her fist as he grunted. They tried to wrestle, but upside-down it felt as silly as it looked. Then there was a loud 'crack' and Brenna's snare instantly went slack. She hit the ground with a resounding 'thump.'

Mitch didn't even try to hide his laughter as she painfully stood up.

"What're you laughing at?" she said in a sarcastically sweet tone. "I'm free. Now what was that about 'being sick of my arrogance?'"

The smile quickly vanished from Mitch's face, "Hey, come on, let me down."

"I don't know, you look pretty good hanging upside-down." Brenna grinned. "And what was that about beating me with a stick? That's a good idea. I'll find a nice big one to give you splinters."

Brenna turned and walked toward the trees, pretending to search for a large branch while Mitch struggled to get free. He suddenly remembered that he had the carving knife that Dawn had given him. He quickly pulled it from the back of his belt, then strained to grab hold of the rope and began sawing at it.

Brenna stood up straight and turned around at the sound of loud 'snap' and 'thud.' She saw Mitch lying on the ground, moaning as he struggled to his hands and knees. When he caught sight of her, he leapt to his feet and charged.

Brenna wasn't sure what to do at first, then she met him head on. She was shocked when she felt herself shoved backward until she hit a tree. Mitch held her there and brought his face close to hers.

"Now what was that about splinters?" he growled just under his breath.

Brenna wasn't certain what she should do. All she could do was stare into his blue-gray eyes. Even now as they glowed with anger, there was a deep sorrow that she just couldn't identify.

Mitch felt his breathing slow as he stared into her dark eyes. His lost love had dark eyes like the Wolf Princess, and she'd looked at him this same way when she was trying to hide her fear. His gaze suddenly began darting back and forth between her eyes and her lips as he started to close the distance between them.

"What're you doing?" Brenna asked in alarm.

The urgency in her voice seemed to bring him back to earth and he froze, then leaned back questioning what he was doing himself. He blinked his eyes and shook his head slightly, as if he were trying to wake himself from a dream.

"Would you two make up your minds already." Dawn almost snapped from a branch above. She'd obviously witnessed this last bit of drama between them. "One minute you're ready to kill each other, and the next you're playing kissy-face. You humans are so bazaar."

At the words 'kissy-face' Mitch leapt away, then pointed at Brenna and said, "She started it!"

"I did not!" Brenna growled.

"Did too." said Mitch.

"Did not!" she stated.

Dawn rolled her eyes and began looking around for some more dandelions to stuff in her ears, muttering under her breath, "Humans."

Candy could see a strip of green up ahead of them. She could tell that it was solid ground and she quickened her pace. All three figures came to a sudden stop at the sound of a long, high-pitched whistle. Candy slowly turned and saw a large mud-whistler with the torn piece of her sleeve hanging from its lower jaw, its eyes focused on her.

"Run!" Candy screamed, turning and running toward the strip of green.

She ran about five steps before she felt something slimy wrap around her right ankle, and then she fell flat on her stomach. She screamed as she felt herself being dragged back toward the reptile. She clawed uselessly at the mud, trying in vain to grab hold of something, anything to save herself. She found a tree-root and took hold of it. She heard an angry whistle from behind, and felt herself being pulled on harder.

CHAPTER TWELVE

CHOICES AND CHASES

D ritt came stumbling up to the splintered gate exhausted, just as the party of men who'd been hunting Brenna, Mitch and Dawn came riding up to the outer wall. They all entered the courtyard and marched inside to the great hall where Griff sat feasting noisily on roasted mutton, making an absolute mess. The small tuft of a beard on his chin was thick with grease now as he ate ravenously.

"More wine girl!" he bellowed, sending a spray of loose meat and breadcrumbs in Erica's direction.

Erica came forward and filled his cup, then went back to stand by the wall as before. She watched and listened as the men entered and gave their reports.

"I saw her, but had to run because of the lizards." Dritt explained.

"I don't care about that one!" snarled Griff, spraying the one-eyed man with half-chewed food. "What about that dark one, Brenna?"

"We saw her and that boy you hired, Mic, Mit, Mac?" said one of the men, scratching his head.

"Mitch, the Northman?" said Griff after issuing a loud belch.

"Aye sir," said the man. "They were crossing the Roaring Eagle River when we shot them."

The man ducked as a platter was hurled at him from the table and clanged against the tapestry-covered wall, then clattered loudly on the floor.

"You idiot! I want her alive!" bellowed Griff, anger burning in his sapphire-blue eyes.

"But sire, we don't know that they're dead! They fell into the river and we didn't see if they came back up!" the frightened man said quickly, still cowering on the floor.

"Then why are you here?" Griff roared, sending another platter of food flying across the dining-hall in the cowering man's direction. "If you don't know whether she's alive or dead, you've nothing to report!" Griff stood, "Is Dritt the only one here that's competent enough to make certain that someone is alive or dead? Get my steed ready! If you want something done right, you've gotta do it yourself! You there, slave-girl, clean up this mess!" he bellowed at Erica before draining his cup, belching again, then storming from the room, quickly followed by his men.

Erica came forward, knelt and began cleaning up the scattered food around the overturned platters. Once she'd finished, she gathered as much of the unspoiled food as she could with the middle-aged maid, Fiona, and MacKurk's betrothed, Elsa. Then they made their way down to the dungeon. Erica carefully passed the food through the bars to Konroy, while Fiona did the same for Kavan and Elsa did the same for MacKurk in the cell next to them.

Kavan and MacKurk had been placed in this cell along with Angus, Darsy, and a slowly healing Bricker, who was much better now thanks to Darsy's efforts.

"It's not much, but it's what we could find." Erica said apologetically.

"It's plenty. Thanks." Konroy said, taking her hand in his.

"I'll try to find some more later." Erica added. "I also have some news about your sisters sir."

Konroy's eyes widened with interest, "Are they alright?"

"I'm not sure. Lady Candace is traveling west through the swamp, and the Wolf Princess, Lady Brenna, was headed north toward the mountains." Erica explained.

"Was?" asked Konroy, barely above a whisper.

"The Raves shot at her as she crossed the Roaring Eagle, and they don't know if she's alive or dead. But there are rumors that she was shot last night after she escaped. They say that she went over Murky Falls and survived." Erica told him.

A small smile crossed Konroy's face, "That sounds about right. She's most likely traveling to Uncle Allen, and if Candy's going west through the swamps she's probably headed for Uncle Garvey's. Any word on Lewis?"

Erica lowered her eyes and shook her head sadly, "None."

"I hope he's alright," Konroy sighed, "and the girls."

"I'm not sure that hope will last too long sir," Erica's voice was sad, "Laird Cray is going out to hunt down the Wolf Princess himself."

"Oh I feel sorry for that one." Konroy said, shaking his head.

"Worried about your sisters sir?" Erica asked kindly.

"No, I feel sorry for Laird Cray," Konroy said, "and I'll feel even more sorry for him if he catches her."

Candy's muddy fingers were slowly slipping from the tree-root as the Mud-whistler pulled harder and harder on her ankle. She cried out in pain at the feeling of her body being stretched.

"Leave her alone!" Nick yelled, rushing toward her cries.

Candy screamed as she lost her grip on the tree-root and began sliding on her stomach through the sticky mud toward the huge lizard.

Nick tripped over the root that Candy had clung to just a moment before and fell flat in front of her. Nick raised his mud-covered face listening as Candy screamed for help. He reached forward and took hold of something that felt like a hand. He knew it was hers when he heard her say in a pleading voice, "Please, don't let me go?" then he heard her sob.

"Don't worry, I got you!" he panted, grabbing her other hand with his.

The Mud-whistler let out a long, angry whistle at the two humans that weren't sliding toward it anymore. Then it gave what sounded more like a high-pitched roar as Marie came swooping low. Time and time again she slapped the huge scaly beast with a hefty paw. Marie screeched like an eagle in triumph each time she smacked the monster across the eyes. Then she made a half howl, half chirp-noise, mocking the beast's angry roars of pain and frustration.

"Has it stopped pulling on you yet?" asked Nick.

"I, I think so." Candy gasped, trying to catch her breath.

Nick cautiously released Candy's hands. Nothing happened. She didn't start crying out or sound as though she was sliding away even slightly.

Nick slowly got to his knees and asked, "Are you all right?"

"Aye." Candy gasped, half sobbing. "But that thing's tongue is still around my ankle."

"Which ankle?" he asked.

"My right ankle." she told him. "Why?"

In answer Nick drew his hunting knife.

"Pardon me," he said, then placed the blade between his teeth, clamping down tightly. Keeping a hand on her, he moved down toward her ankles. Once he was there he closed his right hand over her right ankle and around the tongue.

The feeling of someone's hand on its tongue caught the beast's attention. When it saw the blade raised in Nick's left hand it let out a whistle of anger that was almost deafening. Candy clapped her hands over her ears and screamed fearfully. Marie fell to the ground and chirped once in pain at the high-pitched sound.

Nick almost dropped his knife. He clenched his eyes shut and ground his teeth. He could feel blood trickling down from his nostril, and his head was pounding. But despite this agony, he brought down the razor sharp blade on the slimy flesh just as the monster started to yank on Candy once more.

The severed tongue snapped back into the creature's open mouth, which quickly closed then reopened to issue a loud screech of angry pain.

Nick tore the bit of slime covered tongue still wrapped about Candy's ankle away and tossed it over his shoulder. Then he pulled Candy to her feet.

"Where's Marie?" he shouted above the screech.

"I'm here Nick. The Moss-trail is dead ahead." Marie called.

"Run!" Nick yelled, still holding Candy's hand as he ran forward.

The Mud-whistler came clawing after them, purple blood dripping from its mouth as it growled low in its throat. Its yellow-orange eyes fixed on the fugitives as it pursued.

Candy chanced a look over her shoulder as they ran toward the green strip of moss ahead of them.

"It's after us!" she cried when she saw the large lizard gaining.

"Marie, are the vines still hanging there?" called Nick.

"Aye." Marie said. "I'll chirp as I pass the thick one."

"What's going on?" Candy half sobbed.

"There's a trench of quicksand between us and the trail!" Nick told her as they continued to run. "We need to swing across on the vines!"

Candy's brow shot to her hairline, "What?" she yelled fearfully.

"Trust me!" he called.

Nick heard Marie's chirp less than six steps in front of him. He let go of Candy's hand, hurled his staff forward like a spear and yelled, "Grab onto me!"

Candy wrapped her arms around his neck just as his right hand closed around the vine and his left arm came around her waist.

"Jump!" he yelled.

They both felt their feet leave the muddy ground as the vine went tight. The huge Mud-whistler leapt after them and let out another loud, angry screech.

It had been about an hour since Brenna and Mitch had had their lunch of roast rabbit. They'd been marching in silence for about ten minutes, having finished their argument and now established that they weren't speaking to one another. Though they were not afraid to send each other icy glares and make little discontented grunting sounds.

"There they are." said Griff to his men, pointing at the two small figures far off in the woods. "Let's fly up ahead and arrange a little surprise for them, on the other side of the woodlands."

Several of the men chuckled and nudged each other.

On their winged steeds the group of ten Raves rose from the forest floor and flew over the river and above the treetops toward the mountains. Griff smiled to himself. This was going to be fun, making the Wolf Princess his prisoner.

"Forward!" Dritt bellowed at the score of men that trudged behind him.

Who cared if Griff had ordered him to stay at Castle MacKline? Who cared if he'd taken twice as many men as Griff had? Dritt certainly didn't care. All he cared about was getting his revenge.

Vrant had remained at the castle and could handle things while Dritt got the revenge that he thirsted for so desperately. As for those ugly, giant lizards, those huge reptiles wouldn't stop him this time. They'd go around that muddy, mucky grove and find that girl. That horrid, hated girl.

Candy opened her eyes and looked down. She let out a small cry of fear when she saw the Mud-whistler clawing through the quicksand, still slashing the air between them.

But then she felt slight relief and something almost like pity for the reptile. It was sinking into the quicksand. It was almost too gradual to see, but the large beast was sinking.

"Now Nick!" Marie shouted somewhere in front of them.

Candy suddenly felt herself falling. She screamed, watching as the mossy ground got closer.

"Oof!" she grunted as she and Nick made contact with the earth and went rolling. Somehow, most likely because neither of them had released the other, it ended with Nick on his back and Candy lying atop him. She looked down at him a little concerned.

"Are you alright Nick?" she gasped.

Nick's chest was heaving as he spoke. "I, ooh, my back. Uh, I think I'll live." he panted. "How 'bout you?"

"I'm fine. I think you broke my fall."

It hurt to laugh but they did. They couldn't help it.

"Hey, isn't anyone gonna ask me how I am?" called Marie, a hint of humor in her voice.

The treetops echoed with laughter, then moans. Lastly there was a shrill whistle from the enraged Mud-whistler as it sank into the muck. This made the three on the Moss-trail grow serious. Candy scrambled to her feet and looked at the monster. Only its head was above the quicksand now.

"Poor thing." Candy said sadly.

"Poor thing?" Nick nearly shouted. "That 'poor thing' just tried to eat us! It didn't have to chase us but it did and now it's dying. That's just the way things are out here." Nick took her hand in his, then softened his tone, "Come on, let's get out of here. Where's my staff?"

Candy retrieved his stave and handed it to him. Then the three travelers continued westward, away from the dying monster.

Dritt and his men were just passing Dead Lizard Grove, when they heard Candy's screams.

"Faster!" Dritt roared picking up speed. Now he knew where she was. Soon, very soon, he'd have his revenge. His sweet revenge!

"Would somebody talk?" Dawn said pleadingly. "It's just too quiet."

Brenna and Mitch fixed that problem with gusto. The two started screaming insults at each other so loudly that Dawn couldn't understand a single word.

"Shut up!" yelled the small wolf-like creature.

Amazingly the humans both went silent, crossing their arms and glaring coldly at one another.

"Alright, Brenna how much farther to your uncle's village?" asked Dawn.

"It's right through that valley up ahead." Brenna grunted.

"Good!" Mitch snorted.

"Oh, just be quiet you!" growled Brenna. "Or else!"

"Or else what?" Mitch jeered. "You gonna kiss me again! Ooh, I'm scared!"

"You know what I'm gonna do? I'm gonna . . ." Brenna stopped in mid-sentence and looked skyward at the sound of flapping wings. "Run!" Brenna yelled, bolting forward.

Griff and the Raves landed directly in front of them, and dismounted drawing their swords. The three travelers skidded to a stop not six feet away from them.

"Leaving so soon, Princess?" Griff jeered as he approached, sword in hand. "I was hoping that we could talk."

The group of men behind him laughed.

Brenna suddenly remembered that she had her sword. She drew it from its scabbard and pointed it at Griff shouting, "I'm not scared of you Griffy."

Griff advanced, Brenna retreated, sword raised defensively.

"Really?" he sneered. "You should be." He glanced at Mitch, "Why are you with this girl?"

Mitch shrugged, then lowered his eyes.

"I'll give you a chance to rejoin us lad. Telc, give him your extra sword." Griff called.

A large man came forward and offered a sword to Mitch, hilt first. Mitch's gaze went from the sword to Griff.

"If you're with us lad, take the sword and help me capture the Wolf Princess." Griff continued. "It's up to you?"

Mitch looked toward Brenna. The Wolf Princess instantly regretted her harsh words to him. Mitch took the sword in his hand, testing the balance and weight, then turned in Brenna's direction and took a single step.

Griff's smile was so smug that it made Brenna want to run him through, and Mitch seemed to be gloating. She wanted to run over and punch him in the nose.

"I have one question," said Mitch, looking at Griff.

All eyes turned to him.

"Where were you when I was lying wounded in her dungeon?" Mitch asked.

As Griff contemplated this Mitch turned back with lightning speed and separated Telc's hips from his torso before he could even scream.

Brenna still didn't know if she could trust Mitch as an ally, or if he even trusted her. But she didn't care about that right now. Their enemies were the same and that's what counted at this moment. She rushed forward and gave a half roar, half howl battle cry as she struck out at Griff.

Griff saw her coming and reacted. He raised his sword and met her blow, pushing her back a pace. Brenna kept her sword up, ready for him charge. This wasn't good, he was stronger than she'd anticipated.

Griff came forward and delivered a blow that drove her back another pace, but Brenna's skill with a sword came through for her. She bent her knees and planted her feet. Griff delivered another blow, but Brenna didn't budge from that spot.

After killing Telc Mitch was charged by four more Raves. The first he cut the legs out from beneath. The second he beheaded. The third he dodged, delivering a smack to the Rave's seat as he passed causing him to run straight into the side of a tree and fall flat, completely unconscious. Mitch met the fourth man's blade with his own and sparks sprayed from the steel.

Dawn had slipped behind the harpusia and bitten one on the rump. This sent all of the beasts into a blind panic, gaining the attention of the remaining four Raves who tried in vain to calm their mounts. Dawn was satisfied that she'd helped her companions.

Griff applied more pressure on his sword, but Brenna wouldn't be moved. She stood firm, then looked up and smiled at his obvious frustration before she shoved him with all of her might. Griff fell back a pace and a half, shocked that this mere girl could call up such strength. He raised his sword to block another blow as Brenna came forward and brought down her weapon like a massive hammer.

Griff's anger grew as he began to take advantage of his height and weight. He wasn't all that much taller than Brenna, but she likely only weighed about two-thirds of what he did. She took each blow, but began to feel very tired. She started to bob and weave, ducking and dodging each thrust and swing. She sidestepped a thrust and circled around behind him swiftly.

"Come back you coward!" Griff roared, pursuing her.

"Come and get me Lady Griffy!" Brenna taunted, sticking out her tongue in his direction, then dodging him once more.

Mitch and his opponent were battling hard. The Rave was larger than Mitch, but the young Northman managed to hold up under each bone-crushing blow. But the huge man soon had Mitch backing up until he felt his back against a tree. The giant of a man raised his sword over his head with both hands and brought it down with all of his might.

Mitch's eyes were wide with apprehension. He ducked and dove between the man's tree-trunk-like legs, sliding on his stomach. Pieces of bark and inner wood flew through the air as the giant's sword made contact with the tree's truck. The hulking man pulled his weapon free of the wood and turned around. Mitch rolled to his back and looked up at the giant.

The man struck the ground, narrowly missing Mitch who'd rolled to his right. The Northman had barely escaped the massive blow that sent mossy earth flying. The huge man struck again, Mitch rolled to his left. As the man raised his weapon again, Mitch took up his own sword and thrusted it as hard as he could into the massive ribcage above him. Mitch scurried to his right as the huge form collapsed forward, nearly landing on top of him.

Mitch claimed the extra scabbard from the now dead Telc's body and attached it to his own belt, then looked around. The remaining four Raves had finally succeeded in soothing their mounts and were now looking in his direction.

Dawn was up the rock-face directly behind the harpusia. She pushed a few rocks over a ledge, causing a chain-reaction that led to any loose rocks below starting to slide downward.

The Raves below ran forward madly, trying to avoid being crushed under the rocky avalanche. They rushed toward the woodlands as their steeds rushed passed them, also eager to escape.

The rockslide caught Griff's attention. Brenna took advantage of this by running toward the valley ahead. Mitch saw her and followed, careful to avoid the falling rocks as he went.

Dritt and his men had found the remains of Candy and Nick's campfire at the Fallen Giant, and were now approaching the quicksand. Dritt was wiser now. He took an old, dry piece of wood and threw it into the mud where the trees stopped and watched as it vanished below the surface.

Taking another piece of wood he hurled it across the mud and smiled as it thudded on the mossy ground. Dritt took five steps back, then charged. He leapt, grabbing onto the vine in front of him.

He swung high, then let go and landed on Moss-trail. He turned and gazed back at his astonished men with his one good eye and said, "That's how it's done lads! Come on! Don't dilly dally!"

Brenna and Mitch ran through the valley. The grass and ferns were so tall that they were brushing the two young people's hips as they went.

"Duck! They've got arrows!" Dawn called as she flew overhead.

Brenna and Mitch threw themselves flat and laid still. Brenna looked over at Mitch, who lay about four feet away from her, still feeling uncertain as to whether or not she could really trust him.

Mitch looked over, meeting her gaze as his thoughts following similar lines. Then he knew what to do. He rolled to his back and sheathed his sword, then rolled back to his stomach and looked at her again. He gave a subtle nod in her direction.

Brenna rolled to her back and sheathed her own sword. Rolling back to her stomach she nodded to him.

"Brenna! Mitch! They're lighting the valley on fire!" Dawn yelled.

The two young people looked back and saw the dry vegetation starting to glow. They could smell smoke and hear a faint crackling sound.

"Run!" yelled Mitch, jumping to his feet.

Brenna scrambled to her feet and ran as fast as she could. She could feel the heat behind her as the smell of smoke got stronger and the crackling of flames grew louder.

"Brenna!" she heard Mitch shout. "Over there! We can climb out!"

She looked to where he indicated. There was a rough path up the mountainside. She altered her course to join Mitch at the path. He was already three feet up the rock-face when he reached down and took hold of Brenna's outstretched hand. He gave a straining grunt as he pulled her up next to him. Carefully they both climbed upward. Dawn flew nearby.

"Are you two alright?" she asked.

"Where're the Raves?" asked Mitch.

"They were gonna ride up here, but the flames are too high so they went back." Dawn explained.

"Then how did you get through?" said Brenna.

"The harpusia are more scared of fire than I am." Dawn said rather proudly. "And the Raves have to go where their steeds take them."

"Fly up and see if there's a ledge or anything for us to climb to." Mitch said nodding upward.

Dawn tilted her head to one side and gave a wolfish glare.

"What?" said Mitch, feeling confused.

"Did you ever think to say 'please'?" she said, still glaring.

Mitch raised a brow, "Please?"

"Thank you!" she snorted, zooming upward.

Mitch's expression was still confused as climbed upward.

"Women!" he snorted, shaking his head.

Brenna cleared her throat loudly, shooting him a glare.

"What?" said Mitch, looking at her questioningly.

Brenna rolled her eyes and shook her head as she reached for another hand-hold.

A few seconds later Dawn hovered nearby and gave her report. "We're in luck. There's more than a ledge up there. It's a trail. It's level and wide enough that two horses could trot side by side safely."

Brenna and Mitch continued their ascent until they reached the level trail. They crawled up, shaking after the steep climb. They were so glad to be on solid ground again that they just lay there for a few minutes, grateful to be out of the smoke and ash that was flying up. Brenna lifted her head and looked around, then quickly got to her knees.

"I know where we are!" Brenna exclaimed.

"You do?" Mitch panted.

"Aye. Uncle Allen used to bring me up here with father and Lewis." Brenna was thoroughly excited now. "Come on. We just need to keep heading north on this trail and we'll reach the village in a couple of hours."

Brenna was very nearly skipping down the mountain trail as she moved Northward. Mitch couldn't help chuckling at how giddy she was now as he followed.

Griff was seething with anger as he entered the courtyard at Castle MacKline. He dismounted and stormed into the dining-hall.

He slumped moodily into a chair and rapped loudly on the tabletop.

"Bring me wine!" he bellowed.

Erica entered with a cask of wine and a goblet. She filled the cup and left it with the cask in front of him.

"Would you like me to bring you some food sir?" she asked calmly.

"Aye!" Griff snorted irritably, taking a long draft from his cup and then motioning for her to refill it. Erica did so, knowing that she didn't dare leave without knowing the sort of food he wanted. Griff took another long drink before belching and saying, "Bread and cheese."

Erica refilled his cup once more, left the cask on the table, curtsied, and then left to fetch the food. She smiled to herself. He wouldn't be so angry if he'd caught the Wolf Princess. She hurried to bring the tray laden with bread and cheese so that she could tell Konroy, knowing that he'd be pleased.

Brenna and Mitch walked along the mountain-trail, occasionally glancing down into the now glowing valley.

"This valley's part of Uncle Allen's land," Brenna explained. "I wouldn't want to be in ole Griffy's boots when Uncle Allen catches him."

"Your uncle sounds like a renowned man." Mitch commented, wondering if he truly wanted to meet this man.

"He is." Brenna said very matter-of-factly. "He gave me my jeweled dag, aah!"

"Brenna!" Mitch yelled as Brenna vanished from his sight.

Mitch looked to see that part of the ledge had crumbled under Brenna's weight. He fell to his hands and knees, then looked over the edge. He saw Brenna hanging onto a branch growing out of the mountainside.

"Are you alright?" Mitch asked.

"Do I look alright?" Brenna groaned.

Mitch tried to hold back a smile, "Hold on!" he called, lying flat on his stomach. He reached down toward her, but she was just out of reach. He ground his teeth as he stretched and strained to reach her outstretched hand.

All at once, without warning, the ledge under Mitch crumbled too and he fell. He let out a startled cry, but stopped when he felt a hand take hold of his. He looked up to see Brenna, still holding onto the branch with her left hand, had taken hold his left hand with her right. He reached up and closed his free hand over her wrist.

"Thanks." Mitch said.

"Ow! Don't mention it!" she moaned. "Dawn!"

"Aye?" said the small wolf-like creature, as she hovered in front of Brenna.

"Take the dagger in my right boot and fly as fast as you can to the end of the valley." Brenna explained, gasping in pain. "Find the man the others call Allen, and show him that dagger. He gave it to me when I was learning to throw knives. Tell him what's happened to us and lead him back here as fast as you can. Please!"

The small Bulf went to Brenna's right boot and carefully drew the jeweled dagger with her teeth, then flew northward, swift and straight as an arrow.

"Hurry!" Brenna and Mitch shouted as one.

"Ah, there they are!" Dritt said to his men as he gestured ahead.

He could see the three figures through the trees in front of them. He smiled a cruel smile, touching the scar on his face tenderly.

Soon. It'll be very soon. Sweet revenge. he told himself.

"Draw swords." he said aloud, unsheathing his own Blade. "Do what you want with the lad and that wolf creature, but the girl is mine. Understood?"

The men all nodded vigorously. None would dare to challenge him on this matter. Swords drawn, the Raves started forward as quietly as they could, in order to sneak up and capture the fugitives ahead of them.

Candy was the first to stop at the sound of a twig snapping behind her. She turned and felt her blood freeze at the sight of Dritt. He had his sword drawn and was coming straight at her, a look of utter hatred burning in his sole remaining eye.

"Don't run lass and it'll be over quickly." Dritt's tone was colder than ice and twice as chilling.

Fear gripped Candy as she realized that he meant to kill her. She turned and ran blindly. Dritt pursued, a growl rumbling deep in his throat.

"Come on Nick!" shouted Marie.

Nick and Marie ran away from the score of Raves that came running toward them, swords up.

Blind though he was, Nick knew this area better than any Rave. Marie stayed in front of him, warning him of any new obstacles. But there was something about the voice of that man who'd frightened Candy. Something familiar.

Candy chanced a look over her shoulder and gave a sob of fear as she saw that Dritt gaining on her, his eye gleaming with contempt.

Dritt was overwhelmed with glee. Soon. Very soon. That fear in her eyes, oh how beautiful it was. Oh the hours he'd spent imagining that expression on her face. He quickened his pace, eager to end the chase.

Candy's lungs were aching. She needed to lose him now!

She ran near to a tree, pushing back a thick branch as she passed, then she released it just as Dritt came up behind her, his empty hand outstretched, ready to grab her.

'Thwack!'

The thick branch broke in two as it struck Dritt's chin, knocking him flat. Candy heard him groan painfully once as she started running away without looking back. She intended to put as much distance between herself and the one-eyed man as possible.

Nick and Marie sat high in a tree, the Bulf watching as the Raves searched for them below.

"Where'd they go?" said one.

"I didn't see." said another.

"It's like, like they just disappeared." said a third.

"Like, ghosts." gulped the fourth.

"This place is haunted!" said the fifth. "Let's get out of here!"

Most of the men were very superstitious and fled back the way they'd come, leaving behind the five bravest men. These men didn't believe in ghosts or spirits, or that anything anywhere could be haunted, so they continued on the search, grumbling about how cowardly their comrades had been.

The silence was broken by a shrill scream for help somewhere to the southwest.

"Candy." Nick said softly.

"Come on!" said one of the men below, starting in the direction of the cry.

"Marie, we've gotta beat 'em there or Candy's dead!" Nick said urgently.

"Follow me," said Marie. "The tree-branches are close to each other up here. It's like a bridge through the treetops."

Candy had fallen into a pit of quicksand and screamed from both surprise and fright. She did her best not to struggle. Uncle Garvey had told her that when one struggles in quicksand one sinks faster. She looked around nervously.

She couldn't see Dritt anywhere. She started at the sound of a twig snapping to her left. She felt her heart stop when she saw five men dressed all in black come from behind some bushes. She knew instantly that they were Raves.

The five of them just stood there, staring at her. Then they all began laughing cruelly and sheathed their swords.

Candy watched them like a terrified and wounded animal in trap watches an approaching hunter. She knew that she was in grave danger as one of the men came and knelt by the mud-pit, still grinning evilly.

"Do you want out of there missy?" he jeered.

Candy narrowed her eyes and said, "Wouldn't you?"

The men all laughed.

"Well that's too bad, isn't it lads?" said the man, his cruel eyes dancing with merriment as the Raves behind him chuckled nastily. He stood and continued, "'Cause you're staying put."

Gesturing to another Rave he went to a nearby log. The two men, grinning, hefted the log with great difficulty. The other three men came to their assistance. They carried it to the edge of the quicksand and aimed it so that it would fall on top of her head. Candy tried to get out of the way and braced herself for the crushing blow.

Mud sprayed in her face as the log splashed into the quicksand next to her. She looked up to see the Raves' shocked expressions.

"How could we miss her?" one growled.

"I don't know. It was like the wind shoved us over a little!" complained another.

Candy could feel herself sinking deeper into the muck. She clung to the log and began to pull herself up and out.

"Oh no! None of that!" said the first man, drawing his sword and stepping onto the log.

One of the other men drew his own sword and circled around to the other end of the log, cutting off Candy's only remaining escape. The men on the shore all jeered cruelly.

Candy gazed up hopelessly at the man to her left as he raised his sword. Then gasped as from out of nowhere, Marie came zooming in and knocked the man into the muck on the opposite side of the log.

Candy suddenly felt her heart skip a beat as she looked to the shore and saw Nick dealing out mighty blows on the three remaining Raves.

Candy fell back, dazed as the man still on the log kicked her hard in the shoulder as Marie knocked him into the quicksand next to his comrade.

"Marie, help!" Candy called to the Bulf.

Marie swooped low and offered her forepaws to Candy. "Grab on!"

Candy took hold of the offered paws and Marie began flying upward and backward. Candy found herself only knee-deep in the mud now as she was pulled toward the solid ground.

Marie caught sight of Nick. Two of the Raves had hold of him and the third was raising his sword, preparing to decapitate him.

Marie laid Candy on the shore halfway out of the quicksand.

"I'll be right back!" she said, then leapt at the sword man.

The man holding the sword was caught completely off guard as Marie sank her teeth into his arm. The other two men were just as surprised and accidentally loosened their grip on Nick.

Nick broke free of their grasp and began beating them with his stave. Within a few minutes the three men turned and fled. Marie chased after them, barking and snapping at their heels until they were out of sight.

"Nick!" Candy screamed as the ground beneath her gave way to the quicksand underneath.

Nick rushed to where he heard her cries and knelt. He stretched out his staff over the mud as Candy explained her situation, and he said, "Grab hold."

Candy needed no second bidding. She clung to the rod and allowed Nick to pull her to shore. Tears poured down her face the moment she was on dry ground. She threw her arms around Nick's neck and wept freely against his chest. Nick embraced her, unsure of what else to do.

Candy was trembling uncontrollably. Nick laid his head against hers and whispered words of kindness and comfort until she was calm enough to stand under her own strength.

Marie took some vines in her mouth and flying over the mud-pit dropped them to the two Raves still squirming in the quicksand. The two men pulled themselves from the muck and Marie chased them out the same way she had the previous three. The Raves didn't even try to put up a fight, having lost their swords in the quicksand.

"Are you all right?" Marie asked when she returned.

"Aye." Candy sniffed, nodding slightly.

"Nick?" Marie asked, concerned.

"Aye." Nick said simply, appearing to be near tears himself. "Come on. Let's get out of here."

The three travelers continued westward, a little shaken, but slowly recovering from the ordeal they'd just been through. But the future seemed somehow brighter now that the Raves were retreating.

CHAPTER THIRTEEN
RELATIONS WITH RELATIVES

It seemed like hours since Dawn had left them hanging off the cliff, though it had really only been about ten minutes. But in situations such as this, every minute feels like an hour as it slowly crawls by.

"Have your arms stretched to twice their length yet?" Brenna moaned.

"Almost." Mitch groaned, managing a rather weak smile and half-hearted chuckle.

There was a soft cracking sound and both young people yelped as the feeble branch gave way a little more.

"How fast is your uncle at climbing?" Mitch asked quickly.

"Uncle Allen's a regular old mountain-goat." Brenna stated proudly, then screamed as the branch gave way still more.

"Are you sure?" he asked apprehensively, looking down at the smoldering valley floor far below them.

"Aye. Uncle Allen's never let me down before." Brenna told him.

There was a loud snap and Brenna held a useless piece of wood in her hand. The two young people were suddenly falling, hands still clasped. With a sudden jerk they stopped and Brenna could feel why. A large, rough, sunburned hand had clamped over her wrist. She looked upward and her eyes widened, two words forming on her lips, "Uncle Allen." Her voice was little better than a squeak she was so excited.

"G'day lassie." Allen MacKline grinned. "Pull me up lads."

They began to ascend the mountainside and were soon lying on the ledge panting.

Brenna leapt to her feet and embraced her uncle. "Uncle Allen."

"Here lass." Allen said, drawing a very familiar looking jeweled dagger from the back of his belt.

"Thanks." Brenna smiled, taking her dagger and sheathing it in her right boot. "Where's Dawn?"

"Right here." Dawn answered, sounding rather out of breath. "He's a fast runner, and an even swifter rider, but I've told him almost everything that's happened."

"Aye, 'cause you're a fast-talker." Allen chuckled. "Ah," he added, offering Mitch a hand up. "So this must be Mitch."

Mitch looked at the hand, then at Allen's face, then back at the hand, and accepted the offer. Allen pulled him to his feet in one swift motion, making Mitch groan slightly as his arms were still sore after hanging for so long.

"He's a friend of yours lass?" Allen asked.

Mitch met Brenna's gaze, a worried expression on his face.

"He's trustworthy." Brenna shrugged.

Mitch raised a brow and tilted his head to one side in surprise. He stared at her for a moment before the hints of a smile turned up the ends of his mouth. Brenna stared back, forcing herself to keep a passive expression.

The smile on Mitch's face vanished as the air left him in a rush. Allen had just given him a hearty clap on the back, laughing, "Well that's good to know." Mitch almost collapsed under the force of the huge man's blow.

Allen MacKline was about six and a half feet tall, sporting the same dark curly hair and dark eyes as his niece. His arms were massive with bulging muscles, which caused Mitch to nearly lose his balance when this man smacked him on the back.

"Nigel!" Brenna said excitedly, hugging a young man with dark hair and eyes. Nigel MacKline was the image of his father, only twenty years younger and not quite so muscular.

"Brenna!" he chuckled, clapping her on the back.

"Conlan!" she said, embracing an even younger man with blue eyes and brown hair.

He embraced her warmly. Conlan was more gangly than his father and elder brother, but his strength was his obvious intelligence which sparkled behind his eyes. One had only to look into his sky-blue eyes to see the wisdom that lay within his mind. Brenna had always gotten along well with these boys ever since she was newly able to walk.

She and Nigel would climb trees and have mock duels with sticks in place of swords. She'd sit with Conlan and listen to his stories and made-up jokes. But never had she been able to favor one even slightly over the other.

"It's good to see you." Brenna told them.

"Come. We have ponies over here." said Conlan with a sweep of his hand.

Brenna saw five hearty mountain ponies waiting patiently a little ways down the trail. Two stretchers lay on the ground.

"What are those for?" she asked.

"We didn't know how bad things were, so we brought them in case you were hurt." Conlan explained. "If you're tired, you could rest for a while and we'll lead the ponies down to the village."

Brenna was exhausted. It took every ounce of will-power she possessed to stay standing. All she wanted was to drop onto one of those stretchers and surrender to the weariness that was nagging at her mind and body. But her pride got the better of her.

"I think I can ride for a bit." Brenna told them

"What about you lad?" Allen asked, slapping Mitch on the back again, this time knocking him to the ledge top. "Well that answers that."

Mitch coughed and gave a groan as he struggled to his to his hands and knees, then collapsed again.

"Come on lads, lets lend him a hand." Allen said, pulling an unconscious Mitch up and dragging him toward one of the stretchers. Brenna was mounting up on one of the ponies, when she leaned too far one side and found herself lying on the ground on the opposite side of the horse.

"Brenna!" cried Nigel, running to her side. "Are you alright?"

"Ow!" Brenna moaned as she sat up. "I think I'll live."

"Are you sure that you don't want to lay on the stretcher?" he asked. "At least for a bit?"

"It would make us feel better." Conlan added.

Brenna decided to take the opportunity that her cousins were offering her, "Well if it'll make you two feel better, then I suppose I could."

Conlan and Nigel guided her swaying form to the empty stretcher and laid her down gently. The moment that her head touched the makeshift pillow that Nigel had made from his jacket, her eyes closed and she was lost to slumber.

"There it is!" Candy said excitedly. "That's Uncle Garvey's village just ahead of us!"

They'd left the swamp and were now walking through a thinned out wooded area. About thirty-five yards ahead of them on the open land were several neatly built wooden houses with thatched roofs and a very fine gray-stone castle. There was a great deal of activity in the village, mostly children running between the houses with dogs, and mothers fussing their children for being too loud or getting dirty. Men went about, doing their work diligently.

Nick's ears filled with all the sounds made by the people and animals within the small town. His nostrils were suddenly filled with the scent of roasting meat and freshly baked breads. His mouth watered and his stomach began growling. That marsh duck seemed so long ago, and the food smelled almost too wonderful to be real.

"Come on! Let's run!" Candy said happily, running ahead.

Nick wondered where she got that energy after their escapade in the swamps. But her enthusiasm was so infectious that Nick, with a slight smile playing on his lips, ran after her with Marie soaring above to inform him of any obstacles in his path.

Garvey MacAllister was Lady MacKline's eldest brother. He stood about six feet tall, had green-blue eyes and brown hair, though in his middle-aged state he was in the beginning stages of going bald. He had a beard, which he kept neatly trimmed and a small scar on his left cheek from a battle in his youth. He was a muscular man, with legs as strong as tree stumps.

He was stacking firewood for an elderly widow with his eldest son Nevin when he looked out across the field and saw a very muddy Candy running toward them.

"Nevin look." Garvey said, pointing toward the woods to their east. "Isn't that Candy?"

His son looked and saw the muddy figure racing in their direction.

"What do you want me to do Father?" he asked, a little apprehensive. "Should I call the guards? Is that someone chasing her?"

"No. She's smiling." Garvey pointed out. "She wouldn't be smiling if that was an enemy. Come on."

Garvey and Nevin rushed out across the field toward Candy. She saw them coming and flung herself into their waiting arms, tears in her eyes.

"Uncle Garvey!" she sniffed, trying not to cry.

"Candy, what's happened?" said Garvey. "Did you come through the swamps?"

"And who's that man coming with, is that a flying wolf?" asked Nevin, watching Nick and Marie's approach.

"Don't worry Nevin, they're friends. Uncle Garvey, there's trouble at Castle MacKline." Candy sputtered, trying to explain and catch her breath at the same time.

As they all walked to the village, Candy introduced Nick and Marie, telling Nevin that the winged creature was a Bulf, not a flying wolf, which Marie greatly appreciated. Next Candy told her uncle and cousin the whole story about Griff, Dritt, and the frightening swamp.

She finally finished her narrative when they sat down to a supper of roast venison and fresh bread. In the midst of the meal, Candy turned to her uncle and asked, "So, will you help Uncle Garvey?"

Garvey lowered his eyes and thought for a moment, then turned to his eldest son and said, "Nevin, I do believe that you should call up the guards."

Nevin smiled, "Aye sir." Nevin rose and left the table.

Nick raised a brow, "Guards?"

Candy felt as though she couldn't breath, "You will help then?" she gasped, feeling tears roll down her muddy cheeks.

"Aye!" Garvey smiled. "And I do believe that you need a bath after dinner."

"Brenna? Brenna wake up." came Allen's voice.

The Wolf Princess was reluctant to come out of the restful sleep she was in. As she opened her weary eyes she saw the blurred outline of her uncle and the massive shape of his castle behind him.

It was much larger than Castle MacKline and nearly three hundred years older. It was built into the mountain-side with birch, pine and oak trees closely encroaching on the thick outer walls. The battlements were higher than any of the trees, but the foliage was so thick that the massive fortress would've been impossible to see if not for the outer walls and towers stretching into the blue expanse above.

"Mmm, what?" she groaned.

"Supper's gonna be ready soon. I thought you and Mitch should go wash up." Allen told her.

Brenna moaned and rose irritably, "Mum always makes me wash at home. I thought I could have some peace here," she grumbled. "It's such a waste. I'm only gonna get dirty again."

Allen grinned and said, "Aye. Me own dear mother always made me wash too. But once, I tried to get away without scrubbing me ears."

"I'll bet Grandmother wasn't too pleased." Brenna chuckled, feeling a little more cheerful now.

"She wasn't pleased at all." Allen said in mock fear.

"What did she do to you?" asked Brenna, hiding a smile.

"Oh it was horrible! Awful! Dreadful!" he said dramatically.

"What?" Brenna giggled.

"She washed 'em for me." Allen shrugged.

They both groaned comically and had a good laugh, then Brenna went down to the stream just outside of Allen's village. She knelt, then began splashing water on her face and scrubbing at her dusty hands. She took a long drink before continuing.

She looked to her left and saw Mitch doing the same. His shirt and jerkin were dirty and torn. The right sleeve was nearly gone having been ripped at the seam. But she noticed something strange. There was something emerald-green around his upper right arm.

"What's that?" she asked, pointing to the band of green around his upper arm.

Mitch wiped the water from his eyes with the back of his hand, blinked, and followed her finger. His eyes grew wide and his left hand closed over the green thing.

"Nothing." he said quickly.

"Come on. What is it?" she pressed, coming a little closer.

"It's nothing!" he growled. "Now just drop it and leave it alone!"

Brenna sighed, curiosity burning in her brain. She had to know what that thing was.

"Raves!" she almost shouted, pointing behind Mitch.

"Where?" Mitch said, turning to look.

The moment his hand left his arm, Brenna grabbed the thing and ran up the small stream-bank. It was a necklace. A green piece of silk with a small green gem hanging from it.

"Give me that!" snapped Mitch, chasing after her.

"What're you doing with a woman's necklace?" Brenna laughed, taunting.

"That's none of your concern!" Mitch growled. "Now give it back!" Mitch tried to grab the necklace away from her, but she dodged.

"Come on. Where'd you steal it?" Brenna said waving it at him. "You can have it back when you tell me."

"Alright! It belonged to my wife!" Mitch said in defeat.

"You stole from your wife?" she taunted, too caught up in this game of keep-away to think about the fact that Mitch had been married.

"It's all I have left of her! She's dead now!" Mitch shouted, tears burning in his eyes.

Brenna instantly regretted her words. She lowered her eyes and held out the necklace to him. Mitch took it and went back to the stream. He sat there, cradling the piece of jewelry as though it was the most precious thing in the world.

He crouched forward, resting his elbow on a knee and put a hand to his forehead. Brenna heard a sniff, then Mitch spoke, his voice cracking and halting.

"She died in my arms. And, and like a fool, I, I just sat there. I could've gone for help, but I didn't. I just sat there, cradling her. She was so good. So beautiful. So sweet and kind, and I just let her die. But she looked up at me, so trusting and unblaming. Then she took my hand and put it on her stomach and asked if I could feel the baby kicking." Mitch couldn't speak for a moment, and Brenna heard a sob before he slowly continued. "I did. It was kicking so strongly. Then it stopped, and I knew that I'd lost them both, 'cause her hand slipped from mine. This necklace is all I have left of them both."

Mitch said no more, only wept freely. Brenna stood there, uncertain of what to do. She turned and would've left, but she suddenly remembered how she had wept the previous night and what a comfort it had been to be able to speak with Candy. She also knew that Candy had befriended Mitch and cared a great deal about him.

It was for these reasons that she walked over and sat down next to him, then said, "I'm sorry. I didn't know." She laid a hand on his shoulder comfortingly.

"What do you care!" he snapped, shoving her hand away. "You've never lost a child! You're just a spoiled princess who's lost her castle!"

"What?" Brenna said, glaring at him.

"Just leave me alone!" Mitch growled, rising moodily and stalking away, disapearing into the trees.

"Fine!" she yelled after him, then turned on her heel and stomped back toward her uncle's village and castle.

"And this Laird Griff Cray was the one who set fire to my land?" said Allen, who'd been speaking with Dawn as they sat next to the hearth in his great hall.

The small creature nodded enjoying the warmth from the fire, "Aye sir."

"Well, we can't let him get away with that, can we lads?" Allen grinned at his sons who sat at the long table drinking mugs of hot cider.

The young men smiled back at their father and nodded, a mischievous glimmer in their eyes.

"We should start making preparations to pay him a little visit." Allen said, his smile widening.

At that moment with all of them sitting in the great hall and a large pig turning on a spit over the hearth's open flame, Brenna came marching through the door. The massive oak door made a loud 'clunk' sound as she shoved it open, her face expressing what a foul mood she was in. She growled irritably as she stomped passed them and was began to ascend the stairs when Allen called to her.

"Brenna, lass, 'tis almost time to sup."

"I'm not hungry!" she snorted, continuing up the stairs without stopping or even turning.

Conlan and Nigel exchanged a glance, each raising a brow, then they looked to their father.

"What's wrong with her?" asked Nigel.

"I don't know." Allen shrugged eyes still on the stairs. "Why don't you go ask her?"

"Not me!" exclaimed Nigel. "Conlan, you do it."

"I haven't written my last will and testament yet!" said Conlan. "Besides, it was Father's idea."

"I've got a family to provide for." Allen said.

His sons looked at each other, then back to their father.

"We'll miss you Father." Conlan said, struggling to keep a straight face.

Nigel's countenance twisted as he giggled.

Dawn trotted to the open door and looked out, "Where's Mitch?"

Candy lay soaking in the large wash-tub of warm soapy water. It felt so good to wash the filth away. She ran her fingers through her hair, ridding herself of the last of the caked mud. She sighed, feeling warm and content, then slid completely under the water, submerging her head.

Nick entered the room at that moment. He too had bathed and now wore clean clothes lent to him by Nevin. He cocked his head to one side and listened.

"Candy?" he said.

Candy resurfaced, looked over and saw Nick, then nearly screamed.

"Nick!" she gasped franticly.

Nick bent his knees, holding his stave defensively as he asked, "What? What happened? What's wrong?"

"Whatever you do don't look at me! I'm immodest!" she stated.

"Not a problem." Nick said, straightening up.

"Oh, I forgot." Candy said sheepishly. "Sorry."

"It's alright. I just wanted to say goodnight."

"Is that all?" she asked.

"Well, Garvey and Nevin have been able to gather a large group of warriors, and they all have weapons. But about half of the men have gone to the mountains up north to hunt in this fine weather, and several others have become ill working in the summer heat." Nick explained. "Others are either too old or too young."

"So it's a really small number." Candy said disappointedly, lowering her eyes.

"Garvey says that it's not as great an army as he'd hoped, but he's got five hundred and fifty able bodied men." Nick said kindly. "Would you prefer to continue this conversation later?" Nick couldn't help feeling slightly uncomfortable.

"If you wouldn't mind leaving so I can get dressed?" she said shyly.

"Not at all." Nick said, heading for the door hastily.

'Bump!'

"Ouch!" he grunted as he collided with the door, bumping his head.

"Are you alright?" she asked in a concerned voice.

"I'm fine," he said as he rubbed his sore face, "I'll meet you in the hall."

Nick made his exit just in time. Candy could barely hold in her sympathetic laugh.

He stood in the hall, waiting patiently for Candy. Within five minutes Candy exited her room, wearing a clean white nightgown and a dark green robe lent to her by Garvey's wife Nell, a beautiful short woman with blond hair and eyes like lilacs.

"Was there anything else Nick?" Candy asked.

"Nevin spoke of a man, northwest of here, called Harkin." Nick said.

"My mother's cousin. He's married to a cousin of my father's, Lady Gitta."

"Aye," said Nick, "and Nevin said that if they'd join us we'd stand a much better chance."

"Is somebody riding up there tonight?" Candy asked, sounding almost hopeful.

"No. Not tonight." Nick shook his head. "But Nevin said something about you being more capable of convincing them to join us than anyone else."

Candy was silent.

"Candy, are you alright?" he asked as the silence wore on.

"Dylon." she muttered.

"What?" asked Nick.

"Dylon. Harkin and Gitta's eldest son." Candy explained.

"Do you two not get along well?"

"We were very close when we were children." Candy shrugged.

"And now?" asked Nick, a curious edge in his voice.

"We're still friends." Candy shrugged again. "We're just older."

"So, are we going there tomorrow?" Nick asked.

"I suppose so. Goodnight Nick." she said, before turning and going back into her room.

"Goodnight Candy." Nick answered before turning to go down the hall to his own room. Along the way he nearly had a collision with Nevin.

"Oh, pardon me." Nevin chuckled.

"No, I'm sorry." Nick said. "I should've waited 'til breakfast to talk with Candy."

"You spoke with her about rallying Harkin?" Nevin asked in a surprised voice.

"Aye." Nick said simply.

"What did she say?"

"Something about a fellow named Dylon." Nick explained, raising a brow.

"What did she say about him?" Nevin seemed thoroughly interested now.

"That they've been friends since they were children." Nick shrugged.

Nevin started laughing uncontrollably.

"What's so funny?" asked Nick, feeling as though he'd just missed the punch-line on the world's greatest joke.

"They're a great deal more than friends." Nevin laughed.

"What are they then?" Nick said hesitantly.

"They've been betrothed since she was six months old." Nevin said simply.

"Betrothed?" said Nick.

"Aye. They've been betrothed for nearly twenty years, and rumor has it that he's getting tired of waiting for their wedding day." Nevin continued. "But he's too shy to ask her to move it up."

"When's it set for?" Nick couldn't help asking.

"They're expected to marry before her twenty-fifth birthday." Nevin said. "It would please the Clans if they were to move it up."

"Has anyone ever broken a betrothal in these clans?" asked Nick.

"Never. Such a thing would be a disgrace." Nevin stated. "And she and Dylon are fortunate enough to be friends. Some of my cousins have had to marry complete strangers."

"I see. Well, it's been a long day. Goodnight Nevin." Nick said hastily, turning in the direction of his room.

"Goodnight, Nick." Nevin said, raising a brow as he wondered why Nick had ended their conversation so abruptly.

Nick closed the door to his room for the night, and leaned back against it issuing forth a loud, discontented sigh. He slid to the floor, sitting with his back to the door. One knee bent, he folded his arms across it and leaned his head back against the old oak door, allowing his stave to clatter on the floor.

"Nick?" came Marie's voice. "What's wrong?"

"Nothing." Nick said, in an almost sad voice.

"You can't fool me Nick Garthson." the Bulf said, trotting over and putting a gray paw on his arm. "Talk to me. Please?"

"Candy's betrothed." Nick sniffed quietly.

"Oh." Marie said with motherly understanding in her voice as she sat down next to him. "Well, tell me everything."

Hunger got the better of both Brenna and Mitch. The young Northman was the first to make an appearance in the great hall as Allen himself carved large chunks of roast pork from the boar that had been turning on the spit.

"Ah, there you are lad." Allen called when he saw the young Northman approaching. "Get yourself a plate and get over here. I've a choice cut for you."

Mitch had finished weeping on the stream-bank a few hours before. He had washed his face with cold water to hide how red his eyes and cheeks had become after crying. He did as he was bidden, taking a plate to Allen who gave him a large chunk of roast pork, and then he sat down at the long dining table. A beautiful maidservant with reddish hair came over and filled his cup with a crimson liquid that tasted like strawberries. She smiled at him in a most flirtatious manner, then walked away having been called by a man who'd emptied his cup. Mitch watched her go, thinking that she looked a little like his long dead wife, but not really liking how forward she was being with some of the men in the hall. His wife had never behaved like that.

Brenna descended the stone-carved stairs and entered the expansive great hall. Taking up a plate of pork and a cup of strawberry cordial she found an empty space on a bench between Nigel and Conlan.

About halfway through the meal Brenna caught sight of Mitch, who happened to look her way at that same moment. She quickly dropped her gaze. What was the matter with her? Why did this Northman make her feel so insecure? She was the Wolf Princess and she lowered her eyes for no one, and certainly for no man. Or Northman for that matter. She raised her eyes and stared back at him, raising her chin in defiance of him.

Mitch stared back just as defiantly. The firelight danced in his eyes, shining like light reflecting off of the blue ice in the arctic. He would not lower his eyes for this girl. Not now, not ever. Though her staring at him made Mitch feel somehow uneasy. But he forced himself not to let his discomfort show.

Brenna began to squirm under his gaze, causing her to lower her eyes again, much to Mitch's relief, though he didn't let it show. In frustration Brenna got up from the table and stomped out the door into the courtyard, prompting Mitch to finally lower his eyes.

Brenna went up on the outer wall and looked out over the burned valley, now illuminated by the moonlight. She knew that several of Allen's men had been hurt putting out the fire and Allen only had a thousand warriors, some of which were younger than herself. She knew that Griff had at least ten thousand men enlisted in the Raves.

Her frustration turned to despair as she gazed out across the ash covered emptiness that had once been a fertile green valley. The emptiness consumed her and she felt fear grasping at her heart as hot tears began stinging in her eyes.

Then she saw it. A black horse galloping toward Allen's castle, leaving clouds of ash in it's wake. Brenna couldn't believe her eyes. As the black beast came closer she saw a white zigzagging stripe on its face.

"Open the gate!" she yelled to the gatehouse-keeper as she ran for the stairs that led down into the courtyard.

As the gate opened the horse trotted inside and stopped in front of Brenna, whickering at her. She threw her arms around the black creature's neck, burying her face in his soft mane.

"Lightningbolt!" she almost sobbed. "Where've you been boy?"

The stallion nuzzled against his mistress and gave a soft whinny, showing her how glad he was that they had been reunited.

The following morning Candy went for a walk before breakfast and discovered a pleasant surprise. Nevin came up to her in the cobble-paved courtyard leading a golden-chestnut mare with one white hind hoof.

"Look who I found grazing in the east field this morning." Nevin grinned.

"Dutchess." Candy nearly squealed with delight, planting a kiss on the mare's velvety nose. She hugged the beautiful creature's soft neck and smiled, "Thank you Nevin."

"My pleasure. I took off her saddle, gave her a rubdown and a brushing. So she's right as rain now. Here." Nevin said proudly, offering her the reins.

Candy took the reins and led her pony out through the gate. She mounted up and rode across the fields laughing joyfully.

Nick sat in his room by an open window, listening to the sound of her laughter as it echoed across the fields and around the castle's outer walls. He sighed just enjoying the warm sound. He loved the sound of her laugh.

"Nick, we need to make a decision." Marie said gently, interrupting his thoughts. "Do we go with Candy to Harkin's village or do we go home?"

"I think that we should go with her, then, that Dylon fellow can protect her." Nick said glumly.

"Don't be like that." Marie almost scolded. "She might very well be in love with him."

"That's what I'm afraid of." Nick said quietly.

Candy returned from her ride for breakfast. She sat next to Nick at the table while they ate fresh roasted venison and she told him all about her ride and Dutchess. She also added that she hoped he'd like the pony.

As it happened, Dutchess and Nick got along famously. Dutchess nuzzled him and he patted her neck affectionately, saying how soft she was. Candy felt very pleased.

Candy then saddled the gorgeous mare, checking her sword. It was clean and sharp, just as she'd hoped. Then she mounted up and Nick climbed up behind her.

"My warriors and I will meet you at Blair's village. He was always one of my favorite cousins and he's certain to help." Garvey told them before they rode off to the northwest with Marie flying high above watching for enemies.

CHAPTER FOURTEEN
DYLON AND TRAVELLING ONWARD

N ick hadn't been on a horse in years. His whole body ached by the time they stopped for lunch. After a quick meal of some bread and cheese they were on their way again. Nick couldn't help moaning as he remounted behind Candy.

"Are you alright Nick?" Candy asked.

"Aye." Nick said, not wanting to tell her how much pain he was in.

By mid-afternoon they'd reached Harkin's Castle. It was an elegant tall building made from dull gray stone with wide, high towers and stained-glass windows in the main halls. The courtyard was expansive and there was even a gray marble fountain in the very center of the yard with carvings of silvery horses' heads all the way around it's edge. Candy had always liked this castle and those who dwelled there.

Dylon was the first to greet them. He stood nearly six feet tall, had light brown hair, and bright, clear blue eyes.

"Candy," he said with surprise and obvious pleasure that made Nick feel hot. "It's so good to see you. What brings you here?"

"Dylon, there's trouble at Castle MacKline." Candy said seriously, ignoring his obvious joy.

Dylon eyed Nick suspiciously, "Who's this?"

Nick grew even more hot at the accusing way this question was asked.

"Nick Garthson. Nick this is Dylon." Candy said simply.

Nick and Dylon just stood there facing each other. Dylon looked Nick up and down then looked at Candy questioningly.

"He saved my life Dylon, and Brenna's." Candy told him.

"Oh," Dylon said, sounding more relaxed. "Well I'm grateful to him then. Thank you Nick."

Dylon held out his hand in Nick's direction. Marie nudged Nick's leg from behind.

"You're welcome." Nick said politely.

"Oh," Marie groaned, rolling her eyes at herself.

Dylon caught sight of the winged creature at that moment. "What the, it talks?" he said in shock.

Marie sent him a cold, wolfish glare, "'It' can hear you, and 'it' prefers not to be referred to as an 'it'!" she stated firmly.

Dylon gulped noticeably and Nick couldn't stop the small smile that creased his countenance. He didn't feel quite so hot anymore.

"Is that clear?" Marie asked, still glaring slightly.

"Crystal." Dylon said. "May I ask your name ma'am?"

"Marie," she stated with obvious pride.

"All right then, Marie. Now Candy, and your friends, come in and tell me what this trouble is at your castle." Dylon said, offering Candy his arm.

Candy looked at his arm and then at his face before she accepted and allowed him to guide her inside. Nick and Marie followed. Within an hour Candy had told the entire story to Dylon, Harkin and Gitta.

"I've come to ask for your help." Candy said when she'd finished her narrative. "Will you give it?"

Dylon gave his parents a longing look, then said with an immovable steadfastness, "If no one else will go with her then I'll go alone."

"So will I." Nick said in an almost competitive nature.

"There's no reason for you to go without help from us. I have a thousand strong warriors who can be ready to march to Blair's by tomorrow." Harkin said, standing up from his chair.

"Really?" Candy said, overcome with joy at his words.

"Aye lass. Somebody should go south to Erin's and ask for his help as well." Harkin added.

"Nick, Marie and I can go." Candy said quickly. "We'll go right now. Dutchess can be saddled again in a moment."

Dylon's eyes widened, "I'll come too. I can have my own horse saddled in no time."

He seemed just as competitive as Nick. He turned and rushed out the door to the stables. A short time later Dylon was bidding his parents farewell, and then they were on the road heading south.

Nick's whole body screamed with discomfort, but knowing that Dylon was riding with them he said nothing. Marie flew overhead, always on the lookout for any signs of trouble.

After breakfast Brenna began making preparations for the journey westward to her Uncle Keelan MacAllister, her mother's brother who had married Aine, one of Laird MacKline's sisters.

While filling a canteen at the stream she saw Mitch washing his face. He was kneeling on the bank and after splashing water on his face he leaned back his head, eyes closed and heaved a very heavy sigh. Then turning so that his back was toward her, though he was unaware that she was just upstream from him watching, he leaned forward and pulled his newly mended shirt off.

Brenna's mouth dropped open in shock when she beheld his exposed back. Scars upon scars. The kind made by a whip. She watched as he scooped up handfuls of water and splashed himself. He rubbed at his ruined flesh, almost as though he wanted to erase the scars. The large scar on his chest he scrubbed at the hardest.

Brenna felt the sting of guilt as he washed the wound on his shoulder where she'd stabbed him a few days earlier and saw him wince. Then he looked in her direction.

She dropped her canteen in the shallows, startled when he'd caught sight of her. She turned away, picking up her half-filled vessel. She turned back when she heard footsteps approaching from his direction.

Mitch had put his shirt back on and was now carrying his jerkin in one hand. He sat down next to her, keeping his eyes straight ahead on the opposite bank.

"Morning." he said simply.

"Morning." she replied just as simply.

"I suppose you saw all those scars?" he said, eyes still focused on the opposite bank.

"I did." Brenna said hesitantly, dropping her gaze. "I didn't mean to stare."

"It's alright." he said kindly.

"So, how'd that happen?" she couldn't help asking.

"With a whip." Mitch chuckled.

Brenna tried to hide a smile, "I gathered as much."

Mitch became more serious, "On a ship. I spent three years wrongly enslaved on that ship."

"Wrongly enslaved?"

"I was sold by my brother. He always hated me." Mitch explained.

"Your own brother?" she said in shock, turning to him.

"Well, half-brother." Mitch shrugged, eyes downcast.

"How have you not gone mad after all you've been through?" Brenna asked.

"I was very near it when I met Babbette."

"Who?" Brenna raised a brow.

"My wife. I almost went mad with grief when I lost her, and the child." he said sadly.

"How old would the baby be by now?" Brenna asked gently, staring at the stream.

"A little over two years old." Mitch said, his eyes still lowered.

"I'm sorry about yesterday." Brenna said, looking at him again.

"I'm sorry for my angry remarks." he told her kindly, still keeping his eyes straight ahead. "I hear you're travelling west?"

"Aye." she nodded.

"I owe Candy my life. If you don't mind, I'll go with you." Mitch said, still not looking at her.

Brenna forced herself not to show how pleased she was. She hadn't wanted to travel the mountain-trails alone.

"If you want." she shrugged, hiding a smile as she looked back down at the flowing stream.

Mitch side-glanced at her and gave a small half grin, "Got nothing else to do."

Nothing else was said between them until they went to the stable.

Brenna was leading Lightningbolt out of the stable when Mitch stared and inquired why the stallion wasn't saddled. Nigel and Conlan started to chuckle as they stood nearby.

"I lost the saddle in the woods, besides, I don't need one." Brenna said simply, scratching under the horse's chin. "Is there anything wrong with that?"

Mitch swallowed before saying, "No. There's no problem."

"Have you ever ridden without a saddle?" she asked curiously, raising a brow at him as she hid a small smile.

"Aye." Mitch said, squaring his shoulders. Though he'd only ridden once without a saddle when he was very young, and had fallen off nearly breaking his left arm. Ever since he'd only ridden with a saddle.

"Come on then." Brenna said, mounting up in a swift and professional manner.

Mitch looked over at Nigel and Conlan. They stared back. Mitch walked over and mounted up behind Brenna, then nodded toward two brothers in a smug fashion. The two sons of Allen MacKline rolled their eyes and came forward.

"Safe journey." Conlan said, handing Brenna a saddlebag.

"We'll meet you at Clancy's." said Nigel.

"Until then." Brenna said.

"Hang on tight." Conlan said looking at Mitch.

"And don't fall off." Nigel added.

"What's that supposed to mean?" Mitch said, glaring at them.

Brenna sank her heels into Lightningbolt's ribs and they were off at full gallop. Mitch suddenly found himself with his arms wrapped tightly around Brenna's waist to keep from sliding off.

"Hang on with your knees and loosen your grip! I can't breath!" Brenna yelled as they rode west through a wide valley.

Mitch followed her instructions and it did become easier to stay on, but he wasn't about to admit it to her.

"I wouldn't have to hang on so tight if you weren't riding so fast!" he snorted.

"We've got to get there by nightfall!" she snorted back.

Just then they went over a log and Mitch nearly fell off.

"Easy on the jumps!" he groaned, feeling slightly sick from the rapid movements of the horse. "I almost slid off back there!"

"I wish you had." Brenna grumbled under her breath.

"What?" shouted Mitch, having heard the remark.

"Nothing!" Brenna growled.

"It was something!" Mitch pressed.

"No it wasn't!" she hissed.

"Aye it was!" he persisted.

"No it wasn't!"

"Aye it was!"

They continued to argue for several minutes before going silent, refusing to speak to one another. Dawn flew above them, shaking her head at the two of them. One minute they seemed like they could become the best of friends, the next they were arguing like bitter enemies. Dawn heaved a heavy sigh, knowing that this was going to be a long trip.

Dritt awoke and looked around. He was lying on a cot in the infirmary at Castle MacKline.

"How'd I get back here?" he asked aloud.

"You're men found you unconscious in the swamp last night sir." said a young blond girl. "They carried you back here. Would you like some water sir?"

"Aye. My throat's dreadfully dry." Dritt moaned, touching his bandaged chin and wincing. "My head feels like it's gonna fall off."

Erica brought the water filled ladle to his lips. Dritt drank deeply, coughing and sputtering as he finished.

"I almost had her." he sneered, slamming a fist down on his cot.

"Who sir?" Erica said calmly.

"That Candace girl. She was within my grasp, and then she did this to me!" he pointed to his chin. "She's escaped me again!"

Erica forced herself to remain neutral, "You should rest sir."

"Aye. Rest. Then I'll find her, and kill her!" Dritt growled as he laid his head back and closed his eyes.

Erica left the infirmary and made her way to the dining hall.

"I'll take that in." she said to a dark-haired maiden approaching the door with a tray.

The maid stared at her for a moment, then offered her the food-laden tray, glad to be excused from serving Griff and his men. Erica entered the dining-hall and approached the table. Placing the tray on the table surface, she began setting out the plates and bowls of food slowly so that she could listen to the Raves' conversation.

"Well Vrant my shadow-man, what have you seen this morning?" said Griff, breaking open a warm loaf of bread and taking a bite.

"Well that girl, Candace, went to a village far-west, and now there's a small army gathering. Then she went northwest to another village. There's another army there." Vrant reported.

"And what about the Wolf Princess? Is anything left of her after that fire?" Griff said around a mouthful bread, spraying Vrant with several crumbs.

"Uh." Vrant said reluctantly.

Griff stared at him, "Speak!" he growled.

"She's riding west from a large town in the mountains where another army is being put together, sir." Vrant said, almost gulping.

"She's not dead!" Griff bellowed jumping up from his seat so fast that his chair fell over clattering on the floor. "But how?"

"I don't know sire." Vrant said, stepping back, his eyes on the dagger in Griff's belt. He swallowed as his leader fingered the deadly blade.

"So they're gathering an army." It was more of a statement then a question. Griff's voice was more calm now. "Where are they going next?"

"I'm not sure milaird." Vrant said honestly.

Griff scratched the tuft of hair that served as a beard, "We still have one of their brothers here don't we?"

Erica listened intently at the mention of Konroy.

"Aye sir." Vrant nodded.

"Bring him to me." Griff ordered. "Now!"

Brenna and Mitch had arrived at Keelan's castle in time for lunch. They were served a meal of roast mutton and potatoes by

Aine, Keelan's beautiful wife. As they ate Brenna recounted all that had occurred in the last couple of days.

"I can have five hundred men at Clancy's by tomorrow night." Keelan offered when the Wolf Princess had finished speaking. "Is that soon enough?"

"Aye." Brenna said happily. "That's perfect."

"Will you be staying the night?" asked Keelan.

"There's still some daylight left Uncle. I think we'll go south to Harkin's and ask for some help from him as well." Brenna said.

"Oh." Mitch groaned, his seat and legs sore from bouncing and hanging onto Lightningbolt.

"Surely you'll stop there." Aine said, concern in her voice.

"If we arrive soon enough, I hope to reach Erin's yet today." Brenna said, tearing off a piece of mutton with her teeth.

"Spare your poor horse." Keelan pleaded.

"I have been. Mitch here isn't used to riding bareback on Lightning yet, so we've been taking it slow." Brenna said, slapping Mitch on the shoulder.

"That was slow?" said Mitch, shifting uncomfortably in his chair.

"And what do you mean 'poor horse'?" Brenna said defensively. "I'm talking about Lightningbolt, son of the black stallion of the mountains. Have you ever known him to tire?"

Keelan chuckled, "No. He's too much like his rouge of a father."

Brenna drained her goblet of strong apple cider and refilled it.

"This is excellent Aunt Aine." she commented.

"Thank you Brenna." Aine said graciously.

Brenna popped the last bite of potato into her mouth and in one draught she drained her goblet again, then stood. "See you outside slowpokes." she grinned at Mitch and Dawn, who were only half done with their own meals. They watched as she turned and headed for the door.

"Is she always like that?" Mitch asked, his tone a little annoyed.

Aine and Keelan couldn't help smiling as they nodded.

Mitch sighed and took another bite of mutton. When he'd finished he went to the door and saw Brenna patting Lightningbolt's neck affectionately. Dawn left her plate licked clean on the floor, and came to stand by Mitch's feet.

"I wish I could fly like you." Mitch remarked.

"Huh, it's no picnic keeping up with that black tornado either. "Dawn said, launching herself into the air.

Mitch walked up to the Wolf Princess and her steed.

"Alright then, Lightning, this is Mitch. Mitch this is Lightning." Brenna said.

Mitch raised a brow at her, then said in a slightly confused tone, "Charmed."

"Come on. Pet him. Lightning, be nice." Brenna said firmly.

The horse snorted, then nuzzled against Mitch's outstretched palm, allowing Mitch to stroke his long face. Mitch smiled at the stallion then asked Brenna, "Why are we being introduced?"

"Because you're riding in front." Brenna said simply.

"What?" Mitch nearly shouted in shock, his eyes growing wide.

"Look, you hold on too tight. If not for that meal we just had, I'd be twice as thin as I am now." Brenna said, her hands on her hips as though she were scolding him. "Lightning knows the way to Harkin's, don't you boy?"

She patted the stallion's neck, causing his head to bob up and down slightly. Mitch frowned at them.

"Come on." Brenna said. "Unless you're afraid to ride in front."

Mitch mounted up stubbornly and Brenna climbed up behind him with a grin before they were on their way again.

Darsy had insisted on accompanying Konroy to the dining-hall, so the guards had brought him along. He and Konroy were now on their knees, their hands bound in front of them. Konroy glared up defiantly at Griff.

"You, boy," Griff said, pointing at Konroy. "Where would your sisters go?"

Konroy just glared, his lips drawn into a tight line.

"Alright, you then," he said, pointing at Darsy. "Where are they?"

"Somewhere safe if you don't know." Darsy said plainly, a small smile playing on his lips.

"Give me a straight answer!" Griff growled menacingly.

"What are you trying to accomplish here Griff? This isn't your castle, or your land. Your father's dead. It's too late to gain his approval." Darsy said in a soft, serious voice.

Griff stared at the herbalist in disbelief. How did he know so much about his life?

"Take him to the corner!" Griff ordered. "Away from the boy! And keep your comments to yourself, herbalist!"

The Raves obeyed without a murmur as Griff turned back to Konroy.

"Where would they go lad?" he asked.

Konroy was silent as a rock covered in moss.

"Don't make me ask again boy." Griff growled.

"Aren't you going to ask me about my brother?" Konroy spat smugly.

"Why should I? He's with your ancestors now." Griff smirked.

Konroy's brow shot upward, disbelief and sorrow in his eyes. Lewis, dead?

"Now, where would the Wolf Princess go if she needed help?" asked Griff.

"I thought that you didn't want to ask again." Konroy sneered, having regained control of his emotions.

"Don't play mind games with me lad!" Griff's tone was deadly. "What sort of person is the Wolf Princess? Why can't I catch her? How many times must I kill her before she'll finally die?"

"A force much greater than you is protecting her." Darsy put in.

"I told you to keep your comments to yourself!" Griff warned.

"Why do you go down this path? She'll never join you?" Darsy said.

"Why? She was born under the dark star! She has a dark destiny!" Griff growled.

"You choose your destiny, and you've chosen the wrong one." Darsy continued. "You're on the wrong path."

"And the Wolf Princess is on the right one?" Griff snorted.

"She's at a crossroad. Very soon she will have to choose. But she'll more than likely take the right path." Darsy told them.

"Take him back to his cell! He's only encouraging this boy's insolence!" Griff roared.

The guards dragged Darsy from the room and took him back to the dungeon.

"Now," said Griff, after taking a deep breath to calm himself. "What must I do to capture the Wolf Princess?"

Konroy smiled up at his enemy.

"Tell me! Why can't I catch her?" Griff snapped. "What is she?"

Konroy's smile widened, "She's the Wolf Princess, and she's twice as elusive as a wild wolf. You'll never catch her."

Griff was seething as he slapped Konroy across the face as hard as he could.

Erica looked away, wishing that she had some way of helping him.

"Where would she go in the mountains?" Griff snarled. "Tell me or else!"

"Or else what?" Konroy growled, tasting blood from his now split lip. "If you kill me, you'll get no information."

"Then tell me!" Griff roared.

"Never!"

"Then why should we keep you alive?" Griff sneered.

"Fine! I don't fear death! If that's what it takes to protect my sisters then so be it!" Konroy said, glaring at Griff defiantly as he struggled to his feet, still dizzy after being struck.

"Maybe you don't fear for your life, but what about someone else's?' Griff smirked, quickly drawing his dagger and wrapping an arm around Erica, pressing the blade to her throat.

Konroy tensed, his eyes wide as he stared at Erica. Her face was a pale canvas of fear. Konroy met her frightened gaze and wished that he could rush forward and knock Griff away from her. All he wanted was to erase her fear.

"Do you know where they're going, or do you want her blood on your hands?" Griff jeered, making an awful face.

Konroy's mouth opened, then closed. He swallowed noticeably.

Erica closed her eyes, but a single tear squeezed out from under her lid.

"Come on lad. You can't let an innocent, sweet girl die for your silence. Especially one so pretty." Griff taunted.

"What makes you think that I care about a servant girl?" Konroy said, trying to keep his voice even, though there were tears burning in his eyes.

"Because slaves are valuable." Griff snorted. "Especially pretty ones."

Erica opened her blue-green eyes once and looked at Konroy. Tears streamed down her cheeks and she trembled visibly.

"Give me a map." Konroy said in defeat, lowering his eyes in shame.

Lewis felt like he was dead. He'd been shot in the chest the night he'd escaped and now all he knew was the pain in his wound. He there was also the soothing feeling of something cool and wet brushing his forehead. Then the caress of a soft hand on his cheek.

Is this heaven? he thought.

Then he felt someone kiss his brow, then gently kiss his cheek, then his lips.

It must be. he thought, letting out a small sigh.

He forced his eyes open and saw a beautiful young woman gazing down at him with kind and loving eyes. A moment after he'd opened his eyes, a small smile spread across her face, only enhancing her beauty.

"Are you an angel?" he managed to say weakly, unable to turn his gaze from her face.

"I was hoping you'd wake up Lewis," she said sweetly.

"Colleen?" he said, managing a weak smile as he recognized his betrothed.

"I'm so glad to hear your voice again," she said, tears building in her beautiful eyes. "I was so afraid that I'd lost you."

Her hand was resting lightly on his wound. He covered her hand with his own, squeezing it gently as his eyes locked on hers.

"You could never lose me Colleen." Lewis said kindly.

"I'm glad," she almost sobbed, leaning down and laying her head near his neck. He put his arms around her comfortingly.

"So am I," he whispered, turning his head and brushing his lips against her brow.

Dylon saw Candy and Nick sitting side by side. They'd stopped for a rest and a light meal, and now Candy and Nick sat very near one another on a long fallen tree, talking while they ate. He came forward and sat down between them. There was silence.

"So, Nick, how long have you been blind?" Dylon asked, unable to think of anything else to say.

"Dylon!" Candy hissed, elbowing him in the ribs.

"No, it's alright Candy. I've been blind since I was seven." Nick answered, his voice sounding slightly sad. Then he brightened a little. "So, Dylon, how long have you had that limp in your left leg?"

Dylon's mouth dropped open and his gaze turned to Candy, "Did you tell him?"

"No." Candy said, shaking her head. She was obviously just as surprised as Dylon.

"How did you know that?" Dylon asked, turning back to Nick.

Nick grinned, "It's not very noticeable. Just one step is quicker than the other when you walk."

"But how did you know that it was my left leg?"

"When you were walking toward us your footsteps got louder, and the quick step was to my right, so I knew that it had to be your left leg." Nick explained. "So how'd it happen?"

"A hunting accident." Dylon said, blushing and rubbing the back of his neck nervously. "I took an arrow to my lower thigh."

"Who shot you?" asked Marie, sitting at Nick's feet.

Dylon lowered his eyes and continued to rub the back of his neck, "I was using a crossbow for the first time, and I put it down without locking the trigger properly."

Nick fought to keep his expression neutral.

"And I really shouldn't have laid it down so that it was pointed in my direction."

Nick bit his lower-lip to keep from laughing. Marie suddenly stood then sat again.

"As I was pulling the arrow out a deer came by and just stared at me." Dylon said. "The very same deer that I'd been tracking. Then it came over and sneezed in my face before running off."

"Excuse me." Marie said urgently, jumping up and running off into the woods.

After a few seconds they heard a burst of laughter. Nick shook as he laughed silently, still biting his lip.

"Perhaps we should be on our way." Candy said, forcing a frown as she rose from the log.

The young men rose as well and followed her.

It was about three hours later when they arrived at the village. It was as silent as a grave and there were no signs of life anywhere.

When they went to the castle gates they found them locked and saw no signs of a watch on the walls.

"There's something wrong here." Dylon said, looking around. "It's like the whole place was completely abandoned."

"They must've had somewhere to be." Candy said simply.

"But where?" asked Nick, Marie trotting at his side as she sniffed at each door they passed.

CHAPTER FIFTEEN
DANGER AT THE OLD GORGE

Brenna and Mitch had been riding for an hour, a little bit slower than when Brenna had been in front. Brenna had her arms around Mitch's middle and tightened her grip each time that Lightningbolt performed a jump over an old fallen tree. This road had obviously not been used in a few years and was horribly overgrown.

"Now who's holding on too tight?" Mitch gasped after a particularly high jump.

"I'm just showing you how it feels." Brenna snorted.

Dawn came winging in overhead and said, "You'd better hurry up."

"Why?" Brenna asked, raising a brow.

"I just spotted five Raves coming in over that mountain to the east." Dawn panted. "They're coming like the wind on those strange flying horses."

"We need to get across the bridge at the Old Gorge before they get there." Brenna said urgently.

"Old Gorge?" Mitch asked apprehensively.

"It's a huge crack in the ground, too deep to see the bottom and too wide to cross without a bridge." Brenna explained. "If they get there first they'll cut the support ropes for the bridge and fly back to block our way out through the valley."

"Will the bridge hold a horse?" Mitch asked, leaning forward as Lightningbolt reared to perform another jump.

"I think so." Brenna said when they were racing across the ground again.

The woods suddenly thinned out and they heard the flapping of wings rapidly approaching. They looked up and saw the five Raves Dawn had told them about. They were preparing to land and block their way.

Dawn flew at the men, one after another, knocking them from their steeds to the ground. Barking ferociously she chased the winged beasts back toward the mountaintop.

The Raves, now on the ground, leapt to their feet and drew their swords chasing after Brenna and Mitch. Brenna chanced a look over her shoulder and saw them running. She glanced ahead and saw the bridge. It was a simple construction of four thick ropes, two suspending several short yet thick boards to provide a walkway, the other two were attached to waist-high stakes that held the entire bridge up while providing a barrier to keep people from falling off.

A sickening thought came to the Wolf Princess. Those men were right behind them. What if when Lightningbolt was halfway across the bridge these men cut the support ropes? She couldn't let that happen.

"Whatever happens don't stop 'til you're across that bridge!" she called to Mitch as she slipped her right leg over Lightningbolt's back to the left side.

"What'd you mean?" Mitch called back, but Brenna never answered. She slid from the stallion's back, landing on her feet. She drew her sword, prepared for battle. She met the first man head on. Their swords clashed once, then Brenna relieved him of his head.

The four men behind him skidded to a stop and stared at her. Brenna glared at them, fire flashing in her eyes. She raised her sword, roaring like a lion she charged toward them. The Raves were completely surprised by this and retreated.

She chased them about ten feet, then turned and ran as fast as she could toward the bridge. The Raves slowed to a stop, realizing that she was no longer behind them and pursued her.

Mitch was two thirds of the way across the old rope-bridge when he glanced back at them. He saw Brenna making a mad dash for the bridge with the four remaining Raves close behind her.

Lightningbolt stopped as soon as he was on solid ground. Mitch leapt from the horse's back and yelled, "Run Brenna!"

Brenna somehow managed to sheath her sword while running, and within a few seconds she was in the middle of the bridge, still running at an amazing speed. One of the Raves ran after her, hot on her heels.

Mitch grew pale with sickening anxiety, knowing that there was nothing he could do. It was the same ill, helpless feeling he'd felt when his beloved wife lay dying in his arms. He was startled when something thudded at his feet. It was a small quiver of arrows and a crossbow.

"Pick it up!" Dawn called urgently from above, her wings beating the air as she hovered there. "I took it from one of their saddles! Hurry!"

"I don't need to know where it came from," Mitch said as he picked up the weapon and loaded it. "Just that it works."

He looked across the gorge and saw that the three remaining Raves were cutting the support ropes. He took aim and fired, instantly killing one of the men. He reloaded and fired twice more, effectively ending the lives of the last two. He felt guilt for doing it dispite the fact that he'd had no choice. But it was too late. The ropes had been severed. One moment the bridge, Brenna and the last Rave behind her were suspended in the air, the next they'd all vanished from Mitch's sight, the sound of their screams echoing in his ears.

"Brenna!" he yelled, dropping the crossbow and rushing to the gorge's edge.

Falling to his knees he looked down to where the dangling bridge clattered against the steep wall. He gave a sigh of relief when he saw Brenna clinging to the closely tied boards. She climbed slowly but surely toward him. She was within his reach when she cried out. Mitch looked passed her and saw the last remaining Rave climbing up. He had hold of Brenna's ankle and was twisting it mercilessly. She started kicking at him in vain, shouting, "Ow! Let me go! Lemme go! Ow!"

Dawn chirped like a bird then dove into the gorge. She flapped around the man's head, smacking him with her wings and clawing at his face, yelling, "Let her go and we'll help you up."

The Rave put up his free hand to protect his eyes, still clutching and twisting Brenna's ankle. The Wolf Princess cried out in pain, clinging to the fallen bridge.

"Get away you little monster!" the Rave roared as he slapped Dawn away, nearly sending her into the gorge wall. "I'm taking the Wolf Princess to the bottom with me."

He's insane. Mitch thought, then started when he heard a loud snap. He looked and saw that the old ropes weren't holding up as another one broke under the strain. A third one snapped and Brenna gave a startled cry as the bridge shifted.

Dawn flew back and sank her teeth into the man's neck, then wisely flew away as he struck out at her. He made the mistake of striking out with both hands and he fell. He gave an angry cry as he plummeted beyond their sight.

Dawn snorted, then flew high above the gorge and performed a summersault before landing next to Mitch.

Mitch reached down toward Brenna and called, "Take my hand."

There was a resounding snap as the last rope gave way under the strain. Brenna released the bridge and took hold of Mitch's outstretched hand. The old rope-bridge fell away into the blackness below. Brenna gave a little cry as she swung slightly, nearly hitting the rock-face. She looked up at the man who held her hand.

"Don't let go." she said fearfully, her voice trembling.

"I won't." Mitch promised, shaking his head slightly.

He gave a grunt as he pulled her up. He backed away slightly to make room for her. Once she was on solid ground Brenna shocked them both as she suddenly found herself clinging to him trembling. Not knowing what else to do Mitch put his arms around her and just held her until the shaking ceased. It felt strange, yet good to have someone near after going through so much.

"Are you alright?" he asked after a moment, his voice a little husky.

"I will be," she panted, slowly releasing him. "We should get moving. Harkin's village isn't far."

They rose and mounted up on Lightningbolt again, then continued on their way.

They soon arrived at Harkin's village and noticed that carts and wagons were being loaded.

"Maybe this means they can help you sooner." Mitch said hopefully, trying to get Brenna's spirits back up after crossing the gorge.

"Or that they're too busy to." Brenna said glumly, obviously still a little shaken.

Harkin greeted them warmly and informed them that Candy, Nick and Marie had already been there and told him about Griff Cray. Then he explained that they and Dylon had ridden onward to Erin's castle in order to ask for his help.

This news seemed to lift Brenna's spirits instantly. She was overjoyed to know that Candy was all right. She hastily thanked Harkin and they started toward Erin's village.

Dylon had started a small fire in the hearth of one of the abandoned houses, feeling fairly certain that it was the home a hunter due to all of furs and animal heads mounted on the walls. He poked at the embers with a long stick, stirring up sparks and bits of ash as he scanned his surroundings.

"We'll need more wood before nightfall," he said after a few minutes, "I have some wrapped meat in my pack. I'll start cooking that if one of you will go gather some more firewood."

"I'll go." Nick said.

"Me too." Candy added.

"So will I." Marie put in, trotting toward the door.

Dylon watched them go, eyeing Nick suspiciously, uncertain whether to trust him or not.

Candy and Nick walked within a few yards of each other, gathering pieces of dead, dry wood. Marie trotted on the ground wherever she pleased, sometimes with Candy, sometimes with Nick, sometimes in between them.

"Marie," said Nick, "why don't you scout ahead a little."

Marie heard something in his voice that caused her to run off without question. Nick walked so that he was closer to Candy.

"Uh, I was thinking that, maybe after we gather the wood, Marie and I should probably go back home." Nick said softly, his voice a little nervous and unsure.

"What?" Candy's voice was surprised and unhappy.

They both halted then.

"It's just that, this is none of my business." Nick said calmly.

"It's Dylon isn't it?" she said, an edge of frustration in her voice.

Nick was silent.

"Don't let him scare you." Candy stated. "Dylon's just, protective. Please don't go?" she said, gently resting a hand on his shoulder.

"Do you really want me to stay?" he asked, trying in vain to hide the hopefulness in his voice.

"Aye." Candy said, her voice a little shy.

They were both silent for a moment as small smiles crossed their faces.

"Well, then I guess we should gather up the wood." Nick said, walking ahead of her.

Candy's smile broadened as she watched him walk.

A strong wind suddenly came through the forest, sending down a shower of leaves. There was a loud groan, then a cracking sound. Candy looked in the direction of the noise and saw a large tree falling directly toward Nick, who had stopped to listen and was trying to decipher what that cracking sound was.

"Nick!" Candy called urgently, rushing in his direction.

Nick turned in her direction just as Candy launched herself into the air. For a second she was four feet up, parallel to the ground. She put out her hands and shoved Nick out of the path of the falling tree, but didn't have enough time to get out of the way herself. The tree-trunk came down like a hammer on her back, throwing her to the ground in mid-flight.

Nick landed on his back, the air leaving his lungs in a rush. He gasped and forced himself into a sitting position.

"Candy?" he called, having heard a crash.

Fortunately for Candy, there'd been large rock to her right and while she lay flat on the ground, she was shorter than the rock. The tree fell slightly impaling itself on the rock, saving Candy from being crushed. There were about three inches between the bottom of the tree trunk and the top of her back.

"Candy are you alright?" Nick asked, a little shaken.

Candy raised her head and groaned, "I think so. You?"

"Aye. What happened?" he asked.

Candy crawled out from under the tree with an effort and explained what had occurred. Marie came bounding through the bushes and managed to hear the whole story.

"Are you sure that you're alright?" asked Nick.

Marie walked over and sniffed at Candy's back.

"I don't know." Candy said. "My back hurts. I don't think it's serious though."

"Nick, you should probably carry her back to the house." Marie said calmly, in the motherly tone that she often used in these sorts of situations.

"I think I can walk." Candy grunted as she got to her feet.

But Nick shook his head as he stood, then scooped her up and marched back toward Erin's village. Candy protested at first, then complied by putting her arms around his neck and laying her head on his shoulder. Her lips lightly brushed his cheek in thanks, causing him to blush and give a slight smile. Candy was soon sitting by the hearth resting comfortably as Marie looked at her back.

"You'll have an ugly bruise and a sore back for a couple of days, but you'll be fine." Marie told her kindly.

"Thank you Marie." Candy smiled.

"Just rest for a while and don't do anything too strenuous." Marie instructed.

Dylon was none too happy that Candy had received such a blow. He watched jealously as Nick removed his coat and bundled it up into a cushion shape with a couple of fox furs before placing it under Candy's sore back.

Dylon cut some of the meat he'd been roasting and placed it on a plate before taking it over to Candy, bumping Nick slightly with his arm.

"Here." Dylon said, handing Candy the plate. "I saved the best meat for you."

"Uh, thank you Dylon." Candy said, noting the eager look in his eyes which caused her to become too shy to inform him that she wasn't hungry. She graciously accepted the offered plate, then turned back to Nick, "Thank you for carrying me Nick."

Nick blushed again and gave a slight grin, "It was no difficulty."

"Speaking of difficulties," said Dylon, "It's difficult to keep a fire going without wood."

"Marie and I'll go." Nick said, the smile gone from his face. He rose moodily and headed for the door, Marie trotting at his heels.

When they were gone Candy shot Dylon a cold glare, "What's the matter with you?"

"Nothing." he almost snorted, going back to the fire.

"Dylon, I've known you since childhood, and even then you couldn't hide it from me when something was bothering you." Candy said a little more kindly. "What's wrong? Why don't you like Nick?"

"I never said I didn't like him." Dylon snorted again.

"Then what's wrong?" she pressed.

"I don't want to talk about it!" he growled.

They were quiet for a while. The only sound was the crackling of the fire and sizzling meat as it cooked. After about ten minutes Candy broke the silence by saying, "Do you remember that summer when we all went swimming, and Brenna shoved Lynch into the pond for trying to kiss her?"

Dylon kept his back to her so that she wouldn't see his smile.

"He certainly came out of that water in a hurry." Candy continued. "Remember how he had all of those old wet leaves sticking to him?"

"Aye," said Dylon, unable to keep silent. "He ran crying to his mother that he was covered in leeches."

The two of them started chuckling.

"And you stole my boots and shirt, then threw 'em up into a tree. I had to climb up dripping wet to get them back." Dylon said accusingly in mock anger.

"Ah that was Brenna, not me." Candy said in self-defense.

"Right," he said sarcastically, "and I suppose that Brenna's the one who splashed me in the face too?"

"No, I'll take the credit for that one." Candy grinned.

"You'd better. I swallowed half the pond thanks to you."

"I was just trying to help." Candy said sweetly. "You looked thirsty."

They laughed for about five minutes, then ceased when Nick and Marie walked in with a bounty of wood and laid it down by the hearth. They all sat down and ate a light supper of meat, bread, and cheese, then washed it down with mulberry cordial.

CHAPTER SIXTEEN

THE MYSTERY OF THINGS THAT GO BUMP IN THE NIGHT

After their meal they all made their beds around the house. Since they planned to be on their way at first light, Candy went into one of the back rooms rather than upstairs.

The young men made their beds on the floor near the hearth, but not too near each other. Dylon made certain that Marie was between them as she stretched out as near the flames as she dared. She kept one eye open as she watched Nick like a mother-hen.

"Goodnight Nick." Marie cooed.

"Goodnight Marie." Nick answered. "Goodnight Dylon."

Dylon only snorted and rolled so that his back was toward them.

Nick sighed and settled in for a good night's sleep. He didn't know how many hours he'd slept when Marie woke him in the middle of the night.

"What's wrong Marie?" he whispered.

"Shush. I heard riders coming. It sounds like two at least." Marie whispered back.

Nick slowly sat up, listening intently.

"I don't hear a horse." he said with bated breath.

"They've stopped and are on foot now. There's two and some kind of dog I think." Marie explained. "Can't you hear them?"

He listened again, then he heard it. Footsteps just outside the house.

"You should wake Dylon." Marie whispered as she stalked toward the door, her head low and teeth bared.

Nick crawled over to where Dylon lay and covered his mouth before waking him.

"Dylon, we've got company outside." Nick whispered, having shaken Dylon awake. If Dylon's mouth hadn't been covered he certainly would've cried out.

Dylon sat up and looked around. The fire was little more than some dying embers. It made the large room seem very dark and almost eerie as the mounted animal heads stood out from the wall.

"I can't see much." Dylon whispered to Nick, then rebuked himself for saying something like that to a blind man. "Sorry."

"It's alright. Do you have your sword?" asked Nick.

"Aye." Dylon said, drawing the long blade.

Nick guided Dylon to the door, stave in hand. They positioned themselves on either side of the entry, their weapons raised. They could hear the footsteps outside coming closer. The people out there were coming up to the door. The old wooden door's hinges creaked as it slowly opened.

Nick struck out with his stave, catching the first intruder in the stomach. He heard the man gasp as he bent double. Nick brought his staff down on the man's back and heard him hit the floor. The second intruder entered, the moonlight glinting off his sword as Dylon met his opponent's blade.

Their swords clashed three times in the dark before Candy came rushing out of her room and yelled, "What's happened?"

"Candy?" came Brenna's voice.

"Brenna?" Candy cried.

"Mitch?" said Nick, having pinned his opponent to the floor.

"Nick, get off me! You're knee's crushing my gut!" Mitch gasped.

"Ooh sorry." Nick said, removing his knee from Mitch's middle.

Dylon made his way back to the hearth and lit another fire so that they could see each other.

"Where's Dawn?" Marie asked, looking around.

As if to answer her question, Dawn came skipping in chasing a tiny brown moth.

"Get back here you!" she growled playfully as she swatted at it.

She'd been pursuing this moth since she'd arrived. She'd chased it to the outer reaches of the town and back determined to catch the small fluttering creature. But Marie was the only one interested in any of this.

Brenna and Candy had the rest of the room's attention as they embraced tearfully, glad to be reunited.

It took nearly twenty minutes to sort it all out. Brenna and Candy finally calmed down enough to introduce Mitch and Dawn to Dylon.

Another hour was spent exchanging stories and eating some cold meat. Then Mitch made a bed for himself on the floor and Brenna went back to the room that Candy was sleeping in, the two of them chattering about anything and everything. Dawn trotted over to the hearth, feeling quite pleased with herself having finally caught the moth, and curled up next to Marie who raised her head and affectionately licked Dawn's face.

"Goodnight Whirlwind." Marie whispered.

"Goodnight." Dawn said cheerfully after licking the older Bulf's nose.

Then they put down their heads and went to sleep.

In the back room Brenna and Candy were lying on a pile of thick furs giggling.

"I didn't see Dutchess. Where'd you put her?" Brenna almost chuckled.

"We put her and Dylon's horse in a stable to the west. Where'd you put Lightningbolt?" Candy asked with a happy giggle.

"In a barn to the east." Brenna explained.

Lying side by side on their makeshift bed, they talked for about an hour, just as they'd always done at home since they were small children. Then Brenna started a tickle-fight and they laughed and rolled for about another ten minutes. It was something that they did from time to time. Finally overcome with exhaustion, they called a truce and fell asleep.

The lads and the Bulves were the first awake. While the Bulves went hunting for breakfast, the young men built up the fire. It wasn't too long before Dawn and Marie returned with a plump stag.

Dylon and Nick seemed to be getting along with each other much better today. Ever since Nick had awakened him the night before, the two of them had an unspoken trust. Mitch and Nick were acting like the best of friends, but somehow Dylon was fitting in perfectly. As they skinned and cleaned the stag, they talked and joked until the girls came out giggling about something.

"What's so funny?" asked Mitch.

"Oh, nothing." Brenna said, trying not to laugh.

All three of the boys suddenly turned in their direction, feeling curious. Brenna and Candy both burst out laughing, then exited the house.

"We're gonna go for a walk before breakfast." Candy called over her shoulder.

After about five steps Brenna chuckled, "What did I tell you? If we walk through laughing they'd be curious and confused."

"That was horrible." Candy said, trying in vain to sound serious. "But they are easier to trick than Lewis and Konroy."

They both giggled for a few seconds, then couldn't help growing serious at the mention of their brothers' names.

"Do you really think that we'll rescue the castle." Candy asked.

"I'll fight 'til my last breath for our home." Brenna said confidently.

"But what about Mum and Da'?" Candy's voice was trembling. "And Konroy?"

"Candy, we're gonna rescue them. I'm the Wolf Princess, it's what I do." Brenna stated. "It'll all work out. You'll see. All right?"

Candy sniffed and nodded.

They returned to the house and enjoyed a fine breakfast of roast venison. Then they packed up their supplies, mounted their horses and rode southward to their uncle Dacey's castle on the sea-cliffs.

CHAPTER SEVENTEEN
DARING RESCUES AND
CONVERSATIONS

As they topped the ridge that stood between Dacey's village and the grassy fields that lay inland, they couldn't believe their eyes. The village was burning and the sound of battle was thick on the air.

"Is it the Raves?" asked Nick.

"No," Mitch said, going pale and looking as though he was about to be ill.

"How do you know?" asked Candy.

"Look," he said, pointing to the sea where five large Northland ships lay anchored in the shallows.

Mitch was in front of Brenna on Lightningbolt, watching as three Northmen on fat mountain-ponies rode around the flaming buildings laughing. Brenna felt Mitch tense.

Mitch felt something snap inside of him as he dug his heels into Lightningbolt's ribs. The stallion reared before charging down the ridge.

The three Northmen on the ponies had spotted a small boy running toward the open fields to the east. They chased after him whooping and hollering like wild animals.

Mitch steered Lightningbolt in between the invaders and their would-be victim. The black stallion reared and bellowed at the sky to show his strength to the stocky round ponies, who skidded to a sudden halt.

"Get out of our way boy before you get hurt!" snorted the man in the lead.

Mitch fumbled inside his shirt and drew forth the gold medallion he wore. Holding it up so that the trespassers could see it clearly he shot them an icy cold glare.

The Northmen all drew back in fear of something. Brenna didn't know if it was Mitch or the medallion, but she was certain that they were afraid.

"Leave and don't come back! Go!" Mitch yelled, his voice thundering with anger.

The Northmen turned their ponies and galloped back toward the shore, shouting to their mates that it was time to go.

Mitch dismounted and Brenna followed. Dylon, Candy, Nick and the animals all came down the ridge after them. They quickly went to work helping wherever they could.

Brenna and Candy soon discovered why Erin's village had been deserted. The warriors had come to Dacey's aid led by Erin, while the warriors' families had gone to Blair's village for safety.

No longer doing battle with the Northmen, whose ships were now disappearing over the horizon, the warriors had only the wounded to care for and the fires to put out.

In front of a cottage engulfed in flame they found a woman on her knees wailing, "My children!"

Mitch took one look at the house then charged, kicking in the door as he entered the burning building.

"Mitch!" Brenna and Candy both screamed.

It was absolute torture waiting as the minutes crawled by. The doorway was completely swallowed up in flame and they didn't dare follow to help him.

Dylon and Nick came rushing passed them with buckets of water which they threw on the fire, then ran back to the sea to fetch more. Brenna and Candy ran after them to help.

As they dumped their pails of seawater on the flames Mitch came bounding through the extinguished door, an infant in his arms and a small girl on his back. He fell to his knees, coughing and sputtering. The girl dropped from his back and lay on the ground completely motionless. The infant wailed.

The woman rushed forward to the little girl crying out, "Elsie! Elsie!"

Nick knelt and breathed the breath of life into the child's lungs as he had done for Brenna after pulling her from the river. The girl coughed and opened her eyes.

"Mumma?" she gasped.

"Elsie!" the woman sobbed as she hugged her daughter, then she opened her arms so that Mitch could hand her the wailing infant. "Bless you lad. Bless you." Then she kissed his cheek and went back to cradling her children.

"You're most welcome ma'am. Just keep 'em safe." Mitch panted, then rose and went off to help where he could.

Brenna watched him go, hoping that he'd be more careful. Then she nearly chuckled when she saw Nick blush as the woman kissed his cheek to thank him for saving Elsie.

It was several hours before the entire village was extinguished and all of the wounded were in the infirmary. While carrying in the wounded, Brenna and Candy came across a familiar face.

"Lewis!" they both squealed, assaulting their brother with hugs.

Brenna suddenly jumped back and punched him in the arm in mock anger saying, "You rat! You scared me! I thought you might be dead!"

"Glad to see you too," their older brother smiled, still embracing Candy who was so overcome with joy that she was crying.

Lewis told them the whole story of what had happened to him over the last three days. That first night he'd been shot in the chest, but fortunately his horse had carried him safely to Clancy's village where his wound was tended. Then he explained how his beloved Colleen had sat by his side until he was well enough to stand, and how they'd received word that Dacey's village was under attack and went to help defend the people.

The girls were telling him about their adventures when Colleen walked passed with an empty water-bucket, obviously planning to refill it. As she walked by she gently brushed her free hand against Lewis's elbow. He smiled and took hold of her hand for a moment, before releasing his grinning, blushing betrothed. It was such a tender moment that it even made Brenna blush slightly.

"While I was recovering, I asked Clancy for his blessing," Lewis whispered, "and he gave it. I'm going to ask for her hand as soon as I can get her alone." He seemed almost giddy and there was a great affection in his eyes as he watched his betrothed walk toward the door.

Colleen was just exiting the room when Brenna said, "I just remembered something that I need to do."

"Alright. We'll see you at supper." Lewis said, still looking at the door.

Brenna rolled her eyes and groaned before also exiting the room.

"I hope that we'll have something to celebrate at dinner tonight." Lewis added, winking at Candy happily.

Supper was a late affair of rich mutton stew and warm bread. People received some food and a mug of water, then went to sit wherever they found room in the dining-hall.

Brenna had missed lunch while fighting the fires, so she didn't worry about manners and finished eating in record time while Candy ate slower with ladylike grace.

"Where's Mitch?" Candy asked, looking around.

"Mitch? I'm not sure. I haven't seen him since he saved those two children earlier." Brenna said honestly.

"That was him?" Lewis said in shock.

"Aye." the girls nodded.

"The Northman from the dungeon?" he asked, still in shock.

"Aye." Candy almost chuckled at his disbelief.

"The same one that Brenna stabbed?"

"Aye." Brenna nodded.

"And he's the one who saved those two children?"

"Lewis," said Candy, half in amusement and half in frustration. "There's an awful lot about Mitch that you don't know."

"I'll say." Brenna said softly.

"What do you mean?" asked Lewis.

"Uh, I'll see if I can find him." Brenna said, rising from the carved wooden bench. "I'll be back."

She left the castle and ventured through the town. Many of the houses were just charred shells of what they'd once been. The few people who hadn't been harmed and several that had been cared for were now searching through the remains of their homes.

It saddened her heart to see so much waste and suffering. Brenna quickened her pace, not wanting to see so much grief and sorrow.

Brenna searched for the better part of an hour and still couldn't find Mitch. She went down to the beach hoping to find a clue.

In the last rays of the setting sun she saw him sitting on a rock gazing out at the sea. His shirt was ash-covered and torn, the right sleeve completely gone. His jerkin lay on the sand, little better than a tattered rag.

"Pardon me Miss?" a small voice said, pulling her attention away from Mitch.

Brenna turned and saw the young girl that Mitch had saved.

"Aye lass?" she answered the child. "Elsie, isn't it?"

"Aye ma'am." the child said then paused, staring at the tall woman before her. "You're the Wolf Princess aren't you?" said Elsie in wide-eyed wonder.

"I am indeed." Brenna said proudly.

"When the other children and me play battle, I always say I'm you." Elsie said with a large smile.

"Is that right?" Brenna grinned, kneeling down so that she was eye-level with the child. "I'm most honored."

"Aye Miss." Elsie nodded. "Uh, I was wondering ma'am if you knew where that man what saved me life is?"

"I do actually. He's right over there." Brenna said, nodding to where Mitch sat.

"Thank you kindly ma'am." Elsie said, curtsying politely before walking toward Mitch holding her small back straight and trying to stand as tall as she could. It was then that Brenna noticed Elsie was holding a flower.

The small girl walked over to Mitch and held out the flower. Mitch looked at the flower, then at Elsie, then back to the sea.

"I wanted to thank you for saving me sir." Elsie said. "I don't even know your name."

"Mitch." Mitch said simply.

"Sir Mitch."

"No." Mitch chuckled, shaking his head. "Just Mitch."

"Well, Mitch, I don't know how to thank you for saving me and me brother." the little girl said.

"Just stay safe and that will be thanks enough." Mitch said simply, giving her a kind smile.

"I will." Elsie promised. "Thank you again."

She laid the flower on the ground next to his feet respectfully, then she curtsied and walked back up to what was left of her village.

Mitch's smile slowly faded from his face. He looked down at the flower and saw that it was a large daisy. He picked it up and just held it for a few minutes, turning it over in his hands as he examined the pale petals.

Brenna watched him for a moment before walking over and sitting down next to him.

"Evening," she said.

"Evening," he replied, eyes straight ahead.

"You missed dinner," she commented, looking out to sea as well.

"I wasn't hungry." Mitch shrugged. "I just needed some time to think."

"About what?" she asked gently.

Mitch took the green necklace off of his right arm and held it with the flower, just gazing at them. Then he said with slight grief in his voice, "I was thinking about Babbette, and the baby. How I could save Elsie and her brother from the fire, but not my wife and child."

"That wasn't your fault." Brenna said kindly, turning back to him though his eyes were on the objects in his hands.

Mitch looked back out to sea, as silent and still as a statue. There was a deep sorrow in his eyes that tugged at her heart.

"When you get hungry, come up to the castle." Brenna said, unable to think of anything else to say. Then rising she put a hand on his shoulder to help herself up. Mitch winced and grunted. Brenna suddenly noticed that there was a small burn on his right shoulder.

"Mitch this needs to be looked after." Brenna scolded, hands on her hips.

"I've already washed it with seawater." Mitch said simply.

"It needs to be bandaged!" she stated.

"I'm fine!" he snorted.

"No you're not." Brenna said.

"I am!" he insisted.

"You're not!"

"I am!"

"You're not!"

"Just leave me alone!" he growled, standing up and walking away.

Brenna stalked after him, "If you want any peace from me you have to get that wound looked after!"

"No I don't!" he snapped.

"Aye you do!" she replied.

"Don't!"

"Do!"

"Let's not start that up again." Mitch groaned, quickening his pace.

"I grew up in a family with three other children, I can keep this up all night." Brenna snorted proudly, still following after him.

"So what! I grew up in a family with eight other children!" Mitch called over his shoulder.

Brenna froze in mid-step, "Nine children?" she gasped in shock.

"In the Northland we raise large families." Mitch said, maintaining a steady stride.

"Why?" Brenna called after him, still in shock.

Mitch halted about ten feet in front of her, keeping his back to her. She thought that she saw his head and shoulders slump ever so slightly as he answered.

"Because the more children you have, the better the chance that you'll have one of them outliving you." Mitch said, then broke into an easy jog across the beach.

Brenna watched him go thinking of everything she'd ever heard about Northmen. She knew that they were a warlike people and that the land they lived on was cold and harsh, especially in the winter. But she hadn't thought of how hard it was for their children.

She turned and slowly walked back to the castle, wondering if the harshness of the Northland was why the Northmen sailed down here to do their raiding.

I wish there was a way to resolve this, she thought.

Colleen was carrying some linens into the infirmary when she nearly collided with Lewis.

"Oh, sorry Colleen," he said blushing with embarrassment. "But I am glad to see you."

"No, it, it was my fault." Colleen stuttered, refusing to make eye-contact.

Lewis raised a brow at this and asked, "Uh, I was looking for you. I wanted to know if maybe you'd like to go for moonlit walk on the beach?"

"No thank you. Excuse me." she said, pushing passed him and walking away briskly.

Lewis watched her go. He opened his mouth as if to say something, then closed it again. Candy came forward from where she'd been watching around the corner.

"Did you two have an argument?" she asked, curiosity in her voice.

"What?" he said, looking at her as his brow furrowed.

"It's just that, well, it's like she's afraid of you." Candy said simply.

Lewis shrugged, "I don't know what's wrong. She took care of me until I was well enough to travel. But just this evening, she's started almost avoiding me and acting like, like that."

"Really?" said Candy with a small half smile.

"Really." Lewis said, sounding sad. "Do you think she dislikes me?"

Candy chuckled, "I doubt it. But she might want to see if you like her."

"What do you mean?" he asked, sounding confused.

"She might be testing you, to see if when she withdraws, if you'll pursue her. Some girls are like that. Though I never thought that she was." Candy said thoughtfully. "Or maybe she's just feeling shy for some reason."

"I thought she knew that I loved her. What do you think it is?" Lewis asked still sounding slightly confused.

"I'm not sure. You know her better than I do." Candy said simply. "Though it seems strange that she's suddenly become shy, and only around you. It's a mystery. See you later."

She turned and walked down the hall to the chamber that she and Brenna were sharing with Colleen.

I'll soon solve this problem, Candy thought as she came to the door.

Candy and Brenna were sitting on their bed talking later that night, when Colleen entered the room. She paused at the door, staring at Brenna for moment before speaking.

"Hello. Am I interrupting?" she said in an almost timid voice.

"No, come on in." Candy said in her kindest voice.

Colleen closed the door behind her slowly, her eyes darting to Brenna and then dropping as she walked over to her small cot. She sat down, keeping her gaze on the floor.

"Colleen?" said Candy.

Colleen looked up, a startled expression on her face as she said, "Aye?"

"Would you like to sit with us?" Candy asked, wondering why Colleen looked so frightened.

Colleen's eyes darted once more to Brenna, wide with something like fear. Candy took note of how Brenna's brow lowered.

"I'm tired. I'd much rather go to bed." Colleen said, lying down on her cot.

Candy looked at her sister and noted Brenna's satisfied expression.

"What's going on?" she asked.

"Nothing." Brenna shrugged, trying to seem relaxed.

"Colleen?" Candy asked without taking her eyes from her sister.

Colleen was silent for a moment as Brenna's face grew tight with intensity. Colleen finally said, "Nothing," and rolled so that her back was toward them.

"See?" Brenna said, forcing herself back into a neutral expression.

"Perfectly." Candy snorted. "Brenna, may I have a privet word with you?"

Candy rose from the bed and walked out onto the balcony, Brenna following reluctantly. Out in the open night air the two sisters just stood side by side staring out at the starry expanse as it reflected on the constantly moving ocean. All was quiet except for the rippling waves and whistling breeze.

Candy suddenly turned to Brenna and slapped her hard on the upper arm.

"Ow!" Brenna said, rubbing at her now sore arm.

"What did you do?" it was more of a statement than a question as Candy stood glaring at her sister.

"I didn't do anything." Brenna protested innocently.

"Liar!" Candy accused, putting her hands on her hips in a scolding manner. "Lewis said that she didn't change until this evening. So what did you do to her?"

Brenna was silent then said, "Ouch!" as Candy delivered another smack to her arm.

"Tell me or else!" Candy growled threateningly.

"Or else what?" Brenna smirked.

"Or I'll never speak to you again!" Candy snarled. "Now what did you do?"

Brenna's eyes were downcast as she quietly spoke, "I told her to stay away from Lewis or she'd regret it."

Candy heaved a disappointed sigh, "Why?"

Brenna raised her eyes to meet those of her sister, "Can you tell me honestly that you want Lewis to leave and make a huge hole in the family?"

Candy was silent for a moment before answering, "If he loves her, then aye."

Brenna was dumbstruck.

"Besides," Candy added, "they're betrothed."

Brenna grew hot at these words. "You're one to talk." Brenna snorted.

"What do you mean?" said Candy, stiffening.

"You know exactly what I mean." Brenna almost growled. "You don't love Dylon. Are you still gonna to marry him?"

"I don't see what this has to do with Lewis and Colleen." Candy said, her voice almost trembling.

"But do you have any true feelings for him?" Brenna pressed.

"Dylon is a good man." Candy stated. "He's a very good friend and any woman would be lucky to have him."

"But do you love him?" Brenna growled.

Candy thought for a minute then said, "I do love him. He's like a brother to me."

"But girls don't marry their brothers!" Brenna stated very matter-of-factly, crossing her arms.

"Don't make this about me!" Candy snapped. "There are worse things in this world than marrying Dylon!"

"Aye! Like marrying Lynch!" Brenna growled.

"No! Like driving a wedge between Lewis and Colleen for your own selfish desires!" Candy almost shouted.

"Are you saying that you wouldn't change your betrothal if you could?" Brenna snarled. "Honestly, wouldn't you?"

"I know my place Brenna MacKline!" Candy roared. "Do you?"

Brenna was silent, then looked away from her sister's face. Candy took a deep breath and closed her eyes to calm herself before speaking again.

"Brenna, you need to mend this." Candy said a little softer, tears in her eyes. "Please?"

Brenna, still refusing to look at Candy, turned and stormed back into the chamber. She stomped to the door, Candy calling after her, "Where're you going?"

"I know my place Candace!" Brenna bellowed at her twin. "I'm the Wolf Princess! Who're you?"

Brenna stalked from the room, slamming the door behind her. She stormed down the corridor, fire flashing in her eyes behind the hot tears.

Candy flung herself onto the bed and wept bitterly. Colleen rose from her cot and sat on the edge of the bed.

"I always wanted a sister until tonight, because I'd always quarrel with my brothers." she said kindly, gently stroking Candy's back.

"We've never fought like that before." Candy sobbed.

"I'm sorry for you." Colleen said softly.

Candy sat up and hugged the older girl, "So am I," she sniffed.

Brenna stood on the beach hurling stones into the surf, watching as they splashed.

"Wow," came a voice, "I didn't know you had such a good arm."

She turned to see Mitch coming down the rocky path that led to the castle.

"What do you want?" she groaned turning back to the sea. She tossed a particularly large rock at the waves making a rather dramatic splash in the shallows.

"I just wanted to show you my new bandage." Mitch said, showing his newly bandaged shoulder to her.

Brenna looked at the dressed wound, then threw another stone at the sea. Mitch bent and picked up a rock of his own.

"I heard you and Candy arguing," he said a little more seriously as he hurled the rock into the surf.

Brenna stared at him. "You were spying on us?"

"I didn't have to." Mitch said, throwing another rock into the salty, swirling water. "Your room's right next to the infirmary and I was at the window. I didn't hear all of it, but I heard about what you did."

Brenna sighed, her gaze on the surf, "So, do you think that I was wrong?"

"Depends." Mitch said, tossing another rock into the waves.

"On what?" she asked, turning back to him.

"Does your brother love her?" Mitch said simply.

Brenna was silent.

Mitch chuckled after a while, throwing another pebble into the surf. "It's ironic isn't it?"

"What is?" she couldn't help asking.

"You were down here about an hour ago telling me to tend to my wound, and now Candy's telling you to 'tend' to your brother and his betrothed." Mitch continued, giving another chuckle.

"It's not funny." Brenna said, crossing her arms and turning away.

"Aye, 'tis." Mitch grinned.

"No it's not!" she growled, turning back.

"It is!"

"Is not!"

"It is!" he snickered. "Don't challenge me Princess. I grew up in a family of nine children, I can keep this up all night."

Brenna tried in vain not to smile.

"Is that a smile?" he ginned.

She turned away, but he followed her.

"It is." Mitch said triumphantly, his grin broadening.

"I hate you," she said, trying not to giggle. "You're making me laugh when I don't want to."

Mitch chuckled, "Good!" then added a little more seriously, "You know you need to fix this."

Brenna lowered her eyes, "Aye. But does it have to be tonight?"

Mitch shrugged, "That's up to you. I wouldn't leave it 'til passed breakfast though. Goodnight, Wolf Princess."

"Goodnight, Mitch." Brenna called after him as he walked back up the path toward the castle.

She stared out at the roaring surf and just stood there for a few minutes. It felt so peaceful right there at that moment.

When she did return to the chamber that she shared with Candy and Colleen, she found the two of them asleep on the large bed, leaving the cot empty. Brenna wanted to yell at them for hogging the bed, but restrained herself. Instead she walked over and laid herself down on the cot.

She awoke the next morning and found that she was the only one left in the room. She rose and put on her belt, leaving her sword and scabbard in the room for safekeeping.

She went down to the dining-hall where everybody was eating hot porridge with fresh strawberries, cream, and cold milk.

She filled a bowl for herself, then took up a mug of fresh milk and went off in search of a seat. She found one at the table where Mitch, Nick, Dylon, Candy, Lewis and Colleen were all sitting. She sat down between Mitch and Candy, across from Lewis. Candy scooted away slightly, refusing to look at her sister.

Brenna ate silently, eyes downcast. She was startled as Mitch nudged her with his elbow. She looked up at him and whispered, "What?"

"Don't give me that," he whispered back. "Fix it."

"Alright, fine." Brenna growled, then gulped as she looked up at Lewis, "Uh, Lewis, I need to confess something."

All eyes turned to Brenna, even Candy cocked an ear in her direction.

Brenna looked around, "Are any of you Lewis?"

Everyone but Lewis turned away.

"What is it? Can it wait until after breakfast?" Lewis asked.

"Aye, ooh!" she said, feeling Candy's foot connect with her shin. "I mean no. I, I did something, very foolish."

"What?" he asked. "You didn't punch someone or knock them out of a window again did you?"

"That was only once!" Brenna stated in self-defense.

"It was a stain-glass window! In a church!" said Lewis.

"He was trying to kiss me!" Brenna stated again.

"He was a novice and it was the kiss of charity." Candy put in. "But that's not what she did, is it?"

"No." Brenna admitted, hanging her head.

"Then what did you do?" asked Lewis.

"I told, someone, to stay away from someone else." Brenna said, her voice halting.

"Who?" Lewis asked, a hint of knowing in his voice as his brow lowered.

Colleen perked up her ears but kept her eyes on her food as she listened intently.

Brenna was silent.

"Ooh!" Candy and Mitch both elbowed her at the same time. She glared at the two people on either side of her, then looked into her brother's dark eyes before dropping her gaze and admitting softly, "Colleen."

"Who'd you tell her to stay away from?" he pressed, a sharp edge in his voice.

Brenna swallowed hard, "You."

This was the first time that Mitch had ever seen the Wolf Princess look so timid. He himself even felt a slight shiver as he watched Lewis glare coldly at Brenna, fire flashing in his eyes.

"I'm sorry." Brenna said sadly, watching as her elder brother stood up. "Where are you going?"

Lewis didn't answer or even look back as he stalked away angrily, his fists clenched at his sides.

Candy elbowed Brenna again.

"What now?" Brenna whined.

"Don't you have something to say to Colleen?" asked Candy, her eyes boring into Brenna's.

Brenna looked at Colleen who was sitting and just staring at her half-eaten bowl of porridge.

The Wolf Princess gave her sister a pleading look, but Candy sent her such a stern glare that it caused Brenna to say in a low voice, "I'm sorry Colleen."

"Apology accepted Brenna, thank you." Colleen said graciously.

Brenna gobbled down her food hastily, then left the table with her cheeks burning. She went to the stables and began grooming Lightningbolt to cheer herself up.

Candy entered the old barn after a while and started brushing Dutchess's coat. They were both silent.

"So, are we friends again?" Brenna finally asked.

"Aye." Candy smiled. "Thank you."

"Whatever." Brenna snorted. "Any word on where we're headed to next?" she asked a little softer.

"Aye." Candy sighed, then paused.

"And?" asked Brenna, raising a brow.

"Blair's." Candy said calmly.

Brenna's eyes were wide, "What?"

"I'm sorry Brenna, but Blair has a huge army." Candy said sympathetically. "Between Clancy, Dacey and Erin there're only sixteen-hundred warriors. Blair will have more. Where're you going?"

"I need some time alone." Brenna snarled as she stormed out of the stable, passing Nick, Dylon and Mitch.

"What was that all about?" asked Nick.

"Oh, she's just upset about going to Blair and Flanna's." Candy sighed.

"Why should that bother her?" asked Mitch.

Dylon started to snicker and Candy's face was strained to keep from smiling as she scolded him, "Dylon that's not nice. Now stop it."

"What is it?" asked Nick.

"That's where Lynch lives." Dylon said in a teasing tone.

"Oh do shut up Dylon." Candy groaned. "It's not funny."

"You're right. It's hilarious!" Dylon burst out laughing only to be silenced by swift smack on his arm from Candy.

"Hold on. Who's, what's-his-name?" Mitch asked in a rather confused voice, raising a brow in interest.

"Lynch." Candy corrected, then quickly silenced Dylon with a glare. "He's Blair and Flanna's son."

"Why should that bother Brenna?" asked Mitch, thoroughly interested now.

"Because," Candy sighed, "he's Brenna's betrothed."

Mitch's brow shot upward. This was the first that he'd heard of Brenna being betrothed. Nick seemed surprised as well, saying nothing for a moment.

"Doesn't she love him?" Nick asked when at last he'd recovered from the shock.

Mitch listened intently, wondering what sort of man was betrothed to the Wolf Princess.

"No." Candy said, shaking her head sadly. "She doesn't care for him at all, and I don't blame her."

"Is he an unkind man?" Nick said, scratching his head.

"He's not unkind, but he's rather, uhm." Candy's voice trailed off as she thought of how best to describe Brenna's betrothed.

"He's as annoying as a finger in the eye." Dylon snorted.

"Really?" said Nick, trying not to laugh at Dylon's bluntness. "He's that bad?"

"Worse!" Dylon chuckled.

"Oh, you two are horrid." Candy growled, trying in vain to be angry with the jocular young men. "Just leave Brenna alone, all right?"

An amused murmur of agreement came from the three lads, though Mitch seemed half distracted.

"Are you betrothed Candy?" he asked after a few seconds, his curiosity getting the better of him.

Dylon's countenance grew serious and he put his arm around Candy's shoulders, almost possessively as his eyes narrowed at the Northman. Nick coughed uncomfortably, almost like a warning, and Candy's cheeks turned beet-red with embarrassment as she lowered her eyes.

"Dylon and I, have been betrothed since I was about six months old." Candy said haltingly.

Mitch met Dylon's narrowed gaze with his own as he raised his chin. He glanced at Candy, then back at Dylon. Mitch drew himself up to his full height and said, "Congratulations." Then he tightened his jaw before adding rather smugly, "I hope that you two are happier than Brenna is."

"We are!" Dylon almost snapped at him.

Mitch raised a brow and gave Dylon a rather smug though small grin before turning to go. Nick cleared his throat as he turned to follow, moving his stave back and forth in front of him to make certain that the way was clear.

Dylon and Candy just stood there for a few seconds alone before she shrugged off his arm.

"I think I should go find Brenna." Candy said softly, moving toward the door and leaving Dylon alone in the stable.

CHAPTER EIGHTEEN
LYNCH; THE BETROTHED OF THE WOLF PRINCESS

After Candy found Brenna it was announced that they would be leaving for Blair's village directly after lunch, which made Brenna all the more irritable. Her mood only darkened as the day went on.

Lunch consisted of fresh venison stewed with potatoes, carrots and onions in a rich gravy, with warm bread for dipping and sweet cider to wash it down.

As soon as the meal ended everybody saddled their horses, except for Brenna who insisted on continuing to ride bare back. Mitch groaned slightly as he climbed up behind her, though it wasn't as painful as when he'd first started riding saddle-free.

They arrived at the village shortly before suppertime. As they all dismounted in the courtyard Mitch noted that Brenna's eyes were constantly darting here, there and everywhere.

"Something wrong?" he asked, trying not to smile.

Brenna glared at him, "Candy told you didn't she?"

"Told me what?" Mitch chuckled.

But Brenna didn't answer as someone suddenly yelled from across the courtyard in a gleeful voice, "Brennaboo!"

They all turned in the direction of the one who was yelling. Mitch beheld a young man who was about his own age, with a messy mop of blond hair atop his head and a large smile on his angular face. He was running toward them, arms outstretched.

Brenna rolled her eyes and heaved an annoyed sigh. As the young man closed in, it was obvious that he intended to hug Brenna. Just before he reached her, the Wolf Princess dodged to one side and put out her leg, tripping him. The young man landed with a loud 'thud' as he hit the ground.

To Mitch's amazement the lad rose smiling at Brenna. Brushing himself off he said, "You're warming up to me. I can tell. You only tripped me instead of throwing me. That's my Brennaboo."

Lynch's servant Delaney stood nearby rolling his eyes at his young master, who was dusting himself off.

He came forward, arms outstretched, lips puckered and eyes closed. Brenna put up her hand and grabbed his face roughly. The young man's eyes went wide with shock, his arms still outstretched.

"Lynch!" Brenna snarled. "Let's go over the rules, again! No pet-names! No hugging! No kissing! No signs of physical affection what-so-ever! And most important, no, I mean No Brennaboo! Do I make myself clear?"

Lynch nodded fearfully and said, rather muffled by Brenna's hand, "Aye ma'am."

"Good!" Brenna nearly snarled as she shoved him, then turned and stomped away angrily, Candy following in order to calm her down.

Lynch landed on his back at least three feet from where he'd been standing a few seconds earlier. Lynch coughed, then raised himself up on one elbow as he watched Brenna go.

"What a woman," he whistled. "I like 'em fiery."

Mitch looked at Dylon with a surprised expression. Dylon shrugged as if to say **'get used to it, this happens all the time.'**

"How can you be in love with her?" asked Nick. "It sounds like she shoved you at least three feet."

"But that just proves it. Last time she threw me five feet. I'm winning her over." Lynch grinned, lying back down and folding his arms behind his head as he gazed skyward dreamily.

Mitch looked at Dylon again, who was rolling his eyes, and Nick tilted his head in their direction looking confused.

"Don't listen to him." Dylon shrugged, shaking his head. "She's just distressed about her family."

"Otherwise it would've been nine feet." Lewis's voice came from their right.

Dylon walked over and shook hands with him. Lewis seemed better tempered than he had at breakfast, though he only nodded at Mitch while he shook hands with Nick. Mitch returned the nod, knowing that though they weren't friends there was a mutual respect between them.

Lynch lay where he was, still smiling at the sky as he heaved a contented sigh, "Ah, Brennaboo."

The four young men who were standing nearby walked off in the same direction that the girls had taken, some shaking their heads and others snickering at Lynch's behavior.

After a fine dinner of roast-beef and fresh bread, Brenna, Lewis and Candy all thanked Blair and Flanna for their hospitality, then asked for their aid in recovering Castle MacKline.

Blair turned to his son Lynch, who was gazing at Brenna in a rather lovesick way, and said, "Lynch, gather the warriors and tell them to prepare for war. We leave at dawn."

"Can't Delaney do it?" Lynch asked, obviously not wanting to leave.

"I'd be happy to sir." Delaney put in, stepping forward from where he stood by the open doorway.

"I believe I asked my son to do it." Blair MacKline said, his tone dictating that he was not to be questioned in any way.

Lynch left reluctantly, eyeing Mitch suspiciously since the young Northman was sitting next to Brenna. Mitch stared back, then rolled his eyes as Brenna gave an unhappy grunt.

Delaney nodded to Blair once before exiting the dining-hall to follow his young master.

"You'll really help us?" Lewis said in disbelief.

"Aye." Blair said simply, then added as he glanced at the Wolf Princess, "My family has a stake in this as well."

Brenna wrinkled her nose at him, knowing that the laird was thinking about the dowry Lynch would recieve upon marrying her.

I'm not a piece of property! she thought bitterly, glaring as she crossed her arms to show Blair her displeasure. She wanted to throw her goblet of cider at him when the laird's only reaction was to smirk at her.

"Well, let's make some plans." Lewis said, wanting to change the subject.

The remainder of the day was spent preparing to be ready to leave at sunrise. Before nightfall the rest of the clans arrived. Brenna and Lewis added up the troops and found that all together they had a fine army of five-thousand people.

All of the Clan Leaders moved into the great hall of Blair's castle to talk, closely followed by their heirs, the three eldest MacKline children, Mitch and Nick. As Allen, Clancy, Dacey, Blair, Erin, Harkin, Garvey and Keelan all took seats at the head table, they began debating about who should lead the army. Brenna stood and raised her right hand for silence. When the hall was quiet, she said, "I think Lewis should lead. The castle is his inheritance and it's our family and friends who're being held captive."

"I agree." Candy and Mitch proclaimed together, standing up at the same moment.

"As do I." Nick put in. "I may be blind, but I can see that he's the right man for the job."

A murmur of agreement ran around the table of Clan Leaders. Then Allen rose and asked Lewis to stand. Lewis did as he was bid, a questioning and somewhat nervous look on his face, but he kept his back straight and behaved as a true son of a laird.

"Lewis MacKline, you stand before eight lairds, the leaders of eight mighty clans and one day you will join us. Tomorrow, you will face a foe in order to win back your rightful inheritance. Come forward and kneel." Allen said, extending a hand to him. "And hand me your sword."

Lewis did so and watched as his father's eldest brother held the blade high, then spoke, "Lewis of Castle MacKline, do you vow to,"

"Wait." Lewis interrupted.

A murmur of confusion spread through the room until Allen held up his right hand for silence as Brenna had done then looked down at his nephew.

"My father told me about this vow and I think that my sisters should be allowed to take it as well." Lewis explained.

All of the lairds looked at one another.

"Are you certain lad?" asked Allen.

"Aye." Lewis nodded.

Allen looked over his shoulder for approval. There was the sound soft whispering and debating. After what felt like a long time Clancy stood and said, "After some deliberation, we have come to the unanimous decision that the Wolf Princess and her sister have as much right to take this vow as their elder brother."

There was slight cheering as Brenna and Candy came forward at Allen's bidding and knelt on either side of their brother. Lewis kept his eyes straight ahead, but they could both tell that he was glad to have them beside him. Then the room went silent once more.

CHAPTER NINETEEN
THE VOW OF THE CLANS

"Do you vow to be just in all of your decisions, especially those involving the Clans? To be loyal and true in the face of danger? To be good warriors? And above all, to defend those who are weak and to never attack the ones who are weaker than yourself? Do you vow, upon your honor?" Allen said, touching the sword flat to Lewis's right shoulder.

"Aye." Lewis said, eyes fixed on those of his uncle. He then bowed his head as Allen raised the sword and touched it to Lewis's left shoulder.

Then Allen rested the sword on Candy's right shoulder.

"Do you vow this?" he asked.

"Aye." Candy answered, then bowed her head so that he could move the blade to her left shoulder.

"Do you vow this?" Allen asked, resting the flat of the sword on the Wolf Princess's right shoulder.

"Aye." Brenna said, then lowered her head as her uncle raised the weapon then gently touched her left shoulder with it.

"Rise, all of you." Allen said, pride evident in his voice.

The three eldest children of Laird and Lady MacKline rose from where they knelt and stood before the Clan Leaders.

"You now stand amongst equals. From this point on you will sit with us at all of the Clan gatherings when we make decisions." Allen announced, then the entire room burst into applause.

Nigel and Conlan, who were sitting with Nick, Mitch and Dylon, stood and howled gaining a small smile from Brenna.

Dylon nudged Mitch and Nick, then told them, "You're both very fortunate to witness this event. We've never had anyone outside of the Clans present for one of these."

"What just happened?" asked Mitch.

Conlan turned to him, "They've just been dubbed worthy of being Clan Leaders. They're the first in our generation to be given such an honor."

Mitch watched as Allen returned the sword to Lewis, who held it aloft causing the crowd to cheer even louder.

Lewis looked around, beaming with pride, then blushed to the roots of his hair when he saw Colleen watching from the doorway into the great hall. She was also beaming with pride, but then she blushed and quickly exited the room. At that moment Lewis felt something in his chest, something different, and all he wanted was to go after her.

When the applause finally died down, Lewis, Brenna and Candy all sat down at the long table on the dais with the Clan Leaders.

"Now," said Erin, "to the business of forming a plan."

"Aye." Dacey said. "How do we get in?"

"We could rush the gate if the it's still splintered." Clancy offered thoughtfully.

"I doubt it." Brenna snorted. "If ole Griffy Cray is half as intelligent as I think he is, he's probably rebuilt it by now."

"Aye." Candy agreed. "He probably knows that we're rallying the Clans to face him."

"We can't simply charge and storm the walls unless we have a way in." Harkin said. "Any ideas?"

There was silence. Everyone's thoughts were focused on the main gate and how to get through it. Mitch stood up cautiously and all eyes turned to him, making him even more uneasy.

"I know that I have no right to speak here, but I think I know how to get in." the Northman said.

"How?" Lewis asked curiously.

"The escape tunnel." Mitch shrugged.

A murmur ran through the room, then the Clan Leaders all nodded their agreement, including its newest and youngest members. Brenna and Candy both smiled at Mitch, causing him to blush slightly as he reclaimed his seat. Lewis nodded to him again, this time with something like admiration shining in his dark eyes. Mitch nodded back respectfully.

It was decided that somebody would take about a hundred men and enter through the tunnel. Once inside the group would signal the main army to charge, then the inside men would open the gate and run down to the dungeon to release all of the prisoners, thus adding to their numbers.

Several people volunteered to lead the way into the tunnel, one of which was Candy. After some debate she won out, under the condition that Dylon helped her to lead, a decision that made both Dylon and Candy blush slightly.

Next it was discussed how to signal the main group.

"Dawn and Marie." Nick said.

"What?" said Dylon.

"They can fly over the castle and look down, then do a flip or a summersault to signal everybody-else outside." Nick explained. "Someone can put out a piece of cloth or something when it's time."

This was considered to be a good plan by everyone.

"Brenna and I will be at the front," said Lewis, "to distract Griff Cray."

Brenna looked at her elder brother, then smiled like a child who had just been offered a special toy. "Really?"

Lewis simply nodded. He had truly forgiven her for what she'd said to Colleen.

"Is that safe?" asked Keelan.

"I'm the whole reason that he attacked the castle." Brenna said, lowering her eyes. "He wants me. So if I'm outside and in front it'll draw his full attention. Candy and her group will have a better chance then." her tone became dangerous as she added, "But one thing must be made clear, once we're in, nobody comes between me and Griffy. Nobody."

They all stared at her, seeing the fire of battle in her eyes.

"He's mine." the Wolf Princess said simply.

"But why?" asked Lewis, who was the only one that dared to ask.

"He wants me on his side. If I defeat him he'll have to retreat with his men." Brenna explained.

"Can you beat him?" Candy asked, concern in her voice.

Brenna swallowed before answering, "I faced him in the woods, I can do it again, and this time I'm ready for him."

Lynch came in and informed them that the army would be ready to march within an hour, so being ready by dawn wasn't a problem.

The Clan Leaders decided that they should march through the night so that they'd arrive at Castle MacKline by sunrise. Nick knew of some caves in the woods where he'd lived once that the entire army could sleep in before the attack.

The hall emptied and everybody went to prepare for the trip.

Mitch found Brenna in the stables brushing Lightningbolt's coat. She seemed distracted.

"Something wrong?" he asked kindly, leaning against the stall-door.

"No," she said quickly, though not angrily.

"Really?" he said skeptically.

Brenna turned to look at him, then dropped her gaze, "Promise not to tell anyone?"

"Of course." Mitch promised.

Brenna sighed uneasily, "I, I'm afraid. When I face Griff Cray what if I can't beat him? What if he defeats me?"

"You faced him before." Mitch said encouragingly.

"I know. But if Dawn hadn't started that rockslide, I don't know what would've happened." Brenna said, almost fearfully. "What if I can't do it Mitch?"

"You won't know unless you try." Mitch shrugged.

Lynch entered the stable smiling, though the smile vanished when he saw that Brenna and Mitch had been speaking alone in the stable.

"Northman," he said loudly.

"It's Mitch actually." Mitch corrected.

"Northman, I'd like to speak alone with my betrothed." Lynch said with a cold edge in his voice.

"Anything you want to say to me you can say in front of Mitch." Brenna snapped, not wanting to be left alone with Lynch.

Lynch narrowed his eyes at Mitch and walked passed him, intentionally knocking into Mitch's shoulder with his own. Lynch winced in pain, realizing that Mitch's muscles were more solid than his own.

"I have a gift for you my beloved." Lynch said, trying not to grit his teeth as he grinned at Brenna.

"What did I say about pet-names?" Brenna growled, coming out of Lightningbolt's stall.

"Just look in that stall." Lynch said, gesturing at another stall.

Brenna looked and saw a fine palomino mare with four white stockings, a diamond shaped star and a snip on the very tip of her velvety nose.

"Father said that she's the best he's seen in years and told me that I should give her to you." Lynch stated proudly. "So she's yours."

Brenna reached across the door and touched the horse's face.

"She's beautiful. Thank you." Brenna said blankly. "So I can do as I please with her?"

"Anything you wish will only make me love you more my darling." Lynch said dreamily.

Brenna cringed, then asked, "What's her name?"

"Whatever you want to call her." Lynch sighed happily.

"Hmm, what would you call her Mitch?" Brenna said smugly.

Mitch pushed passed Lynch and looked at the mare.

"Well, she looks fast. If it was up to me, I'd call her Thunderstorm." Mitch said thoughtfully.

"Then Thunderstorm it is, 'cause she's yours." Brenna smiled.

Both of the young men were stunned.

"What?" said Mitch in a disbelieving tone.

"What're you doing my dove?" Lynch whined.

"I like my horse and I won't demean him by taking another, and Mitch saved my life several times in the last few days." Brenna stated firmly.

"But this mare is worth so much." Lynch complained. "A fortune."

"Are you saying that my Lightningbolt isn't worth a fortune?" Brenna snarled. "Or my life?"

"Oh no my beloved rose."

"What did I say about pet-names?" she growled, taking a threatening step toward him. "Just get away! Go!"

Lynch ran from the stables like a frightened dog with his tail between his legs.

"Good riddance." Brenna said, sounding relieved. "I thought he'd never leave."

"Why are you so nasty to him? I think he really likes you." Mitch said, stroking Thunderstorm's soft neck.

"He likes me about as much as I like him." Brenna almost snorted. "His father knows that I have a fine dowry and he's somehow convinced Lynch that we're perfect for each other."

"Are you sure?" asked Mitch.

"Aye. I can't even get along with him as a friend. Each time we touch it makes me feel ill. That's not love." Brenna told him.

"I can't disagree with you on that." Mitch said, scratching behind the mare's gold colored ears.

"She really is yours." Brenna said kindly.

"Truly?" he said in disbelief.

"Aye," she said simply.

"But she's a laird's horse." Mitch pointed out.

"So what? She's yours now." Brenna shrugged. "I don't need another horse anyway. All that would do is make Lightningbolt jealous."

Mitch hugged the mare's neck as she stuck her head out of the stall-door.

"Thank you," he said gratefully, burying his face in the cream colored mane.

Colleen was helping to wash the dinner plates in the large underground kitchen. She was doing a fine job despite the fact that her thoughts were elsewhere at the moment.

She was remembering how well she and Lewis had gotten along when they were children. They'd been as close as two people could be, but in the last few years she'd been uncertain about how to approach him. He was so tall, handsome and muscular now.

Colleen had learned one of the hard facts of life. When you're a child you love everyone as a friend or a family-member, but as an adult love between a man and a woman is added to these. This emotion was new and strange to her, even a little frightening. It made her feel shy whenever he was present. They'd kissed more than once, but even that didn't take away the shyness that she felt. She couldn't stand the thought of being with any other man, but she still blushed whenever she thought about being married to him.

She was so deep in thought that she didn't see or hear when Lewis entered the underground kitchen. Nor did she notice how all of the other people in the room ceased working and looked at him.

Lewis nodded toward the stairs behind him and all of them filed out, leaving Lewis and Colleen alone. Lewis strolled over to stand next to Colleen. He had a rose in his hand which he offered to her.

Colleen jumped, feeling startled when she saw him.

"Lewis!" she exclaimed. "What're you doing down here?"

"I wanted to give you this before I leave." Lewis said, feeling sorry that he'd startled her.

Colleen blinked in surprise, "You're leaving? Tonight?"

Lewis nodded, "Aye."

"But, I thought," her voice trailed off.

Lewis held out the flower. Colleen seemed to take notice it for the first time. She quickly dried her hands then gracefully accepted the rose. She raised it to her nose. She sighed, then looked at Lewis tenderly, tears in her eyes as she spoke.

"Thank you Lewis. You remembered." she smiled.

"How could I forget." Lewis smiled back. "It was that day you cut your knee after we'd gone tree-climbing wasn't it."

"You wiped away the blood then hugged me until I stopped crying." Colleen added, blushing deeply.

"And you told me that someday, the man that you'd marry would bring you a red rose to show his love." Lewis's cheeks were turning as red as the rose while he spoke. "Colleen, I'm about to go to war, and this is not the time to speak of love," he continued slowly, "but I need to know if when I return, if you would be willing to,"

Colleen dropped her gaze and lightly bit her lower lip as he spoke, then jumped, "Ow."

"What happened?" Lewis asked, feeling concerned.

"Nothing, I just pricked my finger." Colleen said, examining her injured digit.

"Let me see." Lewis said, gently taking her hand in his.

A small thorn stood erect in the very tip of her longest finger, a tiny bead of crimson building around it. Lewis gently took the thorn between his index finger and thumb, then looked at Colleen.

"Put your hand on my shoulder," he instructed her.

She obeyed.

"When I tell you to, squeeze my shoulder as hard as you can. Alright?" he said.

Colleen nodded and closed her eyes.

"Now." Lewis said kindly.

Colleen applied pressure to his shoulder and Lewis pulled the thorn free of her flesh.

"You can open your eyes now." Lewis said, holding up the thorn proudly.

"Thank you." Colleen said, then blushed to the roots of her hair as he kissed the tiny wound. She'd pulled thorns from her hands on her own already and had experienced higher levels of pain, but she couldn't bring herself to tell Lewis that his chivalry wasn't necesary.

"Are you sure you're alright?" he asked, his eyes fixed on hers.

"Aye," she said breathlessly.

Some instinct within him caused Lewis to reach up and stroke her cheek. Colleen leaned her cheek into his palm, closing her eyes and giving a small sigh of contentment. She opened them again and gazed lovingly at him.

Lewis slowly began to close the distance between them, his eyes darting back and forth between her eyes and lips. He couldn't help thinking that if his heart pounded any harder it would leap straight out of his chest.

Colleen thought that she was going to faint or wake up to find that this had all been a dream. She couldn't decide which was worse.

They were almost touching. For an instant Colleen was certain that she could feel his lips brushing hers.

"Lewis we're ready to, whoops!" Candy said, stopping at the bottom step. She just stood there staring at them, then asked, "Should I leave?"

The two young people both raised a brow at her.

"All right then." Candy said. "I just wanted to tell Lewis that we're ready to go. Bye."

Lewis and Colleen both gave a small sigh of relief as she turned to go. Lewis wanted to crawl into a hole and die as Candy turned back and added with an approving smile, "Oh, and congratulations on your engagement." Then she turned and quickly ascended the stairs.

Even after she was gone Lewis and Colleen both just stood there, silent and blushing deep shades of crimson. Finally Lewis said, "I'm sorry."

"It's not your fault." Colleen said kindly. "But for what it's worth, I'm sure that the answer to your question will be to your liking."

Lewis smiled as he lowered his eyes.

"Maybe you should go." she said kindly, gently touching his arm.

Lewis nodded, raising his eyes to meet her loving gaze, "I hope to see you soon."

They embraced then looked at each other with great tenderness. They would've kissed if they hadn't heard Brenna suddenly yell down the stairs, "Are you two done smooching yet? We're waiting!"

Obviously Candy and Brenna had been talking. Lewis rolled his eyes.

"Well, good-bye," he said, turning to go.

"Lewis?"

"Aye?" he said, turning back.

"Be careful." Colleen said softly.

"I will." Lewis promised.

It was a long ride to Nick's caves. Lewis was silent, his thoughts on Colleen. Brenna rode between Mitch on Thunderstorm and Candy and Nick on Dutchess. Dylon rode on the other side of Candy, while Dawn and Marie led the group to the caves.

It was late in the evening when they finally reached their destination. Nick had been correct, the caves were quite large and spacious. They made camp, watered their horses and bedded down for the night.

Brenna had trouble sleeping, her thoughts on the coming battle. She rose and went to Murky River to get a drink, hoping to calm her nerves. She knelt and scooped up handfuls of water, drinking deeply. She splashed some water on her face to refresh herself.

She looked up and saw Mitch across the river with Thunderstorm. They didn't seem to know that she was there. She watched as the man and horse stood together, acting like old friends.

Mitch stroked the mare's beautiful mane, then said softly, "You know, I had a horse once. His name was Thunder. He was the best stallion I'd ever seen. But he was shot out from under me in the land just north of here. I won't let you get shot out from under me tomorrow. That's a promise girl."

Brenna rose from the riverbank, unintentionally drawing Mitch's attention. She froze and felt her cheeks reddening.

"I came for a drink," she explained, watching as he mounted up.

Mitch rode across the river to where she stood. He looked down at her and said, "Still having doubts about tomorrow?"

Brenna lowered her eyes in shame then said, "What if Griff is right? What if I do have an evil destiny?"

"It's been my experience that you make your own destiny. Whether a person is good or evil is their decision." Mitch said, wisdom in his voice.

"I suppose so." Brenna sighed glumly.

Mitch thought for a moment, then leaned forward a little. "Wanna go for a ride?" he asked.

She looked up, half-surprised, then asked, "Really?" with childlike-wonder in her voice.

Mitch smiled, nodded and extended a hand to her. She took it and he swung her up behind him.

"Hold on tight." he said.

They were off at a full gallop, the wind whipping through their hair. They didn't know why, but they both started laughing.

Candy watched them go from where she sat at the mouth of a cave. She sighed, her mind also troubled.

"Are you alright?" came Nick's voice from behind her.

"How'd you know I was here?" she asked.

"I could hear you breathing heavily, and that suggests that you're not feeling well." Nick explained. "So what's wrong?"

"I'm worried." she admitted.

"About what?" he asked sitting down next to her.

"About tomorrow. What if something goes wrong?" she said fearfully. "What if we get captured? What if we don't get the gate open in time? What if,"

"What if the sky falls and lands on your head?" Nick interrupted. "You'd get the worst headache in history."

They both chuckled.

"Listen Candy," he said kindly, "You can say 'what if' and worry until your hair turns gray. But what good would it do?"

Candy thought for a minute, then said simply, "None."

"Exactly." Nick smiled. "It doesn't matter how much you worry. All you can do is your absolute best. What's gonna happen, is gonna happen."

"Then why should we even go? We're most likely going to lose." Candy asked, almost sobbing.

"You won't know unless you try." Nick said simply. "I was scared the first time that I went into the swamp. But I did it."

"How?" she sniffed. "Where do you get the courage?"

"By accepting that what comes, comes." he shrugged. "Courage isn't the absence of fear, it's not being overcome by it."

They sat in silence for a while, just listening as the crickets in the woods chirped, the river babbled and the leaves rustled in the breeze.

Candy reached over and brushed his hand with her own. Nick opened his hand to hers and lightly squeezed it. Then he felt her head resting on his shoulder. It felt strangely good. He leaned his head against hers and felt her squeeze his hand a little harder.

Brenna and Mitch had made a wide circle around the caves, and were now back where they'd started. Thunderstorm splashed into the river, slowing her pace to an easy trot. Brenna and Mitch were still laughing. Thunderstorm stopped and snorted before taking a drink.

The two young people dismounted and Mitch began playfully chasing Brenna. He caught her around the waist and started tickling her mercilessly.

"Aah! Stop!" she squealed.

Mitch finally stood up straight, hands on his hips and asked, "Are you still afraid about tomorrow?"

Brenna took a deep breath and sighed, "Aye. But not as much as before."

"Good." he grinned.

"And I'll promise you this," she continued, "if we win tomorrow, if we survive the skirmish, I'll kiss you."

Mitch stared at her in disbelief, "Really?"

Brenna stepped a little closer, smiling at him while biting her lower-lip. Mitch's eyes widened as she brought her face close to his, then she grabbed him roughly by the shirt-collar and said, suddenly glaring, "And if you tell anyone I said that, I'll beat you into the ground. Understood?"

Mitch smiled, then nodded.

"Good." she said. "See you in the morning Mitch. And thanks."

"Goodnight." Mitch called after her, watching as she walked over toward the cave she'd been sleeping in.

Brenna was worn out now. She laid back down on her mat and looked over at Candy, who was lying by her side. Candy felt much better after her conversation with Nick and was able to sleep now, but she opened her eyes when Brenna said her name.

"Hmm?" Candy sighed.

"Promise me that you'll be careful tomorrow." Brenna said softly. "I don't know what I'd do if anything happened to you."

"I'll promise if you will." Candy whispered.

"Alright. Spit shake?" said Brenna.

"Ew!" Candy wrinkled her nose.

"Alright, just shake then."

The two of them shook hands heartily, or at least as heartily as they could while lying on their sides.

"Hey, look. Our stars are out tonight." Candy whispered, pointing to the mouth of the cave.

"Aye, they are." Brenna smiled, looking heavenward.

There the two stars were. Side by side as always, Dark and Bright.

"Goodnight Candy." Brenna yawned, closing her eyes and still facing the sky.

"Goodnight. Oh, and Brenna?"

"Mm, what?" Brenna said without opening her eyes.

"Go easy on the Raves tomorrow. I want a chance at 'em too. Alright?" Candy grinned.

"I'll do my best, but I'm not promising anything." the Wolf Princess chuckled, and was lost in slumber until morning.

CHAPTER TWENTY

THE GREAT BATTLE FOR

CASTLE MACKLINE

"Konroy? Konroy?" came Erica's voice from outside of the cell. The sound of his name being called stirred him into wakefulness.

"Hmm, what?" he moaned, sitting up painfully.

"I brought you some more water and little breakfast." she explained. "How's your back?"

Konroy winced as he flexed his scared back. Until two days ago his back had been smooth and whole, but now he bore a long scar that started under his left shoulder blade and stretched a foot long, pointing like a finger toward his right hip. He'd received this wound as thanks after marking on the map where to find his sisters.

The wound had burned the previous day, but this morning, amazingly, it only ached. It throbbed though each time he flexed, but he knew that his mother was listening and didn't want Erica to see his pain, so he said, "It's better today."

Laird MacKline came to the bars, "Any word on my daughters?"

Erica shook her head sadly, "None Milaird. The party that was sent out after the Wolf Princess never returned. Just their steeds."

"They were riderless?" asked the laird.

"Aye sire." Erica said hopefully. "I don't think the princesses showed any mercy."

Lady MacKline sniffed in the back of the cell.

"Is she alright?" Erica whispered.

"She's been in despair ever since we got the news about Lewis." Konroy replied, lowering his gaze sadly.

Erica handed them the food and water through the bars, then said, "I pray that her Ladyship recovers swiftly. Oh and here."

Konroy raised a brow as Erica stood and unfastened something. There was a resounding 'Clang' and a 'Clatter.' Father and son beheld two sword-belts on the floor. Their sword-belts. One held an axe, the other a sword. She slid them through the bars to their rightful owners.

"Hide them under the straw until later. The other maids and I have been sneaking weapons under our skirts to the warriors in the cells all morning while delivering their food." Erica explained in a whispering tone. "I know where the keys are too. When the time is right, I'll let you out. If that's alright with you Milaird?"

Laird MacKline shook his head in admiration, "Aye. You're a marvel lass. If all goes well, you will be granted your freedom."

Erica's heart leapt. Freedom? She felt such joy at the very thought. The MacKlines hadn't been unkind to her, but to be a free woman, it sounded almost too good to be true. She met Konroy's gaze, and they both blushed as they lowered their eyes.

"I have to go before I'm missed." she said, turning. "But I'll be back."

Konroy watched her go and sighed, leaning his head against the bars. He cleared his throat and sat up straight when he caught sight of his father's knowing smile.

The sentries on the wall above the newly built gate were dozing in the first rays of light. It was warm and they'd been on duty for several hours. Their eyes drooped and their heads nodded forward. One began to lightly snore, but that didn't last long.

There came a sound like thunder from the open land in front of the castle. The three men on the wall rubbed their eyes and stood to look out toward the woods. They all gasped when they saw what was making the thunderous sound.

Brenna and Lewis were in the lead, four-thousand, nine-hundred troops on horseback following them. Lewis raised his left hand and the company halted. Lewis and Brenna continued forward until they were halfway between the army and the castle.

"You there, on the wall, I want to talk to your master!" Lewis bellowed.

"Why should my master bother with you?" roared Vrant, who had come up onto the battlement to see what all of the noise was about.

Brenna drew her sword and held it so that the sun reflected off of it. She angled it just right and the light hit Vrant in the face, momentarily blinding him.

"Tell Lady Griffy what's-it to come and atone for his sins. Now!" she yelled at the top of her voice. "The Wolf Princess and her brother have a bone to pick with him!"

Vrant blinked at them.

Lewis drew his own sword and held it the same way that his sister had, then yelled, "GO!"

Vrant turned and ran to fetch his master.

Brenna and Lewis sheathed their swords and looked at each other. They started snickering like two naughty children.

"Did you see how scared he was?" Brenna giggled.

Lewis chuckled as he nodded.

Candy and the group of one-hundred warriors were deep inside of the tunnel. They'd come ahead of the main party and slipped unnoticed into the mouth of the hidden tunnel.

Candy opened the small door into the stable just a crack and looked around. There were some men saddling harpusia. The minutes crept by as the beasts were saddled and led out into the courtyard. When the stable was empty, Candy and the rest filed in and hid in various places.

Candy got as near to the mouth of the stable as she dared and peaked out into the courtyard. About a hundred men had mounted up and were sitting straight in the saddle ready to ride into the sky at a moment's notice.

Nick sat next to her, well out of sight.

"Are we ready?" he asked, scooting a little closer.

"Not if those riders and creatures don't move." she whispered. "There're so many of them."

Candy and Nick were sitting a little too close for Dylon's liking. He quickly moved over and sat between them.

"I wonder what they're waiting for?" Dylon said casually.

"Shh. Griff Cray's coming, and so is Dritt." Candy gasped, ducking though she didn't need to. Fear gripped her as the image of Dritt chasing her in the swamp came back to her. Hatred and revenge burned in his one good eye.

Griff and Dritt went up on the wall and looked out at the two figures on horseback. Brenna recognized Griff the moment that she saw him.

"So, have you reconsidered my offer Princess?" Griff smirked.

"Never!" Brenna bellowed. "I've come to issue a challenge with my brother Lewis."

Griff fought to keep himself calm. That lad was supposed to be dead and decaying in the forest somewhere. Yet there he was by the Wolf Princess's side, looking every bit as fierce as she did.

Word quickly spread that Lewis still lived. Erica was in shock when she heard. She tried her best not to draw attention to herself as she moved toward the dungeon stairwell. It was time.

"You dare to challenge me?" roared Griff from where he stood up on the wall. "You and what army?"

"That army!" Lewis yelled, gesturing at the four-thousand, nine-hundred people on horseback behind them.

Griff studied the group just in front of the tree-line and laughed.

"That's not an army! This is an army!" he shouted, raising his arms. "Raves, arise!"

All of the men on winged steeds rose into the air and began circling like vultures. The men on foot ran up to the battlements and into the watchtowers, then screaming their battle-cries they waved their weapons in the air menacingly.

Brenna and Lewis felt overwhelmed at the vast number of Raves within Castle MacKline.

"Fire!" Griff bellowed.

As a shower of arrows rained down on them, Brenna and Lewis steered their horses back toward the tree-line and out of range. Even there they could hear the mocking laughter of their enemies.

Lewis noted the fear and doubt on the men's faces. Quickly he rode up and down in front of the makeshift army that he and his sisters had gathered, calling out encouragement.

"Friends, I am not a laird. I am the son of a laird, and my father taught me what it is to be one, and that man on the battlement is no laird. He believes that it is only power and land that makes him a laird, but it's more than that. It's standing for truth, for justice. It's protecting those who can't protect themselves. That man protects no one but himself, and if we don't drive him out now, soon he will seek to conquer you and your lands. Will we stand for it?"

"NO!" the crowd shouted in response.

Brenna started calling out as well, "We did not come here to listen to his mockery! We came to rescue those that're held prisoner!" She waved her sword in the air, then Dawn and Marie launched themselves from where they perched in the treetops and flew toward the castle.

"We stand for truth and justice. And the truth is that the villain on the battlement has taken something that he has no right to and no claim on. And justice demands that he return it. But when given the chance, he refused." Lewis called, riding up and down the line of soldiers with Brenna at his side. "Will we stand for it!"

"NO!" the crowd shouted.

"Will we take the castle?" Brenna shouted.

"AYE!" the word hung in the air like a bell ringing.

Marie and Dawn narrowly avoided the Raves on their winged beasts as they looked down for a signal. Candy quickly spread her lace-hemmed, white handkerchief on a barrel top just outside of the stable. The Bulves flew high and both preformed perfect summersaults. Brenna saw this and nodded to Lewis.

"Now let us ride!" Lewis called out, steering his horse so that his and Brenna's steeds stood side by side facing the castle ahead. "Be careful." he said, extending his hand.

Brenna took his hand and shook it, then said, "Be careful yourself."

Candy and Dylon looked out into the courtyard. There were almost no men left there. They were all either on flying steeds, on the battlements or in the watchtowers.

"Now!" Candy whispered, and she and Dylon rushed out to the main-gate.

Brenna and Lewis both drew their swords and shouted, "Charge!"

Four-thousand, nine-hundred and two sets of hooves pounded across the open ground toward Castle MacKline's newly repaired main gate.

"Hurry!" Candy gasped as she began to climb toward the second bolt that was at least seven feet above the ground.

Dylon worked quickly, unlocking the bottom bolt. Candy lifted the second bolt and jumped down to the ground.

"Pull!" she groaned, trying her hardest to pull the heavy door open. But it wouldn't budge.

Dylon was already pulling his side of the gate wide open. The thunderous beating of the charging horses' hooves was getting louder. The two young people could hear the twang of bowstrings above and knew that the Raves were firing at the oncoming riders.

Tears filled Candy's eyes as she strained to open the huge door. She let out a small cry of pain and frustration. She was ready to collapse to her knees in despair, when she felt a hand brush hers. She looked up to see who it was.

"Nick!" she exclaimed, overjoyed to receive aid.

"Come on!" he said, pulling at the heavy gate which was just starting to move.

The gate was opened just in time. In poured the riders led by Lewis and the Wolf Princess, howling her battle-cry.

The moment that the Raves had realized that the gate was being opened they rushed down from the battlements and out of the watchtowers. Several of them were trampled under the clans' horses as they filled the courtyard.

Griff watched from around the corner of the castle. He'd rushed to this spot with about five men as soon as the clans had entered the gate.

"Quickly!" he snarled at two men who were rolling a large barrel of oil from the castle corner to the outer wall, leaving a slick trail between their laird and battle.

Dritt was on the ground now, searching for Candy. He'd seen her. He'd seen that hated girl! She was here! He would have his revenge this day! His sweet revenge!

Candy had rushed back to the stables pursued by five men. She drew her sword and prepared for battle.

"Wolf Princess!" Griff bellowed. "Come and face me, if you're not too much of a coward!"

Brenna looked over and saw Griff standing at the ready with his sword drawn. She steered Lightningbolt and rode directly at her enemy, wielding her sword.

She was about fifteen feet away from him when Griff suddenly shouted, "Now!"

A Rave with a torch threw it down on the oil-slick, just before Brenna was about to ride over it. Flames sprang up in front of them and there wasn't enough time to stop. Lightningbolt like all horses wasn't too keen on fire, but he was also a clever beast and knew that he couldn't stop, so he quickened his pace and leapt over the fire-barrier. Brenna held her sword high and gave her howling battle-cry.

As the stallion's hooves touched the earth, four ropes were thrown over his head and around his neck.

A Rave rushed forward and knocked Brenna from the horse's back. She hit the ground with a loud 'thump,' then leapt to her feet, brandishing her sword as the Rave came at her with an axe. With one swift blow his body slumped over dead.

Brenna's head was pounding. She hadn't landed on her head, but she had rolled, scraping her forehead on a small rock. But she didn't have time to think about that as she faced Laird Griff Cray of Castle Cray. He jeered at her, throwing off his cloak and swinging his sword.

Brenna marched toward him with steely determination in her eyes. She didn't turn as the four Raves who had hold of Lightningbolt screamed as they were dragged across the hot, steaming surface of the dying fire. Lightningbolt would not be held by these scoundrels, so he dragged them across the smoking ground.

The Wolf Princess stood about three feet from her opponent, sword at the ready. Brenna glared at Griff as he grinned smugly. She lunged. He dodged to the left and slashed at her. But she shielded herself by raising her sword. The clanging of steel on steel filled the air as they circled. Griff suddenly lunged forward, Brenna bent backward until her hands and sword were flat on the ground, and threw back her head. The blade was so close that she could feel the chill from the medal.

Brenna waited until he drew back his sword to strike, then performed a backward summersault, the toe of her boot connecting with his goat-bearded chin. She landed perfectly on her feet, sword in hand and saw that Griff was rubbing his sore chin.

"Had enough?" she grinned.

"I'm just getting warmed up!" he snorted with a small smile, then charged.

Brenna dropped to all fours as he swung at her. She swept a leg beneath him. He leapt over her sweeping kick and brought down his sword like a hammer. The Wolf Princess put up her sword just in time and sparks flew from the blades as they clashed. Brenna rose up on one knee, testing Griff's strength and knew that she was in trouble.

Candy was backed up against a wall in the stable, five Raves with their swords drawn surrounding her. There was a large net that hung from the ceiling of the stable. It held several barrels of oats that they kept for winter and incase of famine. Candy looked at the net and the rope that held it. She then realized that the end of the rope was tied to a hook near her. She took hold of it and severed it below her hand. Down came the net of barrels, and up went Candy toward the loft. The net and barrels landed on four of the Raves, while the fifth one leapt to one side and began climbing a ladder to the loft.

Lewis was dealing out tremendous strokes left and right. He noted that there was a young warrior who stayed near him, always watching his back. It was a great relief to have an ally in this battle. Then with a terrible shock, he saw the warrior's face.

Colleen? he thought.

Yes it was she. Colleen had disguised herself in mail and a helmet, and caught up with the army in the night while they camped in the caves.

Lewis resolved then and there to stay near and to protect her no matter what.

Dylon had somehow been chased up onto the wall by a huge monster of a man. They battled fiercely as their swords clashed again and again. Each blow from the giant Rave was nearly bone-crushing. Then he somehow knocked the giant off of the wall and watched as he suddenly grew smaller and smaller as he fell toward the ground.

Then Dylon straightened and gulped. He felt the unmistakable point of a sword-tip against his back. There was a sickening sound, like a blade sinking into someone's flesh. But Dylon felt no pain. The sword-point dropped from his back. He turned in time to see the Rave who'd been behind him fall from the battlement, an arrow through his neck.

Dylon looked down into the courtyard to see who had fired the shot. His mouth dropped open. It was Nick with Marie guiding his hand. Dylon raised a hand in thanks, then he saw Marie say something to Nick and watched as the blind warrior waved in his direction.

Lynch wasn't very brave or a great warrior. He'd started hiding in an old empty barrel as soon as the battle became fierce and would issue forth a high pitched scream whenever the barrel was bumped.

Erica had released everyone in the dungeon and they were now charging out into the courtyard. Erica stood just inside the doorway to the dungeon-steps watching as Konroy wielded his axe with expert precession.

She screamed as a strong arm closed around her from behind and the cold, sharp edge of a dagger was pressed against her throat.

Konroy whirled around at the sound of her cry. He started toward them his axe at the ready and shouted, "Let her go!"

"Stop right there!" the Rave yelled.

Konroy halted, his dark eyes fixed on the villain.

"Drop your axe or she's dead!" the Rave sneered.

Konroy reluctantly threw down his weapon and put his hands on his hips.

"Alright. Now let her go." Konroy growled.

"As you wish." the Rave smirked, shoving Erica away from him and charging at Konroy with his blade at the ready.

Konroy reached behind his back and drew the axe-head he carried and hurled it at his enemy. The Rave fell dead, the blade lodged in his chest. Panting, Konroy looked at Erica who was shaking like a leaf caught in the wind.

"Are you alright?" he asked.

Erica swallowed and nodded. Then her eyes grew large as she suddenly pointed behind him and yelled, "Look out!"

Konroy turned just in time to see a huge Rave with his sword raised to strike him down. Konroy bent double and rammed his shoulder into the man's gut. He heard the man gasp as the air left his lungs. While he was still bent double, Konroy drew his jeweled dagger from his boot, then stood up straight as he hit the Rave on the head with the dagger hilt, knocking the man unconscious.

Konroy whirled around at the sound of a grunt. He saw another man poised with a sword. Konroy raised his dagger defensively, but the Rave never struck. Instead the man toppled forward, dropping his sword. Konroy looked down and saw the axe-head that he carried buried in the Rave's back. He gazed at Erica. Her hand was blood-covered after she'd pulled the blade out of the first man's chest and thrown it at the second man to save Konroy. He smiled with relief when he realized that it wasn't her blood.

"Thanks." Konroy said, nodding to her.

Erica nodded back, managing a weak smile.

Vrant stared angrily at Lewis as he defeated each Rave that approached him. But Vrant noticed how Lewis seemed to be protecting a young warrior that stayed near him. Then Vrant was shocked when he realized that it was a girl dressed in armor.

She must mean something to him. Vrant thought as he devised a plan.

Vrant suddenly rushed forward and grabbed Colleen, holding her tightly against him with his sword to her throat. Colleen screamed. Lewis turned and fear gripped his heart. Lewis started toward them raising his sword.

"Halt young laird!" Vrant growled.

Lewis stopped a few feet away from them, his eyes narrowed at Vrant. "What do you want scum?"

"Call the surrender, or she's dead." Vrant sneered.

Lewis's jaw drew tight as a steel trap as he quivered with anger. Colleen knew that he was seething and that he might do something rash. The fear of this gave her desperation, and the courage to do what she did next.

"Ah, come on lad." Vrant taunted. "You don't want to see her blood on your hand, Agh! My ear!"

Colleen had thrown her head back as far as she could and had bitten Vrant's ear. Vrant hollered, pushing Colleen away and clutching at his bloodied ear. Colleen rolled away as she hit the ground and Lewis came forward, his sword held high. Lewis swung his blade in order to decapitate Vrant. But the Rave had seen many battles in his lifetime and was prepared.

He ducked, drawing a dagger and shoved it into Lewis's ribcage, then rose and set his fist to Lewis's chin. The impact was so great that Lewis spun as he fell backward, causing him to land on his stomach.

Vrant prepared to kill Lewis, but the sudden pain of being stabbed in the leg caused him to turn on whoever was stabbing him. It was Colleen, using her dagger.

"You little brat!" he snarled, striking downward.

Colleen scurried backward just in time but suddenly felt the outer wall at her back. Vrant raised his sword, laughing wickedly.

"You're mine now girlie." he snickered evilly as he started to bring down his weapon.

Colleen turned away and put up her hands to shield herself from the blow. 'Clang!' The sound rang through the air as metal clashed against metal.

Colleen opened her eyes and saw that Lewis had somehow leapt to his feet and put out his sword to shield her. Vrant stared in shock at the young man who was now glaring at him, blood dripping his split lower-lip.

"What is she to you? Your wife?" asked Vrant.

"If she'll have me!" Lewis snarled, spitting blood in his enemy's face as he ran him through, killing him instantly. "Not that you'll ever know." Lewis sank to his knees next to colleen, panting, "Are you alright?"

Colleen nodded, then smiled, "Aye. To both questions." Then she kissed him gently on the mouth, careful of his lower lip.

When at last he could speak, Lewis said, "If we survive this, I want to marry you as soon as possible. Alright?"

All Colleen could do was nod.

Candy was at the very edge of the loft now, the last of the five Raves still pursuing her. He stood about six feet in front of her, his sword raised and a smug grin on his face.

"Nowhere to run lass." he chuckled wickedly.

The whole courtyard was spread out behind her and the sound of battle rang in her ears. She looked around for some means of escape. She looked down and saw a pile of hay through the cracks in the floor. Then she noticed where the Rave was standing, on a loose floorboard. She leapt on the opposite end of the board and catapulted the man through the thatched roof.

The man flew through the air and would've flown farther if not for the large man in his path, who was ready to stab Dylon in the back. The two fell in a heap, unconscious behind Dylon and Delaney as they pulled Lynch out of the barrel he'd been hiding in, while Dylon scolded him for his cowardice.

Candy gave a grunt as she plopped down on the pile of hay. Still clutching her sword, she leapt to her feet and ran through the stable-entrance into the courtyard. She skidded to a stop when she saw Dritt waiting for her, sword drawn. Fear gripped her heart as she turned and ran toward the castle, Dritt on her heels.

Mitch hadn't even entered the gates to Castle MacKline. When the charge was called he rode with them for a few minutes before breaking away and riding up a hill to his left. He'd stayed on that hilltop ever since, watching as his new friends battled his old allies. He no longer felt any loyalty to the Raves, but he didn't care to face them in combat either. He was a loner. He had been ever since his wife's death. Though he felt concern and guilt as he watched Brenna battling Griff Cray from the high hilltop.

Brenna and Candy had trusted him, helped him, confided in him. Brenna had even given him the horse he now rode. He despised himself for leaving, but how could he go back? What was there for him if he stayed? It weighed on his heart whatever it was.

Brenna and Griff had been fighting hard and both were tiring. Brenna cried out in agony as a dagger struck the back of her right thigh. She slashed at Griff, causing him to leap back out of her reach, tripping over the dead body of one of his men and landing on his back.

Brenna groaned as she gritted her teeth, pulling the blade from her flesh. She examined the blood-coated blade and saw the reflection of the one who had thrown the knife. It was one of the Raves who was preparing to throw a second dagger.

She turned with catlike reflexes and hurled it at the-would-be assassin, killing him instantly. She quickly turned back to deal with Griff who was up again. The two of them slashed wildly at each other.

Brenna's leg and hands were throbbing as she battled the wicked Laird Griff Cray. Suddenly, he swung his broadsword with such ferocity that when their blades met, Brenna lost her grip and her sword flew from her hands. With another heavy blow, Griff Cray brought his sword back cutting diagonally down from her upper-arm and across her ribcage. If Brenna hadn't leapt back, he would've spilled her entrails.

Griff Cray leapt forward as well and gave her a hard, cruel head-butt that knocked Brenna back against the wall behind her. She let out a moan as she slid down into a sitting position. She sat there, clutching at her wounded arm which was squeezed hard against her bleeding side.

Griff Cray hovered over her, sword raised and asked, "Did you really think you could best me?"

Just around the corner, unknown to either of them, Brenna's twin and only sister Candy was fighting Griff Cray's right-hand man, Dritt. He flipped the sword out of her hand with an unusual twist and kicked her so hard that she fell back against the castle's gray-stone wall. She stood there, knowing that her life now hung by a thread.

Dritt raised his sword and smirked, "Well now, Princess, I suppose this is the end."

Griff Cray looked down at Brenna, watching as the crimson, sticky liquid seeped out from between her fingers, a smug grin on his countenance. Brenna returned his gaze, utter and bitter hatred in her eyes.

"You have a choice Wolf Princess." he sneered. "Join me and become an unstoppable force, or die! Which will it be?"

"I make my own destiny!" she growled as she glared up at him defiantly, then spat in his face. Griff grimaced and wiped the saliva from his countenance before glaring back at her.

"Very well Princess. You've chosen your fate." he snarled, raising his sword to strike her dead.

"First the eyes." Dritt sneered around the corner, raising his sword-point until it was level with her tear-filled eyes.

Candy closed her eyes and let out one sob of despair as she pushed herself as far back against the wall as she could. She turned her head to one side, ready to meet her fate.

"Say goodbye to the light," Dritt said mockingly, drawing back his sword.

The sword clattered against the wall only a few inches from Candy's face as Dritt was struck by someone who seemed to come bounding out of nowhere. Candy looked, not believing her eyes.

"Nick?" she gasped as the two men wrestled on the ground.

Marie had seen Candy's peril and told Nick. Dylon was in the heat of battle and had no idea what was happening, so Marie had led Nick to Candy as fast they could move.

Brenna turned away as the sword came down. In that moment her entire life flashed before her eyes. 'CLANG!' She saw sparks as she turned back. She saw two blades crossed less than six inches from her face, one of the swords blocking the other. One blade was Griff's. The new blade was Mitch's.

"Mitch?" Brenna said in disbelief, eyes wide.

"I want that kiss you promised." Mitch said, giving her a small grin.

"You little traitor!" Griff snarled.

"At least my conscious is clear." Mitch snorted just before punching Griff in the jaw.

Griff stumbled backward, holding his throbbing jaw. Mitch ran after him brandishing his sword.

Nick and Dritt were locked in each others grip as they rolled around on the ground. Candy stared at them too horrified to move or to even take her gaze from the spectacle.

"Get his sword! Get his sword!" Nick yelled to Candy.

This seemed to wake Candy from the trance-like state that she was in. She scrambled to where the blade lay in the dirt. Marie, now joined by Dawn, growled at Dritt overhead, unable to land on the Rave for fear of harming Nick.

"No!" Dritt roared, shoving Nick off of himself and leaping to his feet.

He sent a dive-bombing Marie into the side of the wall with one swift motion of his hand as he stalked toward Candy. Marie lay on the ground, motionless. Dawn landed next to Marie's still form, her mission to protect the humans forgotten as she nudged at her motionless mentor's muzzle with her own.

The moment that Nick was thrown from Dritt, he'd yelled, "Candy, Run!"

Dritt reached his sword before Candy, grabbing it up and pointing it at her throat as he bellowed at Nick, "You little runt!"

Nick couldn't believe his ears. He knew those words. He'd heard them before, many years ago.

"That voice." he shuddered, struggling to his feet. "I know that voice. You're one of those bandits that killed my family! You kicked me! You took away my sight! I know your voice!" Nick was screaming now. All the memories of his family's death came flooding back into Nick's mind. How from atop a horse Dritt had kicked him, knocking him down so that his head hit a rock and had caused him to become unconscious. When Nick had awakened, his head had been pounding and all he had seen was the fading sun shining down on the bodies of his family before his vision was gone forever.

Nick's entire form was shaking now as he stood before Dritt and Candy. Candy saw that Nick's expression was one of vengeance.

"Nick?" she asked, though her voice sounded far off as it reached his ears.

Mitch and Griff were fighting hard. Griff tried to cut Mitch's legs from beneath him. Mitch leapt over the sweeping blade and kicked Griff in the chest, knocking his enemy flat. Mitch also landed on his back but quickly jumped up again. He struck downward at Griff, but the villain rolled to one side and with a sweeping kick Mitch was flat on the ground again. Griff stood over him smirking. Mitch tried to raise his sword in self-defense but Griff stepped on his wrist, keeping him defenseless. Mitch clawed at griff's leg desperately.

"Stop that lad! It's useless!" Griff said smugly, placing his sword-tip against Mitch's throat.

Brenna was moaning as she struggled to her feet. She was clutching at her wounds, leaning against the wall for support. She was gasping and felt dizzy from both pain and blood loss.

Nick drew the sword that Dylon had given him and started toward Dritt.

"Just stay out of the way Candy." Nick almost snarled, listening to Dritt's footsteps.

Dritt was taller and heavier than Nick and Candy, so his footsteps were heavier as he walked. When Dritt swung his blade at him, Nick knew to put up his sword in self-defense. The blades clashed loudly and sparks flew as the two men battled.

Dritt couldn't believe that a blind man was blocking each of his blows. But Nick was too experienced to be bested by Dritt. The Rave tried to use his height and weight to his own advantage, but Dritt felt great fear as he looked into Nick's sightless eyes.

To Dritt's dismay and Candy's shock, Nick knocked the sword from the one-eyed man's grasp.

On your knees murderer!" Nick snapped.

Dritt gulped as he obeyed. "Mercy! Spare me!" he begged as Nick put the blade to his collar-bone.

"My family begged for mercy. Did you spare them?" Nick growled through gritted teeth. "I have no reason to leave you alive."

Dritt swallowed and decided that he'd better change tactics. "You don't have the stomach to do it!" he snarled. "You're not man enough!"

Nick growled and moved his sword downward, cutting into Dritt's flesh. He left a three inch long gash down Dritt's chest.

"Nick, don't." Candy said, barely above a sob. "You're better than this."

If Nick heard her his expression gave no indication. His face was twisted in a glare that was a horrible mixture of hatred, grief and pain. His sword didn't move from Dritt's chest, though Nick's entire frame was quivering with anger as the images of his family's death flashed through his mind. His family, they were always so proud of him. But would they be proud of him now, if he took revenge on this man, vile as he was?

"I won't be like you. Killing isn't what makes a man a man. I'm sure of that for you are no man. You're a monster." Nick snarled, trying not to sob. "I'll spare you if you leave now and never come back! Understood?"

"I understand perfectly." Dritt gulped, drawing a long dagger from the back of his belt. Quick as a cat pouncing on a mouse, Dritt ducked under Nick's sword and slashed at Nick's thigh.

Nick cried out in pain as the blade cut into his flesh. Dritt grabbed up his own sword and was about to rise when Candy came forward and put her own sword-tip to his throat.

"That's far enough Dritt!" she said with much more courage than she felt.

Dritt glared at her with his one good eye. Nick came limping over, sword in hand and stood next to Candy.

"Alright." Dritt said in defeat. "But if I must go, I'm taking you with me!" he bellowed as he raised his sword and stabbed Candy just above her right hip.

Candy didn't scream. She couldn't. All the air had left her as she dropped her sword and held her bleeding side, Dritt's laughter echoing in her ears.

Dritt couldn't help his wicked laugh. He'd finally gotten his revenge. His sweet revenge. His laughter however was his downfall as it told Nick where to strike. Blood spayed from Dritt's chest as it was slashed, his laughter ceasing. The one-eyed man fell back, his weapon dropping from his hand as he lay motionless in an expanding pool of his own blood.

Nick dropped his sword when he felt Candy's trembling hand on his shoulder as she tried to steady herself. The smell of blood was thick on the air around her as he turned in her direction.

"Nick," she whimpered.

"I'm here." he said, cradling her in his arms as he knelt. All he could hear was her ragged breathing. He followed her arm with one hand until he found the wound in her side. He felt ill as he felt the sticky liquid gushing from her wound.

"Nick, tell Brenna, I love her, and give her hug for me. And tell Dylon, that I'm sorry." Candy half sobbed, half gasped. Then she pulled his head down near enough to kiss him, and brushed her lips against his before the darkness surrounding claimed her.

Nick held her limp form to him, unable to stop the shaking in his limbs or the tears building in his sightless eyes.

Mitch glared up at Griff defiantly.

"Goodbye traitor!" Griff snarled, raising his sword.

Brenna had pulled her jeweled-dagger from her boot and was now holding it by the blade.

"Hey, Griffy!" she called.

Griff and Mitch both turned their heads toward her as she hurled the small weapon at Griff's head. Griff ducked, but not quite fast enough.

The dagger thudded into the side of a barrel, pinning a large black wig to it. Brenna and Mitch both stared openmouthed at Griff's shiny bald-head and began laughing as he tried to cover his head with his free hand.

"Shut up!" Griff yelled angrily as he stomped toward the laughing girl.

Mitch, now free, rolled to his side, sat up and lunged at Griff's legs, tripping the older man. Griff began to struggle when he saw that his men were retreating.

"Come back you cowards!" he screamed.

But there was no coming back. The Raves had lost. When they'd seen that Vrant and Dritt were both down with their bodies being dragged from the battlefield, and that Griff had lost his wig they'd started a hasty retreat.

Painfully, Brenna limped over to him and knelt near to his head.

"Give it up Griffy. You've lost. Both your wig and the keep." the Wolf Princess said firmly. "Now I want you to get lost, and stay lost."

Griff glared at her and shoved Mitch off of himself. He leapt to his feet and ran after his men, calling over his shoulder, "You've won the battle Wolf Princess, but not the war. You have an dark destiny and one day you will fulfill it!"

"Ah!" Brenna yelled, sticking out her tongue and spitting while making a rather rude sound as she did. "Go and tell it to your mummy, egghead!"

Brenna and Mitch stood side by side watching as Griff's form grew smaller, then they both burst out laughing.

"Look at him run." Mitch laughed, his blue-gray eyes dancing with glee. Then to Mitch's shock, Brenna suddenly flung her arms around his neck and kissed his scratched cheek.

"There. I kept my promise." she smiled. "I even kissed your scratch."

Mitch raised his brow, then started rubbing at his mouth saying, "Ow, ow. My poor lips."

"Oh shut up. Walk it off and be a man." Brenna said, shoving him playfully.

The two of them chuckled as they walked over to the barrel. Brenna retrieved her dagger and held the wig between her thumb and index finger.

"This is disgusting." she grimaced, then giggled, "It's like a giant rat."

"No, a rat's less greasy." Mitch snickered.

They began walking around the corner, Brenna limping badly. But as they came upon Nick cradling Candy's still form their smiles vanished.

"Candy!" Brenna shrieked, rushing to her sister's side. She fell to her knees and took hold of Candy's shoulders. "Candy? Candy wake up! Come on! Stop faking! It's not funny! Why won't she wake up?" Brenna was half-sobbing now as she held her sister's limp body.

Nick couldn't speak. All he could do was shake his head sadly. Just then Dylon joined them, not believing his eyes.

"What happened here?" he asked, tears springing unbidden to his eyes.

"Dritt stabbed her." Nick sniffed, tears staining his cheeks. "She wanted you to know that she's sorry Dylon. And she wanted her sister to know that she loves her."

The Wolf Princess hugged her sister to her, "No! She can't be gone! She can't! She just can't!" Brenna's voice trailed off as the darkness closed in around her. She didn't feel pain as she fell to the ground. She didn't hear the words of concern from her friends and family as they gathered around. She didn't hear her mother wailing, her father's words of comfort, or Colleen's sobs. She was unaware of her brothers lifting her with the aid of Mitch and Dylon. She didn't even hear Lynch and Darsy as they joined the mourning group.

Nick crawled over to where he heard Dawn whimpering.

"What's wrong?" he asked.

"I think Marie's dead." the small Bulf sobbed.

"What?" Nick said in disbelief as he stroked Marie's soft fur. "Marie." He buried his face in her silky coat and wept freely.

"Nick, you're making my fur soggy." Marie moaned.

"Marie!" Dawn and Nick both said together as they assaulted Marie with hugs.

"Uh, you're crushing me." Marie groaned.

"Sorry. I'm just glad you're not dead." Dawn said, licking the older Bulf's face.

"Hey, where're Brenna and Candy?" asked Marie, still sounding dazed.

Nick sadly explained and Marie licked away his tears tenderly.

"There, there." she said in a motherly voice. "It's alright. Shh."

CHAPTER TWENTY-ONE
THE WOLF PRINCESS AND HER SISTER

Brenna's eyes flew open at the feeling of something wet on her forehead. She gasped as all the memories of the battle came flooding back into her mind and clutched at the wrist that was in front of her face.

"Easy. Easy." came Mitch's voice.

Brenna looked up panting, and saw that Mitch had been bathing her brow. She gazed around at her surroundings. She was on a cot in the infirmary and there were several other wounded people lying on their cots all around her.

Her head ached, her thigh throbbed and her left arm hurt when she tried to lift it. The most severe pain came from her ribcage where Griff had cut her with his sword, but Brenna didn't care about that right now.

"Where's Candy?" her voice was laced with a mixture of fear and grief as she tried to sit up.

"Calm down." Mitch said, gently pushing her back down on the cot. "Relax."

"But where is she?" Brenna persisted, struggling against his grasp. "Don't make me pound you into the ground! You know I can do it!"

"Obviously you're alright." Mitch couldn't help chuckling.

"Mitch, tell me where she is!" Brenna said desperately, taking hold of his shirt collar.

"She's in her room. Darsy's been looking after her." Mitch said, gently prying her fingers from his collar and holding her hand reassuringly.

"So she's alive?" the Wolf Princess's voice was hopeful.

Mitch lowered his eyes.

"No," Brenna began sobbing. "No, she can't be. She just can't."

"She doesn't seem to be alive or dead. Darsy's been tending to her for the last three days." Mitch explained.

"I've been out for three days?" Brenna said in disbelief.

Mitch nodded, "Aye, and it was a real struggle every day to get you to swallow water and milk."

"What?" she asked raising a brow.

"You wouldn't wake up, so we had to tilt your head back and pour water down your throat. Two days ago we started you on milk 'cause water just wasn't enough after awhile." Mitch explained.

"Hey, look who's awake." came Konroy's voice. Brenna caught sight of her younger brother as he called over his shoulder, "Brenna's awake."

Brenna suddenly found her cot surrounded by her parents, brothers, Colleen, Nick, the two Bulves and Erica. Lady MacKline knelt and hugged her eldest daughter, who surprisingly sat up and returned the embrace before groaning as her wounds were bumped.

"Oh, I'm sorry dear." Lady MacKline sniffed, reluctantly loosening her grip on Brenna. "I'm just so happy that you're alright."

"How're you feeling lass?" Laird MacKline asked, a tiny smile playing on his lips and tears dancing in his dark eyes.

"Like a horse trampled me." Brenna moaned. "What about all of you? Konroy, is that a bandage on your head?"

"Aye, one of the Raves caught me in the forehead with the butt of a spear. I'm just glad it wasn't the other end." Konroy explained, rubbing the white strip across his forehead. "But Erica fixed me up." he added with a smile.

Erica dropped her gaze to the floor and smiled as well, her cheeks as red as ripe cherries.

"Colleen took care of my arm." Lewis said, proudly displaying the sling that supported his injuried limb as he wrapped his good arm around a blushing Colleen. "She's also agreed to be my bride as soon as we've all recovered from the battle."

"Have you seen Candy?" Brenna asked.

"We've all been to visit her." said Laird MacKline. "Though there's been no change."

"I want to see her." Brenna grunted as she threw off her blanket and tried to rise. Instantly she collapsed under her own weight. Mitch and Laird MacKline rushed to catch her.

"You forgot about your leg." Mitch said gently as he and Laird MacKline placed her back on the cot.

Brenna examined her bandaged thigh, then noticed that Mitch's wrist was also bandaged.

"What happened to you?" she said, nodding at his wound.

"Oh this. Remember when Griff stepped on my wrist out there? Well it turns out that he sprained it for me." Mitch said, raising his right hand slightly. "Nick and you are both in the same boat."

"Aye." Nick said, tapping his own bound leg.

"Well I don't care if I do have a busted leg. I want to see Candy." Brenna said, looking around. "Does anyone use that crutch?"

Konroy went to the wall where a finely carved wooden crutch leaned, "We were hoping you'd be well enough to use it." he grinned, picking it up and handing it to her.

Brenna leaned on the sturdy wooden support as she stood. She planted it's top firmly in her right armpit and bent her leg at the knee as she took her first wobbly step in three days. She gritted her teeth as her softened muscles tried to support her. But as much pain as she was in she continued forward with utter determination in her eyes.

Mitch fought back a chuckle as he thought, **She's too stubborn to stay in bed.**

It was a long limping walk down the hall and a trying climb to the next floor as the Wolf Princess hobbled along, the wooden crutch thumping on the floor as she went. Her friends and family all followed, concern on some faces, admiration on others.

Brenna paused at the chamber-door, questioning whether or not she really wanted to see what was on the other side. Her left arm was in a sling and her right hand gripped the crutch so tightly that her knuckles were turning white.

All eyes fixed on her right hand as it slowly released the carved support and rose to the door latch. For a moment her trembling hand rested on the old worn latch. So many times she had touched this very latch over her lifetime, but never with such sorrow and dread in her heart. She lifted it and slowly pushed the door open. Brenna froze one step inside the chamber and her mouth dropped open at what she saw.

Candy lay flat on the bed, her hair a tangled web on the pillow and soaked with sweat. Her face was pale like snow and her eyes were closed. Her breathing was ragged, sounding awful and labored.

The group of people behind her filed into the room passed her and stood near the bed. Darsy stood near the bed mixing something in a bowl.

"How is she Darsy?" asked Lady MacKline, tears in her eyes as well as voice.

"I've been trying to keep her fever down, but it keeps rising again." Darsy said as he dropped some dried herbs into the bowl and began stirring again.

"What's that?" asked Lewis.

"Something that can lower her fever and relieve the pain if she'll just drink it." Darsy said softly. "Konroy, Erica, would you lean her head back and open her mouth for me?"

Konroy sat on the edge of the bed and lifted his sister from the pillow until her head was leaned back. Erica sat on the other side of Candy and opened her mouth. Darsy came forward and tipped the bowl over Candy's parted lips. The liquid poured into her mouth slowly.

"There we go. Now close her mouth so that she'll swallow." Darsy said, lifting the bowl away.

Erica gently closed Candy's mouth and they all smiled to hear a soft gulping sound. Candy's mouth opened again and they heard a wheezing sound.

"Is she alright?" asked Konroy.

"That's how she's been breathing for the last three days. She's still in pain. She needs more." Darsy explained, pouring more of the liquid into Candy's mouth as Erica opened it again. But this time Candy began coughing and regurgitated the medicine. After a while she quieted and the only sound was her wheezing.

"She always does that," groaned Darsy, "and I don't know why."

"Brenna, do you have any ideas?" asked Nick.

There was no answer.

"Brenna?" he asked again. "Brenna?"

"Where'd she go?" asked Mitch, looking at the empty doorway.

Brenna had left the moment that Candy had started coughing. She couldn't stand it. She limped to a corner in the hall and sank into a sitting position. Her expression was an awful mix of shock and despair. Tears were burning in her eyes but she refused to let them spill. She held her breath when she heard footsteps. Three maids passed her talking about Candy. Brenna perked up her ears at the mention of her sister.

"I'm amazed that Miss Candace has survived this long." said Fiona.

"She's strong." said Anne. "She always was."

"I think that she's waiting for her sister to say goodbye." Ivy put in. "Everyone else has been to see her but the Wolf Princess."

Brenna couldn't listen to anymore. Once the maids were out of sight she rose and hobbled down the two flights of stairs before limping outside to the sable-yard.

"Hello Lightningbolt." she said, reaching across the fence to stroke the long, black, velvety face that stared at her. "And hello to you too Dutchess."

She patted the brown-gold neck of the beautiful pony while the black stallion nosed at her injuried left arm.

"I'm all right boy." Brenna smiled, then frowned as Dutchess turned toward the castle and whickered. "She's not coming girl."

Dutchess called out again.

"I'm sorry girl, but she's not coming." Brenna told the horse.

Dutchess continued to watch the castle door for another minute before she lowered her head and slowly walked back to the stable as though she'd finally understood the words. Brenna leaned her head against Lightningbolt's large face and began to sob, unable to hold back the tears that stung her eyes any longer. She was startled to feel a hand on her shoulder. She turned to see who was it was and instantly wanted to die.

"Mitch, please go away." she sniffed, turning away and scrubbing at her tearstained face with her good hand.

But Mitch refused to leave.

"If you'd like to talk, I'm here and I'm willing to listen." he said softly.

"Well I don't want to so go away! There's nothing to hear!" Brenna said, feebly limping along the fence.

"It's alright if you don't want to tell me anything, but you should at least talk to someone." Mitch said pleadingly as he followed.

"It's none of your business! Why should you care?" she snorted.

Mitch stopped in his tracks, "Because I've been where you are. I've lost someone too."

Brenna turned and glared at him sorrowfully, "It's not the same! You and her weren't born together! You didn't play together! Or grow up together! You didn't share secrets and schemes! You don't know what it's like to lose your best friend! To not have someone to go riding with! To not see her at breakfast! To, to,"

She turned and quickened her pace, unable to think of anything else to say.

"To wake up and not see her lying next to you." Mitch said slowly.

Brenna stopped and just listened to his words without turning.

"I didn't want to talk to anyone either, not that I had anyone to talk to. But because I didn't talk, I didn't get over it, and I ended up working for Griff Cray." Mitch explained. "He liked my fighting ability 'cause I wasn't afraid to die. My wife and child were gone and I didn't want to live."

Brenna continued to listen but still refused to turn around.

"I didn't feel anything. I wasn't afraid of anything. I couldn't feel fear because I was bitter, and I couldn't bring myself to love or even care about, well, anything." Mitch continued. "I don't want that to happen to you."

She was silent as Mitch slowly walked up behind her.

"Why don't you go and sit with Candy for a while?" he said in a kind tone.

"That wasn't Candy!" Brenna sobbed, unable to hold back the choking, gasping sound. "That was someone else! Someone ill! She's not that pale! She doesn't wheeze like that! And I can't go in and sit with her!"

"Why?" he asked simply.

"Because she's waiting for me to come and say goodbye before she goes!" Brenna sobbed harder. "If I stay away she won't go!"

Brenna couldn't say anymore. She wept freely. She was blinded by her tears as she felt somebody wrap their arms around her. She knew that it must be Mitch and tried to struggle against him, pushing at him with her good arm. It was all in vain. Mitch was too strong and held her tightly in the fold of his arms.

"Let me go!" she sobbed as she struggled feebily.

After a minute of fighting against him, she stopped and allowed him to hold her. She was surprised to find herself clinging to him. After a while she calmed down and pulled out of his arms.

"I'm fine now." Brenna sniffed.

"Are you sure?" he asked.

"Aye." she said, nodding as she drew the back of her sleeve across her eyes and sniffed.

"Are you sure that you wouldn't rather go and spend as much time with her as you can?" Mitch asked kindly.

"I can't! I just can't watch her die!" Brenna said, forcing herself not to cry. "I can't look at her, lying there like that!"

Mitch was silent for a moment before speaking. "If I could bring my wife back I would. I would do it in a heartbeat. But I can't. Yet I wouldn't trade those last minutes with her for all the wealth in the world." he told her, then placing a hand on her shoulder he added, "You should go to her."

"How long ago did you say it happened?" she asked, trying to change the subject.

"Two years." Mitch sighed.

"It's taken you that long to get over it?" she said in shock.

"To be honest, I'm still recovering." he said, his gaze on the ground. "The pain never really goes away, but it lessens. It takes a long time, but it lessens. Treasure the time that you have left." he said, raising his eyes to meet hers.

Brenna silently contemplated his words, thinking that there was great wisdom in this young man.

At that moment Erica came walking by with a large bucket of water. She had just been to the well, and was in a hurry as she thought of all the thirsty people in the infirmary. Her rapid speed and the large, heavy bucket caused her to stumble. She would've fallen flat and spilled her bucket's contents if Mitch hadn't rushed forward and taken hold of the bucket, giving Erica a chance to regain her balance.

"Are you alright?" he asked.

"Aye." she panted, brushing a blond lock of hair out of her face. "Thank you." Erica stared wide-eyed at Mitch's face and gasped, "Oh my word!" with absolute shock in her voice.

Mitch stared back at her and his mouth dropped open. Why they hadn't recognized each other sooner he didn't know. Taking her by the arm Mitch led her away from where Brenna stood, who was watching them with a questioning look on her face.

"Please, don't tell anyone who I am." he said desperately.

"Aye." Erica gulped and nodded.

"Thank you." Mitch said, relief in his voice.

Then he released her and she hurried to the infirmary. Mitch watched her go, hoping that she wouldn't share his secret.

Dylon and Nick stood near the window in Candy's room, feeling the warmth of the sun on their backs. Lewis and Colleen stood at the foot of the large canopy bed while Laird MacKline comforted his wife in a corner of the chamber. They all watched as Konroy assisted Darsy in pouring some milk mixed with medicine into the princess's open mouth. This seemed much more effective than when he'd only poured in the medicine a short while ago. Candy appeared to be in less pain now.

Darsy smiled and nodded approvingly, "That was a good suggestion Konroy."

"I just thought that if she drinks the milk but not the medicine, maybe she'd drink them together." Konroy shrugged, though he was glad that the idea had been his.

They all turned at the sound of someone clearing her throat and saw Brenna standing in the doorway, her eyes lowered.

"I'd like some time alone with her please?" Brenna said softly.

"Alright." Laird MacKline nodded.

As her parents passed her on their way out they each laid a hand of sympathy on her shoulder. Her brothers, Colleen, and Darsy all nodded respectfully as they passed. Nick wrapped his arms around Brenna in a kind embrace.

"We all miss her too." he whispered, then released her.

Dylon came forward and took Nick's arm in order to guide him, then nodded to Brenna. Dylon and Nick's eyes were red with weeping she noted. The Wolf Princess then turned to watch as they all filed out of the room and closed the door behind them.

Brenna limped over to the bed and looked down at the still form of her sister. She was still very pale, drenched in sweat, and every now and again she would shiver. Though she didn't wheeze nearly so much and seemed to be breathing easier now.

"Hi Candy. It's me. Sorry I didn't come sooner, but I was, afraid, of losing you. I don't know if you can hear me, but I'm gonna talk anyway. I keep trying to remember some of the fun times we had, but I can't. All I can think about is how you're lying here, like this. I might've been able to match blows with anyone, but you were always so much stronger than me in other ways." Brenna could feel tears in her eyes and it was now very difficult to speak around the lump in her throat. She dropped to her knees and her crutch clattered on the polished wood floor. She was now kneeling beside the bed, clutching at the blankets.

"I love you!" Brenna sobbed. "And I know that you're not gone yet but I miss you! And I hate you for leaving me here alone. And I love you, 'cause you're my only sister, and I don't know what I'm gonna do without you. I, I wish it was me instead of you, 'cause I know you could survive without me. But I can't! Not without you! I can't! I won't! I don't want to! And I don't know why you're being taken away, but I'd do anything to bring you back! Anything!"

Brenna could say no more. She buried her face in the blankets and wept, certain that when she'd look up again her sister would be dead. Brenna was surprised to feel a hand on her head.

"Would you kiss Lynch?" said a weak voice.

Brenna raised her head and stared at her sister through the burning tears. Candy's eyes were open and she was smiling a very feeble smile at Brenna.

"Candy?" Brenna said in disbelief.

"Well answer the question." Candy was still smiling and there was a glimmer of mischief dancing in her still weak eyes. "Would you kiss Lynch?"

"I'd marry him and have a hundred children with him if it meant keeping you around." Brenna said, starting to laugh and cry anew.

Candy gave a weak laugh, "I'd stick around to see that."

"Too bad. It's not gonna happen." Brenna chuckled.

Brenna finally gathered her wits and struggled to her feet. Hopping to the door she called to her friends and family, telling them that Candy was all right. The door burst open and Candy found herself surrounded by her family, Colleen, Dylon, Nick and Darsy.

It's difficult to describe what happened next. The joyful emotions that were in each person's heart are nearly impossible to put down on paper. But if you've ever been so happy that all you do is laugh or cry, and felt that your body might explode trying to hold it all in yet didn't care, then you know exactly what the mood in this room was like at that moment.

Mitch and Erica soon joined the little celebration, and it was only about an hour before word of Candy's awakening had spread like wildfire through the castle. It was late that evening before the group broke up and everybody went to their own rooms for the night. Brenna stayed and lay next to her sister. They chattered and giggled long into the night before falling asleep, the Dark and Bright stars shining through their window.

Days passed and Candy slowly regained her strength. By the end of the third day she was able to stand for a few minutes. The next sunset she walked across the room and sat at the window, longing to look out at the sea.

"That was even better than yesterday." Brenna applauded. She herself no longer used a crutch, but still limped very heavily.

"Is that Mitch down there?" asked Candy as she gazed out of the window.

Brenna hopped over on her strong leg and looked down beyond the cliffs where a lone figure strolled along the shore at a very slow pace looking out to sea.

"I do think it is him." Brenna said. "He's a Northman. The sea's in his blood. They're always sailing somewhere."

"Do you think he'll go back to sea?" Candy asked worriedly.

Brenna shrugged, "Who knows." But to herself she thought, **I hope not.**

Mitch was asking himself the very same question as he watched the sun steadily sinking toward the water. He looked down at the emerald-green necklace in his hand. He squeezed it once before returning his gaze to the bubbling surf.

For so long he'd traveled, trying to escape the past. The pain. The guilt. The loss. It had been a lonely road, but it was easier than facing his wife's ghost as it haunted his dreams. But since he'd saved Brenna by blocking Griff's blow, his dreams had become somewhat more peaceful. It was as if a great weight had been lifted from his shoulders. Like he was somehow free now. But he couldn't help wondering if he should still continue to run?

No. he told himself. He would stay here and start a new life. He'd never forget his beloved Babbette, but he wouldn't continue to run from his past. Contentment swept over him and he couldn't help smiling as he turned and walked back toward Castle MacKline, his new home.

It was about two and a half weeks later when Brenna approached Candy in their room with a silky white scarf.

"What's that for?" Candy asked.

"To blindfold you." Brenna said simply.

"What?" Candy said, raising a brow.

"Trust me." Brenna said.

Candy allowed herself to be blindfolded and Brenna guided her to the courtyard.

"Alright. One, two, three, surprise!" said Brenna as she lifted the blindfold from Candy's eyes.

Candy gasped at the cheering crowd that stood in the courtyard. There were a few fires here and there with all sorts of things roasting over them. There was Venison, mutton, suckling pig, beef and several different kinds of fowl. There were also barrels of drink as well as plates and cups on the tables that had been set up for this special night.

"What's all this?" Candy asked, a surprised smile on her face.

"It's a celebration in honor of your recovery." Brenna said cheerfully.

Candy's eyes welled up with tears.

"I don't know what to say." she sniffed.

"Come on. Let's have some music," called Lewis, "and dancing."

He grinned boyishly at Colleen as he offered his hand to her.

The music started and what a tune it was. The drums were pounding, the flutes were sounding, and the dance began. It was a traditional country-dance that was fast-paced and lively.

Brenna saw Lynch coming, obviously to ask her to dance, so she took Mitch's arm and said, "Come on, let's dance."

"But I don't know this dance." he pointed out.

"It's alright I do. Come on, I'll show you." she said encouragingly.

Candy found herself dancing between Nick and Dylon, the three of them linked at the arms.

Music and laughter filled the air as they all leapt about in the joyful celebration.

After the dance everyone was out of breath.

"That was fantastic." Candy gasped.

Murmurs of agreement met her ears, then gasps and giggles as Lynch came over and took hold of Brenna's shoulders before kissing her. The courtyard echoed with laughter as Lynch ran with Brenna hot on his heels yelling about all the horrible things she was going to do to him when she caught him.

"Lynch, you cowardly pig! When I'm done you'll be nothing but a pile of bruised flesh, broken bones and cracked teeth!" she roared.

Lynch was obviously afraid of her but wasn't about to show it. Instead he grinned a rather silly grin and called to Dylon as he passed, "Look! The ladies love me so much that they chase me!"

"Who're you calling a lady?" she bellowed at him. "I wear the breeches in this relationship."

Lynch's cheeks turned bright-red but he didn't dare to stop, even though everyone in the courtyard was laughing at him.

As they raced passed Konroy, Brenna's younger brother yelled, "Lynch is running from a girl."

Brenna immediately skidded to a stop and charged at him. Konroy ran as fast as his legs would carry him.

"Now who's running Konroy?" Lynch taunted, trying to save face.

"Well she's not just any girl, it's the lass that stole that dead rat off of ole Griffy's head!" Konroy laughed.

This prompted Mitch to pull out the wig that had once belonged to Griff and put it on his own head.

"I am Laird Griffy Cray, surrender before my baldness!" he growled, changing the tone of his voice to sound like Griff.

Lewis took up the wig next and began to act comically tough and issued forth a high-pitched cry when he saw Brenna who had finally caught Konroy.

"Say it! Say it!" Brenna growled, putting him in a headlock.

"Eel stew and starfish mush are delicious, and I'm in love with a golden-haired mermaid." Konroy said compliantly, looking toward Erica who was filling a cup with cider. She blushed noticeably as she turned away, a small but flattered smile playing on her lips.

Candy and the rest of the courtyard were still laughing at the young men's Griff Cray impressions. Candy happened to look toward the open gate and saw Nick with Dawn and Marie on either side of him. They were walking at a steady pace across the open ground in the direction of the woods.

She crept over to the gate and took off at a run after them.

"Nick, wait!" she called.

Nick stopped and stood still, but didn't turn.

"Where're you going?" she asked, coming to stand beside him.

"Back to the woods." Nick shrugged.

"What? Why?" Candy said, shock and grief evident in her voice.

"It's where I live." he said simply.

"Do you have to go?" she asked, tears in her eyes as she put a hand on his arm tenderly.

"I don't have anywhere else." Nick said, shaking his head as he started forward again.

Candy took hold of his arms and hugged him tightly, begging softly, "Please don't leave Nick? Please? You can live here in Castle

MacKline with the rest of us. Dawn and Marie could too. Please don't go?"

The sad pleading in her voice caused Nick to wrap his arms around her and hold her close. The sweet perfume that she had scented her hair with filled his nostrils and the warmth of her embrace was overwhelming.

"I'll stay." he said softly.

Candy heaved a sigh of relief, "Thank you."

Dylon had seen the whole exchange from where he stood in the open gateway. His heart ached and felt as though it would break into a thousand pieces. He turned and walked sadly back to sit by one of the fires.

Lewis and Colleen were sitting very near one another, speaking in hushed tones. Then Colleen smiled and nodded to her betrothed. Lewis stood and called for everybody's attention.

"Friends, as you all know, Colleen and I are betrothed. Now that Candy is well again, we would like to have the wedding tomorrow." he announced happily.

The cheers of approval were deafening. Konroy looked around at all of the smiling faces. But there was someone missing. He could see his parents sitting near Lewis and Colleen, and Colleen was saying that she'd like Candy to be her Maid of Honor since she herself had no sisters. He saw that Brenna and Mitch were amongst the rest of the party, Brenna hiding from Lynch. Nick and Candy were near the gate, and Dylon was by a fire. But where was Erica? He saw that the door to the large kitchen was open.

Erica was refilling a now empty pitcher with blackberry cordial, since the barrels outside were quickly emptying. She paused to wipe some beading sweat from her brow with the back of her sleeve. She was startled to feel a hand on her shoulder. She turned and saw Konroy standing there.

"Master Konroy." she gasped.

"Just Konroy." he corrected. "You're free now. You know, you don't have to do that anymore." He nodded toward the pitcher.

"I'm just helping." she shrugged.

265

He gently stroked her cheek with the tips of his fingers, "You came from the Northland, correct?"

"You know I did." she smiled, enjoying the feel of his fingertips on her cheek.

"Do you ever, miss it?" he gulped.

"What do you mean?" she asked, raising a brow.

Konroy's hand dropped and he turned away before answering.

"You're free to go back if you want to."

Erica put a hand on his shoulder, "I'm also free to stay."

Her voice was so soft that Konroy wasn't certain that he'd heard correctly.

"Really?" he asked, turning back and gently taking hold of her shoulders.

She nodded, "My family is gone and I was sold into slavery because there was no one to protect me. There's nothing for me back in that land. You, and your family, have always treated me well. I'd rather stay here with," her voice trailed off.

"With whom?" he asked softly, looking into her eyes.

"You." she whispered, then embraced him.

Konroy didn't even try to hide his smile as he hugged her back.

Out in the courtyard there was a thunderous roar of laughter as Dawn and Marie took refuge on the stable's thatched roof. Brenna and Candy's wolfhounds Dooley and Bonnibel had brought out a litter of ten puppies, who were now barking at Dawn and Marie.

"Well, they are wolfhounds." Brenna laughed as she scooped up the puppy nearest to her.

"We're Bulves." Dawn moaned as she rolled her eyes.

Candy picked up a gray, shaggy pup and walked over to Dylon.

"Want one?" she asked kindly.

Dylon managed a weak smile and picked up the puppy that was sniffing at his boots.

"I like this one." he chuckled as the small creature licked his chin.

Everyone was soon fussing over the puppies, feeding them bits of meat and bread from their plates, rubbing their furry bellies and scratching behind their little, scruffy ears.

Brenna was still holding the puppy she'd picked up, when she glanced at the gate. She thought that she saw Darsy walking through the gate with his donkey and cart. She moved briskly to the gate and called softly, "Darsy, where're you going?"

Darsy stopped and turned before answering, "To my Master, to see what other orders he has for me."

"Orders?" said Brenna, raising a brow.

"My Master told me that I would be needed here, but he didn't say why. Well, other than there would be a battle, and the Wolf Princess and her family would show their metal." Darsy explained. "And that I would be needed to help with the wounded."

"He knew that this would happen? How?" the Wolf Princess asked in surprise.

"I don't know how he knows. He just does." Darsy shrugged.

"He certainly grants you a lot of freedom." Brenna said, stroking the puppy's soft head.

"I'm not a slave." Darsy said softly.

"Then why do you return to him? You're free aren't you?" Brenna asked, feeling confused. "You don't have to serve him do you?"

"No. I don't have to. But that means I'm free to serve him." Darsy smiled.

"For how long?" she asked.

"All of my life." Darsy said happily. "He's a very good Master to serve. The greatest King I've ever heard of."

"He's a king?" she gasped.

"Oh, King, Emperor, Judge, Ruler. He and his Son are both good Masters."

"He has a son?"

"Oh aye. The Noblest of Princes. He would gladly lay down his life for one of his subjects." Darsy said proudly. "Anyone willing to do that is truly great."

"He sounds great." Brenna said slowly. "I think that I'd like to meet him someday."

"Maybe you will. But I have to go now, and see what adventure he has in store for me next. Oh, so that I may report to him accurately, how did you like your first real adventure?" he grinned.

"Well, it was frightening, and exciting." Brenna said honestly.

"Would you like another someday?"

"Oh aye, but with less killing. I've found spilling blood, even in self-defense to be distasteful. But I do like adventures." Brenna told him.

Darsy's grin widened, "My Master was hoping that would be how you feel. He doesn't care to spill blood either. He'll be most pleased."

"When will we see you again?" she asked.

"Perhaps sooner. Perhaps later. It all depends on my orders. Farewell Wolf Princess." Darsy chuckled, turning to leave.

"Farewell herbalist." Brenna said, raising a hand to wave goodbye. Then she stroked the puppy's ears again as she turned and reentered the courtyard. The Wolf Princess put down her puppy and went to the stables.

"Where're you going?" asked Mitch when he saw her saddling Lightningbolt.

In truth she just wanted to go for an evening ride. But to Mitch, who was suddenly joined by Candy and Nick, she simply grinned, "Out for an adventure."

Mitch and Candy worked quickly to saddle Thunderstorm and Dutchess.

"All right, now where are you going?" asked Brenna.

"With you." Nick said, standing close to Candy.

"What?" said Brenna.

"Just to keep you out of trouble." Mitch grinned, winking at her.

The four of them rode out across the open land under the star-filled sky, the hills echoing with the thunder of hoof-beats and the four young people's laughter.

Dawn and Marie flew overhead, glad to get away from the wolfhounds. The Wolf Princess threw back her head and howled her wolf howl.

When they returned home Mitch and Nick were given the spare room above the girls' chamber, and soon they had it fairly well set up. They brought in two beds, a washstand and a dressing-table with a small mirror.

Candy spoke of putting up curtains in their window, but they were quickly put off of that idea when Brenna teased them with the threat of using bright-pink fabric. So the window remained bare, and it still is to this day.

Mitch and Nick's first morning in their new room was a rather interesting one. Nick had awoken to the sound of someone tip-toeing across the creaking floor.

"Who's there?" he yawned groggily.

"Shh!" came the reply.

"It's only Brenna." Marie whispered, then yawned a large yawn.

"She's going over to Mitch's bed." Dawn added quietly.

Brenna went straight to the foot of Mitch's bed, then carefully lifted it up as high as she could before she leapt back, dropping it as she yelled, "Earthquake!" at the top of her voice.

The bed made a resounding 'thump' noise as it reconnected with the floor. Mitch was so startled that he nearly flung himself from the bed as he sat up. When he caught sight of Brenna laughing, he leapt up then fell to the floor with a thud as he tripped over his blankets. Brenna dashed out of the room when she saw him struggle free of the tangled mass and leap up to chase her. In the end the situation was only resolved after an extensive tickle-fight, and then laughing about possible pranks to pull on Lynch the next time they saw him.

The tales of the Wolf Princess and her friends go on and on. They had many more adventures, but they're not recorded here. This is simply the first of the legends and it's now at it's end.

Except to add that Candy was Colleen's Maid-of-Honor, and that it was a beautiful wedding. Konroy was Lewis's Best-Man. Brenna served as a Bride's-Maid, and was the only woman present who was wearing boots instead of slippers. Mitch and Nick chuckled over this, only to receive a swift kick from the Wolf Princess as she passed, complaining under her breath about having to wear a pink dress and white lace gloves. This got an extra large chuckle out of the boys because of the curtain incident the previous evening.

Lynch thought that she was lovely, but didn't dare to say so out loud. Though he hoped that she would catch the bouquet. He was sadly disappointed though when it was Konroy who accidentally caught it, then was smiled at warmly by Erica, causing him to blush deeply.

And that my dear reader, is where this tale ends . . . . For now.

Peace and happiness go with you as you place this book back upon it's shelf, and start a new one. If you are wondering how I know all of this tale, the answer is quite simple. It was all told to me by my good friend Darsy.

THE END